Since the much-loved *The Heart's Wild Surf* in 1996, Stephanie Johnson has published six more novels, three of them historical. She is a past winner of the Montana Book Award (for *The Shag Incident*), the Katherine Mansfield Fellowship in Menton and the Bruce Mason Memorial Playwright's Award. She has also held the University of Auckland writers' residency and several of her novels have been long-listed for the Impac Awards in Dublin. With Peter Wells, Stephanie founded the highly successful Auckland Writers and Readers Festival in 1998. Known also for her poetry, plays and short stories, Stephanie lives in Auckland with her husband and youngest daughter.

For Maeve

THE OPEN WORLD

STEPHANIE JOHNSON

VINTAGE

A VINTAGE BOOK published by Random House New Zealand,
18 Poland Road, Glenfield, Auckland, New Zealand

For more information about our titles go to www.randomhouse.co.nz

A catalogue record for this book is available from the National
Library of New Zealand

Random House New Zealand is part of the Random House Group
New York   London   Sydney   Auckland   Delhi   Johannesburg

First published 2012

© 2012 Stephanie Johnson

The moral rights of the author have been asserted

ISBN 978 1 86979 783 6

This book is copyright. Except for the purposes of fair reviewing
no part of this publication may be reproduced or transmitted in
any form or by any means, electronic or mechanical, including
photocopying, recording or any information storage and retrieval
system, without permission in writing from the publisher.

Cover design: Kate Barraclough
Text design: Carla Sy
Author photograph: Gil Hanly

This publication is printed on paper pulp sourced from sustainably
grown and managed forests, using Elemental Chlorine Free (EFC)
bleaching, and printed with 100% vegetable based inks.

Printed in New Zealand by Printlink
Also available as an eBook

A man either says too little or too much
— William Cotton, 'Journals', 1841

... the woman's power is for rule, not for battle, — and her intellect is not for invention or creation, but for sweet ordering, arrangement, and decision. She sees the qualities of things, their claims, and their places. Her great function is Praise; she enters into no contest, but infallibly adjudges the crown of contest. By her office, and place, she is protected from all danger and temptation. The man, in his rough work in open world, must encounter all peril and trial...
— John Ruskin, 'Of Queen's Gardens', 1865

The Missionary must always expect that colonization will follow in his train... not to draw a line around his native converts, within which no contamination shall be allowed to enter. The world will find a way to them, or they will break forth into the world.
— Bishop Selwyn, 1849

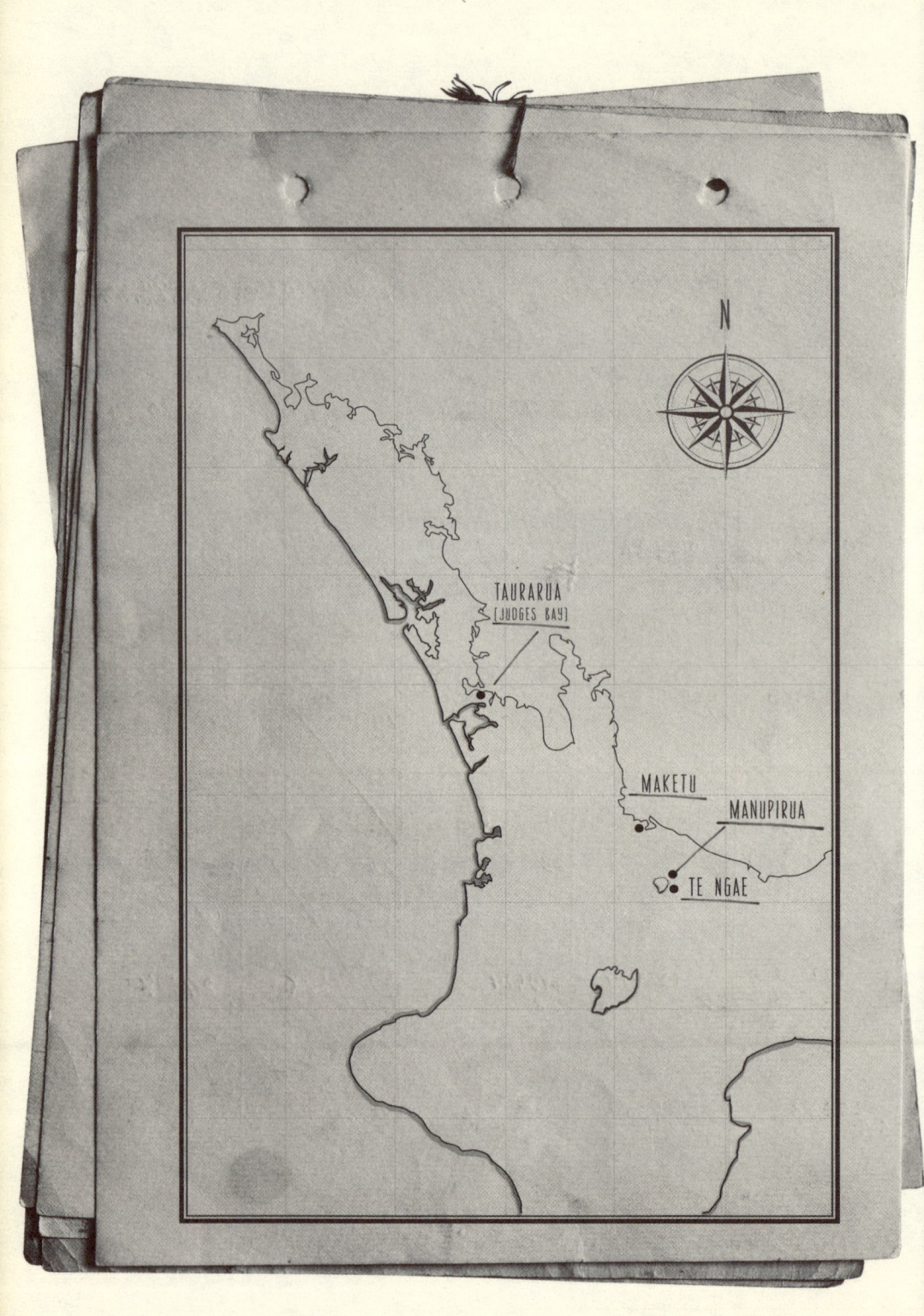

PROLOGUE

Maketu
Bay of Plenty

18 January 1863

HAT PULLED HARD DOWN and wearing an old waterproof of the Bishop's to cut the wind, the Civil Commissioner went out to catch his horse. Some of his children came to the door, and waved and called farewell as he rode her down to the river below the house. He crossed in the shallows, the horse flicking her ears at the sudden roar of the surf as they came up on to the sandspit that ran twenty miles from Maketu to Tauranga. It was Henry's most familiar road, a road eternally shifting with the tides and weather and never the same each time he rode it. On this fine day, the ocean was wide and blue and the current running swiftly along the open sands, the crests travelling faster than his horse and in the same direction. On his other side the spit contained an estuary that changed its shape with every storm, the swamp beyond giving way to tussock and bush until the distant Kaimai Ranges rose dark and steep in the east. But for the wind, the day would have been hot.

He let his horse slow to dawdle and wondered how it was that as a younger, single man he had found these journeys lonely and dispiriting. Now they gave him time to think, time to allow the clamour of his crowded life to still for a moment, to think of his loved ones far and wide. Today he thought of his mother, who this afternoon would sail from Wellington to London, and he was not there to see her off. It would fall to his brother to take her to the ship and contend with any last-minute wavering of conviction. 'You would fly to greater evils,' Henry had told her when she first broached the idea of returning. 'Mother, the subject is exhausted,' he said over and over when it had become an obsession.

Paihereni mumbled at the bit, and her hoofs were sinking a little, so he drew her further towards the water where the sand was harder. The tide was coming in and a wave surged to meet them. The old white mare skittered — he felt a tremble run through her under his aching knee.

The horizon was empty — no friendly sail broke the line. It could become too preoccupying to be always looking for one. In his early years at Maketu, as Native Interpreter, he was for ever hoping for another visit from his mother, en route from the hospital at Taurarua to the missions inland or at Tauranga. He would sit in the garden outside the house, his legs encased in canvas bags for the mosquitoes, smoking like a buck, and translating letter after letter to the Governor and the Colonial Office to put the Native case. He would look up from his labours and out to sea.

There would be no more visits from his mother now, and his heart ached — more than he would have anticipated. It was because he had not believed she could really do it, that she could really board a ship and sail away from them all.

Just past the breakers, fish were schooling, the water boiling and flashing with fins and the white wings of feeding birds. A larger fish — a shark? — broke the surface and disappeared again, and the flock rose, wheeling and crying. The trick would be not to think about her too much but to concentrate on the endless deliberations of his work with the Native Office and on his own growing family. He had asked her 'What do you hope to find in England?' when he should have asked 'Who?' He should have found the courage to weather the inevitable storm. He should have asked 'Will you look for our father?' and insisted on a reply.

The surf was running straight in now and the wind had swung around to kick up a drenching spray. The thick, silvery mist obscured the distant headland that marked the end of his journey.

ONE

London

1866

SHE HAD WOKEN BEFORE DAWN and quelled that familiar first panicked cognisance of the world — *Where am I now? How many more beds must there be?* — then risen to dress in the poor room by the comfort of candlelight, telling herself it was only habit, that there was no lady to serve and no gentleman either and if that were the only advantage of age and infirmity then she should reflect upon it gratefully when bitterness and rage descend.

Amen.

While the sun rose she heated water over a spirit lamp for tea, and set her inkpot and paper on the table under the window. The letter to her son was only half-finished. If she set about it she could post it later, on her way to Mr Griggs's house, but she found herself sitting quietly, warming her hands on her cup and listening to the sounds of the city coming alive. From around the corner on the Hornsey Road a coster's boy shrilled above his father's ruined bark. From just outside on Tollington Park came the slow tread and rattle of a burdened horse, the bump and roll of carriage wheels, the soft call of waking pigeons, and the hurrying footsteps of maids and servants. It was as it ever was — that much at least had not changed — the rich of London sleep on, while the poor who serve them rise.

She picked up the letter she had begun the evening before, only just legible in the soft grey light.

'I hear Mary Ann and Judge Martin are to return to England

and that dearest Mary Ann plans to write a book about our time together and that she may call it "Our Maoris", though they were more mine than hers. I have this intelligence from Bee Cotton, who has it in a letter from Bishop Selwyn. Since I make it my duty to visit Bee, now that he is returned to the asylum, I have seen the letter myself. His madness has not blunted him — he still runs on in his entertaining way — but I would rather not receive my latest advices from a certified lunatic. He has his books around him: you remember his two-volume work on bee-keeping, one in English and one in Maori, and twelve volumes — I exaggerate not — of his New Zealand journals. On occasion he reads aloud from them and most amusing he can be . . .'

But Henry would not enjoy the change in Mr Cotton. They were great friends and allies many years ago.

She shivered and drew her shawl tighter — only early May and the landlady had decreed there would be no more fires in the bedrooms until September. She would most certainly be gone by then. Vanished with the wind. Habit again, too long ingrained to change, and whom would it concern but herself? She would not write of that intention to Henry, still less to her younger son who would berate her for indulging her restlessness.

'Perhaps Lady Martin will write to me if her memory fails,' she wrote. 'Mine is bright to a fault — I find myself teetering on its knife-edge. Indeed, on my visits to Mr Cotton I find myself wondering which of us is the more insane? Mr Cotton's illness makes him either morose or ecstatic, with little shade between; while a facet of my own condition makes the past break into the present more sharply than any mortal should have to bear.'

Elizabeth put the pen down again — she would supply no more details — and sent a fine spray of ink across the 't' of 'mortal', almost as if she'd struck it out. It was immoral too, some of it, some of what came back to her.

The sun was up now, higher than the smoking chimney pots, setting the stone steeple of St Mark's shining. Dearest, long-lost London. How could any heart not built of that same steeple stone not leap at the dawn of another day here in a city she'd believed she could never return to? It was as safe now as it ever could be. Old age is a marvellous disguise — don't all old women look alike with their white caps and collapsing faces, all individual colour and beauty erased?

From across the road came the chaunt of the beggar girl. She had been there yesterday and the day before, in the shelter of the church lychgate, and Elizabeth had given her a penny. Despite the chill of early morning, she opened the window a little now to let the lilting song come in, but she couldn't make out the words — it was a moment or two before she recognised it as Gaelic. A sad song made sadder still by the girl's pure, thin voice.

A door opened in one of the new terrace houses opposite, next door to the church, and a maid emerged, flapping her apron at the beggar as if she was a bird that could fly away. The girl, her song cut off, gathered herself together, wrapped her rags more firmly and struggled to her feet.

Opening her window further, Elizabeth called at the top of her voice, 'Away with you, you flinty shrew — is there any other soul singing for us this morning?'

The maid startled — and searched the third-floor windows opposite until she found Elizabeth — and scowled.

'Let her be!' Elizabeth called.

The lady of the house was at the door now, looking out at her maid, who was no doubt following her orders. In the months Elizabeth had been in Tollington Park, she had only ever seen the mistress once or twice — she seemed a virtual recluse, as so many of her class were now. How did she spend her days in those four walls — at needlework and novel-reading? She almost felt sorry for her. Closing the window, she sat down again at her little table — a traveller with segmented legs that Bishop Selwyn had made a gift of to Henry many years ago.

'Will Lady Martin mention me in her book? I trust she will, since she depended on me more than anyone ever has before or since. If she is to give an account of our Native Hospital, then she must have me central — it was I who did the work.'

But Henry would know that already, because hadn't he watched her at it and on occasion even helped out? It was his mother who bathed the tuberculous sores, applied poultices and plasters, cupped and bled, who went up to the house in the evenings and had Mrs Martin pale at her accounts of diagnoses and doctoring. That lady didn't have the stomach for it, though she had the inclination.

'I have half a mind to visit Lady Martin and offer to assist with her record, especially of the Hospital. Since returning, I have been reading Miss Florence Nightingale's "Notes on Nursing". I reached many of the same conclusions regarding fresh air, cleanliness and the benefits of satisfying patients' fancies. I copy this passage for you as an answer to your challenge against my "silence" in your last letter. "People who think outside their heads, the whole process of whose thought appears, like Homer's, in the set of secretion, who tell everything that led them towards this conclusion and away from that, ought never to be with the sick." You see from this, because I have been so much with the sick, that it is in my nature to be so.'

Allow me my silence, Henry, thinks Elizabeth, or I will go too far.

There were letters she had written in that other country where paper could so often be in short supply and her pen had run away with itself. Unable to take up a fresh piece and begin anew, she had been compelled to delete passages or excise them with her scissors. It was an operation she sometimes performed still on letters received from her sons if they asked her that certain question, or hinted at it. Sometimes she took to letters from other correspondents too, particularly if they concerned themselves with the worrying matter of money. The small room was barely affordable on the twenty-five pounds quarterly sent by her younger son, John Elisha, but there was no rack-rent owing, not a farthing. She paid on time and kept to herself — the lady in a widow's cap, mysterious Mrs Smith who had returned to England after decades of service to Church and State in New Zealand, which any colonist would agree was a very different thing to returning from Australia.

There was an entire quarter of gabby Australians in London, a whole neighbourhood that rested on fortunes made in Victoria or New South Wales, families who lived in one another's capacious pockets. No such ease and familiarity existed for these other old settlers scattered thinly around the British Isles, and a fine thing that was. Even after all these years, it was safer not to have too many associations which could lead to other associations, and so cause complications.

The cheering thing to do would be to make a list of all those she would call on before she was called to Final Rest. She took up a leaf of crisp fine blue paper — so delicious after all those years of stingy cross-writing.

1/ Dear Mr Griggs, of course
2/ Rev. William Cotton — as often as he will receive me
3/ Bishop Selwyn — to speak my mind for once and for all
4/ Mary Ann Martin — to assist the record
5/ Miss Nightingale — to commend her efforts

A knock on the door and the little chambermaid was come to collect the pot from under the bed, dropping a cloth over it as she emerged from behind the painted screen.

'Thank you, dear.'

The child always looked surprised when Elizabeth thanked her — but she persisted because she really was grateful. Where would she be without her? The maid carried the pot out to the pan closet, a reeking sink on the landing with a pipe that dropped to the cesspit in the cellar. Elizabeth supposed it was a sanitary advancement, though not an hygienic one. There was banging and sloshing, the gurgle of the downpipe, the clang of a bucket and the little maid coughing with the rising stench.

She folded the list and put it aside. It was shorter than she would have liked and there were hours to fill until Mr Griggs came to collect her. She could finish her letter to Henry; she could begin one to John Elisha, or to Henry's wife Sophia, or Ish's wife Lilias. She could enclose notes to all the grandchildren. Of all the New Zealanders, she wished she could write to Mokihi, but the world was empty of him.

Some drop was in order, prepared the previous night by

candlelight and so possibly not the most perfectly composed — though hadn't she long mixed medicines in the dark? Her hands were not as steady now.

She uncorked her bottle — her 'beloved little bottle', as Mary Ann styled it — and shook the amber solace into her teacup. The tea was cold, but the drop sweetened it, and gave a faint flavour of aniseed that made it easier to swallow and coated the tongue pleasantly before it travelled on to her otherwise empty stomach. It would not be long before the soft mist rolled in swift as sea fog and all pain would vanish, body and soul.

Among her papers was John Elisha's picture, a mechanical one made two years ago, true to life and worn with caressing — she had rubbed a mark on the dear face. How sad was the resignation in her son's eyes, the early grey in his beard. Melancholy Ish, his grey whiskers long enough to curl into bacca-pipes, his narrow shoulders stooped. He had had the worst of it — he certainly believed he had — but how could she have known that the miles between them in those small, distant islands would prove so great and so many?

From the drawer she took the empty silver frame, bought a month ago but still unfilled for fear it would be stolen, though all she had to do was hide it each time she went out. And who was to say it was real silver anyway, bought more for pity of the hanseller half-frozen on the doorstep? Ish, prematurely foxed and turning up the corners, was at first reluctant to lie flat, but eventually, her stiff fingers fumbling, he was in safekeeping and standing beside his brother.

She could not bear to look at that likeness — Henry at twenty-one: the deep-set, loving eyes, the wide thoughtful brow, the ghost of a smile caught in a clever charcoal made by the Maori gunsmith William Jowitt, the only man Henry would remember calling Papa. The artist's love of his subject had all his kindness and good humour shine through.

Grief and longing rushed in over the miles, over the sea, over the years. Too many miles, too many years, a too vast sea, enough to make a mother wail and cry — though even the most dismissive youth might note the necessary restraint in older people of good character.

And I am of good character, thought Elizabeth.

Beyond the window, a tall man in a worn serge suit was dropping a fadge into the beggar's hand. Watching him, calming herself, Elizabeth peered more closely. The regimental bearing, the quick steps as he crossed the street — it was Mr Griggs come to fetch her. The dear man.

Cup drained, she took up a comb and tamed the wisps escaping her cap, pushed off her slippers and struggled into her boots, a true pair of clamshells that pinched like the devil. If she didn't hurry he would come up to find her in her desolate room, which she would prefer he didn't. There were his footsteps up the stairs — and here he was knocking at the door, which stood ajar since the maid's departure.

'Come in, Mr Griggs!'

It always made a heart glad to look at him. He had a full head of dark hair even in his fifties; his sombre face was smooth, his eyes clear, the blue unfaded. He was certainly well favoured, more so even than Augustus Selwyn in his youth, or than her second husband whose fresh good looks for too long disguised his feckless heart.

No wonder Mr Griggs was preyed upon by certain ladies — he was famous for it in particular circles.

'Are you ready, Mrs Smith?'

'In a moment.' There was her shawl and bonnet to collect from the cupboard beside her bed.

'Who is that?' Mr Griggs asked as she fetched them. He had picked up the silver frame.

'Ish.'

'Who?'

'My youngest son. John Elisha. Don't you remember, we called him Ish?' For an instant their acquaintance seemed more distant than she'd hoped — surely he'd remember that?

Mr Griggs stared.

'But he bears no resemblance . . .' he began.

'He was only fifteen when you last saw him,' Elizabeth offered, and observed her friend for sensitivity curtail himself. No mother likes to believe her son an old man while yet in his thirties.

'I would not have recognised him.'

'You are not so greatly changed. I knew you the moment you came on board at Gravesend. I was happy to see you.'

⁓

They made their slow way down the stairs. At the bottom step, Mr Griggs offered Mrs Smith his hand. Last week he had made the mistake of handing her down from the second step, and she had misjudged her arrival and stumbled.

Her decrepitude still surprised him. It was, he supposed, the interval of twenty or so years that gave him such clear recall of her younger, more vital self — he remembered her as she was when they first met in the early 'thirties. How her good health shone, how her strong fair hair framed her handsome face — the nose too prominent to be pretty, her eyes too deep-set, her brave, too-loud laughter. She was then in her prime, and alarmingly ready to laugh both in good-humoured jest and in mocking judgement; sadly, she had tempered both propensities, when the latter would have been sufficient.

He ushered her down to the street for the short walk to his schoolhouse, which in Mrs Smith's company always took much longer than it should have. First there was the rough terrain of the new street to negotiate — a group of navvies were laying pipes. Then there was the distraction of gauging the progress on houses still in construction. Three doors down, a dusty stonemason knelt at his work on a porch, his crusted hod of cement left lying across their path.

On this particular holiday morning — a holiday at least for Tollington Park School since the boys were home for Harvest, a quaint custom that persisted even in the grinding city — there was a hackney cab waiting outside the church, the horse with its head down, blinking in the sunshine. Mrs Smith stepped out across the street to pat it, then looked back at Mr Griggs with a fair approximation of its expression — inebriated by the late summer warmth, or so he supposed it was: it took him a moment or two to catch up with her. She laughed — and there it was again, that clear picture he had of her as a younger woman in dweebs, bringing her two boys along to the school. A widow of independent means, though he'd never had the details of her jointure.

How unexpected it was — the renewal of their acquaintance after so long lying fallow. There had been a sudden flurry of letters from the lady herself, and from both of her sons, and he had surprised himself by remembering them very well — the fatherless lads who had come to him for instruction in the early years of his school. Mr Griggs could not be expected to remember all his boys, but the Smith brothers — among all the other Smith boys — he recalled. They were not at all alike: one fair, the other dark, one clever and optimistic, the other plodding and given to melancholy. Where he deemed them similar was in their moral character — they were both kind, innately compassionate. Many times Henry's concern for the younger boys was noted and remarked upon by the late Mrs Griggs: 'Oh, but he'll be a lovely father when his time comes.'

Now the widow was edging past the horse to sit on the low church wall opposite, her hand on her chest as she caught her breath. He crossed the road and joined her. It would take as long as it took.

'Animals instruct us so amusingly, don't you think, Mr Griggs?' Mrs Smith said as he sat down. 'There he is, the sensible old nag, enjoining us all to enjoy the sun.'

She spread her work-worn hands over her skirt and turned them palms up.

'And why not, since it is free to everyone. We should love Nature as we love God, wouldn't you agree, Mr Griggs, though they're not at all a thing apart. If I hadn't loved God, then I should have loved Nature as much and so been as intimate with Our Lord by association.'

'One may come to a love of Nature through the love of God,' cautioned Mr Griggs, after a moment, 'but never the other way around.'

She was never so fervent in their early association — or not until the sudden announcement that she was accompanying Bishop Selwyn to New Zealand, and then he rather thought she was playing at it. Now her adherence was strict, though esoteric and a little garbled, as if along with the religion in the Colonies she'd imbibed a dose of pantheism.

He replaced his topper. The sun was fierce but didn't bear remarking on, for the inevitable rejoinder of its being fiercer in that other country — that is, when it wasn't raining, which he gathered was every other day.

'Will there be others joining us for dinner?' Mrs Smith asked hopefully, being an enthusiast for company.

'Only Mrs Stott and Miss Jennings, as always.'

On his davenport in the front room there was another letter from Henry Smith, which he should have slipped into a drawer before coming to fetch the correspondent's mother. She would want to read it, or have him read it to her — and she was too sharp not to notice necessary abridgements. He'd put it away at the first opportunity. All going well, by the time he set about a reply, Mr Griggs would have new information to report.

The lady was standing now and wanting his arm. 'In my situation with the Martins, I rarely sat at table when there was company.'

This was a barb at Mrs Stott, who always did. Mr Griggs, original Chartist and son of a blacksmith, would have it no other way — that is, after Mrs Griggs's passing. Why should the widower and his faithful housekeeper eat separately? At times he regretted his decision, because weren't all women alike in their capacity for needless detail, which stood as antithesis to their otherwise secret natures, although Mrs Stott had not a quarter of the mystery of Mrs Smith, and neither of course did Miss Jennings, on account of her youth and timidity.

Miss Jennings came through to greet them while Mr Griggs was hanging his hat in the hall. She is truly a whiffler, thought Elizabeth — pale, watchful and plain, not bright and welcoming as any lass worth her salt would be, but pale and cow-eyed, looking up at him like a child.

'What a very long time you've been, Mr Griggs,' she said, aggrieved.

Miss Jennings led them into the parlour where Elizabeth greeted Mrs Stott warmly, kissing her cheek, because her disapproval of Mr Griggs's arrangements was directed at Mr Griggs himself, not Sally Stott, who had been with him for over twenty years, since before Elizabeth's departure for New Zealand. She was certainly preferable to his various other 'ladies', of whom there had been a few since his wife died. Mr Griggs was of course decent, a gentleman in all respects, but he was too much a sot for the company of grateful females, as was proved by his taking in of Miss Jennings, who assisted him with the younger boys just as she had herself many years ago, and a great deal more diligently.

They sat together around the small rosewood table, which was jammed among Mr Griggs's piano, bookcases and armchairs. There was scarcely room to breathe, but then there were so many rooms like this in London now — over-trimmed and stuffed to bursting, all the inhabitants' possessions on proud display. It was another fashion Elizabeth didn't like — the Spartan rooms of her childhood were cousins to the colonial ones of her midlife and easier to move about in. On a corner-stand a mongoose fought a snake, the victor not apparent. They had an enviable amount of elbow-room, snarling and rearing under their dusty glass bell. Behind them, among the prints and watercolours, hung a framed map of the world, New Zealand repeated and partially eclipsed at each bottom corner. Elizabeth considered it briefly, as she always did, and had the usual thought that it gave no hint of the true vastness of the globe.

The curtains were drawn against the glare of the day and Mrs Stott, or perhaps the other lady, had filled a large vase with stock. The powerful scent overwhelmed any mild aroma sent up by the cold collation of meats and jellies and aspics.

'Very good, Mrs Stott.' Mr Griggs forked a slice of beef, his smooth brow wrinkling a little, perhaps with concern at the outlay. It was more than the usual fare of simple soups and bread. There were boiled eggs, a fish in white sauce, and strawberries — English strawberries!

What a treat — the first she'd seen since her return. Elizabeth sat one on her tongue, well away from her tender teeth. The berries were small and dark, sharp and strong, not like their insipid, rain-swollen colonial counterparts.

Quite obviously there was supposed to have been another guest. As they'd come up the steps, Mr Griggs had been on the brink of telling her something, but they had both had to concentrate fully on the manoeuvre — her leg had seized at his gate. And when they had first come in, there had been a hurried exchange between Mr Griggs and Sally Stott while Elizabeth was busy removing her shawl, the fringes of which did stick so to the fraying embroidery at the back of her bodice — Miss Jennings had come to her rescue.

'Leave her place set,' Mr Griggs had said. 'She may not be as delayed as all that.'

'Whom were you expecting, Mr Griggs?'

Miss Jennings had flashed her bulbous eyes, being a subscriber to the ever-growing persuasion that held polite enquiry an affront. She sat now with her hands in her lap and would most likely eat nothing. How like Mary Ann she was! There were other similarities too: the slight build, the all-seeing gaze, the bookish brain ticking behind the sickly brow. Miss Jennings could apparently read Latin, and Mary Ann, everyone agreed, had an intellect wasted on a woman. The primary difference was that she was kinder and more curious than this recent acquaintance.

Elizabeth looked more closely. The young lady's bones stood in her face and her skin was pale green. Chlorosis, or anorexy, if there was ever a case of it — so they had that in common too. It was a disease you never saw among the Maori people, since it came from a particular type of misery unknown to them. No doubt, even now, they were learning it.

'Another lady,' Mrs Stott answered for him, since Mr Griggs was taking a very long time to chew his mouthful and then to swallow it. 'She sent word she would join us later.'

'A friend of yours, Mr Griggs?'

He cleared his throat. 'In a manner of speaking. I hope very much that you will enjoy her, Mrs Smith.'

Mr Griggs's smile was watery, almost apologetic, as if he thought this was unlikely. Elizabeth seized on the probability that she was to meet the future, second, Mrs Griggs. If company had allowed, she would have assured him that on the contrary she was delighted that he had an intended, a new wife to tend him into old age. Indeed, if it was jealousy he feared, then he should look closer to home. Hadn't Miss Jennings collapsed further into her chair, her little frame held upright only by her corset?

Elizabeth hadn't worn one of those for years, and neither perhaps had broad Mrs Stott who was seated at her own small table near the door to the kitchen, there being room around the rosewood for only four settings, though it may also have been a concession to herself — it did so make her heart heavy to sit opposite Sally, despite her fondness; it made her heart ache for all the years listening to the Martins and their guests talking in the dining room on the other side of her bedroom wall. Very often her head had rested upon the scrim as much out of longing for relaxed company as it did from exhaustion. Mrs Stott at her own table was a compromise that suited them both.

Miss Jennings began to cough, lightly at first, then more in earnest, bringing roses to her ashen cheeks. With that helpless expression men reserve for displays of frailties in the weaker sex, Mr Griggs remained in his chair while the two other ladies rose from theirs, one to pour water and the other to pat the bony back through bombazine mourning.

'Have you got something stuck in your throat?' Elizabeth asked her. Under her paddling hand the poor little skeleton heaved.

Miss Jennings shook her head and at length lay back, her eyes closed and her mouth turning away from the proffered tumbler. Elizabeth sniffed. There was even the same smell that Mary Ann had so often given off — strange, sweetish, last season's hay after summer rain — though she had recovered, periodically, from greensickness and many other ailments, despite the loathsome cures of the colonial quacks.

For Miss Jennings's sake, she hoped that there were new advances.

'Is she all right?' Mr Griggs asked.

Dear Mr Griggs. He filled the room with stalwart calm.

'I think so,' said Mrs Stott, who sat beside Miss Jennings on the sofa, rubbing the narrow hands between her stout ones while the young woman leaned rigidly against the buttoned horsehair, her eyelids dark blue in her thin face — so blue that Elizabeth had to peer through the gloom to make sure the eyes were in fact properly closed, not open and staring.

Her corsets should be loosened, but let her suffer. It was infuriating, this too-enduring ludicrous fashion, the female desire to starve, to dislodge poor griping intestines and failing organs with pinching stays. She would get her alone and explain to her that those kinds of vapours could be afforded only by married women with wealth, not independent ladies like herself. Besides, old age would come soon enough with all its aches and pains, which Miss Jennings surely knew, if Elizabeth had rightly interpreted the occasional fearful light in her eyes when their glances met: in the older lady the younger witnessed her certain future, if she lived as long.

'Is her heartbeat regular?' she asked Mrs Stott, who had lifted a wing of grey hair to press her ear against Miss Jennings's constricted chest.

'Oh yes,' she whispered, 'I hear it now. Faint and steady.'

'I think she should lie flat,' said Elizabeth, 'and have her gown opened.'

Mr Griggs jumped to his feet, blushing. 'Oh — as serious as all that — I'm sorry I hadn't quite seen how — shall we —'

He and Mrs Stott got the poor limp doll to her swaying feet. For a little they tried to walk her between them, one step, two, until Mr Griggs picked her up in his arms and carried her out into the passage, Mrs Stott following.

Listening to their climbing footfall, Elizabeth considered the lovely picture it had made, a man lifting a woman in his arms — the angled swoop of his shoulders, his bracing legs against her weight: a kind of sacrament in this new doctrine of helplessness. It was what this generation of sickly women craved above all, a moment of purity to be savoured and reflected upon — provided you had come out of your faint sufficiently to be conscious of the man's steady tread beneath you, the cradle of his arms, the soft underside of his throat as he looked ahead for the safest path.

Perhaps they dreamed at night of that rather than the other, closer thing, which she still dreamed of now and again, even now, and counted it a blessing. And besides, who had ever carried her? It was she who did the carrying: Mary Ann, the children she'd cared for, the sick, the dying, the dead. Or wait — at eighteen she'd danced with the sailor Horlock, who'd swung her off her feet and carried her to more than a few beds on land and sea in the short years he'd loved her.

It was all too long ago to be thinking about. If she were to write a book, as Mary Ann was doing, where would she begin? There was too much that went before that must remain untold, or merely glossed over. The story would have to begin with herself newborn at the age of thirty-nine, voyaging across the world.

Oh, but it was close in here. She would open a curtain to let in some light.

Hauling herself to her feet and wishing she'd brought both her sticks instead of relying on Mr Griggs in place of one, she began to make her way towards the bureau, keeping a grip on the edge of the mantelpiece. Under her grasping fingers the mantel cloth slipped alarmingly, nearly dislodging the clock — she pushed on, hand over hand on the back of the sofa to the desk in the window.

There was an envelope, and the handwriting on it was Henry's. The letter protruded, it had been opened — it would be short work to pull it free and read it — but the paper was cross-written fine, and proved difficult to extract without tearing — she would go carefully, carefully — *more haste, less speed* . . .

A knock, muted through the thick curtains of the bay window, sounded at the front door, startling her. The letter was in her hand.

Henry was writing from Opotiki and giving an account of the terrible goings-on there, the murder of Reverend Völkner. Mr Griggs's correspondence had had a slow passage — five months. Henry omitted the part about the Pai Marire men drinking the vicar's blood from the chalice, which Ish had made much of in his last letter. Rather too much. It was gruesome and savage, nightmarish — a trick to living in New Zealand was to put such nastiness out of one's mind as soon as possible. But it was a country of extremes — whatever desolation one experienced could be matched by joy of equal intensity.

The knocker went again, louder. She skipped to the next page.

'I realise you will meet with certain resistance from our dearest mother and can only urge you to persist. She has the greatest regard for you — as do my brother and I — and if you can persuade her to provide you with names and events, then perhaps some gentle investigation may be possible. Our mother must be reassured that the gentleman in question will not be provided with any details as to her own whereabouts and situation...'

The knocker again, and still no response from either the schoolmaster or his housekeeper upstairs. She would have to attend to it — it was the least she could do. Were she ten years younger — five! — she would be usefully employed upstairs, making Miss Jennings comfortable, instead of being left alone to temptation to pry. She replaced the letter, fumbling. It must be returned exactly to the precise angle on the polished wood, the surrounding papers and books undisturbed — a skill she had perfected with years of practice in other people's houses — before she could make the shuffling turn for the arduous trip out into the passage.

She needn't have bothered. From above came Mr Griggs's hurrying footsteps, which strangely grew further and further apart as he descended the stairs, slowing and quietening until she found herself cast into the sofa that had so recently held Miss Jennings, and the approach of his hastening tread came to resemble more the soft scratching of a nib on paper, up and down, round and round, the forming of letters.

TWO

Poreirewa

'It's not as if our story is branded on our foreheads for all to read,' I would tell my sons. 'It is our trial alone.'

If I were to make an account, a companion to Mary Ann's 'Our Maoris', I would have to begin with that, with what would have been branded there — our moko for everyone to read.

Here is where the story would have to begin: we were a tiny band, Ish, Hy and me. Long periods would pass when Mr Hogg was not mentioned, but then one or other of the lads, spurred on by the boasts of a Tollington Park papa's achievements in the world, would say, 'Please tell us about our father.'

By the time they were with Mr Griggs, I was strong enough not to allow my feelings to rise and choke me silent, and I could tell them, softly but firmly, 'He is dead, my little darlings. He is in Heaven.'

And they were not to know that I saw in my mind's eye not one man passing through the Pearly Gates but two, each of them forgiven for their earthly crimes.

'But if our story was branded on our foreheads, Mamma, what would it say?' Ish would ask. 'Did he know us? How did he die? Who is more like him, Henry or myself?' and so on, quizzing me on every detail until I gently chastised him.

Forced to play father, I beat them only sparingly, preferring the biddable nature of happy children to disputative, smarting and sullen ones. And they were happy lads, my boys, curious and hardworking. I recall Mr Griggs's commendation of their amenable natures.

***

By the time Henry was ten years old, the small fortune I called 'my inheritance' came to an end and I had to go out to service. For those long years while the boys were at school, I took positions in houses, my reputation growing, and ensuring that as soon as one case either recovered or died I would be leaving for another. It came about almost by accident, as occupation rather than vocation — and I discovered I was good at it. Miss Nightingale would have it now that a woman must take up nursing as her single cause. She would have us believe that she has single-handedly invented a new vocation — the sober nurse, softly spoken and clean — when there were others like me years before, who came to it similarly in a round-about way. I was never a nanny, but abecedarian to a series of sickly children grown mutually fond, so I ended by nursing them. Enough survived for families to begin asking for me by name as being both clever and tender. In this way I went from case to case. I kept notebooks of observations as much from a desire to save myself work as to ease suffering — the medical men make such a to-do about it all — and so could refer to experience when one set of symptoms colluded with another. Woman's instincts urge her to comfort. Men do not have those instincts and that is why they make cold science of it.

Under Mr Griggs's guiding hand, my sons grew strong and ambitious. For the last two years of their schooling I was in Mr Griggs's employ, tending to the younger boys of his establishment, and so blessed with the daily company of my beloved sons.

'How lucky we are to live in this glorious age!' Henry announced at fifteen, when we saw him off on the coach. 'A man may make of himself what he will.' And so he was, away to Romford to learn the trade of surveyor.

There was talk, even then, of Henry's going to the antipodes with the Wakefields' New Zealand Company to assist in the mapping of that distant land. Almost to the day, only a year later, we were waving him off at the dock: T.H. Smith, Improver, expensively outlaid with theodolites and compass and expansively waving from the deck. I have heard since of mothers throwing themselves into the sea after a departing ship. If I had not still had Ish to care for, I may well have done so. Even now, I miss my smiling son more than any other man before or since.

When Ish's time came, I chose him a profession, securing him an article in the house of solicitor Brockhurst in Islington. I left Mr Griggs's school then myself, brushing off my commendations and adding one from that good man who continued a dear family friend, a kind of uncle to my lads. My first family was in Camden, and a dreary time it was — I regretted leaving my previous post, but Mr Griggs had already replaced me with one of the many sickly ladies who preceded Miss Jennings.

The family was struck down with typhus — it spread from one child to the next and took each to his grave, finishing with the mother, and throughout it all I waged a bitter battle with the quack who attended them. The next case likewise ended dolefully, and it was my misfortune that the same doctor placed the blame on my head, tho' if he had not cupped and bled so enthusiastically the young woman might have rallied. He told stories that spread — of my neglecting to dose the patient with his sickening medicines, or of not sending for him in a crisis.

And so I was compelled to resort to my trifling savings and take lodgings in a house in Cross Street, Islington, not far from Brockhurst's establishment. Aside from my longer interval caring for the lads at the school, it had been my pattern to move from house to house every year or few months or less, to learn its laws and absorb myself in the goings-on of servants and masters with the cheering knowledge that no matter how tragic or unpleasant the situation might prove, it would not be long before I was released from it.

As the weeks went by, it seemed I would be for ever confined in the tiny third-floor room with my few sticks of furniture and only the briefest glimpses of John Elisha, whom Brockhurst worked to the limits of human decency. He was never as good company as Henry — every family has its melancholic, sensitive one, and Ish was ours. Unhappy with Brockhurst, his long face on his half-day off mirrored mine, which made me irritated and sympathetic in equal parts.

My situation was hopeless, and struck me with a certain irony: hadn't I always declined positions that on investigation proved to be more that of companion because I could not bear to be shut away with a poor creature caught in a protracted limbo between life and death? And now I was too much shut away by myself, as if I were myself a useless old woman, not young and strong and able. I came to believe myself older than I was, not knowing then — as I know now — that a woman in her thirties has only the first intimations of old age. I meditated too long on past sins and lost loves, and longed for Henry as if he had died to me for ever.

Poreirewa, the Maoris call it, a beautiful, expressive word: to yearn for absent loved ones.

Tho' I was not particularly religious, I began to attend St Mary's Church, which was a short walk from my lodgings, through the stables and down Dagmar Terrace. A sick-nurse rarely attends service, being needed on Sundays as on any other day at the bedside — tho' she attends more than her fair share of funerals, which will either deepen her faith or destroy it. But I was lonely and the church was close. As luck would have it, St Mary's formed the heart of the Christian Missionary Society and thronged with New Zealand enthusiasts. It was truly as if God had listened to me — everything fell into place. It was there I heard that an invalid called Mary Ann Parker was newly married and needing a companion to assist her to the Colonies. I offered my services, sending word that very afternoon to her father's house — the vicarage of St Ethelburga, Islington, a new, draughty manse of the gothic style the Church favoured building then and now. The invalid sent for me the next day.

There was first a brief interview with her elderly, loving father, before I climbed the icy stone steps to a warm, darkened room where a young woman draped with shawls lay on a daybed before the fire. A little dog rose from its place at her feet and barked wildly until she called from her wraps — the first words I heard from her dear mouth, then, were not of greeting to me — but pleading and ineffectual attempts to quieten the animal leaping and tugging at my skirt. I picked it up and returned it to the exhausted mistress's arms, and saw for the first time the sorrowing eyes of the habitual invalid, the deep shadows in her thin face. Wasn't she precisely the case I had always tried to avoid?

The husband was not then of my acquaintance, but I presumed Mr Martin would be a man of action, of the type given to hard voyaging and general discomfort, for why else would he have appended himself as Chief Justice to a Colony at the furthermost edges of the Empire? It was a mystery as to why he had chosen such a sickly wife. There for the first time was the smell of hay, sweet but cloying, and the sudden conviction at the touch of her hand that the lady was still a virgin.

Henry and Ish would consider this observation indelicate. 'Mamma, that is quite unnecessary,' Ish would caution if ever I gave too detailed an account of a gory case, too graphically described a boil or recalled a ranting fever. Imagine his horror, should I include this in an account of my life! Were my sons more medically minded, they would be curious as to the method of my diagnosis.

Let me merely note that the ability to glimpse the intimate lives of men and women is a knack learned from a way I had of getting on, once or twice, many years ago, when all other ways were closed to me. It is a common enough experience, and one I would not care to revisit in any account of my life. I pray even Saint Peter will not have it on his Heavenly List — for surely I have done enough Good to expunge it.

In any case, my diagnosis of my future employer was to prove correct and at the base of many of her troubles. She had been, so the story went, parted from her husband on the church steps, he going to sea immediately after the wedding.

'Mrs Smith.' Her hand was warm from the shawls and squirming dog, drawing me down beside her while the animal sprang to its feet again and snuffled enthusiastically at the odours of street and lodging house. 'I am so grateful for your kind offer — I will be joining Mr Martin as soon as possible.'

Her grey eyes were moist with longing for him and I thought she might cry, not knowing then that Mrs Martin's eyes belied her blithe spirit and often seemed as if they were about to weep or had just finished doing so — tho' I would wonder at her lipidity since she took almost nothing to drink. She was weary of London life, she told me, which quietly amused me since she had no doubt seen little of it.

'How weary you must be of these four walls!' I responded. 'How ready for adventure!'

'I like you already, Mrs Smith.'

'How long have you been ill, Mrs Martin?'

'Oh, I'm always so,' she replied, with emphasis. 'Always!'

'We shall have to put that to rights,' I said, and told her some of what Henry had told me of conditions in the new Colony, tho' not with any intention of alarming her. At my colourful description of the appearance and manners of the Natives, she murmured, 'Do not frighten me, Mrs Smith,' pronouncing 'fwighten', which childlike attribute I found endearing. Perhaps her father or her sisters had teased or chastised her, because as our conversation went on I noticed she mostly avoided words with that letter, thinking ahead to select another, so that once or twice there were awkward silences while she fished for an alternative.

We talked lightly of this and that, the few people we knew in common from St Mary's, our tastes in music — she was delighted to learn I played the piano well enough to accompany a song or set toes tapping — and in the same light tone my remuneration, which was necessarily small, tho' she promised to begin it immediately. I enquired of her age, which in other circumstances would have been ill-mannered, but if I was to care for her an important factor to consider. I had imagined it was a late marriage, thinking her to be at least thirty. She was only twenty-three.

'And how old are you, Mrs Smith?'

'I am thirty-eight.' It was the closest she ever came to examining my teeth. 'But there are years of work left in me yet. I keep excellent health.'

I remember we met one another's eye then, and caught a corresponding spark of mischief. We were to have an adventure, after all.

When I took my leave of her, I passed the crow on the stairs, arriving with his bag. I did not exchange two words with him — which I regretted in the months that followed. Even supposing he would have allowed me to address him, he might have suggested treatment for her more puzzling symptoms.

John Elisha would have left his article immediately I told him we were to go to New Zealand, but there were still months of preparation ahead. He continued his slog and I moved my traps to a small room at St Ethelberga's, on the same landing as my patient. Very quickly, I grew fond — Mary Ann is universally agreed to be adorable — and just as quickly she held me her 'closest companion', which words contain no 'r's, unlike 'dearest friend'.

'Where were you born?' she asked me one afternoon, while the maid and I sorted linen for the voyage.

'In London,' I replied.

'And your father? Who was he?'

'An educated man. Descended from the Payse family at Painswick. He sent my sister and me to school.'

This was not entirely true, tho' could have been. The maid, a sharp-faced dollymop whose kind I only too well recognised, smirked and caught my eye. I might have been more forthcoming if Mrs Martin and I had been alone, explaining that my father had been a merchantman in possession of a small fleet of traders which plied as far as France. He made enough to keep us warm and fed, and may have gone on to prosper, having his letters and running close accounts. My widowhood interested her more, however, and she would come to it in a delicate fashion.

'And one for you too, Mrs Smith,' she said, during a discussion about arranging for pieces to be made up for gowns. 'Is it for very much longer you must remain in mourning?'

'Oh, yes,' I murmured, for if Mr Hogg was dead, then so I should wear my liberating weeds for not knowing his hour or year — and if he lived, I would do it in anticipation. He could be shot, the bullet flying even as I spoke, or wallowing in dysentery in Calcutta, or clanking chains in Botany Bay. All alternatives were possible and equally affecting, being either tragic or vengeful, depending on my mood and degree of resilience. I seemed to have no middle ground: I wished him dead, I prayed he still lived, I wanted him forgotten, I yearned for him to remember me, I hoped he lived with eternal regret.

The autumn came, and I still had not made my approach to the boy Bishop, the leader of our expedition, tho' I had seen him at a distance. George Augustus Selwyn was young, and blessed with intelligence and boundless energy. He preached enthusiastically at St Mary's and gathered always a large congregation, catching us up in his passionate regard for God and adventure, for settler and savage, for the coming voyage, for the crusading Holy Spirit. Young men would rise in their seats, intoxicated by his call; women would faint dead away. Even Mary Ann was half in love with him — he was one of her husband's oldest friends.

'You are my companion,' Mrs Martin mused one rainy morning as we packed a sturdy crate with a selection of preserves from the vicarage kitchen, 'and so you are not technically one of the Bishop's party. Should we bother him with you, do you think?'

'I am to be your friend, Mrs Martin, not his.'

E hoa, Mary Ann — do you call me friend in your book? You may at least write that word without hesitation. Do you remember how our first Auckland newspaper lost all its 'r's to the *Maori Gazette* — that language profligate with them — and how Mr Cotton would have you read aloud from the *Southern Cross* and fall about laughing while you complied in good humour? Mrs Selwyn arrived scowling one day at the house at Taurarua, and interrupted the game. No favourite of mine, that woman, nor of my sons.

Still I had not met the Bishop when Ish and I boarded *Tomatin* on the mid-winter Thames. She was a youthful three-masted barque and earned our immediate affection for having safely made the voyage to Australia once before. In the company of the servants and intermediate passengers, we sailed in early December from the Docks to Plymouth to meet our betters, who would travel there overland. We were bitterly cold and not yet shipshape for the voyage, but I have never seen Ish so delighted with anything before or since. He was fifteen years old, and from the first day aboard he found all glorious — from the cabin arrangements, to the rigging and workings of the ship, to yarning with sailors and helping with the livestock. I saw the love of it rise in his blood, passed down from our forefathers. He easily stood the sloping, icy decks: Captain McPherson twice called him down from the rigging on the first day. Such a stay-at-home he has been since then, it has puzzled me. He so took to the life I wondered at the time if he would cast aside any notion of career as solicitor and set to sea.

We had thought to be well gone by Christmas Day, but it came and went while we stood several weeks in the Plymouth Sound waiting for the wind. It was tedious in the extreme, the Bishop's party returning to shore for days on end, supplies being eroded and even a beast dying in the stalls — thought healthy enough to butcher, which turned the galley to a charnel house — and led to a complicated and dangerous exercise in bringing a new heifer on board by tackle and sling.

The Bishop's party was several times brought out to the ship and then back to land in the Admiral's barge. The pier had not been built then and the boats brought out the passengers at high tide. The season was colder than anyone could remember. Even there, in the south, the low hills were dusted with snow.

The last time the barge came out to the ship I could see Mary Ann heavily rugged in the stern, her little white face among the wrappings, her lips even from a distance blue. Beside her sat her elderly father, grim countenanced, perhaps as exhausted as his daughter by the journey from London. I had prepared in advance a tonic, but at first glance it had not sustained her — doubtless she had eaten nothing for days and taken little liquid. The sea was grey and choppy, the wind indirectional and undisciplined enough to toss a rogue wave into the laps of the passengers. Mary Ann hid her face in her father's shoulder — she was not enjoying her adventure.

One of the oarsmen caught my eye and exchanged a joyous smile — he was young, handsome, high-coloured, and active in his Bishop's gaiters and short black cassock. He heaved at his paddles with concentrated contentment — there, at a glance, was all the man's vitality and resolve, his refusal at any time to take the easy ride. On deck he was as excited as Ish and almost as boyish, shaking hands with Captain McPherson and greeting his Reverends, most of whom affected the new backwards collar fashionable among clergy of the High Church. I remember noticing among them the rumpled and squinting William Cotton, who was to be chaplain and librarian. He was shorter than me, fine boned, with unruly shining curls and pretty complexion. There was something sardonic about the turn of his mouth — not bitter or malicious, but the mouth of a young man given to chaffer and ready laughter. I picked him out as one I would like to know.

A little to one side of the Bishop there was a nurse carrying a small child. On his other flank stood a tall thin woman with so peculiarly pained a face I could not help but be arrested by it. It was as if she were enduring agonies as unendurable as the first, hellish pangs of birth — but she was perhaps only longing to sit down, or for silence and peace. The strangely impassive gaze never shifted once from her husband — those dry, small eyes the colour and sheen of currants. Many who met Sarah Selwyn were to comment on her appearance — particularly the twisted mouth. Her only beauty was her hair, which was dark and bright, and folded with precision over each ear. She stood in characteristic posture, shoulders rolled forward and arms clasped across her stomach, as if nightly the Bishop overwhelmed her.

Already a divide had formed in the group of arrivals — Mary

Ann's father, the Reverends Dudley and Reay and the others standing aside from the Tory Bishop and his party. The voyagers from St Mary's were mostly Whigs, Low Church, with their collars the right way round, and some of them had connections in the distant archipelago fifteen or twenty years old. For them, George Augustus Selwyn had no understanding whatever of that distant land, was too Roman in his tastes, too young for the post, and at any rate a ring-in — it was his brother the Church had wanted first, not Augustus. The missionaries wanted neither.

In the no-man's land between the two factions stood a little lad dressed in an expensive woollen coat and new leather shoes. He was perhaps younger than Ish — it was difficult to tell his age or even a hint of his temperament. He was the first Maori I had ever seen, far paler than the Africans come to London fleeing slavery in the Americas. Despite his layered coats, he had adopted the easy stance of a seasoned sailor, his hands on his hips and his glossy head tipped back to gaze at the icy mastheads.

George Rupai. What became of him, I wonder? As soon as we reached our destination, he divested himself of his English garb and took to his heels. Uppermost in his mind would have been happy reunion with his people, tho' perhaps his rapid abscondment was sped by his desire to escape the attentions of Sarah Selwyn — who thought him coarsened by his English experience and searched tirelessly all the long voyage for his noble and savage spirit.

But I did not properly meet the Bip even then — at least, we were not introduced. Mary Ann was drenched to the skin and had to remove to our cabin, her father to meet us there when she was changed, for his last goodbye.

'How delightfully squeezy!' she announced bravely at first beholding our poopdeck cabin. She had regained her courage.

It was one of the two largest in the ship, well lit by windows over the stern.

Of the two scotch chests kept back from the hold, I had arranged one as a table, the other as sideboard to hold our cups and plate. Beside that stood her wedding gift from her husband's family — a ladies' companion, a clever folding cabinet of workbox, desk and dressing case, which was to be put to extensive use. The beds were made up with fresh white linen, and a sprig of mistletoe was pinned to a headboard for the Season. Her miniature of the Judge, finished only days before we left London, was fixed to a nogging near her pillow.

She took it all in as I divested her of her wet jacket and dress, her cape and gloves.

'Our home for three months, Mrs Smith. Will we be as fast as all that?'

'That was the duration of the Captain's previous voyage. We can only hope it will be the same,' I said, unhooking her grey merino gown, which was spoiled at the back with saltblack from the barge. I would never learn to enjoy the dreary duties of lady's maid. Even then we were overdue for the discussion on the distinction between that role and that of companion, but the girl was shivering so — both with cold and anticipation — that I let it go and went instead to the galley for hot water.

There is a gap in my recollections then — the dreaming of the past ends with a memory of hurrying out of the cabin to the icy deck, and my nostrils stinging with the cold, tho' surely they never stung as they do now.

Spirit of ammonia mixed with cologne.

THREE

Miss Tripp

1866

Smelling salts, choking and pungent, were being wafted under her nose, and a pair of warm hands — men's hands? — were adjusting her legs so that they lay flat along the sofa.

'Whatever did you think you were doing, Mrs Smith?'

A handsome man was bent over her, a thick-set woman behind him, their faces blurry. She blinked, but her vision would not clear — the salts perhaps. She had never been able to tolerate them, even when it fell to her to administer them to ladies more given to fainting than she was, which was not at all. There was another figure — she could make out the shape of an elaborately frilled bonnet with a fern frond. Or was it a feather, a visiting wahine in an elaborate pōtae?

London. She was in London, in Mr Griggs's parlour. She had been going to answer a caller. Beyond Mr Griggs's shoulder there was a crinoline so absurd the woman could come no further into the room than the door, where she hovered by Mrs Stott's table and abandoned meal.

'You have given us all the most dreadful fright.'

Elizabeth removed her hand from under Mr Griggs's and patted it instead. 'I am sorry, my dear man. Kei te pai. Just give me a minute.'

'Katie Pie!' repeated the woman. 'What a turn of phrase — I do enjoy it! Is that what they say in the Colonies?'

Her voice was familiar, that particular husky fairground tone, as if its bearer used it well — in business or for entertainment. There was laughter in it, and the ghost of lively late-night conversations.

'Do you come in, Madam?' asked Mr Griggs.

The crinoline turned to take the door side-on, and Elizabeth closed her heavy eyes. There was the rustling of skirts and a soft 'oops!' from the wearer as one of Mr Griggs's many dusty bibelots fell with a dull thud.

'My sincerest apologies, Miss Tripp.' Mr Griggs had left her side. 'Mrs Smith has had a turn.'

'Can I be of assistance?' came the woman's voice.

Elizabeth managed to shake her head, though nobody was looking.

As he assisted the young lady into a chair, Mr Griggs worried. It was not at all going to plan, the careful strategy for which he had brought his early career to bear: if Mrs Smith could be thought of as an embattled old general at the end of a long campaign, or at the very least a sergeant-major, then how would he introduce her to a young officer intimate with the enemy — and not, he would stress, in any sense an affiliate of the foe, but an agent able to chart the enemy's true condition and state of mind? It was helpful in this matter to regard Mrs Smith as a man — she had after all lived independently for as long as he'd known her, and had learned to think like one. She was a fellow who played by the rules. Of Miss Tripp he was not so sure, that lady now dipping into an embroidered reticule tied with ribbon at her waist, and producing a small brown bottle of chlorodyne.

'If Mrs Smith should require it,' she murmured in that soft, husky voice he'd found so alluring at their first and only other meeting.

She smiled, showing a row of even white teeth. If she really was who she said she was, then she would be, by his necessarily rough calculations, in her late twenties. He poured her a glass of Moselle, glad of the opportunity to wrest his gaze from her face — she was certainly beautiful, but precisely why was difficult to define. Her hair, now that the extraordinary bonnet was removed, showed itself to be black and lustrous. Above the little chin the mouth was too full and the bottom lip out of proportion with the upper; her brown eyes were too deep-set, her colour too dark — but it was a face that made his heart glad, though he supposed there were many reasons why it shouldn't.

He curtailed his admiration with the observation that if Mrs Griggs were still alive he could never have made this little party — she had always had her suspicions about Mrs Smith, and the discovery of Miss Tripp would only have confirmed them. He would have had to engineer the introduction differently, hire a room or suggest meeting in a public place, which could only have widened the circle of involvement. This way, it was only his household and John Elisha and Henry who knew about it, though the letter alerting them to Kitty Tripp's existence would barely have reached the Bay of Biscay and could languish in Sydney for many months.

'Where is Miss Jennings, the lady who accompanied you to the Pavilion?' Miss Tripp was tossing her hat onto the curled arm of the sofa, at Elizabeth's feet.

A bonnet so frilled and flounced was no doubt expensive and should be preserved. What if Mrs Smith's boots bore malodorous evidence of the street? He wished Mrs Stott would come to remove them and hang the bonnet in the passage, but he could hear her clattering still through the two thin walls between the parlour and the scullery. He wished he could afford another servant.

'She also ah . . . she also suffered an attack of some kind and is upstairs in her room.'

The pink curl of ham halfway to Miss Tripp's lips lowered to rest on her plate. Anxious eyes scanned the multitude of dishes and seemed to deem none of them safe — she withdrew her narrow hands to her lap. He had lost his appetite too: the gelatine of fish was grey around its moulded edges and lurid amber at the uppers — where had Mrs Stott got it? She must have bought it in — neither the cramped kitchen nor her culinary skills extended far enough for its manufacture.

There — he had caught Miss Tripp's eye and smiled now to show he understood: one could not be too careful these days. The summer had brought an unholy trinity of panics. The miasma from the Thames had reeked for miles, bringing fear of another cholera, which had not so far eventuated; the second and third terrors were of poisoned food and of garrotting, the former no more prevalent than before and the latter a new fashion among the more murderous of the footpads and thieves. From his correspondence with India and New Zealand, he gathered the fad had not reached the Colonies.

'This is all very lovely, Mr Griggs. I hope my delay has not inconvenienced you further.'

He would have preferred the conversation to drift towards one or other of those too common preoccupations, rather than to the matter directly at hand, which was Mrs Smith in a dead faint. Miss Tripp was angling her chair so that she could more conveniently gaze on the poor face, mouth slack over sparse teeth, the eyelids fluttering.

What if Mrs Smith only seemed to be fast asleep? What if she were to overhear a bald statement of identity before he'd been able to approach the subject delicately — but not so delicately as was his wont, wherein the subject could be entirely eclipsed? Mrs Stott, for instance, had likely got the wrong impression — all these comestibles were designed for a joyful reunion, which it wasn't at all: the ladies had never met.

The new arrival returned his smile, and he saw a sudden resemblance to Henry — the way the light shifted in her large eyes as humour dawned, the softening of her high brow.

'So that's her, then. We thought she had passed on,' she murmured, and she shook her head. 'I would have thought that, all things considered, she would have been a great beauty. My mother was, you see, and so it follows that this lady would be more so . . .' Her cheeks flushed.

'Oh, but she was, indeed.' Mr Griggs came to her rescue. 'Very handsome — or handsome enough, I should say, and by that I mean . . .' Oh, but he hoped Mrs Smith was deeply asleep . . . 'I have been of her acquaintance for many years.'

'Has she had a very hard life?' This last said with a touching sympathy.

In Mr Griggs's time he had viewed a number of corpses — fallen soldiers on the battlefield, the loss of some of his frailer boys, his own father and mother. The more senior of the departed often looked younger when they were laid out, as if the years of work and worry had fallen away. Mrs Smith, who approximated the same position with her hands clasped on her chest but was now breathing stentoriously through her considerable nose, looked, if anything, older — but then, she was not yet dead, and perhaps that eerie youth fell only in the last hours.

'An effect of the climate in the Colonies,' he told Miss Tripp. 'You have surely seen other such casualties of the sun.'

'Oh yes, particularly in India ... My goodness — her poor hands!'

He had noticed before, of course, how Mrs Smith's stiffened and arthritic fingers struggled to clasp knife and fork, or pen. Her last letters from New Zealand were almost illegible.

'I think, Miss Tripp, it would be as well to ...'

She took his meaning and averted her gaze. All was quiet, save for the ticking of the clock in the pauses between Mrs Smith's exhalations and Mrs Stott's distant efforts in the kitchen. His house had the atmosphere of a hospital.

'It's very peaceful indeed, where you live, Mr Griggs,' Miss Tripp observed after a moment. 'I like to be more amongst life — but I suppose the fresh air is more wholesome for your students.'

Mr Griggs nodded. He would like to know more about her, other than the few facts he had. From where, for instance, did the name 'Tripp' arise? Had she adopted it as a necessary disguise, or was it her professional name? Or the name of her benefactor? His informant could assure him only of her paternity.

'Should you not call a doctor?' she asked with a faint gesture towards the incumbent on the sofa.

'Mrs Smith has no great regard for physicians,' he replied warily. 'I did so once before and earned her wrath.'

'These turns are frequent, then?'

'Fairly so.'

Miss Tripp lifted her hand as if she was to take up her glass, reconsidered and dropped it again. Did she also suspect the

Moselle? It had gathered dust for years, and Mrs Stott's request to decant it had rather taken him by surprise — but then the depletion of his cellar was synchronous with Mrs Smith's return.

'Miss Tripp, I have been thinking of how we may approach the sensitive matter of the introduction.'

She nodded.

'I think — if you will agree — I will introduce you as my cousin, or distant relative, and leave it to you to win her trust. Once that is achieved, we will proceed.'

'To what?' Miss Tripp's perfect brow striated.

'In our investigations. You and she could perhaps pool what information you have on the gentleman . . . Hush!'

Mrs Smith was stirring.

'Where is Mr Cotton?' Mrs Smith's eyes were open and sightless, primed upon the ceiling.

'Who?' asked Miss Tripp.

'We are to have a party in his cabin. The Cup of Grace. We will all go together. Me haere tahi tātou.'

Miss Tripp flashed her eyes in alarm.

'What language is that?'

'Maori, I do believe. Mrs Smith offers living proof of the foolhardiness of long voyages. Not all of us are born Captain Cooks.'

'Whatever do you mean?'

'The chickens are all dead!' exclaimed Mrs Smith dolefully.

'I mean —' Mr Griggs leaned across the table and lowered his voice — 'I mean that the dear lady has travelled almost as far as it is possible to do so on our Earth, and back again, and seems to have left a part of herself behind.'

Miss Tripp's response was rapid.

'But that is not right!' she cried. 'It is cruel to let it continue.'

She was on her feet and, before he could prevent it, bending over Mrs Smith to rouse her.

FOUR

Tin Kettle

I NEVER WAS ONE FOR SITTING about, even when I sustained an injury and was under instructions to rest. Look to Nature — how the bird with injured wing persists in fluttering until the end, how the lame horse tries its step. Mankind, with the gift of apothecary, may accelerate his healing. His intelligence raises him above the dumb suffering of the beast. I taught my sons that pain is the enemy and must be mettled, with the result that both display great fortitude. Bishop Selwyn's wife, on the other hand, was of a mind to succumb to every pang and disapproved of stoicism on principle, tho' worshipped the unholy reserves in the possession of her husband.

I am sitting about now. Look at me, cast on Mr Griggs's sofa, an elderly whale. I find myself hardly able to shift a muscle but feel, strangely, as much at peace as I was after a long day's drudge at the Martins' house and Native Hospital, or the Missions further south.

In the evenings at Taurarua we took turns to read aloud. If we women were alone, we favoured Elizabeth Gaskell and Miss Bremer. If Judge Martin was there, he read to us from his collection of old chronicles and Indian lore, and twice through entirely we heard *Don Quixote*. We would gather in the lamplight in that frail, leaking wooden parlour above the Waitemata Harbour — Mary Ann, the Judge, myself, and whoever else was in company: very often Mr Cotton, Sarah Selwyn, my dear Henry, our loquacious lawyer neighbour Mr Swainson, all of us resting our weary bones — but I was never to be come upon reading a book during the day. One has to be born to that.

How much more indolent must it be to spend one's hours writing one? I might never have the patience. Both Ish and Henry in their Gideonite capacities — in their *enslavement* to the Colonial Government! — spend countless hours of every day hunched over desks writing letters. As young men they wrote endlessly to one another, Ish from Wellington and Hy from Auckland, or Maketu, or Rotorua — the stay-at-home solicitor and tireless Native Interpreter keeping one another abreast of developments. It was a fierce attachment, made fiercer still by the absent father and dearth of siblings. It grew less as they grew older, as all loves do, be they of marriage or blood ties, and the letters grew sparser. When Henry was with me in Auckland and young Ish was first articled to Wellington, they each posted weighty packets that would often go partially unread by the busy recipient — or, as happened more than once, were sunk on a leaking coastal trader little better than a hulk. It was the immediacy of conversation they craved, and letters were a poor substitute.

My account, should I make one, would be a poor substitute for tender recollections better shared in conversation with distant friends, the few I possess.

Shortly before I left New Zealand, I complained to Henry of how lonely my life had been.

'My dearest mother,' he replied distractedly as he searched for a lost paper on his chaotic desk, 'it has been the opposite. You have led a life so crowded over that, because you find it now a little less so, you think it empty always.'

He was correct, the most sapient of my sons, the first-born — tho' the misunderstanding came about through misuse of language. I did not mean 'lonely' as in a life of solitude; I meant a life unloved. It was because as a young woman I had delighted in love in all its guises — and like a fat man who has gorged through his youth and now suffers gout and intestinal disturbances must subsist on invalid pap, on arrowroot and soft bread, never a tasty portion of meat and sauce.

A poor analogy — I am doing my dear ones a disservice! They have never deprived me of affection. It was hardly a subsistence diet. What I mean, if I am honest, is that when I boarded *Tomatin* I was not yet forty and could have passed for much younger — my hair still thick, my complexion fine enough. My secret hope was that a good man might come to love me — the Colony thronged with bachelors and was bereft of spinsters. Perhaps a man of middle years might form an affection strong enough to throw in his lot with mine, and he and I could make our own home. I longed for that above all else. A home of my own. To be mistress of my own household. It was all I ever wanted.

Briefly I was allowed both a man and a home, tho' not together at the same time and only through my own efforts. The love was secret and the cottage almost universally disapproved of, particularly by Bishop Selwyn.

There is a young woman rousing me, trying to shake me from my reverie. I don't know who she is. She's certainly not on the inventory — I recognised all the passengers early in our voyage.

Away with you, young lady! I am remembering that earlier crew and in particular the Bishop, whose sharp face floats through my recollections as often as any lover or husband.

Finally, at long last, I made my personal acquaintance with that man over a sickbed, as I did with so many gentlemen. He had any lady praise the Lord for his very existence — such masculine beauty, such perseverance, such vigour! — and, shortly afterwards, to give thanks that he was not one's husband.

On the evening of St Stephen's Day, the twenty-sixth of December, Captain McPherson gave his command to haul the anchor. Waving his hat from the poop, the Bishop and one of his divine associates called Latin exaltations — 'Floreat ecclesia! Floreat Etona!' — back and forth between ship and retreating longboat so enthusiastically that I feared I was putting to sea with a pack of adventurous schoolboys with the Bishop as Chief Monitor.

There was the brightest moon imaginable casting shadows of the masts across the icy deck where so many of us gathered, unable to believe that our adventure was at long last beginning.

'Sir Walter Scott!' exclaimed William Cotton, who walked beside me. He pointed to a head-shaped cloud, which at that moment was beginning its traverse across the moon. My heart grew cold at the profile. I did not know Sir Walter in the flesh or in any portrait. For me, the cloud bore an uncanny resemblance to a man I had tried to forget. Here was his likeness rising illuminated above the mastheads to bid me goodbye — or foretell certain death, or worse the loss of his living son — while I should linger Earthside and despairing. Mr Cotton had my arm and walked on unheeding while I stared up, barely able to contain my horror — and caught my foot in a coil of rope and fell heavily, wrenching my ankle.

Mr Cotton called for Hussey, his manservant, and between them they carried me to the cabin I shared with Mrs Martin, where — once I had soothed her consternation — I did my best to dismiss the ill portent. Was he dead then, is that what it meant? Or by leaving England had I foregone any chance of ever seeing him again? I had not thought I cared so much. It was perhaps the lying off Plymouth that had rekindled my sentiment, since that was where we had met and from where we had eloped to Bristol. I had not once gone ashore for fear of meeting someone who remembered me.

While I lay in my berth, I heard the rush of feet overhead: all hands were on deck to turn the ship's head south, for the appearance of that cloud was somehow contiguous with the sudden lifting in the sails that pleased the Captain and decided his course. I did not like the synchronicity — the portent deepened and took hold. I would often think of it and the warning it may have offered.

In Mr Cotton's journal, which he kindly allows me to read from on my visits to Doctor Tuke's asylum, he has it that all but the Bishop and the few of us seasoned from the Thames suffered seasickness until January the second — the date the Bishop decreed the sickness would stop and his regime of learning and worship begin. Mrs Martin had never before gone to sea, not even across the Channel, for her delicacy. She was one of the worst affected, and of the ladies I the least, but my injury prevented me from properly assisting her.

Sedulous in his preparation for life among the Maoris, the Bishop occupied himself with the printed grammar and texts and George Rupai, our 'walking dictionary', and hardly enquired after Mrs Martin's wellbeing. Ish — already dubbed 'Young Smith' by Mr Cotton — proved an excellent nurse, bringing basins and flannels, and perching on the edge of Mary Ann's berth to feed her soup, which very often he carried away again to feed to Blackie, the ship's dog. Ish shared a cabin with Edward Arnold, one of the Bishop's six servants, and the Maori lad. By such close proximity he picked up the language more quickly than most, and was assiduous in teaching me what he learned when I could leave Mary Ann's side. She was ill for the first two months — how glad I was of her father's gift, the field chest.

In London my lady and I had prepared it. We had filled its various compartments with pharmacopoeia: the grains, tinctures and potions I had come to depend upon in my professional capacity, as well as the many favoured by Mary Ann during her varied and colourful illnesses.

'I do so love laudanum!' she'd announced brightly one day as we designated that substance to its place.

'It's not worthy of love, my dearest girl, only gratitude for its existence,' I told her, surprising her and myself with not only the stern admonishment but also the endearment, one of my earliest for her.

Laudanum eased her convulsions, tho' I had to be cautious against exceeding the dose — I had seen fever cases choke when too heavily tranquillised. A side-effect was bouts of weeping for England and for the Judge, for whom she had formed — during their four brief days of unconsummated marriage before his departure — an intense, romantic and innocent devotion which I believe never altered nor left her.

When finally I begin my account, I shall be sure not to so digress but draw close more speedily to the matter of my first interview with the

Bishop. He paid us a visit after Mary Ann had failed to appear for the second day of his classes, sending with Ish a message of his intention.

My patient was poorly, but heartened at the prospect of his company. We brushed her hair, Mary Ann taking the brush from me for the sensitive hair around her face — as she was always to do — before I replaited it in two scrawny braids over her shoulders. When His Lordship made his entrance she was propped pale against her pillows.

Selwyn was as unsure of himself as I had seen him, tho' Mrs Martin was the wife of his oldest friend. I saw at a glance that for all his enthusiastic religion he was a man who could not regard a woman in bed without a certain quickening of the pulse. For all his endeavour to ignore it, he failed — and was pleased to divert his attention to me after offering only the most cursory solace to the invalid.

'Mrs Smith.'

I have heard people say that the eyes are the windows of the soul. If this is true, then it is important that a woman such as myself, on meeting the eyes of a young man such as the Bishop — searching, clear, judgemental, fervent — must indulge in a degree of obfuscation. It was essential that he believe me a good woman, and one who had always been, so I met his scorching gaze only briefly. He helped by not offering me his hand, as he would a woman of equal standing: I was forced to drop an ankle-paining curtsey.

'I have met your son. An impressive young man.'

'Thank you, my Lord.'

'When did he lose his father?'

Mary Ann's shawls required rearranging over her thin form.

'Many years ago. He has no real memory of him.'

'Indeed?'

I would not look at him. Mary Ann too was searching my face. I longed to run and hide — an impulse the Bishop would often engender in me.

'My Lord?' she ventured, whether knowingly acting the decoy I could not tell. 'Could you ask Mrs Selwyn to visit me? I should love to see her. I am assured my complaint is not infectious.'

'My apologies,' said the Bishop in so irritated a voice I risked a glance in his direction. 'I will order her to call on you straight away.'

'No, no,' Mary Ann said in that same pleading voice she had previously reserved for her little dog — left, thankfully, to live out its natural life in England. 'I mean for you just to mention that I am well enough now to receive her.'

She was always taken with Sarah. The attraction lay in the children the Selwyns had in quick succession, most notably the firstborn, Willie, who was two years old for the duration of the voyage. Everybody doted on him, particularly Mary Ann and Mr Cotton, who knew all the children's songs — 'Buy a Broom' and 'Froggy' and 'Isle of Beauty', which we were surely sailing towards.

Soon after, through the thin wall that separated our quarters from the Selwyns' we heard Sarah Selwyn's sharp tones of defence: 'If it was fever I could have carried it to Willie.'

'She is seasick. That is all. You are too concerned for your own wellbeing.'

'I am not, Augustus. That is most unfair.'

'You will not speak to me so. I forbid it.'

Mary Ann lay in her white bed, her eyes flashing alarm at me, whispering, 'Oh dear. I did not mean . . . oh dear dear . . .'

Mrs Selwyn wept, the child woke and cried, there was consternation from the nurse, the child was put back to bed, and Augustus took a walk upon the deck before evening service, which Mary Ann and I did not attend.

Hours later, while I plied a sleepless needle to the swaying lamp, out of the dark came the music of matrimonial faddling, Sarah emitting a series of high-pitched mews, while the young Bishop performed a froglike bass.

'Froggy', indeed.

'What is that noise?' asked Mary Ann sleepily.

'It is the Bishop performing his callisthenics,' I told her.

'But that other sound? Whatever poor creature is it?' By that gentle query her innocence was proved.

'The ship's cat. She must be wanting to come in.'

There was no privacy on that tiny ship.

At length, Mary Ann was well enough to take daily walks on the deck and to attend the Bishop's classes in Maori language at ten o'clock every morning but Sunday. She was not so fond of the Greek that followed the hour after, or the Hebrew that followed the ship-biscuit and cheese at one, nor less the mathematics and navigation after that, and would draw me away back to the cabin or, if fine, up top. It was not that the learning was too advanced, for William Cotton accorded Mrs Martin's Greek as being 'most excellent for a woman', but rather quite another reason. There was always work for me to be getting on with, laundry or mending, tidying and sweeping. When she was well enough, Mary Ann would sit by as if she had to keep me at my task, and would draw my attention to missed patches of polishing or clumsy stitches, and through it all would give me such glimpses of love and gratitude. She came to have a higher opinion of my scholarly abilities — tho' not as high as she could have done, drudge and design conspiring to hide my light under a bushel. I came to realise she was absenting us for my own sake.

'Lingua Novella Zelandica is all that we require, Mrs Smith. What use have you for those other endeavours that would only have you dissatisfied with your lot?'

We dined each day at three — Mrs Martin side by side with Mrs Selwyn on the sofa in the cuddy, the rest of the Bishop's party ranged around the long table. Ish and I dined below with the intermediate passengers and servants. Very often the Bishop sent down his meat — it was how he maintained his sinew by eating so little of it — which the young men fell upon.

There were fifty-two of us aboard that squeezy barque, all of us young — I was among the elders! — and all of us, aside from poor Sarah Selwyn, full of optimism and excitement. I can state this so categorically because I passed between upper and lower decks more frequently than most. Already an egalitarian spirit infected our band of near-New Zealanders, one that was to grow and spread on landing, to strengthen further that noble sentiment already taken root.

It is perhaps one of the causes of these momentary fits that have come upon me since my return. Where England is changed in so many ways in twenty years — particularly overcrowded and raucous London — it has not changed in that way, or not as society has in our outpost. The masses here persist in chains. Just the other day a toff was bemoaning how the railways shift too easily the working class, how all this moving about overstimulates their minds and could lead to revolution. He forgets life before they built so many manufactories, how the villages emptied. I am old enough to remember that some of us have always been on the road, whether we like it or not. Not all of us have the prophet's blood and like to wander as Moses did — to seek new lands and opportunities. I would have preferred a steady roof — my own home, a home of my own, my own home.

Even I weary of the versicle. I keep as antidote a letter from Henry: 'Providence has not so arranged for you that you can have the society of those that love you and also be mistress of your own house — you can have either but not both — either here or anywhere else.' Now, in London, I have neither — such a bleak truth I cannot face it. I would remember better the long-ago voyage out, our joyous delight with the unfolding adventure, and how our attachments deepened. I will remember Mr Cotton and how we came to call him Bee.

William Cotton rose from his berth after seven days, one of the earliest to recover from seasickness. He was one of the Bishop's closest adherents and possibly even more energetic, if that was possible. When not wood-turning at his lathe — at which he excelled — or at bookwork or Bible-reading, he was tending his bees, which he was planning to introduce to New Zealand, that country not being yet the land of milk and honey he would have liked to anticipate. As soon as my ankle healed and my duties allowed, I would seek him out. He was marvellous company, being always full of laughter, arcane pieces of knowledge and humorous observations. He maintained his spirits for almost the entire long six months of the voyage, with only the occasional palest shadow of melancholy — even at the failure of his experiment. We had not yet seen his demons — they came to light much later.

Mr Cotton's hives were housed in ingenious devices of his own making — double-walled, felt-lined barrels which could be cooled in the Tropics with ice, and held warm in the chill at either end of our voyage. He showed Ish and me how the inhabitants could pass easily in and out on fine days but be corralled when the weather was intemperate. We assisted him in mixing the sugar syrup that nourished them in place of nectar. The hogsheads were kept apart from the warm livestock in another part of the ship, near the 'castle, which did not please the sailors — there being an ancient superstition that bees bring bad luck at sea. Mr Cotton maintained that this arose only from a primitive fear of the sting, dating from earliest Creation. I proved a worthy ally, being adept at removing the dart without depressing the tiny sac of poison. It was really only on one occasion that the sailors were stung in any numbers.

It was the day that Captain McPherson decided he would not put in to Cape Colony for water. Hot and still, *Tomatin* wallowing, we made slow progress. Early in the morning the sailors were set to holystoning the decks and sail-mending. Among the intermediates and servants at the tubs I attended to the laundry — all of us looking forward to our time ashore. While Ish drew up buckets of water and I soaped and scrubbed, we dreamed of Africa — elephants and giraffes parading the streets, organ-grinders with monkeys of every size and hue. We had been at sea for two months.

When the Captain made his announcement from the fo'c's'le, I observed from my position at the saltwater trough that the Bishop stood close behind him. I wondered if he had been instrumental in the decision, there already being gossip among the passengers and servants about disagreements between the two on our course and speed. Nor, we had heard, did the Captain appreciate Augustus's habit of going among the sailors to give them lengthy advisements that kept them from their work.

A collective rumble went up, and the first mate spoke sharply to the sailors around him. They responded angrily — there were raised voices — some shoving — and suddenly a fight broke out near Mr Cotton's hives, which were open for the still weather.

A cabin boy — a tough, stringy little creature with whom His Lordship had taken to sharing his prayer book at Matins in the cuddy — was knocked by a flying limb into one of the barrels. The bees flew out in an angry yellow-and-black swarm, alerting their fellows in the barrels still standing. At their approach, I had the presence of mind to drape myself head to foot in one of Mary Ann's nightgowns, wet and slicked with saltwater soap. Above the shouts and consternation I could hear the buzzing — I emerged only in time to see Mr Cotton's barrels being heaved one after the other over the side, where at first they floated before the sea found their openings and so dragged them down. The apiarist erupted in sudden, wild laughter and had to be ushered below by his friend William Bambridge and his servant Hussey.

His response endeared him to me more — I knew that urge too, for hadn't I laughed like that on that long-ago night when my fortunes changed for ever, when my dreams of the future were shattered? The woman at the door had put her hands to her ears.

While Selwyn strode fearless among the crew to break up the brawl, the ladies screeched for the bees. Heedless of stings, Ish burst from the galley with an earthenware jar and tin saucer, and did his best to trap the insects still clinging to the mizzen and ladies' dresses, and took them later to Mr Cotton's cabin. By his report, our friend had his face turned to the wall and gave scarcely a murmur when Ish came in and placed them carefully beside him. They must have been quietly disposed of later. Neither the hives nor the bees were ever mentioned again. Mr Cotton let Ish mourn enough for both of them.

I was left to tend to my son's stings and wipe his tears for the loss, just as I soothed him when all the chickens died, and a newly whelped bitch — tho' we saved her pups. Fortunately, the lad was at Greek testament in the cuddy when a goose flapped loose from her pen to be bloodily devoured by a shark — and neither did he witness Mr Cotton throwing from his porthole a piglet that had developed the habit of rootling in his cabin on its frequent escapes. Poor Ish felt it all so keenly. The Bishop spoke sharply to him once or twice as a father might — 'Be a man, Elisha!' — and each time the lad brooded for hours or days, or at least until the daily catches were brought on board. These were taken from the sticker rigged out from the bowsprit, an accommodation to allow easy hunting — as many as twenty sharks and dolphins in a day.

Young Rupai excelled at catching sharks, attaching seabirds or dolphin meat to an iron hook and fighting the beasts up to the fo'c's'le deck. There, as the huge fish died, he would kick them and talk furiously in his native tongue. It was Mr Cotton who listened carefully enough to translate — it seemed he was berating the monsters for his fated journey to England, which he had neither wanted nor enjoyed. They were taniwha, a type of monster. They were whiro — of bad character. Mrs Selwyn saw Rupai's rage as a display of ill temper and would try to restrain him — until she herself was restrained by men in the company who found the lad's savagery amusing. I felt sorry for his distress and tried once to draw him away with promises of cake and cordial, but he roughly shoved me away and went back to his game of revenge and blame.

It is the shared laughter I am nostalgic for — the good spirits roused by evening games and charades in the poop, a part of the deck that offered comfort with a canvas roof and places to rest. There we had songs and chants, Bambridge at his flute or violin and the Bishop's student Fisher entertaining us — he was a gifted mimic and performer. Between rounds of Post-boy, Puss-ill and 'Linka linka linka!' he would do imitations. His Bishop was priceless, and he had Mr Cotton's habit of pushing his spectacles to the bridge of his nose and Sarah's peculiar grimace to perfection.

One night, some weeks before the bee incident, while we stood in the doldrums some distance off St Paul's, Mary Ann organised a game of dress-up charades. We lent the student Mr Fisher his costume for the occasion. It was my slop gown, the only garment we had that would fit him — and rank it was, tho' after so many months at close quarters our noses were dulled. We trimmed it with a clean white apron and set it off with bonnet and fall, pinning at the back one of Mary Ann's hairpieces. Mr Fisher made a pretty girl and, once he had settled upon her saucy tongue, was a lass to set even the dullest party sparkling. Little Mr Bambridge was at the violin — he had borrowed a sailor's costume, a round jacket several sizes too big and canvas trousers rolled. The evening was further enlivened, if I may be so bold, by a tincture of my own manufacture that I served in tiny quantities for its potency.

'What is this called, Mrs Smith?' asked Reverend Reay, who was jigging to the violin after his second cup. 'It does so give me dancing legs!'

'The Cup of Grace.'

It came to me in an instant. It was a night for inspiration, there being a full moon, and so clear and still that the horizon met the heavens without delineation. The vast, surrounding ocean reflected the swathed galaxies — our ship floated among stars.

'The Cup of Salvation?' asked Mr Cotton, bright-eyed. From two pieces of whalebone borrowed from a corset he had fashioned on his lathe an ingenious pair of antennae fixed to a band around his head. The carved and painted baubles hung one from each extreme, bobbing over his face.

'Of Grace, Mr Cotton.' A scrap of scripture floated to me as I raised the bottle for another round. 'Ye shall indeed drink of my cup!'

'Matthew chapter twenty, verse twenty-three,' supplied Reverend Dudley from under a Turk's cap, tho' fairly subdued as if he risked blasphemy and looking about to see if the Bishop had joined us — but the Selwyns were not yet in attendance.

Young Fisher snatched the bottle from me and inserted it beneath the veil, swigging more deeply than strictly was wise.

'Babylon hath been a golden cup in the Lord's hand, that made all the earth drunken!' It was a female voice — but different to the one he had invented in our cabin.

'That's you, Mrs Smith!' giggled Mary Ann, who was Titania in gauzy shawls and crown.

I laughed with the rest so as not to seem ill-humoured — but it galled me. There was my mother's soft Gloucester burr, mixed with the harsher tones of the cockney chavvies who shared my childhood years and, worse, the false Kensington hoot I had consciously copied from my first employer on the impulse to improve myself. And was there also a hint of Horelock's persuasive Scots lilt? A right softie I must sound like, I thought, half off my brain.

Or perhaps Mary Ann had recognised only the familiar gesture of holding up one finger, a habit gained from a decade of bedside exhortations.

'Are we to know the compound?' asked ship's doctor Butt, who so far had not partaken.

I shook my head. 'Suffice to say it will not harm thee, Doctor.'

But the crow was not convinced, as crows will never be by their inferiors, so I swigged another daffy to prove it safe.

Then there was dancing and general merriment until ten o'clock, at which time the still-absent Bishop's rules decreed that ladies should turn in. As spirits were still running high and conviviality coursed among us, I departed to our cabin to fetch another bottle.

All was quiet in the Selwyns' quarters next door, and likewise in the adjoining nursery where slept little Willie and his nurse, which was pleasing. An enthusiast for every wholesome activity, Augustus was a Marplot at *soirées* and parties — a wet blanket, a drain on proceedings. We had so very much more fun without him.

'Sweet slumber, dear fellow!' I whispered, hurrying back towards the poop, the corked brown bottle clasped to my breast.

But there — just as I emerged onto the main deck, I heard voices. It was the Bip himself, tying a tin kettle to Frederic Fisher at the foot of the Companion Ladder. Fisher had removed his bonnet, his face was stricken, and the hairpiece lay at his foot like the dead rat it is named for. Above us the music had stopped, and Bambridge and others were come to the rail to look down.

'Shame on you, Fisher!' A blue tendon twitched along the Bishop's sharp jaw and his eyes in the moonlight were bulging with rage. 'I presume you wear your own clothes underneath? Take it off.'

Fisher made a gesture that meant — here? Now?

Selwyn nodded. I would have waited in the shadowy door, but

the young man was shamed as a sailor caught with a she-shirt, and tore at my only slop gown so desperately that I feared for its future utility. As careful as if it were an egg, I propped the bottle in a coil of rope and came forward to assist his disrobing.

The gown was hideous, a grey cast-off from a prior mistress, with three torn rosettes drooping at the neckline and a sharktooth mend at the shoulder — did the Bishop recognise it as mine? I had more than once hurried past him in it, bent on some odious task.

'Ah. I should have guessed. Mrs Smith.'

'My Lord.'

'What is this "Cup of Grace" they are drinking in the poop?'

In my account, of course, I will mention well before now that I was dressed in Fisher's second-best coat and trousers — we had made a fair swap — so that my readers, that is, dear Henry and Ish, can picture the scene more clearly. Ish will have his own recollection — he may have another version for his brother; he watched wide-eyed from the poop while I fumbled at the hooks and eyes, scarcely more adept than Fisher had been.

'It was an exchange. Don't be looking for more than that in it,' I said, as soothingly as I could.

'Enough from you, Mrs Smith. You will not tell me what to think.'

As I reached around to free the apron, I caught a glimpse of Fisher's gormless face above the gown. I had seen the same expression on the faces of organ-grinders' monkeys when a crowd of children grew too boisterous — a rictus of fear and alarm.

'This is not at all amusing, young Fisher.'

'No,' agreed the Bishop's student, part of whose stricken brain had not yet fully abandoned his role. 'My 'umble 'pologies, sir.'

There was a burst of hastily stifled laughter from the rail above — among it the high-pitched, slightly hysterical giggle of Mr Cotton. Without looking at them, the Bishop thundered an edict.

'Everyone turn in!'

Under my fingers, Fisher's sweating back trembled with laughter or tears — he was in such a state I doubted he knew which himself. At length I managed to loosen the strings at the bodice and haul the stuff from his arms while the assembled made their departure, ladies first down the Companion Ladder. Mrs Lister and old Mrs Liddel were first, both with their eyes averted — when the Bishop was roused, no one wanted to draw his individual attention. Mary Ann, lifted down between two men, came to stand anxiously beside him.

'My Lord?' she tried. 'The fault for all of this must lie with me.'

Selwyn plainly thought the admission absurd and made a sweeping, dismissive gesture in her direction, which set her bright veils moving.

'You will explain, Mr Fisher —' he began.

'No, I must insist!' In the clear moonlight, Mary Ann's thin face was flushed with indignation. 'I chose the game. We were playing dress-up charades.'

'Indeed. And who were you, Mrs Smith?'

'Wordsworth,' I replied, and so I had been, wandering lonely as a cloud.

A sudden breeze caught the mizzen quartersail and the ship rose over a long smooth billow; Mary Ann lost her tentative balance and fell against our interrogator — tho' regained it as quick as I'd ever seen her.

A midshipman set to nightwatch was rousing himself from the shadows and looking about, his boots scuffing on the timbers directly behind me. As he passed behind the mast, I feared for my brew.

Quietly, the Bishop made a show of viewing the passing parade. William Cotton had removed his antennae; Bambridge's wife had divested herself of the baby's bonnet and concealed the feeding bottle under her shawl. Earlier she had supped her Cup of Grace from it — any dregs left to mix with her baby's milk would with luck lend her a peaceful night. The Bishop's profile was inscrutable.

Fisher's disguise was now entirely removed; he stood in his trousers and undershirt. I shook the ugly thing out and folded it with the pinny over one arm, offering the other to Mary Ann — her flush had left her and she looked more knocked-up than ever.

The Bishop laid a heavy hand on Fisher's shoulder.

'I will see you at six o'clock in the cuddy before morning prayers and we will discuss your peculiar proclivities.' He gave the student a little push. 'Could you see Mrs Martin to her cabin? I am not finished with you, Mrs Smith.'

Obediently, without even a glance of solidarity, Mary Ann took the proffered arm and disappeared into the shadows. At first it seemed the Bishop was to follow them, because he passed behind me — but it was to pick up my bottle from the coil of rope. He held it aloft.

'The ingredients, please.'

I hesitated — did he want the full recipe? He tapped his Episcopal ring against the glass.

'Mrs Smith? Were you in female garb I would invite you to sit down, but as you assume hideous and ridiculous masculinity, you can stand.'

It sounded like a challenge — how tempted I was to square my shoulders and throw out my chest. I had a sudden desire to see the Bishop laugh — the effects of the Cup, no doubt, which just as quickly vanished to be replaced by my suddenly aroused maternal affection. I would soothe away his unnecessary sadness, more suited to a sickroom than the last moments of what had been, after all, a marvellous party.

'It is cordial,' I told him, 'an orgeat I made in London and brought on board.'

'Almonds and rosewater?' The Bishop sniffed at the cork. He removed it and sniffed further. 'I think not. But thank you, Mrs Smith.'

'With some additions.'

He was never going to allow me to chaff him. Once more he tapped his ring against the glass, the tiny sound preternaturally loud — it was the opiates coursing through my veins and the weirdly still night. Around the furled yards the stars whirled.

'Rum. Wine. Cloves. Sugar. Kendal's Black Drop. Godfrey's Cordial.'

The Bishop didn't waste a second.

'You must be Coleridge, then? Wordsworth makes public his disapproval of the Black Drop — a sentiment I share. You chose the wrong poet for your charade.'

The thoroughly modern man strode away to empty the bottle

into the tide, his busy little body bent forward in that characteristic way of his, leading with his jaw as if his legs couldn't carry his head as fast as it wanted to go.

'Bliss was it in that dawn to be alive, But to be young was very heaven.' My poet's lines rose on my tongue and could have taken shape between us as a plea for clemency, but the Cup of Grace poured out, a steady amber stream to the ocean, the still air carrying the scent of spice and port, and all hope was extinguished.

'Now I know you for a liar,' he said, so quietly I only just heard him.

How I would have loved to melt away into our lovely cabin, where the moonlight would be streaming in at the panes on the stern — but I was held there as if I was a chastised child, one that knows the scolding has time to run yet. He had taken me at my word and called me a liar.

The Bishop of New Zealand knew Elizabeth Smith for a liar! I was sick with shame. How one necessary untruth spawns another less necessary, and another less still, and another merely sporting — until one is capable of lying out of habit.

The Bishop spoke again, louder. 'It is such a pleasant evening that perhaps we could engage one another in light conversation.'

He gave the bottle a little shake, which unbidden brought to mind the way a man will shake the last drops from his cod after urinating. I only just managed to quell the gust of laughter that threatened to erupt. How glad I was he didn't observe the convulsion it cost me — I wished the Cup gone from my blood and equanimity returned.

'If you like.'

'If you like, *my Lord*.'

He had taken against me, that much was certain. But it was often so with this new breed of men, who coupled with their fervent religion an abhorrence of spirited women. He gestured for me to join him at the rail, and together we looked out over the star-sparkling sea for some moments in total silence. The full-bellied moon spilled its golden path low on the horizon.

Beside me, eventually, at length, the Bishop took a deep breath, and I thought for a moment that the serenity of the night had brought him to prayer — so used was I by now to his patterns of speech that I knew which breath preceded what, for hadn't I listened to the charming but conceited fellow for hours? He only occasionally relinquished his pulpit in cuddy or poop to High and Dry Whytehead or Cotton, never to Low and Slow Dudley and Reay.

But I was wrong.

'I understand you have another son in New Zealand.'

'Henry Smith. He is with the Wakefields at Port Nicholson.'

'And that is why you have engineered your place on this voyage, no doubt. Mrs Martin describes you as her old friend, but you are not of so long an acquaintance, are you?'

All my longing for my clever, sweet-natured first-born rose in me yet again. How the yearning for a departed son may pain the heart as deeply or worse as for a lover! I had known some dark days — but those that had passed between Henry's sailing and my taking of the position with Mrs Martin were the bleakest in my life. In those cold, empty hours on the too-partitioned top floor of the Cross Street lodging house I survived only by conjuring him as a babe in arms, as a little lad set round with his playthings, as a boy of twelve, as he was as a young man of eighteen bent on adventure, and back again to babe, and even the happy months I'd carried him. I had missed the lads during their schooling, but never so sorely until an ocean opened between us.

'Smith,' mused the Bishop. 'You could perhaps have settled on a more inventive name. The Colonies teem with Smiths, and most like you — with something to hide.' He turned his lofty gaze on me.

He had the most extraordinarily powerful eyes, our dear Bishop — one moment loving, enhancing of whomever he beheld; the next arctic, censorious, dismissive.

'My husband died when the children were small boys. I managed on an inheritance until they were of an age to go to school, and was compelled then to go into service, first as a governess, later as a nurse.'

Men's clothes allow easeful grace — it's scarce as if they wear clothes at all after the dragging skirts of my own sex. I found myself leaning again against the rail, one arm hooked through the rigging, while I embarked on the same chronology I had given the Reverend Parker on the day I first met Mary Ann — a story I'd worn smooth through scores of tellings. It has more the qualities of legend than myth. There are truths, half-truths and inspired invention, its origin only a spectre glimpsed through the mists of time — an ancient tower rising ruined on a foggy hill. There is the obfuscated first chapter, with the conclusive, fateful parts more vivid — and the bald, unadorned style of recount.

I confessed to my failure at bringing the family in Camden through typhus fever, and alluded briefly to a triumph over Asiatic Cholera. His Lordship's interest quickened at that — medicine counted among his lesser interests, tho' pursued nevertheless with all his intelligence. He knew enough not to confuse typhus with typhoid, one spread by fleas and the other by water and believed by too many people to be one and the same. He had seen a case of it at Cambridge and could have been drawn into describing it — but he brought the subject, firmly, back to Henry.

'The matter that concerns me, Mrs Smith, is my understanding that you will not break your trust with Mrs Martin. She will live in Auckland — you will not abandon her to be with your son?'

'Oh — I would so love to see my son, I would so . . .' I could not go on.

'Composure, Mrs Smith.'

How foolish to allow the Bishop to rouse these feelings in me. I would never be his friend, his intimate. He could always dismiss me.

'Yes, of course I would love to see him, to gaze upon his dear face. But not straight away. He may join me in Auckland when his cadetship with the New Zealand Company is over.'

The Bishop nodded, vindicated in his earlier suspicions, but he spoke gently. 'My son is as yet only an infant, but I know already the bonds of that attachment.'

'The lads are everything to me.'

'Perhaps you could tell me truthfully the circumstances of their birth. I trust Mary Ann's father saw your marriage licence.'

'Forgive me, my Lord —' there was a tremor in my voice — I willed it away — 'but it is not your concern.'

The blue tendon in the jaw again, a flush of red in the cheek above it.

'You are a member of my party!' He had raised his voice and earned the full attention of the nightwatch.

'I belong to Mrs Martin, it is true, and she most certainly is under your governance. I have, perhaps, a degree of independence, being neither fish nor fowl.'

'I don't quite have your meaning, Mrs Smith.'

'I am neither servant, nor member of your party, nor intermediate passenger.'

Gently, *Tomatin* lifted her head slightly — there was the creaking of stays and the wind shifting in the little sail we carried. The mirror hours were ending.

In my account, I could be tempted to invent an exchange between the Divine and me that allowed for some confession. I would like to show myself as bravely giving a version of my first love and the loss of it, and how I had made my way after — a common enough story of our times. I would like to pretend that I had learned by this time that God forgives, that he offers a second and sometimes a third chance to those who would take it. I took up with Nick Horelock because I loved him, and my second husband because he loved me.

Fresh from his Oxbridge life of sporting challenge and scholarly endeavour, accelerated through the ranks of the Church to take his distant Bishopric, my companion was only yet a cabin boy on the ship of compassion. I was wise enough to see that, and did not appeal to his absent magnanimity. He ended our interview with a prayer, as I thought he would begin it — 'Guide thee thy servant Elizabeth Smith', etc etc, interminable — but mercifully stopped short of having me kiss his ring.

After he bid me goodnight, a good few minutes passed before I could gather up the dress and flag, rat and empty bottle, and follow.

FIVE

To Chiswick

1866

THE CONJURING OF LOST CHILDREN was something best kept private if she was to survive the long hours she necessarily spent alone. In London, all this time later, she found herself come full circle to how she was at Plymouth forty years earlier, when the longing for her first-born overtook her in her duties and made her fall silent and still. Then, it was a yearning salient enough to help her believe she was as captivated by Captain Hogg as he seemed to be by her; it made her brave enough to risk everything on the chance she would have a father for the child three months gone, that she would have a home of her own, that she would once again hold her only daughter in her arms.

Now the yearning took hold again, so that she would imagine herself brushing the child's hair, dressing her in the clothes they had bought after they took her home to Bristol. She longed for the little thin-armed embrace, she remembered the blue lights of her eyes — and all the longing would culminate in a sudden shift in the air, and she would feel the child come unbidden to sit in her lap, and oh — how she welcomed her — but she couldn't now, not in company.

Go away, dear.

Impervious, Katie nestled in, wearing still the brown smock of the orphanage and carrying the rank smell of that place in her hair. A smut persisted on her nose, and her little cracked boots rested on Elizabeth's knee. It was a development that unnerved her. She forced herself to concentrate on Miss Tripp.

Since their first meeting in the spring, Miss Tripp had twice visited Elizabeth's rooms at Tollington Park. This, her third visit, was the day she had elected to accompany Elizabeth to Chiswick, to call on Bee Cotton. Quite why she was proving so attentive a friend, Elizabeth did not like to question. She supposed a lady such as herself, who had voyaged to the farthest regions of the southern oceans, offered exotic appeal. The younger woman professed to being a kindred spirit — or even closer.

'I should like you to think of me as a daughter,' Miss Tripp said as they sat over tea and cake at the table by the window.

At that declaration, Katie's fetch retreated. The sudden abandonment was chilling.

'Did you hear me, Mrs Smith?'

'And why should you desire that?'

Miss Tripp was young enough to be more granddaughter than daughter, though none of the little New Zealanders was nearly as grown-up — Henry and Ish were both late progenitors.

'Because I am like you, Mrs Smith. A woman of independent spirit — though not of independent means as you once were. We both of us understand how difficult it is to have one without the other.'

'Indeed,' said Elizabeth, uneasily. Mr Griggs was desirous that she accept Miss Tripp's companionship, and she would certainly like to please him — he had been so generous since her return — but his judgement was not always to be trusted. Lord, he had trusted in her all those years ago, and she could so easily have failed him.

What exactly this young lady's living arrangements were, she was uncertain. Did she expect Elizabeth to now take up the conversational thread of means, independent and otherwise? Miss Tripp's means were obfuscated. There was, no doubt, a gentleman who kept her in the West End — but Elizabeth would not elicit a confession, and hoped only that the gentleman was kind. If her work in the Colonies had made her less likely to judge her sisters, much of the company she'd kept had made her more so. She regarded Miss Tripp, and thought again what a laughing mouth it was. There was no denying that she was quite adorable, charming and capable of great tenderness. As Elizabeth had come back to herself on Mr Griggs's sofa, it was to the cooling sensation of Miss Tripp's light hands on her brow and a welcome sip of manufactured anodyne, sweet with molasses.

Her new friend took up the teapot to refresh their cups and Elizabeth had a sudden image of a crinoline trailing through winter mud, the young face above intent on the coming ordeal of delivering another baby of an exhausted and ill-nourished missionary's wife — as she had herself on many occasions. The incongruity made her smile — Miss Tripp would never be so much a daughter as could follow into her chosen profession. Today the gaudy bird wore a short blue jacket and a wide yellow skirt looped up in the new style to show her striped scarlet petticoats.

'That's better,' said Miss Tripp, glancing up from her ministrations at the tea tray. 'We ladies must make the most of precious friendships. Have you many?'

Elizabeth shook her head, the wide ribbons from her widow's cap flying perilously close to her cup.

'I have had,' she supplied, 'excellent friends of all kinds and descriptions.' She was thinking of Mary Ann, of her fellow nurse Mary Potene, of Bee Cotton, of the missionaries Mrs Spencer and Mrs Chapman. 'Though not so many in England. Friendship for independent women in this country is still difficult and ever will be.'

'But not for you and me. How else could it be, given how we have made our way?'

'You still have quite a way to go.' Elizabeth took a bite of shortbread and allowed it to melt in her mouth, for the employment of her teeth would result in discomfort.

'Perhaps, perhaps not. A lady can never be sure how much longer a lady has in this world.'

Oh lady, lady, lady, thought Elizabeth, what bosh! We are neither of us ladies. And Miss Tripp must understand by now that there was no money to be had from her. She would ask the question again, having not yet had a satisfactory answer.

'How did you first come to be of Mr Griggs's acquaintance?'

'He came to see me at the Pavilion and later we met with mutual friends in Soho.'

Word for word it was the same reply she had given before — she was not such a good actress that it did not sound rehearsed.

'Mr Griggs at the theatre and chop house? Mutual friends? I don't think so.'

'His tastes have changed. You have been away such a very long time, Mrs Smith. Almost my whole lifetime!'

Miss Tripp rose from her seat on the only other chair and went to the basket she had brought with her. On arrival it had disgorged Eccles cakes and shortbread. Now she brought forth a lump of coal wrapped in newspaper. Mrs Smith beamed and Miss Tripp — that is, Kitty Tripp, aspiring diva — pulled the footstool close to the hearth and sat on it, her wide skirts billowing around her, and tended to the fire.

The more she and Mrs Smith grew mutually fond, the more difficult it would become to maintain the façade.

'Shall I roll out the carpet for you? Why do you keep it against the wall?'

Her hostess, she understood, was in possession of one hundred pounds a year. It was certainly not riches, but surely enough to live with a little more sense of permanence. She blew on the coal, but it would not take — she stood to flap her overskirt at it.

'No. Never mind, dear,' said Mrs Smith.

'But I do mind, Mrs Smith. It is too damp in here.'

Mould speckled the wall, though it was faded since the last visit now the weather was warmer. An attempt had been made to wipe the spores away — the resulting smudge was spread behind the screen that partitioned off the bed. The green silk screen was very old but retained its colour, embroidered over with lords and ladies and hunting scenes. It brought the only bright spot to the room, the curtains being much travelled, a dull grey that may once have been blue. Set by the window was a small table now crowded over with tea things, and the likenesses of the old lady's distant sons propped on the sill above it. Henry and Ish, a charcoal and a daguerreotype.

The fire was hopeless. She would have to go downstairs and ask the landlady for kindling, unless there was something else she could use. On the mantelpiece there were carelessly arranged mementoes and souvenirs — a small carved wooden box set with tropical iridescent shell, a cheap wax seal with a poorly executed bird, some folded letters, a pen and an ancient stained ivory inkpot, its surface crazed and flaking. There was a battered book of Maori songs, an old compendium of remedies interleaved with handwritten notes, and two Bibles of extra weight. If she were alone, Kitty would place one on either shoulder to perfect their almost perfect slope. She lifted one to test its weight — a curious flat figurine had slipped underneath. She picked it up for a moment and examined it — it was made of a green stone, with carved wide eyes, odd little fingers and bent legs.

'What is this?'

'A tiki,' answered Mrs Smith, with no further explanation.

'It looks a little like a monkey,' said Miss Tripp. 'Is that what it is supposed to represent?'

'Not at all.' The New Zealander sounded offended. 'I do believe it represents life itself, its continuation. Fecundity and fertility.'

Kitty dropped it as if it had burnt her, and had the sense that behind her Mrs Smith was smiling again. The old witch. There would be none of that sort of thing for her, not if she could help it.

Her new friend had preserved so little of her long life. Perhaps in the part of the room that served as bedchamber she had objects packed away, as surplus to requirements as the carpet. Boxes and boxes, perhaps. Of silver, pewter, china, lace. Her eye fell on a nosegay of wild grasses with falling seedheads and small blue flowers, dry and crackling, pressed flat as if they had been inside a book.

'These should take.'

'No — they were a gift from Henry — they are precious to me!'

Kitty gave up and sat down again. A sudden draught followed

her from the chimney, scattering ash across the floor. After a moment Mrs Smith said, in a calmer voice, 'We must go soon in any case.'

From her little bottle, she was adding a few drops to her tea. They had that in common too, though Miss Tripp preferred the milder anodyne of similar composition available at London apothecaries — Doctor J. Collis Browne's Chlorodyne, with Indian hemp and oil of peppermint. Her friend's tincture was of her own manufacture and of varying strengths and proportions. On her last visit, she had watched the measuring and mixing of quinine, chloroform, morphia and ipecacuanha, nutmeg for heat and flavour, and a drachm of sugar — all drawn from the battered field medicine chest kept under the table. It had apparently been a parting gift from the father of the woman she had cared for in New Zealand and it seemed to be her most treasured possession.

Jolly old chlorers. It did so give one a lift.

'Did you keep the carpet rolled all through the winter?' Miss Tripp rose to her feet.

'Oh yes. I won't be here long.'

'Why is that?'

'Because it has always been my pattern. The longest I have lived anywhere was with the Judge and Mrs Martin at Auckland, for four years.'

'And after that?'

'And then I worked and lived wherever the wind blew me, wherever I was wanted — the Mission Station at Te Ngae, or to my sons at Maketu or Port Nicholson — Wellington, I should say. I've never quite arrived at the new name.'

Miss Tripp shrugged her sloping shoulders, catching her reflection in the mottled, dusty mirror above the mantel. The Pavilion had had a picture made for the hoardings and she had sat for it. It had pleased her — the dauber had exaggerated the angle from her neck even more than was natural. Perhaps today, when they caught the omnibus, she would be able to point one out to Mrs Smith and Mrs Smith might compliment her on how true a likeness it is, and Kitty would be able to tell her that when she had first beheld it she had thought, only for a second, that she was regarding a portrait of her mother. And perhaps Mrs Smith would then look more closely at the hoarding and begin to make certain connections.

'I cannot imagine any of those places. I was born in Calcutta, Mrs Smith, but my recollection is hazy — I was only a child when we left. Is Wellington like London?'

'Not in the least, though they endeavour to make it like.'

Mrs Smith has not been tempted by the mention of India. 'I have heard Auckland described as being more like San Francisco, with its inebriate ruffians and wooden houses. One may as well live in a tent, the wind whistles through so. At Taurarua, which is very close to Auckland, books would fly open and fires blow out, though all the doors and windows closed.'

'In England we would call that ghosts!' Miss Tripp exclaimed. 'I have a sister with the gift for it — my father encourages her. She draws quite a crowd.'

'Ah — ghosts!' Elizabeth was only half-listening, turning her gaze across the road to St Mark's.

It was raining softly, the stone steeple slicked and gleaming. She had a sudden longing to be inside, watching the rain stipple the face of Christ. There was one stained-glass window at the back of the church, where she most often sat for Matins, which showed Christ carrying the lamb. His glass skin and that of the lamb were of the same pale opalescence. In His right hand was a crook, which held the ewe against His scarlet robes. The mother looked away, tranquil and protected, while her lamb gazed devotedly into His loving face.

She could sit there now with Katie. She would wrap her in her shawl and warm her skinny flanks and tell her how stained glass glistens in New Zealand, how if it has been raining and the sun comes out immediately, it stops, blazing and hot, and the bright Pacific light makes jewels of the quivering droplets on the panes — rubies and sapphires, beryl and amethyst. She would tell her how one could sit in Mary Ann's little chapel at Taurarua and imagine the world beyond washed clean and crystalline, the tough little harbour town beyond transformed into the Celestial City. It would be so quiet she would be able to hear the soft, wondering breath of the child; she would revel in her wide-eyed wonder, see her attention caught by the gold of the altar, all the pretty cloths.

And there shall in no wise enter into it any thing that defileth, neither whatsoever worketh abomination, or maketh a lie: but they which are written in the Lamb's book of life.

She never took the child inside a church until the end. She would atone by including her in the account, should she write it. It would be an honest appraisal of her time on Earth and those she had loved. The Lamb's Book of Life indeed.

How easily a stranger could mistake Miss Tripp for her lady companion, thought Elizabeth, as she received from those hands her cape and purse, and allowed herself to be chivvied out the door and down Tollington Park. An unpaid lady companion, that is, for there was none spare from her allowance — and what a ludicrous notion that a widow who had spent her life in service to others should, at the end of her life, be herself waited upon!

On the corner of Hornsey Road under Miss Tripp's red umbrella they had a moment's disagreement about the route. Miss Tripp had devised a scheme that involved train and omnibus, and there absolutely should be neither. The asylum at Chiswick was about ten miles from Elizabeth's door, which on previous occasions she had covered by cab for the twin fears of maltoolers fanning her pockets for her money on the latter and an unforeseen plunge underground on the former. From a cab it was possible to observe vast areas of London dug up and destroyed all for the sake of a new railway, and also engines and carriages stalled on completed tracks for the obstacle of a fallen carthorse, or lumber, or bricks, or for no obvious reason — just because they were stopped — while their load of trapped humanity must grow ever more impatient. It was another item to add to the list of changes, many of which did not seem to Elizabeth sensible. The cab fare brought about a steep decline in the weekly budget, but hadn't she always put friendship first in her concerns — the distances she'd travelled on that account by foot, ship and carriage! It was a refrain throughout her life — travelling first for love, then for friendship.

The medicine gave the day a sparkle and dulled her aches and pains. In a barrow at the corner, rain-slicked apples glowed to draw the eye. How strong the scent that billowed from damp violets in a lofty flower-box, how pretty the crowing baby passing in a nursemaid's arms. It gave her a smile wider than a tiki's. Miss Tripp, though it hardly seemed possible, was more adorable than she had been at morning tea. The brollie lent her already flushed cheeks further bloom, and a squib of black, polished hair had come loose from her bonnet to curl becomingly against her throat.

'Come along, now.' Miss Tripp had her arm and was leading her towards Seven Sisters station. 'We'll take the train to Maiden Lane and the omnibus from St Pancras. It'll be quicker and cheaper.'

She was walking too smartly for Elizabeth, whose tendons and sinews complained. Her heart thumped, a gouty toe screamed from inside its tight boot, and the young woman's grip on her elbow was vice-like. On her other side, her friend carried the second walking stick and the brollie, the protrusion a danger to people approaching from behind. It would take more strength than she had to disengage. They flew past St Mary's workhouse, where a group of thin and ragged children looked up from their game of stone-rolling on the steps to gaze at Miss Tripp's bright skirts and swift buttoned boots. Elizabeth was glad of their pace, despite her agonies, the better to draw past the high walls. They could hear the paupers at their work inside, a dull hammering of granite, the odd blow that rang above the rest. There was the shout of the overseer, a voice the children recognised because they looked towards it in fear.

This end of Hornsey Road was built up, though green fields still showed now and then between the row of houses on either side of the street — villas and terraced houses that owned to the status of their holders. Some, divided up into rooming houses, were broken, jerry-built of brick and plaster already crumbling and damp. Others showed the prestige of the families they were intended for, with neat gardens and lace curtains — and, no doubt, one cruelly overworked servant. If there was any advice to give to young women going into service, it was to never take a sole position unless driven to it. Too many maids laboured alone, snatching their sleep in bug-infested kitchens, working long days for women little better than themselves. She could never have borne it. They should all sail to the Colonies! All of them. Australia, for preference, since the other place was ruined. They might have better luck than she had.

'Please, Miss Tripp, I must take a breath —'

She forced them to a halt at the mouth of Thurle Street, which like much of Upper Holloway had been intended for the multiplying clerks and their families but never finished. It lay unpaved still, rubbish piled from corner to corner and a stink of ordure that rivalled the Thames at its midsummer worst. A woman with a baby under one arm and a gin bottle in the other begged outside the first house. A gaggle of ill-clad infants clustered around her, hollow-eyed. One of the small number of cows that had escaped last year's cattle epidemic stood in the gutter, ribs sharp as piano strings, nosing at a pile of rotting cabbages the size of an armchair. The air that forced itself noisily down her throat was probably thick with miasma. What mortifying disease was she catching?

Fear forced a nod, and they were suddenly away again, past the waterproofing factory on the corner that pumped black odorous smoke into the low grey sky. Unseen, thudding machinery sent vibrations beneath the pavement, hastening their pace even more — her legs could give way from under her. There was a group of men hefting bales of oilcloth into a cart in the dock — one of them called and whistled after Miss Tripp, who turned to bless him with a smile. He didn't call out again and neither did any of his workmates.

'Struck dumb!' laughed Miss Tripp, well aware of her effect.

They turned the corner at Seven Sisters Road — it was surely not much further. The performance was hardly worth it. By now they could have been riding in a cab, the driver above them and the horse below, the reins bisecting their view of a painlessly passing street. Beforehand, Elizabeth would have taken the opportunity to pat the horse, and to dig in her purse for the lumps of sugar she kept for the dear, patient loves. She would have noted as always the state of the horse's front teeth as he pursed his lips to take in the sugar — she could never help herself, though very often regretted it. The sad state they were most often in! There were more horses in London now than before she'd gone away, but not as many as there were clerks and streetwalkers and hawkers, a generally frightening increase of people.

'The increase of horses is not commensurate with that of the population,' she planned to tell Ish in her next letter — as a soft-hearted boy he had wept for the misery of the coalman's pony.

In the ticket office was a low form against one wall. Elizabeth sank onto it while Miss Tripp stood in a lengthy queue to buy two tickets. There were unruly children with a pinch-faced governess, two footmen in old-fashioned livery joshing with one another and, just ahead and trying to ignore them, a thin-boned man of the cloth who seemed bowed under with the worries of his poor parish, if not the world. The footmen would remind her she was in London, should she need to be reminded; the others could just as well be waiting for a coach on Shortland Street in Auckland. Would that paradise one day be as overrun, as populous, as familiar?

The train, once they boarded it, was crowded. A passenger more elderly than herself, with a shiny seat to his trousers and an unfortunate scalp condition crusting over his bald head, insisted on standing for her. He stank of oil of turpentine, which Elizabeth had to breathe. The carriage smelt abominable. It would be capital to be able to bottle it and send it to those colonists who complained after visits to the pah of 'dirty Maoris'— snuffle this up, she would like to say, and then make your pronouncements.

Elizabeth felt herself retreat from the press of passengers — perhaps London was now a city to be enjoyed from indoors — and emerged again only when she found herself wedged in the Turnham Green omnibus that waited at busy St Pancras. There had been no time to pat the horses, Miss Tripp hurrying her aboard so that they wouldn't have to wait for the next one. Elizabeth leaned her head on the window and would have closed her eyes but for the immediate enquiries to her wellbeing.

'I'm all right. The sooner we get there the better.'

'I always enjoy the journey more than the arrival,' pronounced Miss Tripp, which could only be a modern opinion.

'You have not journeyed as much as I have,' replied Elizabeth.

'If I enjoy the lunatic priest as much as you do, then I shall come again — we could take a boat along the river. There's a landing at Chiswick.'

Elizabeth sighed. 'William Cotton is not a spectacle, Miss Tripp.'

The omnibus rumbled towards its destination. As far as Elizabeth could tell, there was no one aboard who could answer the description of thief — but then they came in all shapes. There were only two other passengers, a young, smeary couple who reeked of the fish markets and were so exhausted they sat with their heads inclined together, dozing. She would sleep too, but didn't imagine for one moment that Miss Tripp would welcome her heavy head on the delicately sloping shoulder.

'Mrs Smith.' Miss Tripp had taken one of her hands and was stroking it. 'Tell me how changed this all is for you. Have you come this way since you returned?'

Elizabeth glanced out the window at the shops and terraces of Marylebone Road and the people thronging in and out.

'I've had no call to. The cab drivers take a different route.'

Miss Tripp was looking at her with an alert and indulgent expression as if she were a painting by a child, or a dog that could do tricks.

'Tell me all the changes.'

'Well . . . there is more of everything, but at the same time less.'

'Less?'

Elizabeth thought of her earlier observation of the horses, but decided against sharing it for fear the indulgence would deepen. She would be robbed of what vestiges of dignity were left her in possession. The inevitability rankled.

'For instance, the moat around the Tower has been filled in. That was reported in our newspapers in New Zealand.'

Miss Tripp laughed, the high fluting note of it ringing above the noise of the crowded street and bringing even the driver's head around.

'And why should that bother you, dear Mrs Smith? Oh — the Tower moat! You are a caution. What else?'

'Well . . .' She pointed at a pillar-box. 'Those. We did not have them before.'

'Really? How extraordinary.'

'That is a fine improvement.'

'What else?'

'Well. There are so many. The outlawing of child chimney-sweeps.'

'So they say,' Miss Tripp said, her voice lowered, 'but just the other day we had one — a tiny little flue-flaker, not six years old.'

Another opening, thought Elizabeth, a chance for her to enquire 'Who is "we"?', but she let it go.

'There have certainly been advances,' she said instead, 'not to mention the fine clothes.' She patted Miss Tripp's collapsible crinoline. 'We had nothing so eye-popping.'

And she preferred the more delicate fashions of her youth, she could have said — but didn't. Miss Tripp adjusted her collar and tucked the escaped strand of hair under her bonnet.

The rest of the journey passed uneventfully, without a single hoarding, and Miss Tripp was compelled to draw from her purse a small volume of verse and read quietly. Elizabeth watched the buildings and streets give way to green fields, and back to streets again, some rich, some poor, but none so mixed as Hornsey Road, until they reached Turnham Green. It was only a short walk from there down Chiswick Lane to Dr Tuke's asylum.

As they passed through the fine iron gates of Manor Farm House, they could see William Cotton himself standing under a tree and gazing up into its canopy. The rain that had fallen earlier in the day in Holloway seemed not to have reached Chiswick. The garden, though lush and finely attended, had a delicate veil of dust over leaf and petal, and the air seemed heavy, more like late August than mid-June. A sluggish breeze brought them the river from the landing at the bottom of the lane — a ripe, mordant stench that wasn't nearly so stifling and nauseating as further east, but unpleasant enough for Miss Tripp to raise a delicate hand to her nose.

'There he is!'

Miss Tripp followed her gesture — Mrs Smith was not so vulgar as to actually point. The gentleman was all in black, as befitted a priest, but had left off his collar. He was stout, short, balding, his frill of curly hair and beard entirely white. The three-storeyed house behind him, with gables, low eaves and mullioned windows speaking of the style of a hundred years ago, gave off the serenity and timelessness of squiredom. The old man could have been mistaken for a gentleman, and this his estate.

'It does not have the feel of an asylum,' Kitty remarked.

'Quite right — it is a class above. Mr Cotton's expenses are paid by his elderly father.'

The women began their progress across the lawns towards him, and though their feet fell silently and neither spoke — as if they were coming upon a skittish cat, thought Miss Tripp — the priest turned to face them. At the sight of Mrs Smith he smiled widely, showing a few blackened stumps.

'My dearest Mata Te Mete! Haere mai, haere mai!' He was hurrying to take his old friend in his arms. There was something childlike in the way he embraced her — his eyes had filled with tears. Miss Tripp looked away.

Two men had come out from the house, one holding firmly to the other, who lifted his face and snuffled at the air like a foxhound at the start of the hunt — then he took off suddenly, his keeper in pursuit. How enlightened to allow him into the garden at all, Kitty thought, and realised she knew almost nothing about the care of the bewildered, since she had never before sought out their company. The running man wore a strange garment, a jacket of fustian or canvas that held his arms to his sides.

'Come, come —' Mr Cotton was tugging at Mrs Smith's hand to lead her back towards the tree he had been gazing into. Miss Tripp followed behind them to stand beneath a fine, ancient oak.

Once a person had seen a land taking shape, as Elizabeth had, the felling and the filling in, the building up and tearing down — it could put her in mind of how her own country had once been. This tree could be part of a long-vanished forest that would once have spread to the riverbanks.

Mr Cotton was pointing high into the rustling green. 'A tui. Do you see?'

High on an upper bough was a starling, dusty and greasy, looking west along the river. It would be able to see for miles — towards London, towards the open sea. Keeping hold of Bee's arm, Elizabeth wondered how far it strayed, if it was a stay-at-home or a traveller. It was said that starlings come in two different kinds, like people. It was easy to see how her friend had succumbed to his delusion — it was a big specimen, and the feathers had some of the iridescence of the New Zealand parson bird.

'But where is his collar?' she asked gently.

'I heard it talking. It's tame. Do you remember Mokihi? He had one that could talk. Kihi, kihi. Kihi, kihi —' He made kissing noises towards the bird, and offered his palm as if it held seed.

'What does he think he can see?' asked Miss Tripp.

Mr Cotton turned to stare at her. His spectacles, thick as paperweights, had a crack through one lens. The glass was dense enough to fracture in layers, making tiny underlying prisms.

'It's not what I think, young lady. It is what is. Who are you?'

'I'm so sorry, Bee — forgive me. Mr Cotton — Miss Tripp.'

Theatrically, Miss Tripp held out her hand and smiled, dimples forming in her cheeks. It seemed she had determined to win Bee over. He inspected her closely — and his expression went from one of intense irritation to affectionate delight.

'Henry! You look just like Henry!' He took Elizabeth's shoulders and pulled her around to face Miss Tripp directly.

'See — she has your lad's wide brow, and here —' he extended a grubby forefinger and touched one of her nostrils — 'just there. Not the entire nose. And when she smiles —' He was smiling himself, broadly. 'Do you see, Mrs Smith?'

Oh yes — she did see. She saw more than Bee could imagine, even in his most indiscreet phases. It was not Henry's face that rose before her, but quite another.

Her own face, she hoped, remained impassive. 'You haven't seen him for many years, Bee. You have forgotten.'

'Henry!' He was patting Miss Tripp clumsily on the head. 'Brow. Chin. Just like him. What is your Christian name, Miss Tripp?'

'Katherine,' said Miss Tripp, 'but you may call me Kitty.'

From the tree above them came a cackle and little choking sound, as if the starling was suddenly as short of breath as Elizabeth found herself. Katherine! Why had Tom Hogg settled on that name? The shaded bower in the open air was as hot and airless as a ship's hold in the doldrums. Hadn't she already recognised the voice when she first met Miss Tripp at Mr Griggs's? It had the same husky, emphatic tones of Henry when he was a boy, though none of Ish's, whose childhood voice was gentle and high. And neither lad ever had dimples, or eyes so dark or deep-set, nor lit so calculatingly with the effect they had on others. Their mother could wish them more aware, given the snake pit of colonial politics.

How strange, that Kitty was more like Henry than Ish. It's not what she would have expected. Neither would she have expected that any of Mr Hogg's other children could be so pale.

'Kihi. Haere mai,' whispered Bee to the starling. When it persisted in giving no response but to pick at its wing with a frantic beak, he hurried away in his odd lumpen tread towards the open door of Manor Farm House. A distance off he slowed, gesturing wildly for the women to follow.

'Where is he taking us?' asked Kitty Tripp, picking up her skirts and departing at such a pace that she left Elizabeth behind.

'For tea,' Elizabeth spoke to her retreating back, and part of her wished it would retreat for ever even as she saw the resemblance there too, straight and narrow. There was something also in the set of her shoulders, familiar and beloved — it was not as if she had not observed those traits in the decades since she had last laid eyes on their originator. Henry had the same build, and before his knee injury the same gait. It made the breath catch in her throat. She would have to play this very carefully.

A bell rang from a room on the lower floor, the room Miss Tripp passed beside. It had pretty casement windows, surrounded by pink and white climbing roses, open to the garden. Inside, there was a long refractory table set with teapot, bread and butter and a fruitcake. Mr Cotton was already seated, his plate and cup before him. There was a long form on either side of the table, and above the wide fireplace a large portrait of a kindly faced, elderly man whom Kitty supposed was the original Doctor Tuke. Hard on her heels came the two men she'd seen in the garden, the attendant and patient in the restraining jacket.

'Good afternoon, Doctor,' said Mr Cotton.

The doctor was perhaps in his fifties, his face set melancholy. He barely acknowledged them.

'Will you sit down sensibly and take your tea?' The madman writhed and giggled as the doctor began to untie the ribbons at his sleeves.

How very entertaining, thought Miss Tripp, taking her seat. She smiled at Mr Cotton, who was chewing enthusiastically on bread and butter. Mrs Smith was only now coming along by the windows and Kitty supposed she should have waited for her. She felt a momentary pang of guilt — but then she should have missed the entertainment.

'Lord Ramsay is as mad as a parrot but perfectly harmless,' Mr Cotton said soothingly but loudly. 'He and I are the only guests at this hotel.'

Hands freed, Lord Ramsay stood over a plate to more easily cram a slice of bread into his working mouth. He was young and fairly glowed with excellent health. While he ate, he fixed his eyes on Miss Tripp — with rather a lascivious expression, she thought. If he were sane she'd slap him. Where was Mrs Smith? She half rose to go and find her, but there she was arriving at the door, putting out one stick and then the other, her mouth pained.

'Do sit thee down, Mrs Smith!' Mr Cotton was up from his seat again to usher his guest to tea.

'Good afternoon, Doctor Tuke!' Elizabeth held fast to Bee's

arm as they gained the table.

'And to you, Mrs Smith.' The doctor was still intent on his patient, who was attempting to insert a hand down the front of his trousers. They were tightly belted and sewn into his shirt to prevent him indulging in what was doubtless a favourite pastime. Elizabeth had nursed young men who in early illness or late convalescence could have benefited from the method — but it would require trousers set with a trapdoor. On investigation he appeared entirely sealed. She pitied his poor nurse — and more the laundress.

'That's enough, sir!'

Seymour Tuke sported a battle scar — a deep scratch down one cheek, a day or so old. It certainly appeared a difficult case, but doubtless the doctor trusted to recovery — the nobleman was strong and hearty, inhaling a slice of cake and goggling at Miss Tripp. If it were up to her, thought Elizabeth, she'd give the poor fellow a dose of bromide and put him to bed.

Suddenly the lunatic dropped to his knees and scuttled under the table, emerging in a crouched run and heading for the door, straightening his back and extending his stride, the doctor once again in pursuit.

Miss Tripp laughed delightedly. It was infectious — a spirited, musical chuckle, very like Henry's when he was truly tickled.

Susceptible to mirth as much as to desolation, Bee joined Miss Tripp, giggling as the chase passed the casement.

'Come, come, Mrs Smith,' said Kitty, 'you must admit it is amusing. If I were not blessed with the voice of an angel I would nurse in just such a place. One would laugh through one's daily work!'

'What an absurd notion, you silly girl.'

'Mr Cotton was telling me he is the only other inmate,' Miss Tripp went on, unperturbed, gathering three cups and saucers and pouring out. 'It will be peaceful, then, from now on.' Her tone was slightly regretful.

They sat quietly, eating and drinking, and Elizabeth wished they had had tea in the garden as they had on her last visit. A servant had brought out table and chairs, and the old friends had talked as they always did of the Colony and their friends there. Mr Cotton had brought forth a bee from his pocket — Doctor Tuke had not allowed him his hives and he had to make do with occasional captives. He had blown on it gently to revive it, his face so full of concern for the tiny creature's wellbeing that she had got to her feet to plant a kiss on his bald head. Her affection had encouraged him, and he had embarked immediately on a recollection of a punishing journey he had made with Bishop Selwyn — how his glasses were broken and his trousers torn, how the Maori Renata carried him up and down mountains upon his back, and how the Bishop inflated his Mackintosh bed to float across a river while leaving Mr Cotton to advance on a submerged bridge the width of a rod, an inconvenient invention of the Natives. Selwyn had driven his party on as demonically as he ever did, from four in the morning until after nightfall, up hill and down dale, across marsh and swamp and flint. That evening he amused himself by swimming three miles up an obviously dangerous river to explore. All had been on tenterhooks until the boy Bishop returned — but of course he always would have. He was as strong and agile in that environment as he was on land.

The presence of Miss Tripp hindered his amusing recollections and their mutual story-telling of all that had passed since Bee's premature departure, insisted on by his father. Once or twice in New Zealand he had shown Elizabeth the Pater's letters, weeping at their contents, the endless castigations against his profligacy. There was never a loving word for the clever, generous and endearing son who made friends wherever he went. In the Colony he was considered near genius — a linguist, botanist, poet, explorer, apiarist, woodturner, sailor and humorist — his only fault, as Sarah Selwyn said, 'a want of ballast'.

Elizabeth leaned across the table to give him a little pat.

While Miss Tripp chattered to Mr Cotton about her performances at the Pavilion, where she specialised in the comic song — good heavens, she was singing for him high and wavering, and he was beating time with a teaspoon — Elizabeth conceived of an adventure. When he was cured, as he would be, inevitably — she had easily seen Bee as mad in Auckland, where he went untreated but for prayer from the Selwyns and affection from herself — *when* he was cured, she would take him on the journey to Lichfield to see the Bishop. It would be better if the endeavour was sooner, rather than later, as there was something brewing in London — a pot Miss Tripp was stirring with a very long spoon.

'Bee, dear,' she began, 'would you like to—'

But he interrupted, having a train of thought that he was not about to let go.

'How sweet of you to visit with your aunt,' he was saying, 'for surely this lady is your niece, Mrs Smith?'

She shook her head.

'Your sister's child?' he persisted. 'Or is the relation from Mr Smith's side?'

'Do you have nieces?' Miss Tripp came to her rescue. There must be an agreement with Mr Griggs and the boys that she should not divulge her true identity. How imperceptive they must judge her.

'I imagine so. My sister married a wool merchant and went back to Painswick. She wrote to me in New Zealand to tell me of the birth of a daughter. But I have not had word from her for many years. Since our mother died. She is quite possibly no longer among us herself.'

'Your only sister, Mrs Smith?' asked Miss Tripp in shocked tones, as declamatory as Cordelia. 'Do you not love her?'

How did Miss Tripp's world remain so simple, given her chosen career — or was Mr Hogg grown so dissolute that he tolerated a daughter taking to the stage? The Hoggs were military people, not a tribe sprung from the grimy lights of the penny gaffs.

'As children we were very close' — Elizabeth would not have answered but for the fact that Bee was waiting on her response as keenly as Miss Tripp — 'but as women we grew apart.'

'Why was that?'

'It really is none of your business.'

Bee was shaking his cup into his mouth for the last few drops. When he was sane, his table manners were not much better — she suspected his infancy was spent more in the servants' hall than at his father's table, much as little George Rupai's during his English sojourn. As he pushed his cup across to Miss Tripp for replenishment, Elizabeth saw the young woman's eyes were smarting and pretty lips pursed.

'My only surviving sister is many years older than me,' Elizabeth said, more gently. 'She had married and gone while I was still growing up.'

'It seems that if we are to love Mrs Smith,' announced Mr Cotton, 'then we must know nothing about her. Do you remember, my dear, when I tried to have your story?'

'You tried more than once.' The subject was making Elizabeth's heart race. She wished it could be let alone.

'Do you remember the first time?'

Did she? Elizabeth wondered.

'Was it on board *Tomatin*?'

'No — there we were always in company, either with your son or Mary Ann or any number of others. I waited until we were alone.'

'At Taurarua then. Do let's talk about something else, Bee. Have you had other visitors?'

'No, before that!' He had turned it into a game. He beetled his eyebrows at Miss Tripp.

'Have you finished your tea? Shall we go out into the garden and see if your tui is still there?'

'There are no tuis in England, Mrs Smith. Don't be silly.'

Mr Cotton had a fleck of butter on his whiskers. When she went to wipe it away with a napkin, he reared backwards, a sly, chaffing look to his face.

'It was at Port Jackson. After the Drama Night.'

'Drama Night?' Miss Tripp said.

'Oh, yes. Dear Mary Ann went wild for her husband, so near and yet so far, just the other side of the Tasman Sea.'

'Mr Cotton, that is quite enough.'

'Quite a surprising performance. None of us could believe she had it in her.'

'She was singing for her husband?' Miss Tripp asked. 'Or reciting?'

'Until one has made that arduous voyage, one has no conception of the tedium and discomfort, even with all of the Bishop's lessons to pass the time,' said Elizabeth. 'Mrs Martin had been at sea for three months and the accident to the keel undid her.'

Bee burst out laughing.

'The keel undid her! You are so funny, Mrs Smith. It wasn't the keel — it was desire. Desire!'

'It was because of the broken keel we were delayed, Miss Tripp. At first Sydney was a delight for all of us. As we came through the Heads, we were met by the harbourmaster's boat with a crew of Maoris, fine handsome warriors in white duck trousers and jackets, with straw hats tied under their tattooed chins. It was when we sailed up to our anchorage the accident happened — we dragged the keel on the harbour bed — but we did not realise then the full import.'

Elizabeth took her little bottle from her pocket and added a few drops to her tea. Mr Cotton was nodding — he would remember it all.

'When we went ashore, there were receptions and parties and concerts. Ish and Rupai, being of an age and three months cabinmates, were thick as thieves — I had a deal of difficulty in controlling them —'

'— or Mrs Martin,' put in Bee.

'Rupai had a fascination for the blacks of that country, and would go among them in their camps, Ish following doggedly in his stead.'

Dogged he was still, the Wellington Solicitor, Sheriff, Receiver of Taxes and reluctant father of five. His Australian adventures at the age of sixteen were perhaps his only remembered freedom.

'But how often is it,' Bee persisted, 'that a person has one character at sea and another on land?'

'Quite so,' agreed Elizabeth. 'A voyage either draws out an aspect or drives it inwards, so that different traits come to the fore.'

'I am like that,' acknowledged Bee, 'but not so you, Mrs Smith. You are always the same. It is because you keep your true nature hidden.'

It was an aspect of his illness that he freely made personal and hurtful remarks. Miss Tripp, bright-eyed, was gazing at her intently.

'I helped you carry Mrs Martin from the room, do you remember? We were all at Bishop Broughton's residency, that grand house above the Sydney harbour. Mary Ann decided to make her feelings known.'

Bee leaned forward confidentially. 'As the Bishop — our own, that is — proved immutable, so Mrs Martin grew hysterical — until Mrs Smith and I helped her to another room and a doctor was called.'

'Was there not another ship to take her to her husband?' asked Miss Tripp.

'That's exactly what happened, in the end,' said Elizabeth.

'The doctor called was a favourite with the ladies of Sydney society,' Mr Cotton went on. 'One who specialised in hysteria.'

Elizabeth stood up sharply. What Mr Cotton knew or did not know about that evening could not bear recounting. They should go back into the garden and find a distraction. Bee could be made to absorb himself in a species of flower or insect for hours.

'He knew the very latest remedy.'

'You have got off the subject, Mr Cotton,' said Elizabeth, having used this particular cure in similar situations before. It was his greatest fear and never failed to pull him up shortly for a few seconds while he cast back for his abandoned topic.

Miss Tripp was tying her bonnet strings, which she had earlier loosened, and was hurrying around the table to take her arm.

'Ah! True Nature!' Mr Cotton clapped his hands together smartly, and both women startled — he had remembered the subject at hand. He hurried to his feet and took hold of Elizabeth's shoulders.

'Tell me — is Mr Griggs any further along in his investigations? I had a letter from Henry last year. A long time ago now. He said a certain Mr Griggs was kindly assisting him in looking for a certain gentleman . . .'

Elizabeth stepped away from him, freeing herself from his scrutiny, which was oddly malicious and now trained on Miss Tripp rather than herself.

'What do you say to that, Mrs Smith?' he said archly, as if they were playing a parlour game.

'Come along now, Reverend. We would like to go into the garden.' Miss Tripp was firm.

Bee Cotton laughed, as if she had made the wittiest riposte — and hurried ahead of them out into the afternoon, as rapidly as if he had a train to catch.

SIX

Mary Ann's Drama Night

It is long past the hour for candles, and I would make my way to bed but the page lies blank before me, despite my resolve as we left Mr Cotton in Chiswick that I would at long last begin my account tonight. By the time I bade farewell to Miss Tripp at King's Cross and reached my lodgings, it was as much as I could do to coax to life her gift of coal and draw a weary chair to it, the page on my knee and toes curled on the fender.

She must know where he is. She is perhaps twenty-five, more than ten years younger than Ish. Mr Hogg could have made his way back to the British Isles, just as I have, bringing his children with him — or just Kitty, born after he was returned to his legal wife. Did he look for me when he had the chance? Is there to be another chance now, one I will deny?

I never went looking for him then, so there is no cause to do so now. I could not bear it, to see our youth lost, the wide span of years we could have had together, raising our children. Do my sons and Mr Griggs think I have forgiven him? Even if I had, what on Earth do they think we would talk about?

There is only one man I have ever searched for, and that was in Sydney in 1842. I had thought it possible I would hear his name spoken in the street; I had let myself hope I would have news of him. As *Tomatin* creaked and groaned through the nights, the closer we grew to Australia I allowed myself just before sleep to remember his dear face, to hope that I might once breathe the same air, and feel myself lying in his arms.

I never did long for my second husband in quite the same way.

A certain gloom settled over all of us as we approached Port Jackson — two sailors had drowned only days before, one drunk and the other sober, the drunk man full of grog stolen from the passengers' supplies and the other knocked to his death during the attempted rescue: the ship had rolled while the crew grappled with hooks and tackle. The lost sailors were Tom Brown and Alec Dick, and I'd exchanged scarce a word with either, but Ish had, and so had Rupai, both of whom streamed with grief. Tears came easily to each of them, for different reasons — Ish from long habit and Rupai from an irresistible urge to display his passions.

It was because of their despair, perhaps, that I was too lenient on landfall. I could not find it in myself to be stern — besides, none but the dreariest spirits could have failed to rise at the Maori paddle-song that was our harbour greeting. We all experienced a steady renewal of the optimism and pleasant temper that had blessed us for most of the voyage. The canoe was one of many craft that flocked to meet us. A scow bore Bishop Broughton in full Episcopal regalia, his purple and red robes billowing like a topsail. Our more modestly gaitered Bishop called out to him, and the Reverends and their wives joined in a rousing rendition of 'God Save the Queen', their voices floating away and dissolving in the wide sky and buffeting wind.

The colour of the Australian sea and sky seemed to our English eyes startling, with the effect that one's senses reeled as if under the influence of an exhilarating drug. Beside me at the rail, Ish and Rupai talked of how, if they were grown men, they would set out over the land now enclosing us on either side. They pointed west and north over the eternal grey-green forest, which had a haze hanging over it. Mr Cotton, who stood with us, said the mist was of evaporating eucalyptus oil. The air was warm and heavy with other scents of life

— an animal, breathing smell, as if the land itself gave off heat and sweat, as if it had a gut, a heartbeat. There was wood smoke, sap, the late fruit of the harvest, a hint of ordure. Rupai snuffled it through his nostrils enthusiastically, his eyes dancing almost with delirium. It was almost autumn here.

Then, as we followed the pilot to our anchorage, *Tomatin*'s keel was broken, dragging along the harbour bed and breaking off half its length. We none of us understood the extent of the damage, not at first...

Mary Ann's Drama Night. How much does Bee remember, I wonder? How much do I?

It was a week or so after anchoring, and we were guests of the Bishop of New South Wales at his grand but already dilapidated house, 'Tusculum'. It stands high on the Darlinghurst ridge, looking west to a broad plain and distant mountains, north down the gentle slope of the ridge dotted with other grand houses, and east towards the harbour's mouth. Water glints on three sides. The reception room is broad and light, with french windows looking out over the hillside garden to Woolloomooloo Bay. I remember it as idyllic.

On that day, our first official reception, the crew of the harbourmaster's boat were gathered in the garden among the roses and English trees. Under an oak a table groaned with ham and bread, wine and cordial. I was presently transfixed by them, these representatives of the people I would live and work among, and — tho' I did not realise it then — give the best years of my life. Far rather would I have been talking with them than sit trapped, as I was, on a settee in the window between the Governor's wife Lady Gipps and Mary Ann. How handsome they were, the Maori boatmen, how at ease. Once more arrayed in their white duck and panama hats, they lounged about the lawn in the merry company of women in bright dresses and men of less quality than the nobs who assembled inside.

There were perhaps thirty to welcome us — Governor Gipps and his wife, a tattoo'd Maori chief who wore a feather cloak over his trousers, several of his upper liegemen, Sydney clerics, officers, sub-officials, colonial Divines and their wives. With sullen demeanour

Mrs Broughton's convict servant waited on the three of us who ranged beside one another like broody chooks on a perch. Our chatter had fallen quiet since Lady Gipps had admonished Mary Ann.

'You should not allow your servant to participate in our conversation with such immodest enthusiasm, Mrs Martin. I never heard such a bellwether!'

Mary Ann was greensick and wan, and only present on account of Sarah Selwyn's bullying. I had been speaking for both of us, recounting some aspects of our journey which I thought entertaining. There were the puppies we fed through the night after their mother died; there was Mr Cotton climbing the mast and afterwards composing a poem on pellucid waves and wheeling birds; there were Rupai's murderous performances with the sharks, the escape of Mr Cotton's bees, the death of the poultry — but Lady Gipps was not amused.

'We can all tell such stories, Mrs Smith,' she said, as if she had better tales but neither the spirit nor inclination to recount them.

At her elbow stood our Bishop with Bishop Broughton, with Governor Gipps making the third party in their discussions. In our silence we listened as they contemplated the slim likelihood of finding a replacement ship to take us the last leg to New Zealand. It seemed almost an impossibility, tho' the Governor thought he had heard of a ship leaving in the next month that could find berths for the Selwyns and their nurse and no more.

'And me!' Mary Ann cried out, on her feet suddenly and hastening towards them. 'You will include me, Augustus?'

The Bishop, flushed with the heat and unaccustomed wine, coloured further. It wasn't the young woman's words so much as her tone — earnest, yearning, intimate — as if she spoke to her husband and not of him. When the Bishop did not answer immediately, Mary Ann gave a long wail and fell to her knees, her hands clasped and gaze beseeching. At the Bishop's obvious consternation, she began to whimper, which altered almost imperceptibly to quiet sobs and built quickly to whooping convulsions — she rolled about the marble floor, by now the sole focus of the throng. Church and State, Native and Englishman, convict and free man stared.

'To your duties, Mrs Smith,' said the Bishop, turning his back.

With Bee's help, I hastened to remove her to one of Mrs Broughton's private apartments. A servant rode down to the town for a doctor.

In seclusion, Mary Ann grew more and more wild, accusing Bee and myself of a conspiracy to keep her from her husband. She conceived of the idea that he was ill, or that his melancholic nature had driven him to the kind of despair I have long feared would assail Ish. She struck out at me, even as she begged for the truth. Her agonies were pitiful to behold — heartbreaking wails and fits that would subside to be followed shortly after by an unfamiliar chuckle, languid and private, while she rocked gently to and fro on the bed. It was too much for dear Bee, who removed himself to the door to deter the ladies arriving in twos and threes to enquire after her wellbeing.

When the doctor arrived, he was ushered into the room by the same sullen convict servant who had earlier served us. Gossip in the kitchen a day or so later taught me that the doctor also had crossed the herring pond, but I would challenge even Sarah Selwyn to detect his convict past at first meeting. Of Dutch build, immaculate, his yellow hair curled becomingly around his sunbrowned face so as to merge profusely with oiled Newgate whiskers, his hands were among the cleanest I have seen on any crow. Without hesitation he opened his bag among the clutter of Mrs Broughton's sideboard, and lifted from it a heavy brass syringe.

'We will require towels and cerecloth,' he said, quick and light — a Scotsman like my lost Mr Horelock, 'and the gentleman will leave the room.'

Mr Cotton and I went out together. By the time I returned with the towels and oilcloth, the doctor had removed Mary Ann's outer clothing and she lay quite still in her petticoats as if in a trance. On his instruction the cerecloth was placed under her hips, her petticoats folded over her upraised knees. The doctor took up his position with the douche, which I saw had been filled with warm water from an earthenware jar brought in by a servant in my absence. It steamed gently beside him.

His intentions only then made themselves clear to me.

'Perhaps the crisis has passed,' I ventured, but he shook his head.

'She is merely in one of its phases — hysteria has many guises. I will induce a paroxysm.'

At the first jet of warm water, Mary Ann moaned and arched her back. I stroked her head — her cheeks were flushed — she shifted away from the tonic.

'Keep still, Mrs Martin,' instructed the doctor, intent on his target. 'Perhaps you could hold her steady?'

'No! You may go, Mrs Smith,' said Mary Ann, suddenly sensible, giving me such a look from that aroused, tousled face. She would rather this was a private matter — and so would I.

'I will wait outside,' I told the doctor quietly, and took my leave to join Mr Cotton who hovered outside the door.

I drew him away further down the passage, but the walls were not thick enough to disguise the tenor of Mary Ann's building excitement — a rhythmic moaning that swelled and quietened. A faint sweat broke out on Bee's upper lip, and his hand, when I took it to reassure him of the application, was hot and dry. His eyes held such a soulful but distant gaze, such as will take hold of a man when the woman he loves lies beneath him — and it struck me that perhaps, when a man who is not of a medical persuasion hears the intimate, private voice of a woman he respects, he is for ever after in possession of a secret that has him love her. It was such a splendid idea that it warmed me from the tips of my toes up the full length of my body and made me cry out with pleasure. I was more affected by Mary Ann's delirium than I knew.

'Mrs Smith! Why on earth are you laughing?'

'Come away into the garden, Bee.' I led him down the hall to a side passage until we came to a flight of servants' stairs that deposited us at the kitchen gardens. There he strode anxiously among the scorched cabbages and herbs, now and again turning his attention to Mrs Broughton's open window, but the light lay so brightly against the lace curtain that we could not discern any movement inside, nor anything other than the tones of the doctor's voice, soothing and instructional.

'Should we trust that fellow?' he asked me, coming to sit beside me on a bench seat, before going on, more to himself, 'Would the Judge trust him?'

'I suspect that Mr Martin is as much a babe in the wood as she is.'

'Whatever do you mean, Mrs Smith?'

I did not explain but merely gave a little smile that was lost on Mr Cotton, tho' after a moment, when his colour returned to his cheeks, he turned to me and asked if I was also a babe in the woods.

'How could I be, dear? I am three times a mother.'

'Three?'

'My first-born died.'

His expression was sympathetic but direct. 'And were you a loving wife, Mrs Smith? Do you mourn your husband?'

I met his eyes and some of the truth must have showed itself, for Mr Cotton's colour heightened further and he looked away towards Mrs Broughton's room, where it seemed the doctor was resuming the treatment. First the rush of water, then the rhythmic, involuntary moaning and sobbing. This time the crow effected a cure. At its apex the patient was fairly howling and Mr Cotton put his hands over his ears.

Mary Ann's treatment was, as Mr Cotton told Miss Tripp, the very latest from Europe — water played hard on the loins to induce an hysterical paroxysm — and I would be the last to deny that Mary Ann was improved by it. She gave no more trouble of that nature, but pursued her case with the Bishop in a serious and dignified manner. It was as if the fit left no memory of its earlier phase — the opening scene of the Drama Night forgotten. Neither did we ever discuss the palliative method, but then Mary Ann would often surprise me with what she chose to ignore and what she chose to make a fuss about. She secured a place for us on the brig *Bristolian*, which would carry the essentials of the party to New Zealand ahead of the rest.

With the promise of the passage and the effects of the cure, Mary Ann regained her gentle good spirits. There were picnics and outings — the furthermost afield being an excursion to Botany Bay, as part of a large company. We found it quite empty, this fabled landing place of the First Fleet over half a century ago. Our guide and host, Governor Gipps, explained that the fleet had only stopped here a few days before shifting the settlement to Sydney Cove. I did not wonder that they had not stayed there — the wide chill sea was too pressing, the flat landscape monotone and for lack of shelter inhospitable.

Ish and Rupai were in hope of convicts dragging chains and were at first disappointed — until the spectacle of kangaroos and large pink and white birds distracted them. One never forgets one's first sighting of a kangaroo. (Mine, unfortunately, had been in the Botanical Gardens, a poor sad creature with matted fur the colour of dried blood, whose pus-brimmed eyes morosely regarded the gawping Londoners.) What exhilaration to see them in the place God fashioned them! A flock bounded ahead of us, like fantastical carriage-hares, as we reached our destination. The strong tail acts as a kind of lever, while the monstrous legs carry the animal many feet ahead with each leap. One of our company had a pistol, and Rupai stood in the brougham to bring down a number of them — he was a crack shot, his patron in England having taken him along as a kind of stirrup cup for many a chase.

Later, while the servants laid out the picnic, I walked away with the lads and several of the younger men. A distance down the beach we turned into the bush, where we came across a group of kangaroos resting in a glade. The pistol was not with us, tho' it should have been, for propriety — a large buck lay on his hip, his legs crossed in the way a man will lie in his bed to peruse a book or gaze at his mistress. At first I thought the narrow protrusion was a part of his marsupial pouch — but it was his organ, a tufted tumescence he palpated enthusiastically with his paws.

Rupai called suggestively to the kangaroo, 'Kaha hoki te tītoi a te kangarū, ka pai!', while Ish laughed as hard as I ever heard him. The only woman in the company, I turned away — blushing! — to return towards the picnickers, while at my back one of the men sharply asked the lads to desist, and the boys overtook me, running fast along the track, laughing hysterically and gasping for air. A parallel sprang between the buck's shamelessness and Mary Ann's cure — I put it from my mind in almost the same instant it occurred to me.

Taken in sparse eucalyptus shade, the picnic was most uncomfortable, Mary Ann and Mrs Broughton's daughter both fainting away in the heat, and the flies sticky and persistent. I was glad to return to the beauty and tranquillity of the harbour.

Every morning during our furlough in Sydney, I was allowed two hours of freedom from eleven until one, when I had to return to the Governor's to dress Mary Ann for dinner. I spent it by walking from Darlinghurst to the town to be among the people and observe how life went on.

The first day, when I went along the beach to the clustered houses and narrow streets, I resolved to make my enquiry, and had the courage to ask one or two people, until his name died on my lips. I looked for him everywhere.

The world knew me now as Elizabeth Smith, the Horelock rusted away after eighteen long years. It was 1862 before I used it again, and only then to differentiate myself from at least four other Elizabeth Smiths in residence in Auckland. 'It would be better to address your letters to Elizabeth Horlock Smith,' I wrote to my sons from Parnell, a year or two before I sailed Home to London — and felt always a thrill run through me at the forming of the word on the page after all those years, tho' I spelt it sometimes 'Horelock'. He was more my heart's love than Hogg ever was.

In Sydney, at the beginning of my antipodean life, I struggled to bring myself even to whisper his name for fear of association with his crime. I thought I was brave, continuing on my single existence with the interests of my sons at heart. I was grateful that the sandy streets never offered him up.

Instead, I indulged in conversation on all manner of pleasurable and interesting topics, and found the people were eager to talk, especially the women, about how it was for them. It was hard, there wasn't enough of anything — of flour, or soap or beef or common regard — and they were greatly outnumbered by the men. But many of the children were pleasingly ruddy and strong, and I thought it would be better to be poor here than in London, even if just for the warmth — which was delicious. I met servants I matched with the nobs I'd met at 'Tusculum', and heard scurrilous tales of intrigue and brutality, piety and spite, crooked deals, fortunes made and easily lost. It was much the same as that which goes on anywhere in the open world.

Rupai and Ish both held a fascination for the Australian Natives, some of whom camped on the edges of town, finding them more entertaining than they did squiring me about Port Jackson. A pretty pair they made — their contrasting good looks caught the eye of all they passed. Rupai had a way of laughing that I was to meet in many other Maori people. It was infectious, generous, offered up to all around him. John Elisha was transformed in his company, prone to fits of giggles and giving voice to thoughts he would otherwise keep to himself. He became in fact more like his brother Henry — who sought Maori company from the moment he was released from Port Nicholson. From the first Henry adored them as a people, and as one does for any love, perhaps, he suffered for it. He thought that they would all be like Mokihi, or William Jowitt and his clever Waiheke friends, or the Te Arawa tribes he labours among. The last have made hard work for him with their arrogance and conviction of their own superiority and physical beauty, their quarrelsome natures — tho' I hear they prove loyal to the Queen in these wars that drag on and on and frighten so many of us away.

So very far away.

It occurs to me now as I carry my candle to bed — and I can't be sure — but I suspect Rupai is the only Maori friend Ish ever had. Once, I think in the late forties, early fifties, he tried to befriend Martin, Te Rauparaha's son — who rejected him as being the paler, less entertaining brother of the true friend he had, further north, in Henry. Wellington abounds with officials and sub-officials even more given to procrastination and obfuscation than the Natives, who excel at it, so it is as well they don't exist there in any numbers together or the capital would stultify — but it removes one race from the other, which does not bode well for the future.

The decommissioned officer has come in to his lodgings below with his rowdy friends — they have not removed their loud boots and the house shakes with their tread. One of them is singing, the words muffled by drunkenness and distance — peace is lost to the evening, and I am sleepless.

My sweet Nick. If the streets of Port Jackson had offered you up all those years ago in 1842, I would have run to embrace you, my heart bursting with love. I would not have been able to stop myself. I would have begged your forgiveness for blaming you for my beloved father's death and for believing them when they said you would hang. I would tell you about how Katie was lost to me, how with Mr Hogg I bore two sons before the truth of his circumstances was made clear — and how I have made the best of my life since then. I would have stood before you strong and loving; you would have forgiven me my second marriage and taken me in your arms.

Go to sleep you old, giddy girl.

SEVEN

To Lichfield

1866

ALL THROUGH THAT LONG hot summer while Elizabeth festered in her bed with one complaint after another, her spirit remained companionable. There was the one caller she expected, the small visitor who came at all hours of the day and night, not always happily. Once, in the early hours of the morning, she woke hot and sluggish to feel the little spirit body cold and light against hers under the bedclothes and somehow resentful. It was a fleeting sensation, lost almost in the moment she was aware of it.

Of Miss Tripp there was neither hide nor hair — it seemed the young woman's curiosity was exhausted shortly after the visit to Chiswick. Their brief friendship had satisfied her: this was her father's second wife, then, this was the fabled Elizabeth.

My father always said she was a great beauty.

Isn't that what Elizabeth had heard as she came out of her faint all those months ago at Mr Griggs's? So Tom Hogg had painted her in a good light? In his cups he might have told other stories against her, and they would have laughed — what a termagant! What wilfulness! What a fool! Did she not suspect?

Mr Griggs, who came regularly, had it that Miss Tripp's neglect could only be attributed to a change in her circumstances, and hinted that these had been brought about by an alteration in a gentleman's affections. It seemed that the schoolmaster took a paternal interest in the peregrinations of his young friend, and afforded a great deal of largesse when it came to her doubtful morals. Elizabeth did not consider he would have allowed her the same lack of judgement when they first met, though she'd played the blameless widow very well — too well, perhaps.

She had no inclination to press him for details of Miss Tripp's situation, just as she did not on the other, more disturbing matter. Let him have the gumption to mention it himself; let him confess to the correspondence with Henry and Ish. They had made him their detective: regimental connections would have led him to Mr Hogg's daughter. Was the bigamist dead then, or at the very least not in England? Let Mr Griggs admit that he had gone behind her back and — yes, it was quite feasible — that he had written to tell her sons whatever Miss Tripp had told him.

The only conceivable form of action was to maintain one's pride, which would be difficult if Mr Hogg was alive and told of her whereabouts. He could come looking for her — he was a man of conscience and feeling for the weaknesses of women, though in other regards too romantic and excitable. If he was widowed, would he want to make amends to her in their old age? It was ridiculous even to entertain the notion. What then? Would they end by recounting the whole story?

In the meantime Mr Griggs was her saviour, bringing her improving books from the lending library, as well as copies of the *Penny Illustrated Paper* and *The Englishwoman's Domestic Magazine*, and the gift of a novel called *Lady Audley's Secret*, in which a woman fascinatingly commits Mr Hogg's crime and many others beside. Though entirely compulsive reading, it left her dismayed for the future of the world. Almost to the end she had believed the lady would be exonerated — how shocking that a woman really could be capable of such hateful actions. Was it now so common that a novelist could write about it? Never had she thought to take her own anger and resentment out on the innocent. 'We are a family not in good repute,' John Elisha had told her more than once. He had made a refrain of it. How much worse it could have been.

A more suspicious person would suspect Mr Griggs's motives for bringing the novel. He read the sensation aloud in his soft clipped voice, sometimes dropping away altogether during passages that embarrassed him, so that she was compelled then to read them herself after he had gone, never mind her aching head. There was a character for whom Elizabeth felt far more acutely than the heroine.

'*Now Mrs Walter Powell*,' read Mr Griggs, '*being afflicted with that nervous curiosity common to people who live in other people's houses, felt herself deeply injured.*'

It had often been a battle not to feel deeply injured — at Taurarua with Mary Ann, at Te Papa with the Browns, at Te Ngae with the Chapmans, in Onehunga with Henry's wife Sophia, at all the houses she worked in that were not her own.

One afternoon towards the end of her illness, when she was well enough to sit up at the table in the window, the little housemaid came up the stairs with a different guest. Bee Cotton was cured and once again out in society. Some shadow of the summer fevers must have shown in her face, because consternation filled his own the moment he saw her.

'Poor Mrs Smith!' He kissed her gently on the cheek. 'If I have neglected you it is because it took Doctor Tuke longer to convince Pater of my recovery than it ever has before. The older he gets, the more he's convinced I am incurably insane!'

Bee was in one of his elevated tempers, his cheeks flushed and eyes sparkling, his body emanating the strange dry and spicy smell that accompanied these escalations. These were his most enjoyable moods, when he was both amenable and volatile, and looking for adventure. In this phase they had sailed together in New Zealand — on a hot, thundery day they had set out from Taurarua and made landfall on Rangitoto, a sleeping volcano that rose steep from the Waitemata Harbour. It was thrilling, dangerous — on their return voyage they had almost capsized in a sudden storm. Throughout it all Bee had remained implacable, utterly fearless.

'Shall we go to Lichfield to visit the Bishop?' she asked him now, in as normal a voice as one would use to invite a guest to remove his coat. Later she would chastise herself for taking advantage, but at the time it seemed a sensible application of Bee's energies.

'Why not?' replied Bee, without a moment's consideration. 'Will he be expecting us?'

'No. And it is just as well. In our case it will be better to surprise him so that he may not turn us away.'

'Ah. You have thought it all through.'

Carefully, Bee took a seat on the spindly chair — how lovely to see him out of Manor House. He had been to the barber and wore a clean shirt.

'I see you are no more settled than you were before.'

He was talking of the rolled carpet, the chest of books, the mantelpiece bare of her mementoes and bibelots.

'Yes,' Elizabeth said. 'Whenever I am well enough, I pack a little more — time to move on.'

'But why so, Mrs Smith? Do you not like it here, so close to the church and your helpful friend?'

'There are other churches, and Mr Griggs makes himself helpful to so many ladies I do not care to become a burden to him.' She feared she already had. 'I may not have much longer, Mr Cotton. Who knows when the Good Lord will call me? To that end I propose to make my last journey.'

'And will you return to London?'

'Oh, yes. I have already arranged alternative lodgings, commencing a week before Christmas, inferior to these but travel is not cheap, is it dear Bee? When one takes into account hotels and dining.'

'I can see you mean to enjoy yourself, Mrs Smith.'

Elizabeth nodded. 'Though penury will follow.'

'As it happens I am allowed my convalescence, so I will most definitely accompany you to Lichfield.'

'And to Torquay, Devon. The Martins are newly settled there.'

'Mary Ann?' Mr Cotton's mottled black and grey whiskers parted for a wide red smile — which just as quickly disappeared again. He was suddenly stricken. 'Though I may be called before that! The Bishop of Chester wants me back in Frodsham by Christmas.'

'The Bishop who called you "the lunatic priest"? I think you should resign your post, dear Bee. Surely you have tried your best and they have found it wanting?'

'Father would cut me out without a moment's hesitation.'

'George Augustus could speak on your behalf and secure a stipend.'

'Whatever makes you think that that is what I desire, Mrs Smith?' A flash of rage. She would not be frightened of him as others had been.

'I will shoulder the plough.'

'Of course you will,' she soothed, 'and take up your rod and staff. Of course you will.'

With purpose, Bee removed a stub of pencil and small brown notebook from his pocket.

'Dates, Mrs Smith. When shall we depart?'

⁂

On a Tuesday in late November they took the train to Lichfield. It was the longest journey Elizabeth had ever made by rail and she was glad Mr Cotton's fearlessness had not deserted him. Once they had travelled as intrepid equals; now she felt herself quailing and nauseous at the noise and speed. Among her luggage in the guard's van was the field chest which contained, among other mixtures, a tincture specified to Bee's requirements should his general demeanour fall away and he prove not so genial a companion. On and off platforms and trains he guided her — leaving the London line at Rugby and changing again at Stafford for Lichfield. It was a tiresome day's journey, which with many delays took part of the night.

'How strange it is, Mr Cotton,' she remarked as they came into Towcester. 'We are not so very far from London and yet the countryside is as unfamiliar to me as — for example — the Middle Island, New Munster, which I never visited.'

'The South Island, I believe they are beginning to call it, Mrs Smith.'

'Oh dear. What do the Maoris call it?'

'Te Waipounamu.'

'The place of greenstone?'

'Loosely.'

'They should call it that, though dreary "South Island" will stick.'

'I have been this way many times before,' said Bee, glancing out the window. 'Have you never?'

'Indeed I have not. Like most Londoners I have an abhorrence of Birmingham.'

'Neither will you see it this time. We turn away well before it.' Mr Cotton laughed. 'And I should think, after your years in New Zealand, you would not use the word "abhorrence" so lightly.'

He appeared to be enjoying his journey very much, his first real excursion since his incarceration. He offered a commentary on everything, from the wintry fields of the Trent Valley, to the extravagant furs of a wealthy woman glimpsed on a platform, to the unruly behaviour of a small boy travelling with his governess. He took delight in a light fall of snow just as the train pulled into Lichfield, where, owing to the element of surprise to their visit, there was no one to meet them.

Directly across the road was a shabby inn. They crossed the icy, rutted street, a porter following after with a handcart, and Mr Cotton exclaiming on the beauty of the snow and how — though he loved the South Pacific — an instinct had always craved the true, agonising bite of an English winter.

'That is the most deranged pronouncement that ever passed your lips,' Elizabeth said, laughing, clinging to his arm, 'and I have heard so many. Perhaps you should return to Doctor Tuke's forthwith!'

Mr Cotton's spirits continued up a pair of broken stairs and through their poor supper of bread and cheese, and for all Elizabeth knew all through the night. Certainly they had deserted him by the time they met at eight-thirty sharp for the short walk to the Cathedral. Neither friend had slept well — Bee troubled by bugs, and Elizabeth by a lumpy mattress as well as her usual dissuasions.

It being dark on their approach to Lichfield the night before, they had not been able to enjoy the spectacle of the spires. Now the murky morning showed three ancient turrets rising into low grey clouds.

'How veiled are the Ladies of the Vale!' Mr Cotton quipped as they passed beside a pond frozen over, the ice thick enough to support a group of larking lads at the centre. Most wore wooden pattens, though one — better dressed than the others — was in possession of a pair of skates, the metal blades flaring brightly enough to draw the eye.

'I never did see the Maoris skating,' remarked Bee. 'But I suppose they had no call for it and so did not bother.'

'I never did see the Maoris bother with a great deal of things,' said Elizabeth, shortly, 'which is not to say they did not do them.'

The warmest boy slid wildly towards them on the seat of his pants, his blades flashing, legs waving before him like a pair of antennae, like a wētā — the terrifying species of giant insect that occupied the walls of the hospital, the thatch cottage on the beach. She had hated them — if cornered, they would stand their ground as rats do.

She drew Bee on around the perimeter of the pool — numbing, damp cold progressing through the thin soles of her boots to her aching bones — to a lane that led up the hill, between the rich dwellings. Who lived here, she wondered? How comfortable they must be, these Princes of the Church. If she had not persuaded Henry away from his vocation, then perhaps he would have accompanied the Bishop and be lodged among them, and she would be living here with him. He might have become devout enough to espouse Saint Paul completely and swear off earthly marriage. She could have been mistress of his house. Henry would have been happy as a bachelor — he had no real instinct for women. How long had he waited for Sophia? Their courtship lasted twelve years! And in all his time among the Maoris there was never a whisper of impropriety. Dear, good, happy Henry. He could be walking beside her now, instead of Bee, who was stopping again, squeezing her arm.

'Why do you want to see Selwyn?' he asked.

It was an aspect of his madness, which was perhaps incurable, only varying in degree, that he hadn't asked the most obvious question until now. And she was perhaps close behind him in her unready answer.

There was a time when she would have been happy never to lay eyes on the Bip again, and Bee knew that: she had told him vehemently of all the Bishop's transgressions — personal and political — since he left. What wounds Selwyn had helped to open up — this war that went on and on, slaughtering the sons and daughters of friends, Maori and Pakeha. And labouring amongst it all was Henry, who had ridden among the Maoris in more than one battle and lost friends on both sides.

There was a letter from him last week, trying to explain the reality of the situation and scolding her for her wish that, after all, a house had been built for her at Maketu, where she could be of service through the troubles.

'I would take the little people under my wing,' she'd written in her last letter, meaning the children and the old women.

'What a strange delusion,' he had replied in his next.

There were places where the ink had run with his tears and her own. If the Bishop had not brought God's House to stand beside the barracks, then the infant nation would have had a chance. For many years Selwyn was openly critical of the vast tracts of land tricked out of the Maori people by the missionaries and the hordes that followed them — he co-authored with Judge Martin a book published in England that defended the Natives' rights — but in the end he sided with his own. So much of what was happening was his fault. On board *Tomatin* he had known her for a liar — an entire race now suspected him as one.

'Mrs Smith?' Bee's supporting arm gave a little shake.

'Are you not curious yourself, Bee?' she asked.

'Oh yes. Oh absolutely, dear lady.'

And so he was, thought Elizabeth. His eyes were shining, he had some of his old colour back, he was committed to the adventure.

They went on, the great Cathedral rising beside them, blackened limestone ornate with carved apostles and saints, papist frippery centuries old. The Bishop would likely love all the trimmings: what Tractarian taonga must lie inside the high walls — robes, gold, luxuries, the library. It would all be to his taste. On this remove he would not have been compelled to arrange his own library, as he had with Bee in the stone store at Kerikeri; he would not have had to contend with mould and moths in his altar cloths; he was not compelled to make conversions of savages, or arduous sea voyages on barely seaworthy tubs. But she knew him well enough to be sure that he would miss going among the people in the way he had in that other place.

Around the front of the Cathedral they went, Elizabeth having to bring all her concentration to bear on surmounting the pain from her legs and thundering heart, her vision blurring so that Bee's pointed finger to the figure above her head — 'William the Conqueror reading the Doomsday Book! My father brought me here as a boy' — showed only as a wash of stone.

Bee hauled up at a gate. 'Here it is. Bishop's Palace.'

How true a promotion this was! Selwyn was indeed a kind of King. The handsome mansion with its many gables and windows drew no comparison with any of his prior residences. To see Augustus in these surrounds would be as incongruous as to behold Te Wherowhero on the throne of England. Their Bishop had certainly laboured — sometimes misguidedly — and this was his sumptuous reward.

A porch so grand should boast a liveried footman, but there was none. A ring of hammers sounded from the rear — there was another gable rising behind the palace, with pale raw framing for a steeple. His passion for church-building had not deserted him, then.

'Wait here,' said Bee, surmounting the steps.

His lack of resentment was humbling. A burst of happiness had him leap two treads at a time and rattle at the banger bold as a bailiff. Here was the devotee since boyhood — an enthusiast for all Selwyn's enhancing reforms at Eton, a willing companion on some of the most extensive and difficult journeys of thousands of miles through bush and swamp — come to visit the one he'd once loved above all, until their paths parted, Cotton back to dreary existence in England while Selwyn grew ever more powerful in the Colony.

Making a pantomime of listening at the heavy door, Bee had one hand to his ear and his posture comically primed as if he were about to spring. He never failed to make her laugh — her accomplice and jester.

Eventually a manservant, who wore only a plain black costume and no powdered wig, opened the door. While Mr Cotton engaged him in conversation, fairly sanely as far as she could make out, her eye was drawn by a twitch of lace in an upstairs window. A woman looked out — a long, sallow face framed with iron-grey hair folded over each ear in rare and antique style.

Sarah Selwyn.

Elizabeth was too far away to be keenly observed, at any rate with elderly eyes, but it seemed that the figure startled — it grew momentarily larger just before the curtain was dropped. The reckless nature of the visit would doubtless disappoint Sarah, though not as greatly as her lost opportunity to deny a polite request for reunion.

'He is supervising the building of the new chapel.' Bee was returned to her. 'We must follow this path around the palace.'

The garden path was yet unformed — a puddle, melting now as the day warmed, slushing and dampening their feet. A brittle creeper snagged at her dress, a marmalade cat bounded ahead of them, leaving prints in a drift of grimy snow. Bee held as tightly to her arm as she did to his — he was limping slightly, having excelled himself at the stairs — he snuffed the scent of fresh sawdust, spicy in the cold air.

'Perhaps a fellow will give me a turn at the lathe!'

He hurried his pace and smiled as a child will at the promise of cake.

There were stonemasons in leather aprons, carpenters in blue shirts, roofers high in the scaffolding, the rasp of saws, and calls of instruction and order. Selwyn had worked his magic — the gang worked as keenly as any synod, as any crew, as any litter-bearing Natives or clutch of missionary explorers. The interlopers were scarcely acknowledged, as if the workmen were used to being visited by curious passers-by and pilgrims come to view the latest palace additions.

The song of the lathe drew Bee away into the darker reaches, just as Elizabeth caught sight of a pair of finely tooled leather boots dangling almost overhead. By his choice of footwear the Bishop was only visiting, not intending to work a full day as he would have in New Zealand, but wanting still to be amongst it all. Elizabeth picked up a small stone and took aim — the ceiling here was lower than in the body — and hit the polished heel. Her deadeye was returned to her — this was a feature of age: old skills suddenly revisiting, and just as suddenly vanishing. Just last night, before bed, Bee had produced his copy of the newly published *Hymns Ancient and Modern* and they'd had some hymn-singing — 'Praise my Soul the King of Heaven' — and she'd found herself in good voice for the first time in years.

> *All People that on Earth do dwell,*
> *Sing to the Lord with cheerful voice —*

Until an irate guest in the next room pounded on the wall, sending dust flying from the picture rail.

> *Hark! a thrilling voice is sounding!*

Her voice was still with her now, and Augustus recognised it!
'Mrs Smith!'
He peered down at her, gravity bringing forward his jowls — though they hung less than they did on many men of his age. He retained his sinewy smile and direct gaze — his pleasure, so far as she could tell, was genuine.
'Good gracious!'
There followed an acrobatic descent — hanging first from the beam by his hands and dropping the considerable distance to the uneven ground, landing lightly with his knees bent.
He had once made such a sudden, light-footed appearance in another chapel — or the remains of one — on a steep hill in that other country, and had half-frightened her to death. She wondered if he remembered. There were reasons the occasion would stick more in her mind than in his.
He took her hands and she bent her arthritic knee, pursing her lips to kiss the ring — and he telling her now to rise and not to stand

on ceremony — and she meeting him eye to eye and observing him in his white shirtsleeves this brisk November morning, and knowing he'd lost none of his heat. His hands were warm in hers, slightly roughened but soft from book-learning too, just the way a man's hands should be — neither too much one nor the other.

'We will have the chapel closed in before the winter begins in earnest,' he told her. 'It's my last. My swan song. What do you think?'

'By its dimensions, very grand. We would not call this a chapel at—' She had nearly said 'home', which slip of the tongue had bewildered her before.

'I have had news of you, of course, from Henry and the Thatchers. You are well, obviously? Your health has improved?'

'England suits me better.'

Even if it didn't, she would tell him so. Sarah Selwyn had foreseen a dismal future here and done her best to dissuade her from the voyage — she had brought messages to the same effect from her husband. Later Elizabeth had written her a letter: 'I would sooner rely on publick charity in England than in this tragic, changeful country.'

'You are here alone?'

'Not at all.' Elizabeth gestured towards Mr Cotton, who had been given a turn not at a lathe but a plane, and was engrossed in making long sweeps along the length of timber set between two saw-horses, curls spilling from it like wake from a surfing longboat. A tradesman hovered anxiously nearby — in his enthusiasm Bee would shave the timber away.

Abruptly, the Bishop let go of her hands and turned to take his coat from where it hung on a nogging.

It had been a mistake to bring her old friend.

'My Lord?'

'Come with me,' he said. 'Fetch Mr Cotton along with you.'

Bee came away from his game the moment she tugged on his arm so they could hurry after the Bishop, who strode along the path at such a clip it took a great deal of pulling together to keep up, following him through a side door of the palace and down a short passage, where he flung open a door.

Sarah was at tea in her morning room, an apartment furnished in dove greys and soft pinks on the eastern side of the house. A bright fire burned, catching on the abundance of silver ornaments and mirrors. With one hand Bee held tightly to Augustus's arm, extending the other in a wide come-hither to Sarah, as if he would embrace husband and wife at once. Rising to her feet, Sarah did little to disguise her expression of astonishment. Old age — for she was now in her early sixties — gave her already twisted face further drapes and folds, so that when she opened her mouth to speak, her chin slipped sideways — which strangely brought to mind a kitchen drawer, the small teeth blackened as tiny pewter spoons.

'Mrs Smith,' she said, 'I had thought I was imagining things — but you really are here. With Mr Cotton.'

'Dearest Mrs Selwyn!' Bee's outstretched fingers beckoned.

'Will you stay for tea, Augustus?' Sarah asked in pleading though steely tones, turning away even as she spoke to ring a little bell on the tea tray. 'I will call for more cups.'

The Bishop sighed — and Elizabeth realised she'd never heard him do that in all their long acquaintance. He had never been a sighing man — disappointing news was only ever received by an almost imperceptible clenching of that fine jaw, or the telling twitch in his cheek.

Engulfed by his pleasure in the moment, Mr Cotton was drawing him to the pink settee and sitting beside him, maintaining his grip and smiling like a crocodile. She would not say anything, Elizabeth resolved, she would bide her time. The Selwyns had always been good at preserving silence rather than risking uncertain conduct. This time she would do the same.

An uppermaid came in to answer her mistress's bell, which Elizabeth saw now was in the shape of a shepherdess with a gilt crook, the striker concealed inside her skirts. There were more shepherdesses clustered on the mantel and on the dresser, with pink and white faces and hooped coloured skirts, a village of them. They reminded Elizabeth of Miss Tripp — the sloping shoulders, the small, pretty faces. They were Sarah's indulgence, some reflection of herself perhaps, as she'd seen her role beside her husband. Elizabeth felt a softening for her, as she had done countless times over the years — though she knew now that it would not be long before a piece of vitriol hardened it again.

Mrs Selwyn lifted a cup on the tray and gestured to it. Immediately the maid hurried to a sideboard with a surface so polished that the opening cupboard caught the reflection of the group — poor Bee looking as mad as he ever had been, Sarah as stricken, the Bishop uncharacteristically ill at ease, and herself — well yes, she would admit it — she appeared to be gloating.

The maid presented three teacups of such fine china that the light showed through at the rims.

'So.' The Bishop took control, as Elizabeth knew he would. 'What brings you to Lichfield, William?' His tone was admonitory, as if any reason Bee could give would disappoint.

'I am here with Mrs Smith!' Bee was fairly shouting. 'We are taking a tour!'

The Bishop nodded, supping his tea, shifting his interrogation to Elizabeth.

'Are you in your professional capacity?' He lowered his voice, as if he would hide his query from his old friend, though they sat thigh to thigh.

'Bee and I take care of one another,' she replied firmly.

'I should like to speak to you alone, Mrs Smith.'

The Bishop's wife glared over her teacup.

'I should enjoy that very much.'

The interview would be extended then. She'd feared it would only be a moment's duration — she had not been invited to remove her shawl, though it was warm and close.

The Bishop sipped at his tea thirstily, as if he had not drunk for days — but he had always been able to tolerate scalding liquids. Elizabeth blew on hers, while Bee drummed an ecstatic tattoo on the polished settee arm to set the contents of his cup rocking.

'You are looking very well, Mrs Selwyn,' he told her, to the rhythmic beat. Elizabeth caught Sarah's eye, though she would rather not have. It was plain the Bishop's wife did not share the same opinion of her visitors. At least the tea was delicious, hot and sweet, and went some way to soothe Elizabeth's rising consternation.

Augustus stood, putting his cup down on a table.

'You will come with me to the Cathedral.' He bent to his wife and whispered in her ear, during which time Elizabeth managed two or three scalding sips before standing and following him from the room.

'Did you encourage kindness from Mrs Selwyn?' she asked as they went down the steps. 'Poor William is so very fragile.'

'You will not assume intimacy with me, Mrs Smith. When we met, you were servant to the wife of one of my oldest and dearest friends. Due to the peculiar society of New Zealand and — I might say — the efforts of your sons, you rose from that position. Here we are returned to our proper places.'

Any allusion to his wife's true character would always set the Bishop blustering. A long time ago, Bee had made a collection of Selwyn's blotting-paper doodles from his desks at Waimate Mission Station and at Tamaki, or left on his portable secretaire in bush settings. Over and over again he had drawn little chapels and portraits of Sarah — her long face and sharp chin, as if he would install the same grace in her as he did the steeples, or at the very least get the measure of her. He succeeded only in lengthening her face and nose more than her Creator had, until she looked like a witch. Bee had made a study of them, cutting them out of the pink blotting paper and gluing them into his journals — a record Selwyn was surely in ignorance of.

'I have approximately half an hour, then I must attend to business.'

He was waiting impatiently at the corner while she did her best to force her pace. The day seemed colder than before — damp air finding its way through all her layers to lie against her skin, moist and chill. The features of a gargoyle swam into focus above the Bishop's head and retreated again just as a small, weightless hand took hold of her skirts. In the pounding of her heart there was the scuff of Katie's tread.

Go away — not now.

'It's lucky that you did not arrive tomorrow — my wife and I are taking a short holiday, and leave this afternoon.'

It was as much as she could do to nod breathlessly as he disappeared, her heavy wrappings weighing her chest and the little hand closing over hers on the knob of the cane now, urging her on.

Shake it along, Ma.

The Bishop stood at a side door, which he was holding open for her to pass through, taking her elbow as she managed the step, worn to a hollow with the tread of centuries.

Katie leaned against her, steadying her, as she passed into the Cathedral, which seemed to gather her in — the lofty roof, the wide ambulatory, the gold and silk and ornament, the worshipful regard of a thousand years.

The dignity and sanctity of Selwyn's ultimate appointment seemed suddenly immense, important, beyond her trifling desire — for what? Revenge? A final attempt to have the man see her for who she was — a woman who could have matched him in determination and vision, who would have been a worthy accomplice had he acknowledged her? Instead she had been his adversary more than once, working quietly against him.

He was hurrying away at a faster clip, gesturing to a pew before the Quire, as if he desired her to sit and wait. She was happy to — there was such beauty here: the stained-glass windows, intricate and brilliant, had her tip her head back to gaze at the clerestory; the high altar drew her eye through the intricate carvings of the rood screen. If a woman loved God, then she must love all this expression for Him, and how could she not love all this beauty? It was so seductive, as seductive as the lunacy of believing her little girl was once again safe in her lap. Elizabeth had come to religion later than most, at first from necessity — as a way of getting to New Zealand and dearest Henry — and later for comfort. Oh, but how easy it was to yield to this beauty, to feel one's spirit fly up — how strange that with one's own beauty gone, one craved it more and more in the world and every variety of it. She forgave the Bishop for his indulgence.

He had completely disappeared.

White robes swishing for an instant against her skirts, a young sacristan passed by, carrying a polished candlestick — she could smell the turpentine — and placed it on the Quire altar, crossing himself on approach. It was her Bishop who reigned here — she was proud of him suddenly, in spite of everything. She too had performed that duty, polishing silver in more than one of the pretty wooden churches designed by Selwyn himself and left as his legacy all over the archipelago. That is, if they had not burned in the current conflagration — along with the flour mills and dairy factories, the schools and barns and cottages. How did anybody know who their friends were now?

Guide us Heavenly Father, guide us.

The sacristan crossed himself again and departed. She had never crossed herself. She never would. Selwyn did, in moments of high piety, and had been frowned on for it by some of the missionaries.

Pale men in long dark robes flitted from the side chapels. She had grown used to priests who grew brown or florid, depending on their complexions, from all their outdoor proselytising. The rest of their bodies stayed white as snow — she had nursed enough of them to see it. Selwyn had insisted they wear their long cassocks up and down mountains, through swamps and marsh, so that they grew as heavy and dragging as a woman's skirts, and as dangerous.

In a tasselled and frilled mauve gown a young woman knelt in earnest prayer beneath what was once a station of Christ. If it weren't for her hoop doing the work of a thousand petticoats she would be anchored there for ever, radiating purity. Elizabeth sensed a quickening of interest in the air that was not entirely her own, a gentle nudging at her side.

Look, Ma — see the rich lady praying.

If the child had lived, would she have been so fortunate? She'd have been twenty years old at the time they embarked for New Zealand and she may have gone with them, or not. She may have prospered here and worn as frothy a gown, may one day have knelt as fervently. The distant high altar gleamed with medieval gold.

Where was Augustus? Was this his ploy — to leave her to contemplate the foolish nature of her journey and confess her sins to God rather than to him? What had he whispered in Sarah's ear? Had he ordered the removal of Mr Cotton back to his asylum? She should hurry back to the palace — how familiar was this sense of panic engendered by the Bishop's disapproval of certain actions or friendships.

But here he was, flying down the aisle towards her, in white collar and plain black cassock. She supposed it was his everyday garb, severe amongst all the frippery, close-fitting at the top and flaring to an abundance of black serge at the bottom.

He was gesturing for her to remain seated and taking a place beside her. Her panic did not subside. It seemed he had planned his interview with her, because he began immediately.

'I do hope you haven't come to ask for money, or to rake over the past.' His eyes rested on the closest crucifix in the choir stalls. His hairline was damp and he smelt of plain soap — he had washed while she waited.

'Has it been as you expected — you have found life easier in London?'

'In some ways. More difficult in others. I had to let go of certain dreams.'

'As have I, Mrs Smith, as have I.'

'If I had been justly rewarded for the work I did at the hospital and missions, I may have been able to buy a home of my own.'

He was looking at her now, impatience twitching at his mouth.

'You are asking for that reward now, in England?'

'Yes, Augustus.'

The Bishop flinched at her familiarity.

'I would not expect it in London, but it could be provided for me in Torquay so that I might be near Mary Ann. Do you not agree?'

'We have talked about this before and I advised you always that you should go to your sons for assistance.'

'Their responsibilities are to their wives and families.'

'However limited are their resources — and they are not as limited as some — they would make provision for you.'

He would paint them in a bad light — she would not allow it. 'And so they do, my Lord.'

'There is no sense in prolonging this interview. We none of us can have life exactly as we would like it. I would not have returned to England had I been given a choice — but I was not! I have wept for it, Mrs Smith.'

His voice broke a little at this confidence, but she would not comfort him even though she could soothe him more genuinely than his wife could: Sarah had not loved the country as she had. He spoke again, so quietly she had to bend her ear towards him.

'I expect you know I was fired upon by Maori troops. You would know that that is how it ended for me, thrown so far back in Native estimation, more than my remaining years of life would ever have enabled me to recover.'

'I remember hearing something along those lines. I was sorry for it.' And she was, though not for the reasons he imagined she would be. He was looking at her intently, as if waiting for her to go on and comfort him. She would — if he would take if from her — but he was dropping suddenly to his knees, taking her with him.

'Father, regard Thee Thy servant Elizabeth who has worked hard in Thy service. Help her to understand the change in her circumstances and to accept the limitations of old age. Give her the blessing of propriety and the wisdom to know her place. Amen.'

The prayer resounded with the one he'd offered on that other day in that other chapel, the ruined one at Taurarua all those years ago. He had arrived among them as alarmingly as if he'd fallen from the broken roof — a second reminder of it in as many hours, a day she would not remember now for fear of reliving its grief. A shaft of wintry sun played about the clerestory above their heads; there was a sparrow flying through it.

'I want to talk to you about Reverend Cotton, Mrs Smith.' Beside her, the Bishop had returned his posterior to the pew. 'What are your plans? Will you return to London now?'

'We are enjoying a tour.'

'In November?'

'Why not?'

'There are some very good reasons. Your health, for one. You should be keeping to yourself, warm and quiet. His health, for the other — he is not in his right mind, as you know very well. You visited him several times in his asylum, did you not?'

She felt a quick flush of flattery — had he kept track of her movements as much as all that?

'His father, whom may I remind you is the Governor of the Bank of England and a man of influence, has kept all his correspondence from the years in New Zealand. At first, he did not remember your name or who you were, so he searched through the letters — mine and those from his son — and found mention. A near-drowning on the Waitemata Harbour. Wild parties where Maori guests were encouraged to play dangerous games. Mind-altering tinctures of your own manufacture. Mr Cotton's inappropriate affection for Mrs Martin, actively encouraged by yourself — though he knew of that from Mrs Selwyn.'

Elizabeth could hardly keep up with the catalogue — not that he would allow her any defence.

'Bee's affection for Mary Ann was that of a brother—' she tried.

'He will not be pleased to know you have taken his son on as a case. Do you have Doctor Tuke's approval?'

'Doctor Tuke discharged him from his care and William came to me of his own free will. May we go through your accusations one by one?'

'They are not accusations, Mrs Smith, but facts. My wife read of Bee's affection in his own hand.'

'In his journal?' How clearly she could see it, Sarah going into his room at the Bishop's College, picking up the leather volume, unclasping the brass lock. She would have told herself she was in search of a cure for him, an understanding of his vacillations.

Augustus had coloured a little.

'It was a means necessary to an end. He wrote tenderly of how '— his colour deepened — 'how a fine gold necklace lay against her throat, of all her moods and preferences.'

'Mr Cotton is a loving friend and that was many years ago, Augustus. I must return to him.'

'You will not take advantage of his kindness. I trust it is his funds you are mining for this venture?'

She took hold of the pew in front and hauled herself to her feet. Her little comforter had vanished — as well she might and who could blame her?

'No. We are travelling as friends and each paying our own way.'

It was as if she had not spoken — the Bishop had risen to

accompany her down the aisle, as in step with her as a bridegroom. At the side door he enquired whether she could make her own way.

She nodded. 'I will write to Henry and tell him I have seen you in person and ask for his petition for justice to cease.'

'He has written to me only once since I returned — hardly a petition.'

It was his victory, of course, though she felt it as her own.

'Goodbye, Augustus. It's marvellous to see you so promoted.'

He helped her down the worn step. 'Goodbye, Mrs Smith. We will not meet again.'

EIGHT

The Native Hospital

'LET HIM RETURN TO the builders,' was what husband had whispered in wife's ear on our departure for the Cathedral. So far from being detained preparatory to involuntary removal to Chiswick, Mr Cotton had spent a happy hour at the lathe.

Sarah herself escorted me to him, having had the maid fetch her wraps and boots. We had all thought she would die long before any chance of return to England, she who so intently detailed every ailment as if her husband's almost inhuman endurance of pain and adversity must be matched by a yielding of equal degree. Yet here she was, spry enough to walk unaided beside me. Having no doubt given it due consideration, she was now of a mind to make me welcome for the little time we had left. On our way through the grounds she entertained me by pointing out the New Zealand trees she had had planted as saplings. At a glance it was obvious that the four kauris — forest giants that require a temperate climate — would not survive the English winter. They were infants, standing only as high as a man; two were dropping their leaves, when at home they were evergreens. The kahikatea, being a type of pine, may well have a better chance, and also a tree I had never seen before: the kaikawaka, Sarah explained, a mountain cedar from the Taranaki, which might enjoy the cold. Near the icy fishpond languished a dismal clump of toitoi, their silvery green quite blackened and none of their wild feathery heads remaining. The Bishop's wife pointed out a place where clematis had once wound around an oak, now died quite away.

When she paused for me to catch up she changed her subject, speaking instead of her children grown to manhood and how marvellous it was to live close to them after all these years. A little flush came to her narrow cheeks. When the boys were sent away to England for school she had suffered great privations, which those who loved her took more seriously than her illnesses. Some of her bitterness for me, I suspect, was born of envy for my proximity to mine.

Now it was my turn to envy her — tho' I could have explained that however dull and frequent were the pangs of loneliness, they were occasionally counterpointed by rare, piercing and exhilarating moments of freedom. If either of my lads had known my plans, they would have tried to stop me. They would not have allowed me this pilgrimage. I would have been reminded by Sophia that the children needed shoes, or that Henry's long-suffering mare Paihereni needed feed through the winter. I would have had word that, in his capacity as Judge of the Native Land Court, Henry required trousers rather better than the ragged ones he'd worn as Native Interpreter and Aboriginal Protector. Or Elisha's wife would complain of yet another hole in their Wellington roof, of a light-fingered maid or sudden inflation in the price of wheat or potatoes — and what profligate, uncaring grandmother would take her hotel bill and train fare from the family purse?

Bee, when we came upon him at a lathe in what would one day be the chapel vestry, was hard at work turning an upright for the altar rail. Thick spectacles bent to the mandrel, he held the emerging barley twist to the blade, carefully and swiftly fluting and shaping. The chapel smelt and sounded of New Zealand — sawdust and sweat and the ringing of hammers — and it brought me up short. It was a joy to see him again so occupied, as I had often seen him since a young man, and I was drawn to stand behind him, my hands upon his shoulders and memories flying through my mind — Bee at a lathe on *Tomatin*, Bee turning chair legs for Mary Ann's chapel, Bee spinning rails for Selwyn's desk for the Bishop's College at Tamaki.

'It is time to go now, Reverend Cotton,' said Sarah very quickly, having never learned that when children or madmen are intent upon a pleasure it is as well to give them warning of some minutes.

Mr Cotton stiffened — and then went on, his foot peddling to power the flywheel, the spindle turning fast enough to blur.

It was my turn to whisper now, *en cachette* in his bristly ear, a conspiratorial plan to fill the afternoon — the hire of pony and barouche to take us into the country for a ride — which so filled him with enthusiasm there was no delay.

And so we took our leave of Sarah, went into the town and paid an idle coachman rather too much for what proved to be a terrifying journey on slushy roads — and more so when Bee persuaded him for a turn at the reins. Amongst it all we reminisced and laughed: did the Bishop still draw his troublesome wife again and again among the chapels and boots and Roman soldiers on his blotting paper? Did he still announce to any listening that he would shortly 'sally forth!'? Did he still whistle tunelessly when he was happy?

'Does he still sit loose as a sack of potatoes in the saddle?' I asked gaily.

'Is he still so light on his feet that he can silently come upon a fellow and fair startle a fart out of him?' asked Bee, delighting in the freedom lunacy will afford.

In the evening we returned to our hotel and supped — rather better than we had the night before — and sang hymns in the parlour with a shiny little man I suspected as a snoozer, tho' why he would thieve from such a poor hotel puzzled me. I had nothing worth stealing and neither did Bee. The thief — if that's what he was — would not let me go once he found I could play the piano, and taught us some new parlour songs that I, at least, had never heard before. On retirement Bee, kissing me fondly between yawns, owned that the day was the most exciting he had had for years.

Now it is late and the lamp flutters black wings on the sagging wallpaper of my room. The fire is low, tho' with real heat in the coals for the parts of me closest. I have procured from the innkeeper a bottle of porter, which bitter, burnt taste is dulled and sweetened with a few drops from a little bottle. Bee's trumpeting snore reaches me now and again through the plaster walls, and from my luggage I have taken my indulgence — a leather-bound book bought new for the purpose, tho' not as splendid as Bee's journals which are prettily tooled and clasped in brass. The paper is thick and white and sweet-smelling.

If I was to tell the story, if I was bothered to get up and search my traps for a pencil, since I have no ink, I would begin with Taurarua in the 'forties. I would set the scene of the Native Hospital and how we lived there together in the house Judge Martin had brought out from England as timber and joinery.

It was a simple structure of eight small rooms with a passage running along on the seaward side. Before our arrival he had selected land a mile and a half from Auckland in a placid crook of the harbour known as Taurarua and later called Judge's Bay. The disaffected of that rough town called it Iniquity Bay, since the Chief Justice occupied the proud swell of the hill protected from the worst of the westerly winds, and Attorney General Swainson the commanding wooded point on the other side of a small ravine. Their holdings were resented by many, Europeans and Maoris alike — and on my frequent trips to town I heard rumblings on the subject. At first I tried to defend their position — tho' in the end proved not so loyal a servant. Mary Ann seemed unaffected by the controversy, altho' she knew of it; even after the gift of pony and trap from her husband, she kept mostly to the house and immediate surrounds.

It is part of life in New Zealand to feel justly at home — of good use and well regarded — and wrongly in residence all at the same time; on so many levels it makes the head and heart ache. Europeans — they call us Pakeha, or Tauiwi, which means stranger — must not allow the dichotomy to overwhelm them. Otherwise . . . what? We must all board the ships and sail away to whence we came?

If you were to stand at our front door — and I am thinking now of you, Kitty, the only one of my likely readers not to have seen it for themselves, tho' Ish's memory must be hazy now — the ground would fall away from your feet in a steep wooded slope. There is a path leading down through the trees to the beach, where stands our hospital — tho' its little raupō roof, only just visible, would not have held your attention. Far greater a pull would be exerted by the Waitemata, a lively band of ocean that lies between the bay and the sleeping island volcano called by the Maori people Rangitoto. In different moods it is foreboding, a frowning presence over rising seas — or protective, embracing, a forested isle humming with birds and insects. When the wind was in the right direction we could hear the birds at dawn, a denser, more distant chorus than the one that surrounded us. Much of our land was treeless, covered instead by fern and grasses, tho' Mary Ann had directed the planting of many English trees — oaks and elms and poplars. They grew quickly and were admired by all our visitors excepting for the birds, who preferred the native trees that remained in the gullies.

And if, Miss Tripp — would you be so obliging — you look now to the east and see how the shining highway of the gulf leads between the volcano and the land, and how distant islands and bays shape that extremity of our world. Were I a painter I could show you the colours and perspective — tho' even the most skilled were challenged to capture the light. Easier for you to imagine, perhaps, is the spectacle that so often blessed us — fleets of waka, the Maori canoes, laden with visitors, produce and patients, skimming across the waters, red blanket sails hoisted high.

A further few degrees south-east and your eyes rest upon the chapel of St Stephen set on the next hill, a narrow ravine between.

Some distance behind the house for fear of fire stands the kitchen, where I spent much of my time in the preparation of food and Physick for all those who came into my care after Mary Ann. Much has already been made in dreary memoirs of pioneering women in the Americas, who endured hard lives labouring on dirt floors, of their hefting of iron girdles, of the heavy two-handled quaich, the iron pots and kettles held over the fire on their sweys, the barrels of flour and chistles of cheese, the invading vermin, the scorched skirts and blistered hands. In New Zealand it was much the same. For isolation and lack of servants, it was so even for some of the gentry.

The only compliment Sarah Selwyn ever paid me was indirect and shared between our cook and me.

'At Taurarua there is always a sumptuous feast,' she told Mrs FitzRoy, the new Governor's wife. 'Always a pudding and never loathsome pork.'

'I shall look forward to it,' rejoined Mrs FitzRoy, a quiet, sympathetic soul who earned much affection for her one contribution to Auckland life — her insistence on removing the stocks from outside the courthouse.

How pleased I am that Sarah enjoyed it, and Mrs FitzRoy too. Dear Henry suffered so when he saw me running backwards and forwards and waiting on them — he did not consider kitchen duties part of my brief. On ordinary nights, when it was just the Martins, Henry and myself — and very often Mr Swainson — we all dined together, with only Cook and the Irish maid managing. We were a family.

But I do not want to give an account of that work, or less the tedious, endless needlework that often occupied me on my evenings — even tho' one of Mary Ann's first gifts to me was the most marvellous invention: a lacemaker's lamp. It was an object delightful for its simplicity and beauty — a globe to be filled with water and set before a candle. Its dispersed, pearly light saved my sight long past the stage I would otherwise have lost it. I made a gift of it to my favourite grandson before I left New Zealand, since he had asked for it as a curiosity.

The work that sustained me at Taurarua, as much as it sustained others, was the work of the hospital. At first, Mary Ann wanted the patients brought up to a small dispensing room in the house, which made for less effort on her behalf, but for many our patients the extra distance was detrimental: those who barely survived the waka voyage from Waiheke or Orere or further away could not climb the hill. We made first a tent for shelter, then William Jowitt's new pah — which means village, Kitty! — at Huruhi supplied us with rushes and uprights to build a three-roomed hut, each with sleeping places a foot off the ground. These were made merely of heaped-up sand, softened with a mattress of fern and topped with a blanket. There were no doors to stop the wind and rain, tho' we did have a single window with joinery.

In this poor place we tended Maori people who suffered the diseases we had brought them — pox of every description, measles, tubercular sores open to the bone. Tuberculosis had been among them for generations, as ancient to them perhaps as leprosy. Mate pokapoka, hura and tuwhenua — names for the worst diseases, those inflicted by evil spirits and demons. Children, men and women — over the years there were some hundreds who came, even after Governor Grey had a proper hospital built during his second term among us. Our patients preferred still Mary Ann and myself — so much so that when, in the late 'forties, Governor FitzRoy asked my employer, 'Who is this Mata Te Mete the Maoris talk about?' the Judge could answer, 'Oh she is an old hen with two chickens which have been taken from her and for want of something to cherish she has taken to bring up a brood of ducklings.'

I have this word for word many years ago from Ish, who had it in a letter from Hy, who overheard the conversation. Faithful Ish would never have kept such an insight from me. Long and hard have I puzzled over it, not for its meaning — tho' the Judge refers to grown adults as ducklings — but for the man's motivation. By his ridicule, he was jealously guarding his wife's reputation, the good she must do, by definition, at the Native Hospital. He would not have me share in the gratitude.

When men work together in the world — a captain and his first mate, say, or a barrister and his clerk — their roles are clear, and tho' love may grow between them, it is not the same as a working association between women. That is an affair of the heart, and subject to tumult and ecstasies that gentlemen's friendship does not allow. Inherent in the Judge's remark there is also the suggestion that I was somehow indiscriminate with my affections.

Here, on this cool thick paper smooth under my hand, I could set the record straight: Mary Ann could never have done the work without me, and I could not have done my part without Mary Ann. She was moral support and adviser — and, when well enough, also performed some of the lighter duties. When I took in the infant Hikipene to live with us — and also Hikipene's father Mokihi — she represented my suit to her husband, who was eventually won around. It was from the Martins' stores came the blankets and bread for the hospital, generously dispensed. And it was from Mary Ann that the money came to replenish our medicines and mustard plasters — the latter so beloved by our patients that they were given names and passed around from wound to wound on different bodies, until they were blackened and filthy and fell apart.

But, in truth, it was only on rare occasions that Mary Ann left off her sofa habits to be of any assistance. The men and women whose suffering we eased knew well who it was laboured sleepless among them: Mere Potene, our Maori boy Josiah, on occasion the Irish maid, myself — and, more than any of us, Mokihi.

He came to us first as a patient, suffering as so many of his people do from an affliction of the eye — they call it toriwai, which is conjunctivitis. The women suffer from it more than the men, being closer to the cooking fires, but all are subject to it from the custom of burning fires inside their houses, with little egress for the smoke. Mokihi was a giant — six foot six. I know this, because he let me measure him when we were better acquainted. A larger bed was made for him and he could not stand upright for the low roof.

The inflammation was well away, sending livid tendrils of infection into the flesh of his cheek, which was not tattoo'd, tho' might have been if he'd lived in his own place. Mokihi was one of the Natives domiciled on the verdant island of Waiheke, which had been emptied by Chief Hongi Hika's rampage some twenty years before. He gardened there with his wife and children and a remnant of a tribe, but as I learned later it was not his ancestral land. His father was one of the Ngapuhi, a tribe a long way north, and his mother, long dead, a Waikato slave. He seemed bereft of strong tribal affiliations and could have been, so thought Attorney Swainson, a contender for a platoon of Friendlies. More than one visitor from the barracks also extended the invitation. He declined.

Softly spoken, silent in his suffering, Mokihi bore his treatment without a murmur — the bathing and the ointment I rubbed into the afflicted orbs. I had mixed it myself from camphor, mercury, and oil of cloves in an unguent of menthol. It was a prescription of the Colonial Quack, who believed the efficacy of medicines can be gauged from the amount of suffering they induce on their way to effect a cure. Previously he had his patient take snuff to ease the discomfort, believing the seat of the disease to be in the nose. I had no faith in either method.

At any event, when he was better, Mokihi went away again with his companion, a bone-thin recent convert with a withered leg, who had taken the name Nathaneal. They were bound for Tamaki, where Nathaneal was loved for his animated preaching and Mokihi for his singing — but he was back within the month.

How will I tell of my love for Mokihi? Or even of his love for me — he detected early that I was not one of the pallid good widows of judiciary, military or church, nor yet another adventurous lowly blow-in from New South Wales. From the beginning I admired him for his strength and gentleness, which same traits he celebrated in me. We were of a similar age and physical type — I was tall for a woman, and broad-shouldered; he was a giant among men, and the most kind and patient I have ever known.

If I were to tell of my heart's journey through my life, then Mokihi would make the third of the trinity — Horelock, Hogg and Holy Mokihi.

Someone is walking up and down outside my door — I can hear his footfall on the thin hotel carpet. The tread is close and steady . . . there — he is just outside and now stepping away again. Perhaps it is the singing snoozer from our parlour hours come to prowl before he tests the doors. I set the poker to stand within easy reach.

At my back the air seems to have formed a solid wall of ice — all is chilled except for the heat of the fire on my hands and face. The slightest movement seems to set the dank atmosphere moving as if I am underwater. In Torquay, we will most definitely take a better class of hotel. This one has jet beetles — there is the rattle of them in the walls, and even my dim eyes can detect their shiny black backs as they traverse the hearth. One of them dares to assault my little bottle balanced on the arm of my chair — I flick it into the fire where it expands and pops.

It is no good. I must be brave enough to remember him without flinching from it. I did not at the time, not at all. I believed our love was our due. If ever guilt rose in me while we conducted our clandestine affair, I would repel it with these words, 'He is my due and I am his', which I believed in all humility. Now it seems arrogant, as if I visited my sins upon him and his upon me. It rose from a desire to keep our affair at a remove — I was in my early forties, it was a last flaring of a fire that previously had burned me, I could scarcely believe it was happening, it was so very wrong. I knew we'd have our day and it would be a short one. We were lucky beyond measure to have got away with it.

In my years in New Zealand there were plenty of incidences of love between Englishmen and Maori women, marriages blessed and unblessed, as well as scandalous affairs such as those conducted by the missionary Colenso, or the Reverend Spencer at Te Ngae, who was seen with his arm around a Maori girl in the dark, long after the hour for candles. I later delivered a child of his despairing wife while he received counsel from fiddlesome Archdeacon Brown at Tauranga. And what of the Greek Yate, who could not resist the sweetest of his warrior converts! But I never heard tell of love our way around, tho' it must have happened. What a wide and tumultuous gulf one crosses to truly love a man or woman of another race. Mr and Mrs Hogg had achieved it — when she came to the door that afternoon, she had eyes only for my husband, and he seemed, in the instant he first beheld her in her bright silks, to regard her also with the most intense, regretful and determined desire.

Henry, your dear whiskery face breaks in on me now, your kind, worldly-wise eyes retreating with alarm — an abnormal response, contrary to any other startle I've ever observed. Or would you never believe it of me?

All this is quite unnecessary, Mother.

Surely you remember Mokihi? He arrived while you were living with me at Taurarua, just before you left for your first appointment as Extra Interpreter at Maketu, after I had rescued you from the evil that was the Wakefields.

'If I am to stay in this country with any conscience,' you wrote to me, 'it is in a position — in either Government or Church — where I may assist the Maori people to strengthen their cause, rather than to weaken it.'

And so I wrote a letter to release you from the thieves and fraudsters that made the New Zealand Company at Port Nicholson, and you were with me by the time you were twenty.

In those long-ago days, there were still so few of us that the Maoris would adopt us, particularly the menfolk, who could form fiercely loving, intense associations — such as that which evolved between you and William Jowitt. He took you with him on occasion to Waiheke, his pah on the other side of the island from the gardens that Mokihi for a time abandoned. It was with Jowitt that you perfected the language and began your dictionary. It was among his people that you first experienced the most addictive phenomenon of that race — the way the clock behaves in their company.

'It is as if you go into a delicious trance — the hours slip by in joviality and argument, labour and song — there is always something to be going on with and usually conducted in manner most festive. It is impossible for me to tell you what we did each day.'

You were his Pakeha, or one of them, and I was Mokihi's — an idea that delighted him one night when we met as arranged around the rocks, on the next half-circle of sand.

'You are my Pakeha,' he said, holding me tight while he fell apart with infectious laughter, eyes streaming, his face creased. I wrestled him onto his back, giggling like a girl and trying to stuff sand into his mouth, while he did as he always did — pretended I was about to win, but repelling me at the last moment, and then kissing me and hugging me and faddling like a lion.

How wonderful it all was, how marvellous it is still a secret.

Mokihi and I certainly laboured; there was more of it than I had known in all my life. We each seemed to know what the other was thinking — we moved among our patients pre-empting one another. We kept our voices low and our touch gentle — and would touch one another in wordless direction when lifting or tending, or in comfort, or to steel our nerves in the face of agonised distress. He became as irresistible to me as the sailor Horlock had been when I was a girl. I do not mean to compare them, only to say how strong my feeling — tho' I sense even the lowest twopenny upright in her tatty feathers would consider it bad taste. Many men have congress with many women in one lifetime and some compare them thus. I have only had three — and blessed I am that they were of loving dispositions, tho' all of them feckless to varying degrees.

And blessed am I too that I did not bear Mokihi a child, which was not more luck than design but the other way around — the eternal design of my sex, that is. God fashioned women for the Change and I must have been drawing close to it.

If Mokihi came to the house of an evening, dressed in European clothes — a blue smock and neat breeches, such as the Judge insisted on for Maori egress to his hallowed library — I had to be careful never to catch his eye for fear of laughing with him at some pomposity of official or priest, or for sharing a sudden silent flare of anger at some old or new cruelty being visited upon his people. How many nights were there in one close room or the other, library or parlour, where we took pains not to allow our eyes to rest on that other strange, loving face? How many nights when Mokihi hung his head as if in shame, and the conversation grew discomforted and then silent. Better by far were the nights in the parlour when Sarah or myself would sit at the piano, and Mokihi, Josiah and the Irish maid would join us in song — we made a glorious choir, even with Mary Ann's fluting and Sarah's tuneless drone.

Periodically Mokihi would vanish south or inland, and often went for long periods to his family on the Waiheke farm. After one such absence he returned with a tiny girl, so gleaming and small

Mere Potene dubbed her Hikipene, which means Sixpence. Her real name was Roimata, which means tears — and seemed to Mary Ann and I too foreboding. Mary Ann would call her Damaris, after the woman Saint Paul converted at Athens, because of the child's innate gentleness and wisdom, which she had from her father.

When we first met her, the child was learning to totter — late for a Native who, being unencumbered with skirts, will learn to walk well before our kind. She was almost two years old, and her ready smile and loving eyes stole all our hearts, especially mine.

It is universally agreed that to fall in love over a child is a most piercing attachment. The same enthrallment had also captured Mr Hogg, who came so to love Horlock's daughter — the first Katherine — as his own that, on his return to India with the real Mrs Hogg, he named a child of that union after her. There is a pattern that repeats itself — even a life of relative freedom, such as I have enjoyed, can be walled in by odd, discomforting symmetries.

Even now I am not sure how much the Bishop saw in the ruined chapel on the hill above the bay — and it is that story I must set down, since it has been drawn forward twice in one morning, even if I am to ball it up and toss it into the fire. Or not write it at all but remember it as if I were telling it to an avid listener, such as Miss Tripp, who could not in any conscience judge me for it.

One night in November 1846, I retired as always to my room, which lay at the back of the house between the Judge's library and the dining room, a few steps away from Mary Ann's so that I could tend the high feather bed if she called for me in the night. Cramped tho' my apartment was, I had among my sticks of furniture a truckle bed for myself and a narrow divan to accommodate either of my sons — I was never so blessed as to have them there together. There was one small window that gave out over ferny dale and scrub forest, an inland view to the volcano Maungawhau, the same as the Judge had from his library, the largest room of the house. I could not see the hospital from my room, which lay the other way but very often if the wind was right I could hear the moaning of the afflicted and the voices of the people camped for the night on the beach. Mokihi had for his own use a whare in the ravine between the house and chapel. It was often his booming laughter I heard above the others from around the visitors' fires.

It was only a few hours' sleep I allowed myself, being consumed with anxiety for Hikipene who was feverish, her wasting disease well advanced and brooking her no resistance to this fresh miasma. In keeping with the understanding of the time — Miss Nightingale would agree we know it now to be dangerous nonsense — we limited her water and her sleep. How barbaric it seems now, but we did it with the best of intentions. Water because we believed too much weakened the system, and sleep because death most often came to children in repose.

At eleven o'clock I heard our voluble neighbour the lawyer Swainson, famous for overstaying his welcome, finally make his departure. The wind had risen — I could hear the loose shutter at the front of the house clipping the frame; the ancient pohutukawa tree that stood between the house and kitchen creaked and groaned. Swainson's farewells were loud and loquacious, his hosts' faint and sleepy. I could hear Sarah's voice the clearest of the three — her odd, throaty giggle which was the strangled expression of her small portion of good humour. We had not seen much of that on this visit — she and the child were staying with us while her husband made another of his punishing journeys and she allowed herself every anxiety.

When I was sure Swainson was gone, I rose from my bed and took up a wrap. The Bishop was expected that very night — the lamp was left burning and the door wide open for his return. Out I crept barefoot down the hill towards the hospital on the beach. It was spring, tho' still cold. Only a few days earlier when Cook and I had crunched through frosted fern on our way to the icy kitchen in the early morning hours before the sun rose high enough over the cottage roof to melt it. Since then there had been a deluge and howling gales — a hurricane. Roofs were lifted from the barracks in town, major repairs were occasioned to the hospital whare, and the first St Stephen's ruined. It was the little chapel built for Mary Ann — who was inconsolable and had taken to her bed.

Once or twice I lost my balance and slid on the blades of my feet — I was glad I had left my boots off, for I would have fallen properly in them. I had not donned trousers since the night of the Cup of Grace, tho' I longed to and would again. At summertime, Mary Ann and the Judge tolerated my bare feet, seeing me rushed off them and knowing good boots were hard to come by. We all of us preserved them. And besides, there were more hours of work in me without their pinch and twist.

Slipping and sliding, I only once lifted my eyes all the way down the hill to feel the growing nor-easter on my face — a cloudy, high sky with the occasional star — and all the way through the trees my heart filled with longing to turn my steps towards the ravine as I had on other nights. How the promise of him could lure me on.

The first night I had battled first my conscience and then my fear — how sure could I be that he would want me? There were plenty of women to choose from, prettier and younger and of his own kind. It was not beyond the realms of possibility that a little miss from any level of Auckland society would throw herself at him from behind a hedge. Everybody loved him. There was a coterie who came to play croquet on the beach and always insisted on Mokihi joining in — he would leave whatever task at hand to oblige them. Had I misread him, I worried, for Mokihi was warm and affectionate with everybody? And I confess I knew also of his marriage, the termagant wife who remained on Waiheke, who had not accompanied such a very young, ill child to Taurarua — I hoped only that their marriage was not a Christian one. In the Maori world a man may blamelessly have more than one wife — it is a shame for Mr Hogg that he was not born among them — and I was never to know how many other women counted themselves as Mokihi's, or where.

That night I was shyly welcomed . . . and then not so shyly. The memory of him jars my heart worse than the termination of my waking dreams.

Let him kiss me with the kisses of his mouth: for thy love is better than wine, sings Solomon.

On this night, the night in question that I must keep returning to, I kept to my dutiful way and was rewarded by a lamp flickering in the hospital window. It was not the Irish maid, not Mere Potene or Josiah or any of the others, but Mokihi, his shape bent over his daughter's bed and his face wet with tears.

A kind of terror greeted me at the sight of his grief, the heart-rending, raw expression of it, utterly alien despite our mutual regard. Shrinking away from him — tho' I cursed myself — what was I thinking? — I hurried behind him to check on the only two other patients. In the far room the men slept undisturbed in the quiet dark. There was a smell of liniment and infection from the fading elderly patient, and of damp vegetation, tho' we had all worked like navvies to replace some of the thatch after the hurricane. I dallied over the young man in the other sleeping place, who had thrown clear his only blanket, and tried to find the strength to go to my loved one, to comfort him, but I felt paralysed by his feeling.

'Ka hemo ia,' came Mokihi's voice from the next room, surprisingly steady, taking hold of me, drawing me in — so I flew to him, put my arms around him, Mokihi bending again to hold the candle close so that I could see her, so close I worried the wax would drip on her narrow starveling face.

The child was indeed dying, her breathing coming quick and shallow, the flesh receded so that her huge eyes, opening now and again to take us in, were emphatic in expression. There was trust, serenity — the worst of the struggle was past now, until the very end.

Suddenly Mokihi lifted her and carried her out, bending for the low door and striding away into the buffeting wind. He did it so swiftly and effortlessly that I was for a moment again struck dumb and motionless before I could follow him.

The bad weather had driven away our recent visitors — they had either decamped to the Maori hostel further around the harbour at Official Bay or returned to their own places. On the point behind us glowed a single lamp in Swainson's house and I prayed his prying nose fully inserted under his blankets so as not to observe me hurrying after Mokihi, who walked intently, his footsteps forming and filling at the edge of the high tide.

I had thought perhaps he was taking the child to his whare, but at the foot of the track up into the ravine he went straight on. Above us, on the crest of the hill, the shattered chapel gleamed for a moment before the clouds gathered again. Mokihi cradled his daughter close to his chest, opened his shirt around her and turned her little face into the crook of his neck. In the dark our ascent was slow and stumbling.

How different this was to the progression we had made up the hill two years before with Mary Ann carried triumphant on a litter, the Judge and Bishop walking behind, Sarah and her child, Josiah, Cook and the Irish maid, William Jowitt, Bee Cotton, Henry, Mokihi and me and a host of singing angels going to give praise and thanks. Mary Ann could now be brought to worship, no matter how indisposed. It was she who I had thought to lose next, but back then I had not yet come to love Hikipene or Hikipene's father.

Braced against the nor-easterly which blew strong at our side, we progressed in fits and starts up the steep slope, with me going ahead now and again since his sight was weakened by the infection. In passing I would lay my hand on Hikipene's back to gauge her breath, and once I brushed my lips against his cheek and tasted his tears — my darling, my poor love, I thought but did not say, my eyes dry, because this is the English way of offering comfort to the grieving, a stalwart restraint that bruises Maori hearts.

The hill that night seemed to go on for ever, until we grew close enough to the chapel to hear wood knocking on stone, an irregular banging in the gusts. It was the door, hanging broken from its already rusted hafts and beating against the toppling belfry — a relic in a new country, where relics are rare. We passed behind it, stepping carefully through fallen tiles of sharp-edged slate to the chancel, which retained a portion of its roof and the eastern wall. The triple arch of stained-glass windows was eerily intact, as if God's wrathful hand had snatched away the rest in one angry swoop. Sturdy and bare, the wooden altar table stood still in its place — the Judge himself had battled through the stormy aftermath to rescue the gold, such as it was: a simple cross, a pewter chalice and plate. There had been some dozen chairs set in rows, one especially for Mary Ann that Bee had made, others given by friends, or bought at the stores — none remained, save two broken ones. That very morning Mary Ann had seen from her bedroom window a number of up-turned chair legs bristling on a departing waka.

Pausing there, Mokihi gazed up at the windows glittering in the moonlight. A scud of wind blew his collar aside to reveal the child's thin face turning towards me, pellucid, all colour drained from it. It was then I took the child from his arms and laid her, without thinking, on the altar table, it being the only place she could lie flat and rest. Mokihi gave out the most anguished cry and lifted her again, staring at me with horror.

'I'm sorry, I'm sorry Mokihi—'

But he was hurrying away, hunched over the child, to the shadows of the sheltering wall, where he sat turned away from me. An interminable moment passed while I burned with my transgression. I had laid the child on a table — not an ordinary one, which would have been for Mokihi offensive enough, but one that had sanctified the Host. I did not know if I had offended more the Christian in him, or the heathen. Whichever it was, it did not matter — I was coarse, heartless, foolish, cruel. I wished the ground would open and swallow me up.

Above the whistle and rattle of the thickening rain, I could hear him breathing steadily, evenly, as if he would soothe the child with the rhythm of it, and I listened too, allowing it to steady me, a stowaway on the ship of his comfort. The child was quiet, she was held, she was warmly wrapped — I longed to go to her, but couldn't. He would never forgive me. I knelt where I stood, and an hour passed; it grew very dark, the moon lost behind black clouds.

'Mō taku hē. Please forgive me,' I begged. 'Mokihi?'

There was a long silence before he answered, 'E noho ki raro,' and I did what he said, coming to him on hands and knees, and sitting down on the floor beside him.

It was too dark to see Hikipene's face, tho' I was sure the child's eyes were open to this strange new world. Mokihi had brought her up here for worship often enough but now it bore no resemblance, except for the stained windows — the shepherd with his flock, the shriven saint, the Three Wise Men. Perhaps she could see their dim, flinty lights from our sheltered place.

Her father began to pray, at first loudly enough for me to hear, beseeching entreaties for his daughter's life, then dropping away to scarcely a whisper, Maori and English words intertwined, on and on, with his head bowed. I felt again that strange paralysis, and could only hold his hand, now and again adjusting Hikipene's wrappings, and worry that she was too hot, or too cold, and lean my head against his shoulder.

We slept and woke, gathered her close, rearranged her fragile limbs, kissed her, murmured and sang to her and to one another, slept again like the dead while the storm blew itself out, and woke at sunrise to find her gone.

I have known fathers to rage at the death of a child, to blame God, to lose their faith in the face of the infant's cruel suffering. Mokihi did not cry out or weep. He was mute, still, as desolate as I have seen any man. He laid her to one side and stood, taking me by the hand and leading me to the naked altar, where we knelt. I knew no other way to comfort him but to hold him close there, to kiss him and whisper endearments, scraps of prayers and psalms, but the praise was bitter on my lips, and Mokihi knew it.

If anyone would ask me the dimensions of my faith, I would say the truest aspect of God is that He shares His gender with the inhabitants of the open world, and so His affections run hot and cold. Sometimes He is with me, more often not, and there is little recourse but to love Him at either distance. That morning He may as well have been on the moon or in the deepest reaches of the sea but still we knelt, side by side and our arms at the other's waist, as the sun rose and the wind dropped and the world beyond grew animate. A chink in the stone hummed a wavering tone; a dawn chorus rose from the ravine; waves broke more gently on the beach below.

There was a sudden shifting in the light, subtle in the early dawn. A faint shadow fell over us, enough to have us turn and break apart to see the Bishop, in the garb he wore for voyaging — an open-necked shirt that allowed rigorous activity, an old pair of woollen trousers, his battered shovel hat and sturdy boots. He was unshaven and sunburnt, and his eyes stood out of his head like organ stops. From behind him came a stumbling through the slate tiles and a hissed blasphemy: 'God be damned!'

Augustus gave no sign of hearing it, his quick vision taking in the small wrapped body, Mokihi's tear-stained, swollen face, my dishevelment and my bare soles protruding from my nightgown. I would have risen to my feet, but Mokihi held me in place beside him. Bee Cotton appeared at Selwyn's shoulder — they must have anchored in the night and now, at first light, come up to see the damaged chapel, it being too early to rouse the sleepers at Taurarua. The storm must have tried them sorely. Bee smelt of salt, damp and vomit, and once again had lost his preservers.

'Is that you, Mrs Smith?' He peered at me myopically. 'Are you all right? What are—'

The Bishop made an exasperated chopping motion with one hand and Bee, blushing, fell silent, tho' he offered me his hand. Mokihi let me go and I stood with the two men above my poor love. In his grief and exhaustion, he seemed not to know where to put himself, but remained kneeling, turning his face away from us.

'His child has died,' I said. 'We brought her up here last night.'

'Alive or dead? With Mrs Martin's blessing?'

I hung my head — and saw to my horror that Mokihi had too, a ruby light from the shepherd's robe playing in his sleek hair. Prayer or contrition? Still I allowed my constraints. I could not touch him; my hands were frozen together, clasped behind my back. What had the Bishop seen? Would he blame me for the child's death?

'I see she did not.'

He rocked back a little on his heels, and looked up into the roof as he did so often when he was preaching that some of his Maori congregations joked they should roost up there to effect direct address. The corner of his mouth worked, the muscle in his cheek stiffened.

'E tū, e hoa,' said Bee gently, and Mokihi rose to his full height at last. Steadily, he met Selwyn's eye.

'So . . . you will bring the child down to the house to be made ready. I am sorry for you, Mokihi.'

At this first sign of sympathy, my lover and I relaxed a little — the Bishop was not so prescient; we were safe in our grief without the other exposure. He came to stand between us, taking one of our hands firmly in each of his.

'Let us pray.'

He did not bow his head until we had bowed our own. Mokihi's eyes brimmed with tears.

'Father receive this child into Your loving care. Give comfort and solace to her father, Mokihi, who loved her greatly. Regard Thee Thy servant Elizabeth who works hard in Thy service. Give her the blessing of propriety and the wisdom to know her place. Amen.'

I wept quietly with grief and shame. Mokihi's face streaked with tears and his shoulders heaved. Bee said quietly, the best solution he knew, 'Let us go down to Mary Ann.'

We returned all together down the hill, Mokihi carrying Hikipene and taking his leave of us the moment we reached the beach. Striding on ahead of us with Mr Cotton, the Bishop did not appear to notice he had slipped away and I certainly did not want to alert him to it. I returned to the house, keeping a distance behind them, and went straight to my room where I hauled on an old gown for the day's work.

At Taurarua we ate at one, so my first hours were with Cook. I felt leaden and clumsy, twice burning my hand and weeping for it, tho' my tears were not for myself but for Hikipene. If Cook noticed I was out of sorts she said nothing, being hot and exhausted herself after the late night waiting on Swainson and his reluctant hosts, and waking early for the ship. Only once the party was at table — and it was a large group, not only the Martins and the Selwyns, but also Mr Swainson, Mr Cotton, Mr Fisher and the students who had accompanied the Bishop to Tauranga — was I able to go down to the hospital.

Mokihi had vanished. Josiah would not be drawn on where, and neither would Mere Potene. I heard later that he had made his way back to Waiheke, where they had buried the infant. By the time he returned to Auckland I was long gone, dividing my time for some months between Henry at Maketu and the Chapmans' mission at Rotorua.

When we were next together, almost a year later, our old intimacy was changed. He was not unkind to me, nor was I to him. We resumed our old complicit understanding in the hospital, feeding and tending our patients together, but that was all. He rarely came up to the house and I did not visit him unbidden. I think his wife had resumed her hold over him — and I had disappointed him. We were for ever at a remove.

What a blessing is this fire and warming drop, for I am chilled to the bone. The footsteps are sounding in the corridor again, clear and steady as a pulse, to my door and away again.

NINE

To Buxton

1866

'I AM LOOKING FOR MY MOTHER, Mrs Smith,' Kitty told the innkeeper, 'who is here with Reverend Cotton.'

The white lie was for emphasis and the addendum unnecessary, for the grubby creature was pointing at the ceiling.

'Third on the right,' he said.

There did not seem to be a maid to send, or at least there was no offer of one, so she was compelled to take the stairs herself.

Even though Mrs Smith seemed to be where Mr Griggs had said she would be, he could still have got it all wrong and sent her off on a wild goose chase. The old schoolmaster wanted her to incept the adventure at Lichfield, rather than attempt to dissuade the travellers later, by which time it might be impossible to effect a positive outcome — so here she was, weary and travel-worn, taking the dark steps with a greasy lantern proffered by the keeper when she passed behind the bar. Gathered in the gloom was a group of men, five or six of them — railway gangers, perhaps, or travelling merchants of the lowest class. They seemed strangers to each other, quiet and hard-faced, watching her disappear into the gloom. She was glad none came to help her with her overstuffed carpet bag, which had narrow straps that cut into her palm and hauled her already slanting shoulder lower still, though allowed her also to gather up a handful of her yellow hem and hold it above her tentative feet while yet holding the sputtering lantern far enough away that it did not smut or burn. It was all such unnecessary effort — had Mrs Smith told her of her plans, then she could have curtailed them. Or tried to.

It was so very cold in her thin coat. She could not go downstairs again with those men there; she would have to beard the lioness in her den, which prospect was alarming. All through the long journey from London, from one icy platform to another, she had fretted and worried over her entrance — it all depended on that. Play it as a lark. You've come into some money. You thought you'd come along.

If Mrs Smith believed that, then it was proof that she really had forgotten what it was like to be young and unfettered — but then perhaps she had never been as independent as she would pretend.

A tilting landing, a shorter, more perpendicular flight of steps and she arrived at the mouth of a corridor only just wide enough to allow her crinoline. It led away into the darkness, a greater traverse of floor than the room below — the inn was larger than it had appeared, its upper storey spreading above the shops on the street.

Here it was, third door on the right, but something compelled her to walk on. If she was clever, there might be an empty room further down that she could occupy free of charge, provided she was up and out of it before dawn — which was only a few hours away now. Then she could approach Mrs Smith calmly in the morning.

Five doors, six doors and all of them locked. The corridor terminated at a stone wall, more ancient and crumbling than the inn itself — remnants of the building that had stood here even before this one, or even part of the old city wall, perhaps — and there she sat on her bag, just long enough to take off her bonnet before she stood again, going quietly with the lantern and pausing outside Mrs Smith's door. A whistling snore emanated from the room immediately opposite which may or may not have issued from Mr Cotton. She pressed a gentle ear against the dusty panel. After a few moments there was the scrape of dull metal and a clatter from within, as though one of the fire irons had been shifted, then a quiet groan and heavy sigh. Elizabeth was awake then, and sitting by the fire.

Back went Kitty to her perch, only to rise again and return two or three times, on each occasion growing a little closer to firming her resolve to knock. If she didn't rally herself, the old woman would go to bed and she would be compelled to wait in the dank passage all night.

On her last attempt she gathered up bag and bonnet, which necessitated two journeys with the lantern, and knocked sharply before she could change her mind. Several minutes passed without result, but at last came the shuffle and prod of Mrs Smith's progress, slow and stiff from the cold and what had doubtless been a protracted huddle for warmth.

'Good heavens!'

Kitty held the lantern higher so that each could gaze on the other's face. Funny old dear! There she was grinning widely with genuine pleasure, showing all her gappy teeth. She wore a greying nightgown and over it a heavy outdoor coat, and carried the poker.

'Kitty Tripp!' She kissed her on the cheek. 'What a splendid surprise!'

No need for a grand entrance then. Kitty gathered up her traps and came inside, where Mrs Smith immediately requested a chair pulled up to the fire and a tin cup fetched from the box and filled with porter.

'Mr Griggs told me you were going to Buxton, so I thought I would join you.'

Mrs Smith looked bewildered.

'Buxton? No, no. Mr Cotton and I are going to Torquay, to visit the Martins.'

'Torquay?' Kitty's heart sank — the tedious train, the cold, the expense, this stinking room, all for nothing. She could have let the expedition go on as planned.

'You look struck all up in a heap, dear Kitty!' The little bottle was uncorked and generously upended.

Kitty took the poker and prodded the peevish lump to a glow. There was no sense in removing her coat — how icy this room was — though she longed to take off her corset, which rubbed on her lower rib enough to cause discomfort so burning that she could see why some ladies elected to have the bone removed, a bone that was in any case extraneous and missing in men.

'Why ever did you think we were going to Buxton?'

Kitty drained her cup and took a careful breath. The situation could still be saved.

'Poor Mr Griggs is so burdened with the worries of his school and the poor invalid Miss Jennings that he must have told me wrong.'

'Oh,' said her companion, 'that is most unlike him. I gave him my addresses.'

'A simple confusion. He must have thought you were visiting Buxton, given the season. Torquay is not so pleasant in the winter.'

'We are going to visit old friends, not to promenade on the pier. What brings you to Lichfield?'

'I thought I would stop a night to call on you — since we have been strangers for — what is it? — oh dear, it is months . . . I'm so sorry, Mrs Smith, I heard you were ill but I have been . . . Yes, I thought I would call on you, see the Cathedral in the morning and then go on to Buxton.'

'I would never have imagined that you have a curiosity for cathedrals, Miss Tripp.'

Kitty emitted a high-pitched giggle, almost a squeal, and Elizabeth saw, for the first time, the mother in the daughter. Not the laugh, for the genuine Mrs Hogg had no cause to laugh that long-ago day in Bristol — it was Elizabeth who had done the laughing — but in the trembling inclination of the vertical shift of her head and a scheming set to her mouth. She was duplicitous. The genuine Mrs Hogg had run away from Bombay under cover of night without the knowledge or blessing of father or brother, but with money for the voyage in her pocket, provided by an English father-in-law whom neither wife ever met but who had more of a backbone than his son. As soon as Elizabeth saw her, she knew she had lost everything.

Miss Tripp stretched her toes to the fire and took a sip of porter, smacking her pretty lips. There are some, thought Elizabeth, who hold half-castes an abomination, and perhaps it is true of some of the races Englishmen bed around the globe — who knows, there are countless, unseen — but the first Mrs Hogg was exquisite, a tiny alluring bird in European dress and fashionable Indian shawl that any English woman would have coveted. How genuine her distress, how palpable her great love for him after an absence of two years. How confident she was in victory, for no other reason than that the second Mrs Hogg was only a raw-boned peasant, while she was quality.

Tom Hogg had put Elizabeth and her sons out on the street that afternoon.

'How many brothers and sisters do you have?' she asked now, the closest she had come to openly enquiring after the girl's family.

'Six,' replied Kitty, blushing, 'though only four living. Three older and one younger.'

As well you might blush, thought Elizabeth. It is high time you were honest with me.

'And all of us girls.'

No more sons then. Elizabeth allowed the intelligence to warm her heart. She had borne his only son.

'What are their names?'

'There are Lily and Emily who are married and living in Calcutta, and Jane who is not and stays at home with Papa.'

. . . who stays at home with *Papa* . . . He is still alive then. How easily and lovingly the word slipped from her lips, this lucky girl who had had her father's love and protection. He had not abandoned her, even for the grave, while poor Henry and Ish made their own way in the world. Perhaps they are the better for it.

Kitty was watching her closely. She would not let her see her consternation. *He is still alive.*

Elizabeth roused herself. 'That is only four sisters.'

'Oh — I missed Pamela. She is only thirteen and has the gift.'

'The gift?'

'She can bring messages from the other side.'

'Can she, indeed?' Elizabeth would not draw her on the subject. Besides, messages were not enough when one yearned for the manifestation of the departed, for their physical presence.

Poreirewa. The word came to her again, as clearly as if it had been whispered in her ear.

Kitty was looking at her curiously. Elizabeth gathered her thoughts and returned to the more immediate subject.

'Did Mr Griggs assist you with funds for your tour?'

'I have my own money, Mrs Smith.' Miss Tripp played virtue

offended. 'You should see how the crowds call for Kitty Tripp at the Pavilion.'

'I will come one night to hear you.'

The girl liked that prospect — a little smile, the lifting of her shapely eyebrows.

'Your father had a beautiful voice,' Elizabeth said. 'It was how I fell.'

Miss Tripp's face clouded again and she would not meet her eye. Elizabeth found she was running on. She was telling her the story. She was telling her too much.

'I was governess to a family in Plymouth, a position I was lucky to get and only because they knew nothing of my past. Mr Hogg was visiting from India with their son, who was in the same regiment. My mistress brought me into the parlour to play for them, since their own daughters were tone deaf. We sang so sweetly together — everyone said we should go on the stage.' That's enough now, thought Elizabeth. It was Henry and Ish who were curious — and now Kitty knew more than they did.

There was a flash of blue at the corner of her eye — Hikipene. She was perched on the coal-box with her toes hooked over the blackened fender, smiling at her. The ghost seemed older than the child had been at her passing, but wore still the faded smock of the day they first met, clumsily embroidered with bright trees and birds. Blue sleeve eclipsing a fraying wing, she pulled from a pocket a stick of peppermint rock and sucked on it, smiling around the sweet so that a sticky stream ran from her mouth and glossed her small brown hand. The other child, her own, stood dreaming against the other greasy chair in a partial embrace of Miss Tripp, her pale cheek resting on Kitty's shoulder.

It was the chloroform: she had too much of that and not enough sleep. It was the cold, and the shock of having Kitty arrive so late at night.

Hikipene got up and came to stare into the depths of her cup. Do the dead experience thirst? She would leave some porter for them overnight and see if they drank it. She would not confide in Miss Tripp, despite her having a sensitive for a sister. The way women made it part of their contest and congress, the spiritualists and so on, took away the truth of it. Fetches were as private as dreams.

'How did Mr Griggs find you?'

'It wasn't difficult,' said Kitty. 'He wrote to an old acquaintance from his regiment who is now an Active Officer — he undertakes such investigations. A distant correspondence had given Mr Griggs the details of my father's regiment and also the sketchiest details of my mother. It was not that difficult — Mr Griggs's acquaintance knew of my real name, under which I began my theatrical career. You would have to be a ninny to believe "Hogg" a name for success.'

'And who was the initiator of the correspondence?'

'I have no idea.' Kitty lifted one finger to the corner of her mouth in the manner she had to prettily express bewilderment. 'One of my most popular acts, Mrs Smith, is my song and veil dance, "The Hindoo Goddess"' — she sang a high wavering tune, a run of close, wordless notes — 'written for me by a gentleman friend with whom I have only recently parted company. It was he the jack first approached. My friend thought there could be money in it, for haven't people returned from Australia, pockets laden with new-found wealth?'

Elizabeth took a deep sip of her porter, thoughtful. 'So why have you befriended me? For money?'

'No — oh no, dear Mrs Smith. Not I. My gentleman friend, from whom I have now parted, thought also that there might be some money, but I . . . no, dear. How little you must think of me.'

'Why then?'

'Curiosity, of course. I was very curious.'

'Curiosity will kill the cat.'

'Not this cat,' said Kitty.

They were silent for a while, the fire flickering. Mrs Smith, who had been gazing contemplatively at Kitty, gave a little startle, and Kitty could have sworn that her focus shifted to watch a figure pass between them and come to settle against her, a small shade that leaned into the old lady's skirts. There was a minute adjustment of her knees, a close, tender glance that met nothing but chill air.

Poor old thing — Kitty saw clearly into her friend's heart, saw the yearning for a child. Was it a particular child she mourned, a child long dead, or a child grown to be an adult who lived but vanished just as surely? For the first time Kitty wondered if Elizabeth had longed for her father as keenly, if she had truly loved him. At first, she had not wanted to meet the woman who had stolen him away from her mother and returned him burdened and guilt-ridden, only to be dismissed from his regiment and find India closed against him — and what hard times they had endured in England. No doubt Mrs Smith had suffered for her association, but she had also been elevated. Look how her sons had prospered in the Colonies — a lawyer and a Judge! The true Mrs Hogg and her daughters had been disgraced.

'I make no secret in London of my heritage,' Kitty announced, lifting her chin. 'My origins are rather higher than yours. My grandmother was Brahmin from Kashmir and my grandfather English gentry — it was poor Papa's adventures that dragged us down.'

'Ah, but do you not have his sense of adventure yourself? Are you married, Miss Tripp?'

'Never. I am certainly in love with an excellent fellow, handsome and enterprising, much an improvement on his predecessor.'

'Love!' Mrs Smith snorted, but Kitty knew it for jealousy.

'Men and women are blessed for what can pass between us, as you well know, Mrs Smith.'

But Mrs Smith scarcely batted an eyelid, indeed gave no sign of having heard her, being at that moment engaged in flicking a black beetle off her little bottle, which was in sore need of replenishing.

'Shall we mix some drop? You can teach me how to do it.' Kitty was on her way to fetch the medicine chest, which sat at the foot of the bedstead.

'There is already a bottle made — next to the camphor. I make it up in batches of three. It does not seem to lose its efficacy provided it is used within five days.'

Kitty would have remarked that three bottles in five days was rather a heavy dose, and so demonstrated some concern for her friend's wellbeing — but the sudden, piercing, selfish longing for tipple blew tender care from her head and had her hurry to unhook the polished drawbridge lid. There was the corked camphor bottle; there was the row of others, smaller and sealed with wax, all neatly labelled 'Chlorodyne' in Elizabeth's scrawling hand. Kitty returned to her chair to dose her last mouthful of bitter beer.

'You have chosen the one I mixed to hasten sleep, with more of the narcotic than the other,' said Mrs Smith — who was beginning to doze and so warned her too late. One rheumy eye opened and regarded Kitty intently.

It was suddenly of the greatest imperative to be unlaced. The drug could come on too quickly, and make her breathless.

'I will sleep here. You are welcome to the bed.' Mrs Smith had seen her anxiety and would mother her. 'Would you like me to help you unfasten?'

How delicious was the melting in her belly in anticipation, that empty belly that had taken the draft swift and strong, which made her stumble a little as she turned to kneel on the footstool before the chair. The slow tugging at her back, the loosening and softening, the quiet observation from Mrs Smith that she had not herself worn a corset for many years sweetened the icy air around them. How would it have been to have been born as this lady's daughter, rather than to the real Mrs Hogg? If her mother had not been so determined to win back her heart's love, then she might have been born to Elizabeth. She would have grown up in England with two brothers to love and protect her from men with an appetite for a willing, blithe spirit. She would have had a pearly complexion as fragile and blooming as that which showed still in the unlined regions of Mrs Smith's face.

As soon as her gown was undone, Kitty went blindly to the foul kife against the far wall and slept like the dead on the teetering, moist pile that doubtless had not been turned or aired for years.

In her chair by the fire, with Katie and Hikipene cuddled close, Elizabeth let her head fall and the Chlorodyne sweep in to swallow her dreamless.

Kitty woke at seven, with a rash brewing in the crooks of her knees, the small of her back and under her breasts, and asked herself what else she could have expected in such a pothouse.

Bliss it was to splash her face with the cold grey water from the ewer, to replace her dress and shoes, and go out of that mean room. She had not passed so cold and uncomfortable a night since the worst of her father's reversals. No wonder the old mare had elected to sleep sitting up, a full cup of porter on the hearth.

'In Torquay we will take a better class of hotel,' said Mrs Smith as they came down the stairs. 'I had hoped we would sleep our second night at the palace — but the Bishop and Sarah are taking a tour.'

In the dining room, Mr Cotton did not seem at all surprised to see her arrive arm in arm with Mrs Smith. The instant he beheld them he began an account of a dream he'd had, a nightmare about a fervent itch and fruitless search for a lost flesh-brush. He waved his hands about and talked at the top of his voice, which garnered the attention of their fellow diners, a pair of men seated at the end of the refractory table whom Kitty remembered from the night before. They were gangers in railway uniforms with shiny silver buttons.

Mr Cotton's dream of loss was prophetic, if only he knew. As he rattled on, the two eavesdroppers at the table end exchanged a glance that plainly said: See the glock! Clock the halfwit!

'Toorey toorey now, Bee, there's a good lad,' said Mrs Smith, or something like it, which must have been Maori for 'be quiet', for the old man fell silent.

A maid, a pretty chavvy of about twelve years, came through bearing a teapot and plate of muffins. If she could turn the clock back, and this was one of the many lodging houses of her childhood, Kitty would have sought her out for company — the girl had an open, soft face and gentle eyes, which would have been welcome distraction from her mother's despair and father's gloom. At least, now, there was not the worry of all that. For years her father had laboured under the delusion that the funds paid from his father's estate to her mother's temporary usurper and the two sons she had borne him had taken up all his inheritance — but when his father died and the payments were stopped, he discovered he had not at all been left penniless. There was a small bequest, enough to buy a livelihood. At least Pa had the sense to do that, for all his failings.

Mrs Smith poured out and passed her a cup, her hand surprisingly steady given her late night and supped narcotics, though she looked tired, more knocked-up than she had at Kitty's arrival. A guilty vision broke in on her of the old folk trailing rain-slicked Torquay streets with all their plans come to nought.

Mr Cotton took up a muffin, curling it to contain its cargo of melted butter, before announcing with his mouth full, 'Today, Mrs Smith, we will see our dearest Mary Ann! Will I recognise her, do you think?'

'I should say so,' said Mrs Smith, 'Mary Ann is changeless — for the reason that she has looked old since she was young. It is you that has changed, dear. You were the most beguiling little elf.'

The image of fat old Mr Cotton as an elf was distracting, but she had made up her mind and began: 'If I could just — you see, the Martins are not at Torquay. It is true they have taken a house there, which is being made ready for them, but at present they are on holiday.'

'How do you come by this information?'

'Mr Griggs.'

'But Mr Griggs has no connection with the Martins.'

'He had it in a letter from your son,' said Kitty, 'which came by the same ship. Henry had this from Mary Ann, whom he visited a few days before they sailed, and they had made the plan then.'

Mrs Smith looked at her suspiciously.

'Where are they?'

There was the tiniest pause while her old mind clicked over.

'Ah. Of course. Buxton. Your destination.'

'We will go to the station and change your tickets directly.'

How odd it was, thought Kitty, to be experiencing what felt very much like relief. It was as well to be kind. She had that lesson from her father — many of his troubles came from that innate quality which allowed generously for others and less so for himself and his family. There were guests at his hotel, old soldiers mostly, who had come for a cure and stayed for months — even years — and were perishingly slow to pay up.

She would accompany Mrs Smith to Buxton and ensure a positive outcome. That is what Mr Griggs had charged her to do. The journey by rail, being only about forty miles, was not so arduous and would give the old people a few hours to mull over the change in plan. It seemed that her previous anxieties were at once assuaged and intensified — it was a little the same as taking to the stage with an act not fully rehearsed or perfected. Here she was about to step out into the lights, there was to be no going back — she would arrive in the glare and had to make the best of it. All she had to do was prevent Mrs Smith and Mr Cotton from visiting a particular establishment.

⁓

'Are we not going to Torquay?' Mr Cotton had asked plaintively, twice, once on the way to the station and again as he took his seat.

Now he gazed out at passing fields and villages and longed for the anticipated sea. Buxton, as he had discovered from a map carried in Mrs Smith's reticule, was entirely inland. He'd known parishioners and acquaintances to take the waters there, but had never visited himself. The idea would never have occurred to him — he had not taken a spa since his youth in New Zealand, where he had languished in a simmering pond with Mrs Smith and Henry and a number of almost-naked Natives, and found that the experience heated his blood to an alarming degree. Henry was a devil for it — perhaps Mary Ann was now too and that was why the Martins were wintering in Buxton.

Mr Cotton sighed heavily. Reunion would be protracted. First they would have to call on the Martins in their hotel for a maximum of fifteen minutes to arrange to meet again very soon and for longer. He hoped Mrs Smith would heed the protocol and not remove her bonnet and shawl almost on arrival — she may assume such intimacy with Mrs Martin, but he could not, not after so many years of no correspondence. He wanted to make sure there would be leisurely time together; he did not want to ruin the possibility. It was curious how his heart still warmed at the thought of her, as curious as Mrs Smith's remark of how Mary Ann had always looked old. He supposed she had — due less to her colourless, dry complexion and dull hair, though they were aging enough, than to the pale grey eyes flecked with silver. They were most unusual and strangely ancient — warm, unjudging, guileless. In her company you forgot entirely what it was to be lonely, so loved and accepted were you for the little time you were allowed.

Dear Mrs Smith was working her mouth while she gazed out of the window, and tugging at the string of the brown velvet pocket that hung from her waist, removing her little bottle and examining the level before replacing it and looking out the window again. She had carried out that very sequence of actions three times in the last hour.

'A question for you, Mrs Smith. Who is it, do you think, you have loved more than anyone else in your life? Do you think it would be Mary Ann?'

'What a preposterous notion, Bee. You can only ask it because you are not a parent.'

'After them, I should say, after Henry and John — in that order. You were particularly devoted to the oldest, as I recall.'

Only because I had him with me, she wanted to respond, only because Ish was an anxious traveller and the Wellington solicitor Strang worked him like a slave before handing him over to the Colonial Government — which worked him even harder. She would not dignify Bee with a reply.

How prettily frozen were the passing fields and trees, yesterday's early snow not repeated, but all with an icy cast. There were a few blackened leaves still clinging, some chilled beasts standing motionless, not yet taken into the barn. It had never interested her to venture to southern climes in New Zealand to see a 'real winter' — she never went further south than Wellington — and why would you, when a temperate clime was on offer in the north? She had not missed the hard weather at all. Today was pleasant, glittering, better than the day before, with a high, pale blue sky.

'Mary Ann is so very adorable,' Bee ran on. 'I feel sure she ranks third. She certainly retained your affections for longer than any gentleman has.'

'Turituri, Bee. That is quite enough.'

'What I mean to say, Mrs Smith, is that you loved her like a daughter since you had none.'

'Oh, but I did.' Elizabeth removed the little bottle again and unstoppered it. 'You remember, Bee — I told you in Sydney how my first-born died. Katie Horelock, from my first marriage.'

Kitty appeared to be paying close attention now, while Elizabeth gave in to her impulse and took a small spoon from the velvet purse for the dose.

'At the time I met my second husband, the child had been three months in an orphanage — I was widowed and had no choice but to leave her there. He helped me reclaim her, but she died not long after. It has always been easier, Mr Cotton, to avoid any recounting of the tale.'

'Who was Mr Horelock?' asked Kitty, but Elizabeth was taking her sip and pretended not to hear her.

'But yes, dear Bee, I love Mary Ann, of course I do. Very much. You will too, Miss Tripp: it will be educational for you to meet a woman of virtue who retains her spark and zest for life.'

'Does she still?' mused Mr Cotton tenderly, heartfelt.

'At least, when she is well enough,' Elizabeth added, for who knew? They could discover Mary Ann very ill indeed, as ill and as pure as she ever was. Women of weak constitution are less likely to fall prey to temptation than those with strength and vitality — and hadn't she proved that by her own experience? She herself had been stronger and more vital even than Kitty, who most certainly burned too brightly for her own good — so vital that she had wondered if she ought to pray for an illness to amend her passions. Now and again during those first few years with Mary Ann, she'd grown envious of her passivity, the safety of her closed world — or rather the world that could be closed, if she so desired it. Mary Ann could take to her bed, she could call for her Mata in the middle of the night, and Mata would come to bathe her temples with Attar of Roses, to heat water on a spirit lamp to mix with port wine, to tell her tales of the Native Hospital and encourage her to take her pony and trap into town the following day, to rub her feet, to soothe.

If the call came at dawn, then Cook would be roused to help boil water to carry to the house for a bath, which would be set with a brass implement rather smaller than the one the hystericist had used in Sydney. When the call came later, to dry the drowsy limbs, Mary Ann would be languid, the prescription filled — and more full than ever of largesse for the day's stream of visitors. In his bedroom at the front of the house, the Judge would only just be stirring.

How sad it had been sometimes to hold out sleeves and to button, hook-and-eye and lace, and know that Mary Ann's pleasure was so solitary. And how absurd it was, she thought, even to entertain the idea of praying for illness. Lord cure the dropsy, she could pray now, take away my toothache, enliven my limbs, make me young again. Give me a man.

The change of destination was to be welcomed. She would most definitely avail herself of the Buxton Baths — a spa in civilised surrounds with a solid roof, clean towels, tiles and assistants, quite the opposite of the springs at Manupirua, open to the sky and insects and curious observers, but which she had come to enjoy in the company of all manner of people, but never dear Mary Ann, whose little face she would very shortly behold.

The crowds made Bee instantly weary, and he felt sorry for the poor invalids in bathchairs, quite a number, who had to be conveyed by the bathchairmen waiting in cavalry rows outside the station. There were so many of them, they interrupted the passage through a narrow gate and so caused a bottleneck. Once on the street, Miss Tripp took control — Buxton seeming to be a town with which she was familiar — and accompanied them to the Crescent, a vast, curved building a hundred years old, built graciously of pale sandstone. There were two large hotels there, occupying the upper two storeys on either wing of the curve: the Old Hall Hotel and St Anne's.

'Oh but this is far too grand!' Mrs Smith had her hand on the carriage door and would have opened it while they were yet rolling to a stop.

The doors of the hotel were imposing glass and wood, flanked on either side by a row of pretty shops — a draper, a perfumer, a hair and wig dresser, a post office and — thank the Lord — a library. It was so much easier to hold the world at bay if one had a book to hand. Bee patted his coat pocket and would have drawn out a most surprising novel that Mrs Smith had loaned him for the train journey, a tale of bigamy and deception written by a woman. The authoress had him enthralled almost against his will, and he was nearly at the end and would read on — but Miss Tripp was pushing past him to be handed down the step by a footman in hotel livery.

'Come along, Bee.' Mrs Smith required his assistance. 'We are to throw caution to the winds.'

Or, worried Bee, to Mary Ann, who could well persuade the Judge to help with Mrs Smith's bill. Or to his own stipend, which was regularly fattened by an allowance from his father — or so he hoped would continue to be so. He should offer right now to meet his old friend's costs while they waited for their boxes, but Mrs Smith had that beady, interrogative look he knew so well.

'Was there a letter for me from Henry?' she was asking Miss Tripp. 'On the same ship?'

'I don't know. Mr Griggs did not say.'

'But he thought it worth your while to come all the way to Buxton to put us right?'

'He wanted to save you from disappointment.'

Mrs Smith did not look convinced. Kitty was turning away and leading them up the steps, under the archway and across the portico to the hotel vestibule, where the desk clerk made the distracting error that Bee and Mrs Smith were husband and wife. Miss Tripp seemed to find this disproportionately amusing, while Mrs Smith was flustered, her hands waving 'Oh dear no — dearie dearie me no —' and Bee's cheeks burned — at his age!

A porter led them towards their adjacent rooms on the second floor, both of which promised views of the Peaks. Kitty watched them up the stairs. It was not until Mrs Smith had gained the first landing and he had half-ascended the second flight that she called, 'Goodbye, dear friends. I will call tomorrow at ten.'

'No — that won't do! It has only just gone two o'clock.'

Mrs Smith executed a shuffling turn on the thick red Turkey carpet.

'Miss Tripp!'

'Until tomorrow — we will go straight to the Pump Room — *au revoir*!' and out she went into the dull cold light of the afternoon.

Elizabeth watched her leave. A band of pain burned across the small of her back — all this moving about, the joggling of the train, the slow passage of the invalids and the crowds, and now this blessed flight of steps and possibly a long corridor after that. Miss Tripp would never punish her body in this way — put it so in the service of others it wears out. How clever she was not yet to have borne a child. Or perhaps she had — and given it away. It was a common enough remedy — and one she had fortunately never had recourse to, at least not permanently.

Here was dear Bee returning to her, forsaking the progress he had made and giving her his arm, helping her up the stairs, and it wasn't so far at all, or not nearly as far as she'd feared and his own room just down the hall.

'Thank you, dear lad,' she told him, before closing the door.

She would gather herself, then go and find Mary Ann. She really could not rise above the disappointment of not going to find her directly.

There was nothing at all amiss with the room. Indeed, it was the finest she had ever been obliged to call her own. There was a Turkey carpet and high feather bed, which on investigation proved to be properly constructed with straw pallet topped by horsehair mattress and binding blanket, the feathers puffed and shaken, and a wealth of pillows and bolsters. Beside the stead stood a most cleverly appointed commode, quite old, of a pale grey ash and, by the whiff on the updraft as she closed the lid again, not altogether clean. There was an oil painting on the wall, so blackened by age as to be of indistinguishable dark shapes that could have been trees or men. Against one wall stood a chest of drawers with a primping glass, and below the window a lady's desk. A wardrobe boasted enough pegs to hold not only her two other dresses but also her coat and nightgown and petticoats, should she be bothered to ferret them out of her traps — which she could not, not yet.

A maid came to light the fire in the grate, and Elizabeth found herself sitting heavily and struggling to remove her boots. The maid proved kind, and assisted her at the last, bringing her reticule closer to hand and agreeing to have tea and biscuits sent up directly.

There was even a footstool — she stretched her stockinged feet before the fire and wondered how she would ever pay for it all. If by chance Mary Ann was gone, or never come, she'd have her elbows out over a begging letter to Ish or Henry.

TEN

Folly and the Yoke

IN MY FIRESIDE CHAIR I dream of fire on the River Thames, a dream that has haunted me for periods of my adult life. At Taurarua there were months of it while I tended Mary Ann through her first long illnesses. It is broken sleep that brings it on.

'Mata! Mata!' she would call, and I would rouse and go to her, appease her, still half-caught in the dream, feeling still my skirts held away from my frantic feet and hearing the furled masts bursting into flame behind me.

In the dream I run hand in hand with Nick Horelock along the riverside. Thick flakes of flaring canvas break free of the sail; there is a crack and boom as the fire finds the mast. Away along the river we race towards Blackfriars Bridge, where the saltwater meets the fresh water and the seabirds give way to sparrows and pigeons; we fly past warehouses and sailors' penny hangs, poor lodgings and inns until he veers away from me, clear into the middle of the river, where he churns demonically above the putrid chop and I am confined to the bank, slipping and sliding in the mud. I know that when we reach the fresh water and dusty birds we will be safe, washed clean — but the bridge is too far west and Horelock too fast for me ever to catch him.

The truth is I was never with him that night but at home with my mother and little Katie and thinking myself the luckiest woman alive. I had loved Horelock since I was fifteen, and Pa approved him at first. My father had two vessels — a scow and a lighter — from which he traded up and down the river and its canals. Horelock had come first into our lives as the man who worked whichever ship my father did not — they were partners in trade. Pa saw our mutual regard and sanctioned it, tho' I was so young and Horelock in his forties. He allowed me to leave my first position to marry him.

Towards the end of Katie's first year, a disagreement between my husband and father arose over some lost cargo and stolen money, and ended with my poor father's ship burnt to the waterline and he along with it. It is too long a story to recount here — save to say that Nicky was caught and languished only briefly on the hulks before crossing the herring pond to meet his death in Australia. He was my father's murderer — and yet, oh how I loved him! In my bewilderment I was vengeful, I was broken-hearted, I was frightened. One night I sailed alone out to the hulk and called for him; I cursed him to hell, I hurled at him all my love and scorn. I saw his dear face hang over the rail and blamed him for our predicament — tho' I scarcely knew the half of it then.

Even if he had lived out his life, Nick Horlock would be dead by now. Nicky at seventy-five? I cannot imagine it. He was a little man, shorter than me but narrow-boned, sinewy, obstinate, with the sailor's indomitable constitution and caustic wit. I never again matched so completely another man — which is why those other dreams come, the ones I will never confess to. They are rare now, but just as thrilling, of how we were together rutting like a girl and her sailor after many lonely months apart, even tho' he was with me more than not. Until our Katie was born, I sailed with him, work I was born to more than I was to nurse and midwife. We would have the boat fairly flying — and the smiles that would pass between us as we drove the little ship! It was the best it can be between a man and a woman. The very best. I draw that old love around me, as worn as an old quilt, still warm enough to comfort.

A maid wakes me, a different one than before, bringing in tea and seedcake. I have her draw the curtains against the dark, finding myself unaccountably weary and content to accept Miss Tripp's plan to delay reunion until the morning. It seems that she has taken charge of Mr Cotton and me — our guide into unknown territory — which is no bad thing.

I drink my tea, eat my cake, and from my trunk excavate my nightgown — which I vigorously shake out over the hearth in the faint hope that any travelling livestock from my last lodging will dislodge from the seams. Then I undress, wash, retire slowly to the marvellous bed and pray the Lord does not send me the shipburning dream again — I do so not enjoy it, tho' I do not wake as dulled with fright as I used to. It leaves now in its stead a certain resentment, a staleness, a query: why this dream again after so many years? The gentle fire flickers in the grate, suggesting still the burning ship and my father's death, my mother's grief and my own conflicted loss. How conflicted! And it is no comfort to wonder, as I have done so often over the years, how many times must it have occurred through history that a man has killed his father-in-law, and his wife is left torn between love and anger, a despairing, impossible longing for them both.

Never have I breathed even a word of Horelock to Henry or Ish, save from resuming his name for those last few years in Auckland. Henry and Ish must think I pulled the name from a hat.

'Why Horelock?' asked Henry, and I shrugged, 'It is a name I like,' and he joshed me when I spelt it variously with 'e' and without, as the unlettered man had himself. It eventuated, during the enquiry, that it was not his real name, but one he had taken from a ship when he was a boy. A man with the most rudimentary education may spell his name aright.

My omission means they hold their father guilty of the crime of bigamy and not their mother, when I could be equally so! Nick and I were properly married in a church. When Thomas Hogg took me for his wife, I did not know whether my first husband was dead or alive. How could I ever confess this to my lads, who have looked to me as mother, father and moral exemplar? I could not bear the fall of their regard.

If we were to know when we are young that this is how we will spend the solitary moments of our last years, mulling and remorseful, then who would pray for a long life? Enjoy the present moment, I counsel my foolish, elderly heart; look where you are, how splendid it all is, how warm. A spa hotel! Once, tho' it hardly seems credible, I had a spa of my own.

Have you begun on your account, Mary Ann? It would feature in mine, tho' not in yours — for which memoirist accounts for the movements of their servants? — that you let me go for good after eight and a half years' hard grind. For most of that time I was with you, tho' I worked for different periods of time at Maketu with Henry, or at Te Ngae with the Chapmans, or Tarawera with the Spencers, or Te Papa with the Browns.

It was in 1849, when you gave me my freedom, that Henry and I had a tiny cottage built of native materials at Manupirua on the shore of Lake Rotoiti, which is in the thermal district of the North Island. It cost the grand sum of six pounds, house and fence, and was named Bath Cottage for its proximity to a spring that bubbled out among the roots of an ancient pohutukawa tree, to which Henry and I would repair both individually and together. There were three pools on that gentle, forested slope above the lake, the hottest at the top closest to the spring and the coolest at the bottom. We each had our favourites, being both so much in need of a rest cure — and we joked that when Ish joined us from Wellington, he would have a favourite too.

But we were never to be all together there. After all our planning and longing, we lived at Bath Cottage for only one month — a little less — only weeks! — before Henry decided he could stand it no longer.

I see now how he was lonely and dispirited. My son found that he did not want to be in the sole company of his mother. Neither did he enjoy the forbidding, surrounding deep bush, nor the continued icy August deluge in so isolated a bay with the nearest company two hours' paddle away at a Native village. If he wanted discourse with his own kind, it was a further few hours to the mission house at Te Ngae. Also, he was in love with little Sophia Baker, his future wife, whom he had met three years earlier at Te Papa Mission Station and whom Archdeacon Brown would not release from her duties. I suppose he longed for her in his own way. Far from enjoying our idyll, we bickered and squabbled, and time weighed heavily for both of us.

If life had played me a different hand and I had accompanied a lady of my own age and experience to New Zealand — a mother! — she might have had the wisdom to advise me not to tie my fortunes to my sons. As it was, childless Mary Ann did not; just as she did not see how often my hand was at the door on my children's behalf — how I played father to them by embarrassing my connections. Sometimes I actively closed those doors, too — it was on my insistence that Henry abandoned his orders at Bishop's College at Tamaki. Disapproval was manifest — Sarah went to see Henry in his rooms and delivered a lecture on how most young gentlemen of twenty-three do not allow their mothers to so dictate to them. She told him he was vain of his abilities and had been spoilt by the Maoris and the missionaries. I should have gone to see her and told her that actually her husband had intimated to me that he did not want the responsibility of an invalid, which Henry had been for two years since a riding accident to his knee on Waiheke. He had spent months bedridden at the College, his knee bandaged and splinted, enduring the attention of three doctors and the most appalling pain and boredom.

At Manupirua both of us were invalids, to a certain degree. Henry's knee had never cured — the leg was swollen ankle to groin and would still sometimes discharge copious liquor, particularly after treatment — and I suffered exhaustion of a far different species than that which had dogged me at the Native Hospital, now a hundred and fifty miles to the north. It is curious, how leaden spirits may overtake the colonist. It is not that there is not enough to be getting on with — the drudge for mere survival is endless — but so often I would find myself sitting on our small verandah, gazing at the weather coming in over the rolling land to the west, at the lake in all her moods, at the steam rising from the pools below the house, or following the progress of a waka or sailing boat, and longing for visitors.

In that short month, before we returned to the Chapmans, we had only one party of guests. Our welcome visitor was Wiremu Tamihana, who came to stay overnight and accompanied us to the springs in the morning, before going on. We had known him before, at Taurarua — a Waikato chief still in his twenties, already with a long history of war behind him. He had a quiet, dignified manner and could readily discourse on any number of subjects, which made him immensely likeable. He had many friends and admirers, and garnered loyalty among the tribes of a most modern and unifying kind.

I last saw Tamihana when I served at the Native Conference at Kohimarama in 1860 — the chiefs Te Rauparaha, Matene Te Witoke and he were my guests at Reverend Pattison's house, which Selwyn had lent me for a few months. It suited him to have me there to look after the place and supervise the preparation of gargantuan meals. By then I was resolved to return to England, and Mr Tamihana was sympathetic to my desire.

'You are old,' I remember him saying. 'It is as well for you to be among your own people.'

He was working towards saving as much as he could for his own. Now he is kingmaker, as I have it in a letter from Henry, determined to create a monarchy to rival Victoria, and my heart aches for him. He had already come to distrust the Pakehas — as had I. As had I! It was an exhausting and conscience-burdening time, Church and State working together to break the Maoris' resistance. Those of us who knew that distant land in the 'forties cannot help but search for blame for how it is now. So much of our hard work destroyed — the schools, the mission stations, the mills — all burned to the ground, as gone to as bitter ashes as my father's ship. How glad I am to be away from it. How so very relieved. It was once so different.

The cottage at Manupirua then, at the end of the 'forties, and Wiremu Tamihana arriving with a woman and two of his men one rainy evening towards dusk. We had watched the small waka come across the lake through the fine mist and wondered who it could be. When they landed at the beach below the house, I knew it was

Tamihana, recognisable for his face being bare of tattoo, and his wife Ruth. He greeted Henry and me fondly, introducing the other men as his brothers and asking us to address him as Mr Tompson, his English name. They were a most handsome couple — Ruth was not bent double with labour or half-blinded by smoke from the cooking fires as so many Maori women are. She was tall and well built, a member of the noble class they call rangatira. She kissed me warmly in the Maori style, nose to nose, and the four of us went inside to the cramped room — the dimensions of which, if I remember correctly, were twelve feet by nine. By necessity, their companions sat out of the rain on the verandah.

Enthusiastically Henry built up the fire for which, had we been alone, I would have scolded him — the poorly constructed chimney was built of sinter, a pretty glittering silica from a nearby spring, and the gaps between the stones heated the thatch roof alarmingly — but it had rained for weeks and did not take. Our visitors rigged their wet cloaks and blankets around the walls, then we each found a perch — Ruth close to the fire, Tamihana beside her, and me on the only chair. Henry was as animated as I'd seen him for months. He limped to our larder, such as it was — three mis-angled shelves built into one crooked corner — and returned with a bottle of porter, which all of our Maori guests declined, even the frozen men outside. It has been only in the last few years that the people have begun to drink — at this time, most of them disliked it for the flavour and more so for its effects. Instead, we had strong sweet tea from the black kettle kept perpetually on the fire.

Tamihana was full of talk about his father, of whom he was inordinately proud. The young chief was of an age with Henry and wanted to match himself against him. As the steam rose from the damp covers and the fire crackled and the room grew close and warm, his tales of Te Waharoa's exploits grew more and more fantastical until I feared that in the next instance the old man could walk on water. Now and again Ruth would catch my eye, then look away again instantly, as if she could not bear the disbelief she saw there.

They had caught us badly provisioned, but I had made bread earlier in the week and brought out a loaf to share among us. From a kete, which is a native basket, Ruth brought forth a parcel of leaves that she unwrapped to reveal a large smoked fish. Henry bowed his head to make an enthusiastic Grace, before eating as heartily as any mother would hope, his pallor dispersing. Much of his misery in that place was for the lack of vittles. Tho' we had plans for gardens and hen coops and a pig with a ring in his nose, we planted and were never to reap.

After we had eaten, Te Waharoa's proud and handsome son leaned back against the side of Henry's battered sofa, its velvet once deep bottle-green now patched and stained, and asked, 'And where is your father? Why does he not live with you and your mother?' before telling his final and most extraordinary story of his father yet, a battle fought with a tribe far outnumbering his own that he easily vanquished.

Perhaps it was because of the company we were in, removed from the social censure of the Martins and the Selwyns; or perhaps it was because of the lengthy two-hour account of that other father, much beloved; or perhaps it was the half-bottle of porter that Henry had swallowed quickly to mix with the ether and opiates he took to soothe his knee — whatever, he embarked on a fictional tale.

'My father is an officer in India,' he began, which once was true of Mr Hogg. 'He commands a regiment in Calcutta' — which never was.

Tamihana and Ruth looked to me for confirmation. The light was fading to a deeper grey at our one smeary window, but my face would have been illuminated by the fire. I gave an infinitesimal but affirming nod.

'Were you born in India?' Tamihana asked. 'I have met other Pakeha who came from that country. It is vast, is it not? And very hot and dry?'

'He was born in Bristol, as was his brother,' I answered, for as any liar knows a falsehood is made more potent with the addition of grains of truth. 'It is a port in England.'

'Does the Queen of England rule all of India?' Ruth asked. The rain had found its way in through the thatch, and to ward it off she had made the addition of Henry's topper to her costume of man's blouse and tartan blanket, with a bright Indian silk tied over it at the waist. 'India! I should like to go there!' Dreamily, she stroked the fine stuff of her sash.

'I should say so, or nearly all,' replied Henry, who was a little out of his depth.

'Is every man a soldier in England?' asked Tamihana, with a degree of irony. 'Are they all born in their red coats? I have seen on a globe how small your country is, smaller even than this one. Archdeacon Brown has a globe in his library upon which our land does not feature at all. There is only an expanse of sea.' Disconcertion creased his brow.

'That globe is very old,' I soothed, 'a curiosity.'

'Yes, and much treasured,' Tamihana agreed. 'It has sailed the world more times than Captain Cook's nanny goat.'

Laughing, Henry refilled his tin cup. 'It is a grand story, that one, is it not? I have told it to children and I will one day tell it to my own sons' — further evidence of Sophia Baker's encroaching claim on his heart — 'how one nanny goat traversed the globe on the first three of Cook's voyages. What a tough old boot she would have been.'

'You would boil her on a slow fire for a night and a day ' — Ruth gave the recipe — 'with onions and potatoes, salt and pepper.' She smacked her lips.

'I have heard you call Wiremu Hoete "father",' Tamihana said suddenly, this having no connection with Cook's goat.

He shifted his gaze to me — if I might say, rather suggestively. I was by now forty-seven years of age and my dalliance with Mokihi long in the past, but I wondered if another, false story had travelled in its place that concerned William Jowitt. How rumours spread in that country where life is an eternal contrast between hard grubbing and idle boredom. Everybody has an appetite for a scandal.

'He is angry that you have come to this place.'

'He must not be,' said Henry firmly.

'Who are you to tell a man so much older than you, who showed you nothing but love, how he must not be?'

The fire flickered, Ruth chewed pleasantly on a crust of bread — if I had a penny for every time I envied a Maori his teeth I would be a wealthy woman — and I could not meet Tamihana's eye nor even look at Henry, whose voice, when it came, was half-strangled.

'I have left Maketu. Isn't that enough to please him?'

'He would rather you were there than here at Manupirua. Do you not feel unwelcome? Where are your friends? Where are Rawiri and Te Haimona?'

'Not far.' Henry inclined his head towards the village.

'Think how difficult it was for you to get here from Maketu — without once leaving this sofa!' He patted its flank as if it were a faithful horse, and his tone was good humoured, chaffing.

Henry coloured, for it was true, it had carried him by canoe and on the shoulders of his bearers, whom Henry had paid fairly for their labour, tho' that miserable little closefist Archdeacon Brown — the man who continued to deny him his bride! — had suggested he substitute soap for coin.

'Did you think you would be welcomed here, that the journey would be easy? I will not speak for Hoete, but you are not pleasing many people by being at Manupirua.'

At that moment the ill-fitting door was flung open. The tarp that formed that part of the floor lifted with the swing and gust, and Henry's multitude of papers flew thickly from the table. One of the men who had accompanied our visitors came in shivering to sit by the fire. Beyond him the trees bent in the wind and there was not a glimpse of the lake through the rain. We were quite closed in.

Henry got up and limped across to close the door, gathering up his precious correspondence, while Ruth retraced my steps to the corner shelves. She returned bearing our only other loaf of bread, from which she broke off a large portion for her companion. I knew better than to caution. Henry could never deny his Maori friends anything — he always had me to understand that to deny without good reason was for them as ungracious and mean-spirited as you could imaginably be.

As if she sensed my stinginess, Ruth took from her basket some late-season apples, which she handed around.

'My mother is pleased we are here,' Henry said with a hard edge to his voice, still gathering his pages and setting them in piles. 'Mamma is fairly dancing with joy. Are you not?'

Holding fast to my wizened apple and quelling tears, I reminded myself yet again that he was frustrated in love, that he was distressed by his agonised knee, that he was ill-tempered because of it, and that only yesterday he had heaved himself from the hottest pool and for several hours lain wrapped sweating and shivering in four blankets before I could walk him to his sofa.

'This — you see, Wiremu — is my mother's dream. To have a house of her own. And as she has just achieved it — and very grand it is too, do you not agree? I must not cease to play the part of grateful son whose regard for his mother is made necessarily more exquisite by the absence of a father.'

Tamihana nodded, tho' his attention had been taken by the pile of books beside Henry's couch.

'I will tell you some more of the story. My mother was handsomely betrayed. He was already married — to an Indian woman.'

Tamihana picked up the first of the five volumes and leafed through it: Carlyle's essays.

'It was a hurried marriage to conceal an illegitimate child, and my father's excuse was that the ceremony was not legal or binding because it took place in a heathen temple. For me to guess at his motivation for returning to that first marriage — and so leaving my brother and me — would require rather a larger dose of ether than Ma has provided.'

I stared at him, but he would not meet my eye.

Tamihana was unperturbed, even supposing he had been listening. 'What do you think of Carlyle?' he asked.

Henry answered straight away, as if he had not just made the most alarming speech I had ever heard from his mouth. 'As I wrote to my brother a week or so ago, he is an admirer of the real, the true, the beautiful, and a severe castigator of folly and hollowness.'

This last was sharply directed at me. Finding myself still standing as if to go out of the room, and realising there was no escape save out into the rain and sulphurous air, I sat down again, but not before Ruth had replaced the apple in my palm, folding my fingers over it.

'I gave you the softest one,' she coaxed, 'for your teeth.'

'In any case, you will not stay here for long,' Tamihana pronounced, 'before you have to move on.'

Taking a pillow from the sofa and another volume from the pile, he lay full length before the fire. 'I had read to here . . .' and he flicked through and found his place, tho' it was many months since he had visited Henry at Maketu and read the first part.

'Henry?'

'Not now, Mother.'

For want of his pillow he lay down flat on his sofa and I could only look longingly towards my bed, where Ruth was making herself comfortable. She patted the quilt as if to say we could both sleep there, then closed her eyes, not stirring even when their second companion made his way inside and lay curled against the other two on the floor, his icy knees against my slippered feet.

There seemed little point in rising to light the lamp. Henry was feigning sleep and Tamihana was nodding over his book. Besides, I was hot and cold, in turmoil for Henry's low spirits and new vengefulness. The fire spluttered and smoked a little when the rain made its way down the chimney, and I longed for a cool draught of fresh water.

'Are you awake, Henry?'

'Not now, Mother. Go to bed.'

'I think I will stay where I am.'

'You will be very uncomfortable — but then I do sometimes think that that is what you prefer.'

'I beg your pardon?'

'A hard bed and discomfort. Lie down with Ruth.'

'Please do not speak to me so coldly, Hy.'

There was silence. Who could tell in the gloom whether any of our visitors were listening — but then how could they not? I resolved not to care.

'Henry?'

'Not now. Our friends are sleeping.'

'How do you know about it? You must tell me. I will not be able to sleep. I feel ill —'

'Mother, I beg you.'

'But it is I who begs you!'

Another silence, then a heavy sigh.

'The letters.'

'What letters?'

'From our grandfather Hogg. John and I found them among your papers at Cross Street. It was just before I left for New Zealand. We read them — an appetite for other people's correspondence being a family trait, as is the ability to remain close-lipped about it ever after.'

'Oh Henry, please!' My voice rose and broke, and Tamihana made a tsking noise under his breath. He sat up to feed the fire while I bowed my head and wept with shame and pity for my sons.

'Mata Te Mete,' he said eventually. 'Did you love this man? Or did you go with him for the things he could give you?'

At this simple question, Henry laughed bitterly, tho' neither Mr Tompson nor I found it amusing. Hy had turned away from the blaze and waited for my answer, but I was too distressed to speak.

'It is not that bad,' murmured Ruth from the bed, after a while.

I calmed myself enough to tell her, 'But I have lost Henry's respect.'

'Haere mai ki te moe. You must talk no more.'

I stood to do as she said — it was the most sensible course — but I had to give Tamihana his answer.

'I tell you I loved him. It was as Henry says — he had already lost his heart to another. She had the prior claim.'

'You should have stayed with him and lived all together,' he replied. 'You were foolish to go away from them.'

'I had no choice. You don't understand — in England a man may only have one wife.'

'Of course I know that, Mata. It is the cause of a great deal of unhappiness.'

'Mother — my rag.' Henry's tone was guarded, warning. He did not like the turn our discussion had taken.

'I am sorry, Mr Tompson,' I said, tho' I didn't know what for exactly, and I went to my chest for the ether and cloth, stepping carefully in the narrow gaps between bodies. Henry held the saturated rag against his face and snuffled, his thin beard moving on his pale, shadowy jaw. As the drug took hold, his blue eyes in the firelight regarded me as impassively as an infant will his nurse, and once they flickered and closed I made my way to lie down with Ruth.

Soon after sun-up we breakfasted on the last of Ruth's fish and some more of the fruit, before departing for the springs, we women going ahead of the men. It was bitterly cold, the ground wet and treacherous from the night's storm, but despite that my spirits lifted — and they could not have been lower, after Henry's disclosure. The pools, brimming to overflowing, steamed cooler from the rain. The lake lay still and grey below us, the further shores and wooded hills lost in the mist.

We had had a simple raupō shelter built beside the moderate centre pool, which was for me the most pleasant. There Ruth helped me to disrobe. All the while she remarked on my garments and so desired a woollen bodice that I gave it to her as a present, tho' I possessed only one other. It was at Bath Cottage that I began my habit of leaving off my corset, but on discovering the shell I had left hanging from a nail, Ruth now desired also a lesson in how to fit and lace it. The eyelets had rusted in the pungent sulphurous air, its strings yellowed and bones curled, but I remedied it enough to be able to give the lesson, carried out with much hilarity. I laced her energetically and threatened never to release her — she swore on stepping free of it that she would never again long to possess such a stifling thing.

When we emerged from the shelter to the pool's edge — a flat stone positioned for ease of entry — we could hear voices. The men had taken the upper pool, the hottest, screened from us by a low, ragged copse of fern and scrub that grew verdant in the sulphurous mud. A glimmer of Henry's thin white shoulders showed through the leaves and steam — Mr Tompson was advising him of his future.

'You must leave this place' — oh well-worn theme! — 'it is not right for you to be alone here with your mother. Are you an outcast?'

Henry murmured something inaudible while I eased myself, shivering, down onto the stone and tightened the old sheet I used for bathing, folded in Ancient style. Ruth entered the pool arrayed in the bodice and little else, and I slipped in after her — the water as always hot, soporific, divine.

'It will shrink in this heat,' I told her and she laughed, hauling the bodice off and laundering it — a vigorous procedure that would reduce it to felt.

'You are not. You are needed to speak for us,' came Tamihana's voice.

Henry mumbled again and Tamihana's reply was inaudible under Ruth's splashing. Perhaps Henry had gestured for him to lower his voice.

Ruth patted the bodice flat against a stone and submerged herself up to her chin so that her long, thick hair floated out around her, a rich, black shawl thrown across the steaming surface. With her shining eyes and healthy, smooth skin, she made the most arresting spectacle. Chiefly women, by dint of descent from men who continually fought to maintain their position and so were of strong constitution and strategising minds, are universally agreed to be of the highest form of humanity. She gave me a warm smile and I returned it as fully, I hope, tho' I worried I would disappoint her. It is easy for an Englishman to feel inadequate in the face of what they call *aroha*. She read something of my reserve in my eyes, and seemed to think less of me for it. She floated away a little.

Between us the mist lifted and dispersed and thickened again, and I longed for the clever child Henry, to whom I could have turned and said, 'Make me a sonnet, lad, on my Greek robe and the Goddess we bathe with.' But the boy was grown and gone and replaced by the despondent man in the pool above, a man who was planning his escape and who could blame him?

'Do you have children?' I asked Mrs Tompson. I had seen her with child at Taurarua. In that condition Maori women do not at all hide themselves away as our foolish women will if their economies allow, but instead go about happy and proud.

Ruth gave an enigmatic smile and drifted gently towards me to sit closer. She spoke softly, caressingly. 'You know my husband is right to advise your son the way he does. You will travel with us to Te Ngae today.'

For a moment I was at a loss for words. Did Ruth see me as a servant to take her orders, having watched me wait on Mary Ann?

By witnessing my work at the Native Hospital, by my care of ailing Mrs Chapman at Te Ngae and Mrs Spencer at Tarawera? I doubted she understood my exact position.

'We will carry only what you need,' Ruth said. 'Your medicines and some of your clothes — only some.'

'No, Ruth,' I said firmly, 'that is a preposterous idea. Henry cannot. He will have to be carried on his sofa and there are no bearers.'

'We will ask Rewiri Manuariki and Te Haimona, who carried him here.'

'Your canoe is not big enough.'

'Do not worry about any of that, Mrs Smith. Kei te pai. We will take care of it.'

'If Henry goes, then so be it. I will stay on here alone for the time being.'

And so I would. There was birdsong from the fern and the sun was now unveiling itself above the low hills on the other side of the lake. I would gaze on that beauty and not on that of Mrs Tompson, this disapproving young woman who thought she could dictate my fate.

She was shivering suddenly, and swam away to be closer to where the water trickled hottest from the pool above, and floated with her eyes closed. The rain had cooled our pond — it was not my obstinacy that had chilled her. At least I wanted to believe that was so, because Ruth had been only ever kind and gracious to me. I felt badly for disappointing her, but could not resign my post so easily. She could not understand that I expected more of myself than had any past mistress.

The men had been quiet for some time, even when Tamihana's companions came to join them. If Henry had his favoured position against the rock with shallow depression, he may have gained such ease as to fall asleep. We had all of us passed a bitter night — Ruth and I, when I had finally joined her in the bed, probably had the best of it with our shared quilt. The hot springs melted the ice from our bones.

Mr and Mrs Tompson left with their retinue in the early afternoon, and Henry did not go with them. Perhaps he would have, had it been possible, but after his bath he was weak and feverish again, which made the decision for him and resulted in some bad feeling. Ruth maintained her earlier distance with me, and Tāmihana would not leave the subject alone until Henry spoke sharply to him, which made our guest very angry.

After our stilted farewells, Henry's from his sofa and mine from the verandah, I spent the afternoon in the vegetable garden. In that part of the island potatoes grow all year round in the warm thermal soil, and altho' my infant plants battled frost, miraculously they survived. There were few pests of the insect variety, but long-legged birds would come to peck the green shoots and pigs gone wild in the bush would break down our fences. Arrayed in an old pair of Henry's trousers and a ragged jersey that once belonged to the Judge, I rebuilt the fence from where it had sagged, and pulled fern from where it had invaded our beds, thinking of nothing but the work at hand and suppressing my usual circular thoughts of how unjust it was that the Colony attracted a certain class of women who had never grubbed a living, and who resented and suffered the labour that came with having homes of their own. I had met women who seemed not to appreciate what they had, or at least not enough to put their shoulders to the plough. I could not picture Sarah with her boot on a shovel.

By late afternoon I was muddy, weary and sore, and longed for another bath. Despite my difference with Ruth, and Henry's barely suppressed rage, the evening promised serenity, if only the thinnest veneer of it. The sky had cleared enough to give us an early rising sliver of moon high above the lake, a pale coronet just present in rapid twilight.

I chose the hottest pool and left off the robe — it was safe to bathe without it since I was the only traveller in that paradise. Henry's favoured rock offered its comfort to my aching back, the moon brightened as the sky around it dulled, the birds were noisy for their first dusk without rain for weeks, and after a time, at length, I recognised some of my quietude as melancholy, the kind that comes with the knowledge that departure from a place is imminent

— a much-loved place. What was it the men had decided there that morning? How I would struggle not to oppose Henry, not to initiate and bear the blame for another quarrel.

When duty called me back to the cottage and my ailing son, I discovered flames leaping high from the chimney.

'We need to talk, Mother.' Henry had pulled his couch as close as it could safely be to the fire.

'In a moment, dearest.'

He had made an attempt to wash up the plate from the night before in a basin, but had seemingly abandoned it halfway through. I completed the job — the hot bath and walk through the cold air had revived me. I swept the floor, set some yeast to prove, replenished Henry's jug from the water butt and stopped to drink a large glass myself. That paradisical water — how I miss it. We drew it fresh and sweet from the lake.

'Did you sup?' I asked.

'I'm not hungry.'

'You are very pale and thin, Henry. Did you make your own rag?'

'Not now. It fogs my mind.'

'Your eyes are fair blazing. Will you take your medicine?' I had already mixed his tincture of potash and iodine for swelling and heat.

'No.'

'Would you like a biscuit? There is a tiny piece of ham—'

'No, Ma!'

Sorrowfully, in the dimmest corner, I put on my nightgown, and then retired to bed. For some time we lay in silence, until I could bear it no longer.

'I don't want you to hate me.'

'You must not pretend to be what you are not.'

'It's how I have got by.' And how I've got you by, my love, I could have added.

'In two days Tamihana is returning with bearers to take us to the Chapmans at Te Ngae. We will be packed and ready to go by then.'

'I love Mrs Chapman as much as you do, Hy, but I must be my own mistress.'

'Mr Tompson has heard she's been very ill. You are needed and you must not give way to your own indulgences. She has been like a second mother to me.'

'Since you are dissatisfied with the one you have, I don't doubt it.'

'You are mine own dear mum, and I don't hate you at all — but you are so very different to Mrs Chapman.'

We lay quietly again, both of us contemplating our near neighbour, who was my antithesis. Where I was brash or ill-tempered, Anne was gentle and good-humoured. She was capable also of great melancholy, which she inflicted on no one save herself, expressing it as a stoicism to rival Selwyn's. Where I could indulge and encourage high spirits, she would always caution restraint; where I would declare an opinion, she would dismantle it with a few well-chosen words. Where I could work like a dray horse, her small frame and poor constitution would have her struggle through a morning of dispensing Physick or schooling infants. Where I would weep at tragedy, she would be silent and dignified.

'She is the dearest old lady I have ever known and needs us to help her at Te Ngae. Also, I hear Mrs Spencer is with child again and will require your attention when her time comes, so you will go on to Tarawera.'

'I am old myself now, Henry.'

'You are not yet fifty! No more now. Let us go to sleep.'

And I would go to sleep now, if I could, in my bed at this English spa, where the rotten egg odour of sulphur does not hang in the air as in that other place, where tomorrow I will share my bathwater with hundreds of others who came before me, where the surfaces of cold marble and arrangement of hoses and douches could not be more opposed to that wild, private and magical pool. But instead I lie sleepless on my sumptuous pillows and remember how we left the only home I have ever owned, just as Henry planned — him carried down to the waka on his sofa, me following behind with the only other woman come to fetch us away, Ana, a girl taken in by the

Chapmans. During the paddle, tears wet my cheeks even as I knew Henry was right, that it was better for us both to return to the yoke. If Ana noticed my misery, she said nothing — I am sure Maori women think us generally an unhappy lot.

As the boatmen pulled us towards Te Ngae, my son on his sofa in the prow, me midships between Ana and Mr Tompson, we could see the various roofs of the establishment set above the shore, the thatched mission house the largest, the schoolhouse and cookhouse set behind. There were the many fruit trees — apples, cherries, plums and peaches — but their branches were bare and black for the season. There were the chickens pecking at the ground below the trees, enjoying the weak sun — and there was Mrs Chapman herself, tottering down the path from the mission house to the shore in her little black prunella boots, her funny brown silk bonnet tied firmly under her chin, and calling out greetings in English and Maori.

'Haere mai, Mrs Smith! Dearest Henry! Haere mai, Mr Tamihana.'

There was another diminutive figure, as dear to our hearts as Anne, racing along the water's edge and waving his thin arms, his mop of curly hair churning in the wind — the most wonderful surprise: Mr Cotton.

If she is your second mother, Henry, then there is my third son, I thought, but forbore to say, the wrench of losing my home now sweetened by the resumption of our friendship.

One of the bearers offered to carry me ashore, but I could never abide that except in unruly surf, such as encountered on the bar at Maketu — I insisted on removing my boots and wading through the icy shallows.

Henry and Bee greeted one another affectionately, with Henry hopping about on his one good leg in the shingle and Mr Cotton, having kissed me on both cheeks, talking so wildly about his most recent adventures that the task of unloading our traps from the waka seemed forgotten. After I had replaced my boots, Mrs Chapman and I walked arm in arm through the cool, grey day towards the mission house. Delightedly, she told me that Judge Martin was also in residence, tho' not with Mary Ann, who had stopped with the Browns at Te Papa — and also that the Bishop was expected any day, making his way by the Kaituna River from Maketu to Okere, then overland to Lake Rotoiti, through the Ohau River that joins that lake to Lake Rotorua, a journey I had made many times myself. It was the same passage the Judge would have taken, without allowing his party to call in to see us on the way. It was extraordinary — he had sailed right by us at Manupirua and not called in. How low his regard for us must be!

Tho' Anne was cheerful, her tiny wrinkled face alive with the prospect of so much company, she was bone thin, there were a number of sores around her mouth, and I could see her teeth pained her. My heart filled with love for her — I could see she was hauling on all her reserves.

Mary Ann has it that Mrs Chapman never overcame her fear of savages. She was so widely revered by them, I am not certain I agree. I saw her devoted service to the children and invalids, her respectful deference to men and women of standing. It was rambunctiousness that alarmed her, whatever the colour of reveller — I remember a night of young English adventurers singing glees and swigging port to the early hours, and her calling me from my bed to mix her a soothing draught.

A large dinner had been prepared for us, for which we sat at two and did not rise until five. Despite the common wisdom that a great deal more was done with less, Mrs Chapman had at that time four Maori girls in the kitchen, Ana being one of them. There was much running back and forth from the cookhouse and infectious high spirits, and the meal was delicious: roasted pork — tho' I never thought I'd long for it! — potatoes and cabbage, then apples from the mission's orchard made into a pie. Large portions were carried outside under the trees, where sat Wiremu Tamihana and his men. This division had come about from Judge Martin's presence and his principle that no Maori enter the house without European clothing. He thought poorly of any other Englishman who did not make the same stand, which he thought was in the Natives' best interest. It surprised me that Mr Chapman had gone along with it. It was most certainly not protocol when the Chapmans were alone, or with Henry.

Doleful as ever, the Judge sat opposite my son and I could not help but observe that throughout the dinner he had scarce a word after him, tho' all the jostling about on the lakes and shores had aggravated Henry's knee and he was visibly suffering for it. From where I sat at the far end of the table, between Bee and Anne, he and I had only one exchange. I enquired after his wife's general health and he admitted sparingly to its being average.

After the meal, Henry, Bee and Mr Chapman went out to sit with Tamihana, who had been joined by Martin Te Rauparaha and one of Te Wherowhero's sons. Were they their fathers, then no doubt they would have been admitted, but the tone of the occasion was set by that other, loftier visitor. I was left at table with Mrs Chapman, the Judge and young Fisher, last described in female garb eight years earlier on *Tomatin*. On our few meetings since the voyage he had had an odd manner with me, as if he regarded me as a corrupting influence. There was no sense now in trying to impress upon him my virtue, that quality in short supply since the Judge disapproved so openly of Bath Cottage.

'What are your plans, Mrs Smith?' William Martin asked me. There was a sardonic lilt to the question, as if I was in no position to have any. 'I am sure my wife would like to hear of them.'

'I have a letter to her half-written.' I had begun it the day before while I waited among our meagre belongings for our departure from the cottage. 'It is as Henry says. I will either stay here or go to the Spencers at Tarawera, wherever I'm needed most.'

Oh Kitty, if you could have been there to hear my sanctimonious servility, which memory sickens me as it would sicken you — or perhaps, like Fisher, it would have amused you. As he got up to assist Mrs Chapman to her more comfortable chair by the fire, a little smile played around his mouth as if he recognised it for more play-acting — which it was not! My intentions were genuine, not least because I was well aware of how short were our funds.

'I should like to think that would be at Taurarua,' said the Judge.

'No, dear.' Anne was settling back, while young Fisher brought her shawl. 'Mrs Spencer is near her time. She's expecting Mrs Smith as soon as she can be there.'

Ana came in with an older woman from the kitchen, and I got up to help them clear away, tho' resolved to take the first opportunity to join Henry and the men.

'Just one moment, Mrs Smith.' The Judge was also rising to his feet, which movement was synchronous with a certain sinking of my heart. 'Would you accompany me to Mr Chapman's library? There is a matter I should like to discuss with you.'

My hands were already full of plates, but he allowed me to carry them out to where Ana and the other women had set to washing up in a series of tin basins in the garden, before I went on to Mr Chapman's library.

It did not compare with the Judge's own, and less with Archdeacon Brown's at Tauranga, which that man had built before even a house for his family. The bookcases were almost empty, due to Mr Chapman's habit of lending his books to flock and friend and never seeing them again. There was a horsehair sofa as dilapidated as Henry's, a heavy Bible open on the desk, and in the corner a pedestal table with peeling sea-damaged veneer, on which sat a bowl of dried grasses. A stained map lifted its corners on the bagging scrim. The fire had burned low and the room smelt stale, close, like a sickroom.

The Judge did not invite me to sit down.

'The Marsh Scholarship,' he began, 'of which your son was the first recipient — a grant to enable him to study for Holy Orders at Bishop's College.'

'Two years ago now, Mr Martin.'

'Yes, and since then he has been either here at Te Ngae or at Maketu — or latterly at your self-styled spa.' His tone was ironic.

'You may rest assured Henry will continue to be of service,' I said, kneeling before the dying fire and taking hold of the poker.

'Whether or not he is of service is hardly the issue.' He sighed, in that infinitely patient way he had which usually made me feel incalculably idiotic. 'You are the one who pulls continually at her binds. Why would you wish that for your son?'

It took me a moment or two to answer. Once the fire was blazing again, I stood to face him.

'Henry continues to gather songs for your Maori compendium and to work on his dictionary. He dispenses Physick. He receives countless visitors who have labyrinthine grievances and no concept of the passage of time, and will give them anything — even, once, his stove door — and for whom he writes volumes of letters every day and travels exhaustively—'

'He did, Elizabeth, he did — and he coped admirably, even with his lame leg —'

'And now he's had a rest cure and is willing to resume his duties. Henry's is a deeply religious character, Mr Martin, as you well know, and he will continue to do God's work. I own that he is not formally studying — but you should see how at Maketu he prays with his visitors, and hear how earnest are their entreaties to a God he makes as real to them as you or me. You should hear how at Maketu he gathers the children together and plays the flute and has them singing chaunts and ditties.'

At this onslaught the Judge was quiet, which rather surprised me, so I went on, 'Henry must not be made to feel he has misused the scholarship.'

'He has not. You have.'

I thought I would be ill — the pork and potatoes, of which I had eaten too much, rose in my throat.

The Judge pulled the chair away from the desk and sat upon it. He did not ask me to sit — and why would he? I was not his equal but a servant to be chastised.

'The general view is that you appropriated the continuing funds for the upkeep of your household such as it was.'

'I have had this already from the Archdeacon Brown,' I managed, for so I had one evening of high feeling at Te Papa, 'who professes to love Henry as a son.'

'And well you might have had that from him, since it was for his tragedy that the scholarship was furnished. If his son had survived, then Marsh himself would have had the benefit and the scholarship would not have existed.'

'Mr Brown has seen how Henry has suffered—'

'It is only a knee. Do you continue the cold water treatment?'

The Judge was referring to a cure that involved pouring cold water on Henry's knee from a great height for a duration of half an hour, a procedure that took a deal of time in preparation and work afterwards, rather than in execution, particularly if performed indoors. The method afforded relief, tho' resulted in excessive swelling.

'No,' I answered, 'we gave it up since we came to Maketu.'

'I think he is the better for it,' said the Judge, 'the leaving it off.'

Do not instruct me in my own profession, I thought, but did not say, for I was tiring of this. I would so have liked to go out to the garden to join the others.

'I continue with the herb poultices and starch bandage, and various medicines,' I said. 'That is why he is better.'

'The Bishop asked me to discuss Henry's future with you — or rather, the question of his autonomy.'

'If I was his father, would you address me thus?' I kept my voice level. 'The world abounds with fathers and sons who go about together and no one thinks anything of it. But I am thought meddling and even greedy by having my son's welfare at heart.'

'Mrs Smith. I have seen the note you sent to Henry that insisted he resign from the college from "affection and duty". There is no wonder that the Bishop and I are concerned.'

There were footsteps along the corridor then, echoing on the bare wooden boards, and Bee Cotton came in, his little face flushed with the cold and conversation. The Judge did not look up, but remained staring at the embers in the grate, his thin upper lip pressed so much into his lower that it almost disappeared.

'There you are, Mrs Smith!' said Bee. 'Mrs Tompson is asking for you.'

'Have we completed our discussion, Mr Martin?' I asked, quelling a desire to lay my hand on his shoulder and so press home my point. 'Believe me, I will allow Henry his own destiny — more than you would, perhaps. From now on we will live independently of one another.'

I went out with Bee to join the others and sat by Ruth, where we entertained one another by telling stories and singing ditties, and very often gaining the attention of the men who left off their dreary discussions of politics and religion to join our song. When the evening grew cold, Anne organised a fire to be set in the schoolroom and we adjourned there until bedtime. Throughout the revelry I felt a weight depart from my shoulders — not of guilt, for I did not feel that, but the negative perception of my betters. It was bittersweet redemption — I knew even then that I would long for ever for our cottage at Manupirua, for what it could have been and what it never was.

Rain is falling, muted by the grand hotel, by the floor above and the distant roof, but I can hear it, and in this place it comforts me. A little before I left New Zealand, I heard from a Lakes tourist that the house has completely crumbled away in the weather, the best of the joinery taken and put to use elsewhere. All that remains is the pink rose I planted by the door, which grows wild there now and is called by the Maoris 'Te Mete'.

All that remains is a rose called Smith.

ELEVEN

To the Pump Room

1866

Mrs Smith proved difficult to rouse — for a full ten minutes by his fob watch Mr Cotton had knocked on her door with increasing force and velocity until she eventually answered, and not before the thought crossed his mind that she had died in the night. Panic welled in his breast and he only just managed to stop himself calling aloud for assistance. Then he had been compelled to wait downstairs for half an hour until his old friend appeared, uncharacteristically dishevelled and complaining of lack of sleep, though evidence of it remained in the corners of her eyes.

'Forgive me, Mrs Smith,' he said, untangling a bonnet ribbon from her collar and lifting her mantle to sit squarely on her shoulders.

'That is quite all right, dear,' she said, retying her bonnet bow at her throat herself — her hands were shaking.

He gave her his arm, and they went out of the hotel doors and along the Crescent towards the Pump Room. The perfumer and druggist were open for business, a glitter of glass and silver in the windows and exotic aromas drifting in the cool crisp air as customers passed in and out. Mrs Smith, he could detect, was tempted — the apothecary being less crowded than the perfumer — but not strongly enough to delay longer than a moment.

'Have you breakfasted?' Bee asked as they walked on, for he had, luxuriously, on ham and eggs and kippers, some evidence of which remained on his shirtfront.

'Oh — I could not eat a morsel!'

She held too tight to his arm, the one that had pained him since a nerve was twisted in the sporting of Doctor Tuke's remedial jacket. At least he dated it to that, though his memory of those episodes was dulled by medicines, which was a mercy.

'Although,' continued Mrs Smith, 'there may well be refreshment available in the Pump Room, or do they only give you Adam's ale? And where is Miss Tripp? Have you seen her this morning or had word?'

'I have not. I had indeed forgotten all about her, she being so recent an acquaintance, and my mind and heart indelibly fixed on the prospect of an old friend and dear.'

Mrs Smith concentrated on her progress, more stilted and halting than ever.

'Did you hear the thunder in the early hours?' He released himself and went to the inside, which was ill-mannered but necessary for his arm, even if Mrs Smith was splashed by a passing wheel. The shallow puddles were frozen solid and the deeper ones breaking up. 'Proper English rain. Very heavy.'

'Of course it was proper English rain. What else could it be?' snapped Mrs Smith, switching her cane to the other hand and stepping shakily on.

'Why was it, do you think, that in New Zealand we longed for English rain when it rains more in that country than—'

'Oh, do let's not talk about the blessed rain! On today of all days.'

She went ahead of him into the Pump Room of the Natural Baths, which lay between St Anne's and another hotel. Tipping his head back, Bee viewed the marvel of the painted ceiling, which though entirely secular brought him to a moment of godliness. The natural beauty of the Peaks and Dales flew aloft, inhabited by fauna — foxes, rabbits, badgers — naiads, nymphs and a distant hunting scene in contemporary costume. He spread his arms wide, so as to be bathed in all its glory.

It was as well Bee had pulled up short, gaping — it gave her time to assess the company. There were perhaps twenty or thirty people gathered, or more — though the further recesses of the room blurred.

Several small counters offered glasses of murky water, as English as the rain had been, with uniformed attendants working the lever taps. No one had removed his coat or cape, for several of the windows stood open to the day and the air was icy. An invalid clutched his rug to his chest with bony fingers; a young mother sat pallid in a corner chair with a motionless, wizened child of five or six in her arms. The pair was rugged for the cold, the mother's cape carefully darned and her boots worn. They were a little above the Charity Baths and a little below the Natural. The guests closest turned their backs. A fashionable trio of young women stood laughing with an officer, who shared his cut of coat with several other gentlemen present: the Duke's men. There was a preponderance of older people, a few family groups — and not one familiar voice or shape.

'Come along, Bee.' She waited again for his arm, and they made their way the full traverse past the row of tall arched windows, Elizabeth peering into the crowd and wishing they had gone on to the Baths, for it suddenly seemed that Mary Ann would more likely be there than here.

Bee found them two chairs side by side with a view through the nearest window of St Anne's Well, the small shrine white-capped with frost. There was a ragged, dark-skinned family holding a cup beneath the spigot and each taking a draught of the healing warm waters: she took them at first to be Maoris — a mistake she'd made more than once since her return, subconsciously — but of course they were not, could not be. They were Ishmaelites, perhaps, gypsies, smaller of stature and with something belligerent in their demeanour. Passers-by gave them a wide berth.

She sipped the salty contents of her glass and practised patience. Ten slow minutes passed, perhaps fifteen, and she was rewarded by the entrance — not of Mary Ann and the Judge, but of the Bishop of Lichfield and his wife. 'We are going away for a few days,' he had said.

Had she told Augustus she intended to go to Torquay to see the Martins? She couldn't remember — but supposed, bitterly, that if she had, it wouldn't have made any difference. As she came in Mrs Selwyn was looking for a lackey to announce her arrival — and

Elizabeth saw by her disappointed expression that it was as she had supposed, that there had been a drop in standards at the spa since her last visit, which would have been twenty or thirty years ago, before the first voyage.

As yet unobserved, Elizabeth watched husband and wife walk towards the pumps, the old, palpable distance between them still there, even though they walked closely. They passed by on the other side of a group of drinkers, and Elizabeth was glad they did not notice her. It was a calamity of sorts: Augustus could well believe she had followed them there.

She tugged on Bee's sleeve: 'Let's be off to the Baths.'

'No, no' — Bee was implacable — 'we should stay here. Mary Ann will be along soon.'

'To your right,' Elizabeth whispered, 'behind the large gentleman with the red beard.'

But Bee was too hard of hearing for such subtle means, so she was compelled to nudge and point at the same time as exercise a restraining hand on his arm to prevent him running to the man he still considered a friend. It was lucky the Pump Room thronged with guests because Bee's loud exclamation was easily absorbed by the chatter. It was not necessary to clap her hand over his mouth, but those who observed her doing it seemed only sympathetic to her plight — she was his aged nurse, his devoted mother.

Away from his See, the Bishop seemed less a giant among men and more an elderly patient seeking a cure. He and Sarah had their glasses of thick water and were glancing about for a place to sit down.

'Oh, this is too frustrating,' Elizabeth murmured. 'Where is our darling? And where is Miss Tripp?'

Bee sighed heavily, his eyelids fluttering. It was a facet of his illness that whenever he was intensely disappointed — something that occurred reasonably often, given his high expectations of the world — a part of his brain seemed to shut down and he would become drowsy.

'Dear man,' said Elizabeth, patting him. His head fell back against the sill. 'It's best the Bishop discovers our presence only after Mary Ann does.'

He nodded sleepily, and Elizabeth felt at liberty to fix her unwavering attention on the newcomers entering at the door.

⁂

Along the icy streets towards the Crescent hurried Kitty Tripp, though her feet of their own accord would turn towards the train station and back to London, since that was home now and not Buxton with all its conflicts and challenges.

At the hydrant she paused and took a sip of chlorers. Lord knows she needed it after her sleepless night in a shared bed. Hotel guests and bathers were passing in and out of the Pump Room, and given it was a half after ten it was reasonable to presume her elderly charges had gone there ahead of her. They would be growing anxious by now, particularly Mrs Smith, who worried rather too much about everything, unless she too had had her soothing drop. Kitty hoped so.

The doorway was blocked by a bathchair, rickety wheeled, manoeuvred inexpertly by an elderly bathchairman. The slender gentleman who accompanied the patient was compelled to assist. His dark hair was streaked grey and white, and Kitty thought him still handsome, though too thin and drawn as if he had recently survived an illness or long voyage. Such tenderness suffused his sensitive face as he opened the conveyance and bent to lift away the invalid, her face hidden inside an old-fashioned bonnet. If what he feared came to pass and he was bereaved, then he could fall prey to a certain type of Buxton girl who snared themselves widowers, being rapid and precise in their attentions after the failure of a cure. Kitty had known a few of them — Buxton born and bred or new arrivals. A spa town could be as much a hunting ground as a Colony. Perhaps this gentleman was already a widower and the patient was his daughter. So fatherly was he, his gentle arms supporting the tiny body while the bathchairman succeeded in loosening the front wheel by vigorously pushing it to and fro.

From long association with the town and the condition of many of her early audiences, Kitty knew the interiors of some bathchairs to be unpleasant, given the foul aroma that lifted from them, but for ease and efficiency it might be necessary to persuade Elizabeth into one later — that is, if they were to go to the theatre. There was a matinee at one. Considering the idea and warming to it as the chlorers took hold — enough of her sensibility remained to suspect the impulse rose from the drug, though not enough to dismiss the idea — she waited while several other would-be imbibers massed behind her. It was not what Mr Griggs wanted, but it would be so entertaining. It would be the final scene of the mystery. She could not contain her curiosity, which Mrs Smith had rightly identified as one of her strongest traits.

The patient at long last re-placed in the conveyance, the father caught her eye and nodded in thanks, and Kitty saw then that she was not his daughter but more likely his wife, though worn enough to be the gentleman's mother. A rheumatic, perhaps, or suffering wasting disease. Kitty could very often recognise Buxton's most common complaints, but this one escaped her. The silvery eyes were of the purest expression, the face very bony and earnest, and Kitty smiled encouragingly as one would to assure an ailing child. She was almost, and it was cruel of her to think it, but it was true — a freak, an exhibit, as if she was a little girl grown prematurely old. The invalid was taking Kitty in — her dainty boots, her costume, the bright yellow silks of her dress and sumptuous velvet of her sister's cloak, borrowed from the cupboard while its owner was yet asleep — and smiling. She had some appreciation of style, then.

Between them the husband and bathchairman straightened the rugs and coverings over the patient in the little carriage while Kitty looked about for Mrs Smith and the Reverend — whom she spotted straight away, because Mrs Smith was rising from her seat at the far end of the room and fairly flying — so far as the old mare was capable — towards her. Surely her arrival scarcely warranted such excitement, thought Kitty, before she realised that the feeling was for the patient she stood beside. Tears and exclamations and endearments issued from both ladies, in English and that other language Mrs Smith had learned to speak, and Elizabeth was kissing the high white brow, pressing her lips against it as a mother would, her cheeks wet.

So this was Mary Ann and the Judge, the subject of so many recollections. The gentleman's face was as tender as before, but had also a new shade of melancholy — whether because he was excluded from the reunion or regretted it, Kitty was not sure. Hard on Mrs Smith's heels, Mr Cotton was doing an excellent imitation of the lunatic at Doctor Tuke's asylum, though without the restraining jacket, pushing through the crowds and running towards Mary Ann as if he would embrace her, but shearing away at the last moment to warmly shake her husband's hand. The Judge gazed at him, astonished.

'Sir William!' Mr Cotton announced, gesturing for Kitty to join their circle. 'This is our young friend Miss Tripp, who has kindly accompanied us to Buxton. We were on our way to Torquay to see you there, but you are here and not there, so all is well . . . yes, all is well . . .' But Mr Cotton could not continue his line of thought, being too intent upon the patient, who beckoned to him, smiling, and held out her hand for him to kiss. The Reverend kissed it, bobbing and cooing, and Mrs Smith drew a handkerchief from her sleeve, blinking moistly and blankly at Kitty as if she hardly recognised her.

Minutely, Kitty smiled at her, and gestured — should I go? It seemed suddenly that it should be the best thing, the kindest thing — though she had heard that in the New World there was a new order and perhaps these people subscribed to it. A Judge! Her father could not fail to be impressed if she made his acquaintance.

'Let us all go somewhere warm, where we may rest before a fire and talk!'

'I don't think so, Reverend Cotton.'

The speaker was an elderly gentleman who had come upon them unobserved, as quiet as a shadow. He had a gathered brow and determined set to his jaw, and under his long, heavy coat there was the high collar of a priest. The drab, thin woman arriving beside him was taller than he was, and had every symptom of a gastric disease, being sallow and of painful expression. Kitty's welcoming smile was not returned, though she could not help staring. Neither newcomer was as old as she'd first thought. The gentleman had something of the sailor about him — seasoned brown skin and eyes narrowed against the weather. He greeted the Martins fondly, but looked through the others as though they weren't there.

'Oh William!' the invalid said, clapping her hands together like a little girl. 'Could we go back to our suite?'

'But we have only just come from there,' said her husband, 'and you have not had your water.' He was pleading. 'Or your bath.'

'Augustus? Sarah? Please, my dearests? This is all so unexpected!' She said 'deawests' and Kitty contained a giggle. She even spoke like a child!

Almost as overcome as Mrs Smith, Bee Cotton wiped his eyes and nose on a grimy sleeve, gathered himself and emphatically hooked Kitty's arm. There was to be no resistance — he led the way through the open door into the brilliant, frosty day.

TWELVE

Reunion

ALL THE WAY ALONG the Crescent, Mary Ann held tight to my hand while the others made a parade behind us — and what a parade! The Bishop and the Judge, Sarah Selwyn, the bathchairman, Kitty and Bee. Mary Ann only let me go at the hotel — our hotel! — when we turned inside, and here we are, the seven of us having a party of sorts in the Martins' small private sitting room. The curtains are drawn against the cold morning; the room is as crowded with dusty furniture and objects as any London room, and as stuffy. A fire glows in the grate, and side by side we sit on the settee, Mary Ann resting her dear head on my shoulder.

'You will forgive me, Mata, for not writing to you with our plans — there was so much to attend to and I had so little time.'

Kitty, who has insisted on standing and so compels the men to remain upright also, hovers dangerously close to the fire in her wide skirts. She shoots me one of her quick, emphatic looks — *And I thought you were as close as mother and daughter!*

'I have not been so assiduous either, dear.'

Was there really only that handful of letters in the years since I left? I began many more. Too often the pen would fall idle in my hand — I had new acquaintances, and Mary Ann knew none of them. If I were to describe Mr Griggs's ladies, for example, with an eye to amuse my correspondent, it would be as it too often was in New Zealand when she was offended by acerbity or ribald humour — 'Oh, your lash, Elizabeth!' If I were to detail my various lodgings and associated tribulations, that would only cause her concern and also validation, because hadn't she warned me often enough against returning? I could only fill pages with sentimental recollections of our earlier lives, which I resisted.

The Bishop and Judge attending, Bee delivers a monologue on his misadventures in Frodsham, and unfortunately, also, his various torpors and manias. Now and again, the judicial eye catches the ecclesiastical, or vice versa, but they suffer him politely.

In our corner, Mary Ann tells me quietly of how it was at Taurarua before they left. She describes the sadness of leaving her many friends, the uncertainty brought by the Wars, how conflicted her feelings on departure. 'We are not all like you, Mata, able to make lightning decisions and then act on them!'

'But don't you remember — it took me years to leave?'

'You had not decided.' Mary Ann is matter of fact. 'You were thinking aloud, as is your wont.'

'Four years from the moment I had decided.'

'Once your sons gave you their blessing, and that took a time. Then you were gone with the wind.'

There is such sadness in her voice that I drop a kiss on the top of her head and breathe her in — still the Attar of Roses, the old faint grassy scent, and the minerals from yesterday's bath. Oh for a sip to nullify guilt and intensify the pleasure of our reunion — but Mary Ann and Sarah would not approve unless I complained first of a pain.

'Are you a New Zealander, Miss Tripp?' she asks, and few could help but smile at 'Twipp'. Kitty is too startled by the question.

'Good heavens, no!'

By her vehemence and high colour the Bishop is distracted from Mr Cotton's irksome tale. 'Why "Good heavens"? Would it be so terrible?'

For the first time in our acquaintance she is hesitant.

'Well . . . I am sure it would very interesting, but do people go there of their own volition or because they are made to?'

'New Zealand was never like that, Miss Tripp. You are confusing us with Australia,' says the Bishop.

'I do believe it will be an eternal confusion.' Sarah works on a piece of lace taken from her pocket. 'It will become part of our nation's character to be for ever distinguishing itself from the neighbour.'

'Your sermon was reported in the papers here, Augustus.' Bee is mirthful as if he is about to tell us an amusing story. 'The one you gave in Sydney on the treatment of the Australian Natives in the 'fifties. Do you remember?'

Augustus draws breath, as if he would cut him short, but Bee goes on in a fair imitation of the Bishop: '"One thing I am sure of, that if the wool which grows on their heads had grown on their backs, you would have found some way of improving their fate." It caused quite a stir in England!'

'I really do not think that is so very comical,' says the Judge sternly, but Augustus shakes his head at him.

'At the time I gave that sermon the nations were governed as one,' Selwyn tells Kitty gently, 'but they are very different. We were never a penal colony and nor did we treat our Natives so sorely. Or shall we say, not at the beginning.'

'And what now? Do you shoot at them for sport?' Kitty's tone has hardened and her cheeks are flushed.

Nobody answers, altho' we are all looking at her and perhaps admiring the beautiful fervency of eyes and mouth. Are her sisters darker, I wonder? When a woman has borne a man's children she is for ever curious about any others in existence, the side issues and secret progeny — their appearance and character. How will they resemble her own? What will there be to love and what to despise?

'We are at war,' Sarah says out of the silence, her attention still on her needle.

'A member of your family, Mrs Smith?' asks the Bishop, staring still at Kitty. 'You have not explained your connection. There is a resemblance—'

Kitty lifts her chin. 'You are imagining it!'

'— and also to Mr Smith.'

'Yes, yes,' agrees Bee, 'I think so too! Dear Henry. The same smile and laughing eyes.'

'What a secret to have kept from us!' exclaims Sarah. 'If I had a daughter half so charming I would not hide her light under a bushel.'

'Miss Tripp is not my daughter,' I announce firmly.

There is a silence then that lasts some time. The clock on the mantel ticks, there are voices carrying from downstairs, footsteps in the corridor. Mary Ann slips a cool, dry hand into mine and squeezes gently.

'"A man either says too little or too much",' she says. 'It was you who made that remark many years ago, Mr Cotton. Do you remember?' Bee nods and opens his mouth to speak, perhaps to extend the sentiment, but Mary Ann goes on: 'And wouldn't you say it is twice as true for a woman?'

'And are you in service too, like your mother was?' Sarah speaks over the top of her, the needle stabs and loops.

'Elizabeth is not my mother,' Kitty replies, and I wish she had not used my Christian name. How foolish we were not to have planned a story — but we were never once alone after the decision to come to Buxton. 'And I am an actress.'

'Good heavens. I would never have guessed.' Sarah laughs that same strained and scornful squawk that I heard often enough through the flimsy walls at Taurarua.

'In fact' — Kitty executes a vivid turn, her wide skirts sweeping coal dust from the fender — 'if you should desire some entertainment, you could accompany me to a small theatre this afternoon, where I will sing.'

'A small theatre?' repeats Bee, his slow smile spreading.

'How wonderful!' Mary Ann turns herself around to lay her legs flat along the sofa, and we arrange the cushions so that she may rest across my lap. 'How wonderful! And what is this theatre called, Miss Tripp?'

The Bishop is speaking in an undertone to the Judge, who nods and picks up his topper from where it is precariously balanced on top of an empty plant stand.

'The Shakespeare.'

'William?' asks Mary Ann. 'Can we go to the theatre?'

'Of course we can,' says William Cotton, but it is her startled husband she addresses.

'No, dearest. I don't think so,' he says quietly, while Augustus places a guiding hand at his back.

'We will leave you women to your own company,' announces the Bishop. 'Where shall we rendezvous, Mrs Selwyn? Downstairs, in an hour? If you are not there, we will find you here later.'

Why don't you take Sarah with you, I think, and it seems she has the same desire because she looks up once from her needlework, sharply, the kind of restraining look that passes too often between wife and husband — but he is set on a course as much as he ever was. He makes his swift farewells.

For a moment after their departure our little group is quiet. At long last Kitty sits, sighing, and Bee settles beside her. 'You women,' the Bishop had said, counting him among us. He does not seem at all perturbed, his hand straying to one of the tassels on Kitty's ornate skirts, which lies beside him. He tugs it familiarly.

'You were saying, my dear? About the small theatre?'

But Kitty only bites her lip and glares at the fire.

'Yes, Bee, absolutely!' I comfort him, for he grows anxious his treat will be snatched away. 'We will go together to Kitty's playhouse. It is too good an opportunity to miss.'

'Oh, it is not a proper theatre,' says Kitty, 'I shouldn't be misleading you — tho' it does have a stage — tho' more of a platform — and it does have curtains, tho' patched — and there are about a dozen chairs. It is attached to an hotel — not nearly so grand as this one, which is called the Shakes—'

'If we are to go to a play,' interrupts Sarah, deliberately, 'then for goodness sake make it worthwhile. There was a proper theatre, as I recall, the Old Hall? I came here for a cure the winter before I was married.'

'Hall Bank,' corrects Kitty. 'They closed it years ago and there's been nothing since, no real theatre. That was my first professional engagement — there have been so many since then!' She sighs, world-weary but alive to any chance of admiration. I remember that impulse in myself as a young woman — the hope that my conversants would be impressed by the depth of my experience but maintaining a pretence of being weary of it so as not to be thought swollen-headed or proud.

'No doubt,' says Sarah, after a certain pause, which lends extra venom.

'You will come, Mrs Smith?' asks unchastened Kitty, jutting her chin. 'You are bound to enjoy it.'

'Let's do, Elizabeth!' says Mary Ann.

'Will you do your Hindoo dance of the veils?' I ask. 'That I would like to see.'

'My costume is in London — but I'm sure I could improvise.'

'I think you should come, Mrs Selwyn, since Lady Martin is,' I risk, tho' Sarah has never once, ever, acted on any advice from me.

'I'm afraid I cannot—' begins Sarah, looking longingly towards the door so recently closed after her retreating husband. Many years ago she confided to Mary Ann — and me, since I was present, attending to some dreary labour, mending or dusting — that she was troubled by endless nightmares of vast terrains of mountainous, eternal forest and forbidding swamps, and passing through it all a vision of the back of her husband's determined head. No matter how she called out to him while she struggled behind, he would not turn around to face her. Sometimes he would be within reach, then as suddenly many miles ahead and she would wake in tears. The dreams plagued her most during her nights at Taurarua after days spent in the front room looking out for the Bishop's ship. Mary Ann and I wondered often if she regretted the solemn pledge that he had extracted from her at their marriage: that she would never stop him going wherever duty called him. She adhered to it, miserably.

'*Lady* Martin!' repeats Mary Ann wonderingly. 'Just listen! It shall never cease to amuse me!' And we laugh together, she and I, for it is delightful and not what we ever would have expected for her labours at the edge of the world.

'We must be ready for the Baths in an hour, dear,' Sarah says firmly. 'We will find William and Augustus there.'

'But we did not arrange that!' Mary Ann pleads, half-lifting from her cushions, a bony elbow digging into my leg. 'I would like to go with Elizabeth to the theatre.'

How quickly did they slip back to their old roles after the reunion,

I wonder? Still Mrs Selwyn, being more forceful, would try to give direction, and still Mary Ann could acquiesce for the sake of peace.

'Without William?' asks Sarah.

'Oh no, I will go. Most definitely,' says Bee.

'Not you — I did not mean you, Mr Cotton. I meant Sir William.'

'*Sir* William,' giggles Mary Ann again. 'It is still so funny to say it!'

'Not at all. It is his just reward,' says Sarah, envious, as if she wishes her own husband could be so civically honoured.

'Don't worry, dearest.' It is the refrain she murmurs most often to those who love her. 'I shall have Mrs Smith to take care of me.' She takes my arm and tucks it around herself as a child will — Mata's arm to warm her and keep her safe.

A maid appears with a tea tray, sent for so long ago as to be before Creation.

We sup and talk of all we knew in New Zealand, those past and those still living — there is the scandal of the Greys — poor, unhappy Lady Grey abandoned by the Governor in South America and still languishing there — the remembered kindness of Mr and Mrs Chapman and the tiresome volubility of our old neighbour Swainson. We talk of the Thatchers, the Browns, the Williamses and several other multiplying families, of Josiah and of Cook and other servants at Taurarua. Mary Ann touches even on Mokihi's gentle spirit and his work at the hospital, and my heart catches in my chest. We come to the kingmaker Tamihana and his tireless campaign, and of Chief Titokowaru and his desperate Taranaki Wars, still raging, and Bee listens intently, one hand bending his ear to catch her quiet words.

'We have come away from all that,' is Sarah's only contribution, 'may we thank the Lord. You have no idea of how tired we grew of it all, Mrs Smith. How the conversation would go around and around and find no solution because there is none.'

'Oh, but there is,' says Mary Ann. 'If there are strong men and clever, and they step carefully and slowly, everything will come right. It will. There are so many good men on both sides they can't fail — men with compassion and integrity and the desire to make peace.'

'My dear Mary Ann. Augustus estimates there are now around

ten thousand troops holding the Colony against the Maoris. Do you have faith in all of them?'

'Not at all. But there are men widely trusted by both sides. Your Henry is among them.' She turns her dear face to me, and how glad I am that we finally arrive at the one I want to hear about most. 'You have every reason to be proud of him.'

'I worry so — he must go between both sides and risk his life. He is away too much from Sophia and the children — and she such a bad manager, left alone with the Maoris at Maketu.'

These are the least of my worries. I could articulate others, but Henry has written to me so often with the same warning that I have memorised it: 'Do not allow your zeal for my good name to lead you into indiscretion.'

Sarah gives one of her snorts designed to warn the speaker against airing her dirty laundry. How familiar the sound is! I have almost missed it.

'Not all families must live cheek by jowl. It is sometimes better if they do not. In that country there is so much work to be done that to live apart is as much part of family life as to live together. At least, that is my observation. You should not rail against it so, Mrs Smith,' she says.

'It is a habit I got into there, to always be fearing the worst. Especially for Henry.'

'But you should see him when he sets out on his commissions, as I have very recently,' says Mary Ann. 'In spite of his poor knee and general' — she smiles a little — 'unkemptness, he cuts a military figure.'

'Ah!' said Bee. 'He gets that from his father.'

'Tho' he is as far from being soldier as you could imagine,' Mary Ann goes on, 'he often has the ear of the officers and warriors, and may ease a situation.'

'He did not succeed at Gate Pah,' snaps Sarah, 'and what carnage ensued there!'

'Henry had quite an opinion of his pater,' Bee recalls. 'I remember a tale at Taurarua of his exploits in India.'

Kitty, who has produced Doctor J. Collis Browne from her purse and is liberally dosing her cup, gives a little start, but goes on with her ministration. Intent as she is on presenting it as necessary medicine, she offers me none — but shoots me one of her potent glances. If I read it correctly, she finds the present company most peculiar and would enjoy it more at a narcotic remove.

'Oh yes —' Bee is keen for the thread to be taken up — 'Captain Smith was quite the hero. My father could not compete, being only the very dull Governor of the very dull Bank of England!'

'Henry never told me anything of him,' says Sarah, her needlework laid aside and a saucer balanced on her knee, 'and I was friend and adviser while he studied with my husband for the priesthood.'

Does she imply my son was lying, or phantasising? I could leap to his defence, but my feelings are conflicted. Excepting for the night at Manupirua with Tamihana, I never heard Henry speak of his father in company either. His imagination was a palliative, I see that now. But he had confided in Mr Cotton, at least to some degree.

'Not all of us have led blameless lives,' murmurs Mary Ann, so quietly I suspect I am the only one to hear it.

'I have never heard of a Captain Smith,' Kitty is saying archly, 'and Mrs Smith and I have talked our way all around the world.'

'Indeed?' says Sarah again, and I am surprised by a glimmer of sympathy in her glancing eye — the merest glimmer.

We are quiet for a moment, Mary Ann sipping her tea and Bee's remaining teeth loudly chewing his cake. A pretty china clock on the mantelpiece chimes the half hour and the fire crackles, and all of us are perhaps wondering at this long silence and why it has fallen so completely. When he has finished his cake, Bee gets up to add a lump of coal to the fire, eschewing the tongs and wiping his black hand on his trouser legs.

'I will go to my room to rest for a little while.' Sarah stows her needle, and stands. 'What time shall you leave for the theatre, Miss Tripp?'

'I should say in an hour, so that we may find bathchairs for both Lady Martin and Mrs Smith. Yes, dear friend,' she insists, 'a bathchair. There is no point in exhausting yourself.'

'Then I shall meet you downstairs in an hour.' Sarah gathers her coat and muff, which are very fine and new. There is a greenstone brooch pinned to the collar, a tiki larger and more splendid than mine, about which Kitty involves her in a discussion as to its origins and value — a gift from Chief Te Wherowhero which she had set in heavy gold by an Auckland jeweller, which in her opinion has far increased its worth.

'I have something to show you,' whispers Mary Ann, and Sarah breaks off her lengthy account to glare down at her.

'You must not whisper in company! I am surprised at you. It is the height of rudeness.'

Alarmed by her raised voice, Bee pulls from his pocket the lady author's novel I lent him in London and opens it at his place — he never could bear Sarah's moods. Sighing heavily, he begins to read, while Mary Ann struggles to sit up again, her elbow bruising the same part of my thigh through my layers of skirts — I wear the three that I possess, and four petticoats, for the very English cold. Still, I feel its point.

'Oh, sweet Sarah! Let us not quarrel. Here — give me your hand!' For a moment it seems as if she will draw Sarah down to sit with us, but instead she kisses the back of it, resoundingly.

'I am so looking forward to our outing, dearest. You will go and fix your hair — it has come loose on one side. If I had a maid I would lend her to you — unless, Miss Tripp, you have skills of that nature?'

Kitty, adrift now on chlorers and staring into the fire, hardly hears the question. Sarah lifts her hand to her silver spaniel ears and it's true, one has fallen, the pin and fine black ribbon awry. Does Mary Ann think she is my maid? She must believe me warmly looked after — how bleakly amusing!

'Miss Tripp?'

'Oh!' says Kitty, eventually. 'I have once or twice assisted Mrs Smith in that manner, but for love, not duty or obligation. You have made a mistake.' Her tone escalates. 'I have never been a servant to anyone and do not intend to start now!'

'For pity's sake!' snaps Sarah. 'I have my maid. She came with me from Lichfield.' She withdraws her hand and looks closely at Mary Ann. 'Do you mean to tell me William is caring for you alone? No wonder he is so pale and thin. It is too much for him. He is much too delicate.'

'There are plenty of people to help me,' soothes Mary Ann. 'The hotel staff are most solicitous. You need not worry. And Elizabeth is here now, aren't you?'

'And she destined for a bathchair the same as you are!' Sarah presses upon her eyeballs, as tho' they ache.

'Poor Mrs Selwyn!' Kitty rises, a little unsteadily. However will she tread the boards? Perhaps, as long as the narcotic is past its first flush, she is the better for it. With a glass of port inside him and a cigar in his hand, her father sang soaring and true.

Kitty escorts Sarah to the door. 'I will see you to your room and then go for my bath.'

'In an hour — downstairs,' repeats Sarah, and she's gone on Kitty's arm.

'Dear, dear, dear,' says Bee. He glances up nervously from his book.

'Will you help me through to the bedroom, Elizabeth?' asks Mary Ann, still with that slight conspiratorial tone.

Limbs stiffened, the halt leading the lame, we make our way to Mary Ann's trunk, which stands against the wall under the window. It was a long-ago gift from the Bishop, an ingenious walnut case that when opened and stood on one end becomes a small wardrobe and chest. Mary Ann slips open a narrow drawer and lifts out a letter.

'If you like, you can wait and read it later. You see, it was addressed to me.'

The paper is of the fine blue tablets widely used in the Colony, and the script is uneven, unfamiliar, with the date at the top twenty-four years past and another date — two years later — in Mary Ann's hand.

'I found it when we were packing to leave and it has weighed heavily on my conscience ever since. I had forgotten about it, you see.'

Below the date, in that other hand, it says, 'My dearest Bess.'

'I would not make the same decision today — to keep it from you. I was young and jealous and would not have willingly given you up.'

203

There are tears in her eyes, whether with remembered sentiment or new remorse it is difficult to tell. 'You see, I put the date I received it here.' Her fingertip brushes the figure. 'It was the day Henry left to go to Waiheke Island with Mr Jowitt, the time he had his accident and damaged his knee.'

I remember that day only too well.

'I vowed that I would give it to you a year hence,' whispers Mary Ann, 'but the year came around and the year after that — too many went by for it to be possible.'

There is a loud thumping in my head suddenly, as if all my blood is gathering there. I feel my cheeks flush and my lips grow cold and ugly. I bite on them and Mary Ann looks away.

'I decided that I — I thought that if . . .' She stops and swallows. 'I assuaged my conscience by keeping it close to hand, and vowing that if I met up with you I would give it to you.'

'If?'

'I wasn't sure if . . .' She seems stricken, as if she is only now coming to understand her reasoning. 'I knew it would be difficult for us to be as close here as we were in that other country.'

She is not being honest, not entirely. She would have worried more that I might become a burden to her and William, that we would regain our mutual need, that I would rely on her again for my living. I don't blame her for that — but this? I turn the letter over in my hand.

THIRTEEN

The Shipburner

Port Jackson, 1842

SHE WAS HERE with two boys, walking around the town and asking for him by name. One boy was hers and the other a Maori, though she looked out for both of them, going so far as to intervene in a stoush between a baker's lads and the New Zealander, who was apparently quick to put up his fists. The English boy, a fine, tall lad of about sixteen, came readily to defend his mate wrongly accused of stealing, and there was a scuffle before Elizabeth appeared and threw flour over them, as she had seen at dog fights on the dock as a girl. She had the Maori turn out his pockets and prove them empty of the suspected bun or scone, then marched them away from the baker and the gathering crowd, back towards Darlinghurst.

Her employer was a guest of Bishop Broughton's at 'Tusculum', and Horelock went there that evening to stand outside. Had it been quiet he might have knocked at the kitchen door, but there was a gathering in that tall limestone house of all the Sydney grandees and he had no business among them.

While he waited some distance beyond the gate — where there were tethered some very fine horses — he watched the last of the guests to arrive on the peninsula, a flogger and a locksmith along the beach together. They passed among a group of New Zealanders, dressed up as English boatmen in white suits and straw hats, gathered around a table in the garden. Some of the ladies among them had gowns as fine as those worn by the English ladies inside, and there was much laughter and excitement. When first he heard a woman laughing on and on, louder than the rest, he thought it was one of the Natives, but the sound came from the house. Then the laughter turned to weeping and wailing, and shortly after a servant rode out for the doctor, whom he recognised when he arrived. It was not the crow who came willingly among the convicts, but the one who put himself above them. For all his clean hands and yellow wig he was a convicted murderer, but clever and favoured by the nobs. Not long after he'd hurried inside with his bag, another servant came out and moved Horelock along.

He picked himself up and went around to the beach side of the house, as if he were to make his way back down to the town, but doubled back and went around to the back, to the kitchen garden. It had a low limestone wall in case the cabbages had a mind to hook it away to freedom. How the rich love walls of all kinds, even for their vegetables!

It was easily breached, and he found himself under a mulberry tree laden with red fruit, much of which had fallen and lay splattered on the flag path — which put him in mind of a man's back flayed after a flogging, and he'd seen a few. What punishment lay in store if he was caught? If only he had fine dunnage of his own, then he would climb the front steps; he would come upon Bess in attendance to her lady and keeping company with her betters as much as he could have been. He could have told her, 'I am one of the lucky Australians — see how I have prospered!'

But shipburners are not easily trusted in a land where ships are valued above all else, and sailing was all he was good for. Ships came and went from the distant north and the near south, bringing the hopeful and the desolate, kauri spars, whale oil and fur-seal pelts. Something of his crime still hung around him and no captain would take him on, though few were old enough to remember it. He was old himself now — a man in his sixties was elderly here — too old to find work at sea.

At the approach of a maid carrying a basket of potatoes up the cellar steps, blinking as she emerged into the late afternoon light, he hid, bruising himself against a water butt that stood close against an outhouse. By its smell of sour milk and yellow cheese it was the dairy.

His luck held in this instance at least. She did not see him, but went on, lugging the basket into the cookhouse, which stood at the far end of the courtyard. The facing wall was windowless, but through the open door he could see servants moving about, hear the cook barking and the whining tones of a young maid. There were kale and lettuce beds, and beyond them a boy burning rubbish who was ragged enough to be almost naked — his own attire was more complete. Bishop Broughton kept so many servants that Horelock thought he could perhaps slip in among them and make his way inside. The smoke from the fire lifted in a clean column into the still evening air and the dirt under his shoeless feet held the heat of the day.

An older convict woman he knew from the port hurried out with a pale of steaming hot water heavy on her scrawny arm. The bucket slopped a little as the old coin-faker — Lady Broughton's maid — carried it through a door and disappeared up the back stairs. A length of time passed while he considered the possibilities and ate plums from a crooked tree that rested its boughs on the dairy roof. The summer had been dry and hot and the fruit had thick, bitter skin his old teeth could barely penetrate, but the flesh inside was sweet and sticky, coating his tongue. He swallowed the skins too, to fill his skinny gut — he knew he'd regret it later.

Had Bess grown bitter? She had every reason to — though her life was no better or worse than the lives of countless other women. And men. Why should it only be women who crave love? At least we knew love, Bessie, he thought, you and I, such as the poets understand it. He'd heard she'd married again, swiftly as she would have had to. The child died soon after. What of the other one she had only just begun to carry? Did it survive? A girl perhaps — called Katie after her sister. Or a son she left behind in England, a son who had not prospered enough to care for his mother? What sort of a man was he?

An upstairs window opened and the crow came to stand in the light, examining a brass contraption he held in his hands, expelling a clear liquid from it that arched and spattered onto the dry dirt of the garden. Satisfied with its mechanics, he turned back into the room.

Horelock decided he would wait until Lady Broughton's maid reappeared and then he'd ask her to bring his wife to the garden. If the old bird began to squawk, he'd be over the wall and under the cliffs before anyone could lay hands on him.

A young man dressed plainly but well came through the door that had latterly swallowed the maid. He wore his collar backwards in that new way young priests had — which at least gave advance warning of their puritanical tedium. The woman behind him gave him a kind of playful push, hard enough for him almost to lose his step. There was an air of high spirits which he sensed before he recognised her.

She walked right past him to sit on the bench opposite the dairy. He had a perfect view of her, eclipsed now and then by her friend as he paced between them among the cabbages. She would be by now almost forty — he couldn't believe he had ever possessed her. Square-rigged in black widow's satin, she wore her thick hair piled on top of her head in a London style he hadn't seen before and, now that he did, didn't much like, though his opinion wasn't strong either way. He wanted to remember her on the scow, on the river and open sea, with that hair flying loose around that playful, loving smile, her skirts wrapping tight against her slender, strong thighs. There was a version of it now, while she soothed and placated the nancy priest. What her actual words were, he couldn't discern — there had been too many beatings around the head that had left him deaf — but he remembered how he'd loved that mouth that formed now around her gentle words, how he'd needed that caressing hand, how he'd kissed the heavy lids of her eyes.

There was another woman's voice coming from the room above, the room that held the crow. It sounded to Horelock as if she was calling the same word over and over again, until he realised it was no word at all but a cry of pleasure such as women give when a man takes some trouble. He shook his head: were the rich so soft and debased they got the medical men to do their tickling? She had a good set of pipes on her, the patient — fluting and mounting cries that at last fell suddenly silent. Through it all he watched Elizabeth and saw the flush come into her cheeks and brow, and it was as much as he could do to stop himself running out from his hiding place and taking her in his arms. But she belonged to someone else now; she mourned him in that black dress, that silver mourning brooch that would likely contain hair from that other man's head. There was the other man in her too: she had grown more like her father — the same strong nose, which she had always hated. The father's face hung before him for a moment, as clearly as if he had last beheld it yesterday. His inadvertent nemesis — it was he who had knocked the oil lamp flying, not Horelock; it was the father who had barred the door to prevent his escape; it was the father who was overcome by smoke and did not escape through the burning timbers as Horelock did. On the hulks and all through the interminable voyage he thought of nothing else but the father and the daughter, nothing else, until he had to think only of survival.

When they stood to go inside, he saw how her body had thickened — she had worked hard, he could see the labour in her, how it had kept her strong. There was her light firm step, her high proud head and guiding arm, which she gave to the poor eunuch, who seemed overcome. Horelock envied him his keen ears — he'd heard only half the song. As they passed by his hiding place, she was almost close enough to touch. If she'd turned that fine head even a few degrees to her right, she would have seen him — but she was too intent upon the choker, all motherly with him, telling him he needed to rest, to eat more, not to fret so. He heard an older reserve in her voice, how she'd polished her childhood vowels, instated consonants, how she'd elevated herself.

'You go and join the party, Bee. I must go and check on Mary Ann.'

But hadn't she always been an adventurer with an eye for getting on in the world? He had been her first prize, a man who would have had his own living if his employer had died in any other way. He should not be surprised that she had bettered herself. He was further away from her than ever.

He waited for a moment after their footfalls passed out of hearing before he got away, back over the wall and down to the beach, a plan forming. He had seen her; she was warm and solid. She was not the thin, beseeching young wife who had rowed herself out to the hulks one icy night, coming close to the broken ship that held him in chains, and calling out for him to show himself. She was no longer the sweet, spirited child who had put herself in his way and had him fall in love with her as soon as possible. He had seen her as she was now — middle-aged and giving herself graces. He had seen her prosperous and warm and widowed.

It was coming on dusk and the light was playing tricks — what he'd thought was a shadow cast on the sand by an old gum separated and took the shape of two approaching boys, one English and the other a New Zealander, sauntering along as if they owned themselves and their destinies. There was a fishing boat pulled up on the beach behind them, with nets spread around it to dry, and beyond that two women ankle-deep in the water, cleaning knives they'd used for scaling and gutting. Smoke lifted from cooking fires in the cove where the Aborigines had their camp — he and the boys were the only people on this curl of Woolloomooloo.

He hailed them. 'Would you be the boys who sailed in on *Tomatin*?'

'Is it any of your business?' asked Elizabeth's son. They were in shirtsleeves for the warm autumn night, and the Maori had taken off his boots, wearing them slung around his neck.

'She's a lovely ship and it's a shame she's scragged,' said Horelock softly.

'True enough,' nodded the Maori lad, who smiled at him so disarmingly it destroyed his reserve.

His agitated mind threw up a single question.

'Who is your father?'

'We have different fathers,' pronounced the Maori boy, 'as you would expect.'

This seemed to tickle both of them. They laughed and pushed each other around, moving away along the beach. He went after them.

'Quieten down now,' he said, and waited until they did.

'Are you a Scotsman?' asked the English lad. 'D'you hear, George, how he sounds like Alec?'

'And who is he?' asked Horelock.

'A sailor who drowned on our way in to Sydney. Are you a convict?'

Horelock stood upright. 'I am a free man.'

'Do you live up there with them?' The Maori pointed towards the humpies. Elizabeth's son laughed in the same vein as he had before, but his friend did not join him. He was looking at Horelock in a way that could have been insolent.

Horelock ignored him.

'What's your name?' he asked the English boy.

'George Rupai,' came his answer, 'and this is John Elisha Smith.'

Further hilarity, though a little subdued. Horelock waited. Smith? He had credited her with more of an imagination.

'How old are you, lad?'

'I have just turned sixteen. At sea!'

'Do you have a brother, older? Or a sister?'

A thoughtful expression replaced what had been a gaby's grin, and the boy regarded him steadily though not suspiciously. He had the same direct, guileless gaze that his mother had at that age. The long face, which lent a doleful aspect despite his joviality, must come from the father.

'Yes I do. Thomas Henry — he is already in New Zealand. And I did have a sister but she died before I could know her. Before I was born,' he added. 'Henry doesn't remember her either and our mother never mentions her. She is a sort of secret.'

Perhaps if his friend had not been there he would not have run on so, Horelock thought. The boy was showing off.

'All families have secrets. Wouldn't you agree, John Smith?' he asked the Maori boy, indulging their game.

The boy shrugged, his face shadowy.

'How fast it grows dark here!' said Elizabeth's son. Was he her last-born? Had she been a widow since then, careful with herself?

'You have sailed a long way,' said Horelock lightly, 'for one so young.'

'I am sixteen!' He was indignant. 'Before we left England I was articled to a solicitor, and Mother says I will be articled again as soon as we find one in our new country.'

'A lawyer!' He was impressed and a little appalled. 'What of your brother? Is he a sailor?'

'Of course not! Why would he be? He is an improver with the New Zealand Company. We went to school and did better than our father, or at least Mother says so.'

George tugged on his friend's arm, eager to be away.

Our father?

'Your mother had her letters. She could read and write,' said Horelock. She had gone to the parish school; she had a grandmother who had been a governess.

'Do you know my mother?' asked the boy.

Horelock said quickly, 'I'm thinking that she would have, since she deemed you should have yours.'

'Come on, Ish,' said the other lad, 'let's go back for our supper.'

For a moment, in his inquisitorial gaze, Horelock saw the young lawyer, just a flash of it, before the boy took off after his friend who had left before him. He returned to his falling hovel, where his loveless woman was waiting, and asked if there was ink and paper to be had. She borrowed some from a neighbour and knew by his mood to leave him alone. There was work to be done, a rough copy to be laboured over, and once it was as good as he could make it, to be taken to a mate who could spell.

FOURTEEN

Mary Ann

Taurarua, 1844

It was hard to think of a place to hide the letter. Elizabeth could so easily find it, having ready access to all of her belongings. In Archdeacon Brown's library at Te Papa she had seen a hidey-hole roomy enough to conceal three or four people. Mary Ann wished for one rather smaller at Taurarua, but the floorboards in her room were solid — none squeaked underfoot. She swept aside the pink calico frilling of the packing-case chest and opened a drawer — stockings and chemises — then closed it again. Nor were the books at her bedside safe — Elizabeth could well take one up and begin to read it aloud, which she did very nicely for one so rudimentarily schooled. The quality endeared her to the children at the new Infant School, but Mary Ann preferred to read quietly to herself like Saint Augustine and often suggested another activity as soon as Elizabeth searched for the place. Even so, Elizabeth could find the letter during the night, if Mary Ann was sleepless and called her to sit with her. She could pick up whatever book came to hand to pass the time.

Her companion must never come upon them, the soiled and crumpled pages William had brought back from town with the rest of the mail, having called into the ship's office after his court session. She was glad he had handed the letter to her in haste, being on his way to his library to finish his day's work. If her husband had encouraged her to read it immediately and share it with him, then he may have decided on a course of action that did not concur with hers, which was to conceal it and wait until a course suggested itself. The letter was dated April 1842, the same month they'd spent in Sydney. Where had it lain for two years? Mary Ann dipped her pen and added the date of receipt above that — 14 May 1844 — so that should she decide to give it to Elizabeth, her friend should understand the length of its concealment and not blame her for it.

Lord Byron. Why hadn't she thought of that before? Where Mary Ann prized him, Elizabeth detested him. Mary Ann had always thought it should be the other way around — Elizabeth being more of Byron's cynical and worldly persuasion than she was, if she would but own to it. The book fell upon at a canto of 'Don Juan'.

> *Man's love is of man's life a thing apart,*
> *Tis a woman's whole existence.*

As she recalled, it was that sentiment that enraged Elizabeth more than any other. She closed and opened the book again and this time her eye fell upon —

> *One of the valorous 'Smiths' whom we shall miss*
> *Out of these nineteen who late rhymed to 'pith'*
> *But tis a name so spread o'er 'Sir' and 'Madam',*
> *That one would think the first who bore it 'Adam' . . .*

Given the circumstances, Mary Ann thought that apt. The letter made no mention of 'Smith'.

She went out of her room and along the corridor to the porch, where Elizabeth wielded the teapot. The Maori gunsmith William Jowitt sat on the bench under the window, his long legs stretched before him. Beside him sat young Henry, newly released from the New Zealand Company in Port Nicholson. He had fallen into Mr Jowitt's thrall and would leave this afternoon for a protracted visit to his pah.

That was another reason she hoped the Judge would stay in his library — he was of the opinion that Henry should stay in Auckland in case he was needed at the Barracks. She could not bear it when they quarrelled: lines were drawn not only between the Judge and their young guest but also between Mrs Smith and herself out of loyalty to the men, and it was very difficult.

'Where have you been, Mrs Martin?' asked Elizabeth jovially, pouring her a cup.

The men stood to greet her, and Mary Ann hoped that none of her discomfort showed on her face. Deception did not come easily to her — but surely it was the kindest thing. If this man, who had signed himself only 'Nick', and in a different hand from that which had written the body of the letter, had truly been stranded in the Colonies since 1824, then there was doubtless a good reason for it.

On the beach below, a little of the westerly that tipped over the sheltering hill blew about the clothes of the Natives and filled the red blanket sail of the three waka being made ready for the voyage. Fronds on the thatched roof of the hospital lifted and fell with the gusts, and the two fires alight on the beach billowed smoke across the water towards Rangitoto. The volcano's bush-clad flanks showed scudding shadows of swift, shifting clouds. The beauty of the place was unearthly, unsettling.

She took the chair next to Elizabeth, who was seated opposite her son in order to gaze at him most fully. This was their stirrup cup before he departed. Did all mothers love their sons so? Elizabeth was always animated in Henry's company, laughing indecorously now at Mr Jowitt's gentle impersonation of the Bishop in the saddle. He conveyed all of Augustus's ineptitude in the smallest of gestures — an expression in the eyes and a wrinkling of his brow, a slight rise from his seat. Mary Ann pressed her lips together — really he should not! — but it was amusing.

The men ate and drank and ran on with their plans. There was to be a stop first at the coastal settlement of Orere, where there was to be a large gathering of Maoris, and then on to Waiheke Island and Mr Jowitt's pah. She saw how excited Henry was at the prospect of two whole weeks among the people, all the going about and talking, the work and laughter among likely new friends. The prospect of horse racing along the beach had him fairly whooping and jumping. He had a remarkably open cast of face, his bright eyes and clear complexion showing all of his mother's constitution and so little of his brother's. At first she had thought the boys alike, John having exhibited some of Henry's exuberance during the voyage out. But landfall had shaken the younger brother and made him sombre, mostly because he had quite fallen in love with little George Rupai and never recovered from the boy's immediate disappearance. At least that was her own opinion, and she was as an aunt to him — that is, until Elizabeth sent John away to Wellington and he disappeared almost as surely as his shipmate had done. Now she was aunt to the older son, and with greater devotion than her husband was uncle, which was unfortunate and difficult to balance harmoniously with other affections.

William emerged from the door into the light, squinting a little and tugging at the bottom of his slim waistcoat. He looked pale and worried, just as he had when he had handed her the letter. She wished he didn't shoulder his burden so heavily. Did any friend in England really understand what it was to be Chief Justice in this lawless place?

'Will you have a cup, Mr Martin?' asked Elizabeth, but he declined with a shake of his head as infinitesimal as Mr Jowitt's imitation of the Bishop had been.

'So I see you have decided to go.' He nodded at Henry's haversack and blanket roll that leaned against the wall. 'Even after you have been to the blockhouse and sworn to serve the Queen, you have made this decision?'

He had that sharp, nasal tone that so alarmed her; Mary Ann shifted uneasily in her chair, suppressing the urge to run to him. What had happened today at the court? His conscience was so often troubled enough to make him ill.

Elizabeth let her cup clatter in the saucer and took a breath as if she would speak up, but Mr Jowitt was asking softly, 'What discussion was this, Henry?'

'Mr Martin was reminding me that we are in a state of emergency,' said Henry, with no lessening of his excitement or sign of apprehension at the Judge's irritation — Mary Ann wondered at it. 'He impressed upon me that it was only weeks ago that Hone Heke cut down the flagpole and that I should not once again jewed out —'

'I did not use that expression!'

'— of going to drill by a request from a friend for my company.'

'Nothing will happen now,' said Mr Jowitt, 'not in the time Henry is away. Mr Heke has gone quiet.'

'For how long?' asked William. 'How do you know?'

'Hei aha,' said Mr Jowitt. 'Do not worry.'

Henry was leaving the table and opening his haversack to take out two notebooks, both of them bulging and misshapen with interleaved pages.

'This one is for the songs and this one is the dictionary. I will be collecting for you — I won't be idle, Mr Martin.'

The Judge suppressed a smile — he was beginning to be caught up in Henry's enthusiasm, though Mary Ann fancied she was the only one to see it. There was a flash of him as he was when they first married, when he was weighed down only by his father's expectations — and he had always felt those too keenly. Henry was fortunate. Not having had a father he could remember, he was never put in that way of thinking of demands and limitations. He would go with his friend and have his adventure with an open heart. Look at poor William Cotton, driven to despair with every arriving patrimonial letter. He was further proof to her theory, if she needed it.

'No, I don't imagine you will be idle,' her husband was saying softly. 'It's not in your nature to be so.'

Beside her, Elizabeth sighed. The crisis was over. Henry regained his seat beside Mr Jowitt, and the Judge was smiling that dear, beloved smile. If only he would more often look at her like that, instead of with his usual painful concern. This last long illness of hers had put them further apart than ever but had increased his brotherly tenderness. How very, very brotherly he was! She wished again that she could go to him and that he would put his arms around her and hold her close, but they were in company, and even if they were not, he would not. It was not in his nature to be so ...

To be so what? He was not cold to her, not exactly. She had no way to describe it, except as an absence even when he was in residence and not travelling the length and breadth of the Colony. She could not imagine him ever writing to her in the way the illiterate man wrote to Elizabeth from Port Jackson, as if his life depended on her.

A Maori woman was making her way up from the beach along the track and passing swiftly through the trees at the edge of the gully. Mr Jowitt waved to her, and she called out to him, 'Wiremu Hoete! Kia tere mai!' Instead of approaching the house, she stopped a distance off and stood with her hands on her hips. Without her spectacles Mary Ann could not recognise her, but the woman appeared to know the rule: no admittance to the house without European clothes. She wore a hybrid of a man's blue smock and a grass skirt, with the addition of a bright Indian shawl as overskirt. It was a kind of fashion among Maori women. The Judge maintained his post as if he would block her way, which he surely would not do if he thought about it. He was so often uncomfortable in himself.

'Come and join us, dearest,' she said quietly, but Henry was speaking too, in an undertone.

'Mother,' said Henry, 'if I am not very much mistaken, that is my blue shirt. I searched for it this morning.'

'Mrs Jowitt needed it,' said Elizabeth shortly, as if that were reason enough to give it away.

Mr Jowitt got up and went down the stairs to offer the woman his hand, and Mary Ann saw that Elizabeth was right. She was Mr Jowitt's wife, Sarah. Even now she sometimes found it difficult to tell their Maori friends apart, which made her ashamed of herself. She had thought at first that she was Ruth, Mr Tamihana's wife, whom she did in part resemble, though Ruth was taller and more queenly. Sarah was softer, more given to smiles and was perhaps from a lower class, though the distinctions were puzzling to an English mind. Today she wore an earring of carved white bone that flashed against her dark hair.

Mary Ann got up and held out her hands to her, and their friends came up to the porch then. Sarah clasped Mata's hand in passing, coming close to Mary Ann and pressing her nose gently against hers.

'You are up and about, Mrs Martin? It is good to see it.'

'I am, thank you, Mrs Jowitt.'

'Soon there will be children here,' she announced as if it was an imminent fact, and loudly enough for William to hear. 'It is sad for you to be alone here with only sick people and old people and no babies, while your husband goes all day to decide who shall live and who shall die.'

William's face was scarlet with embarrassment — and yes, when Mary Ann met his eye, anger. It seemed the truth of their marriage was laid bare among them all.

'Goodbye, Mamma!' Henry leaped to his feet and kissed his mother again, and then also, resoundingly, Mary Ann. She felt his young lips press against her cheek and breathed in his fresh healthy scent, the yellow soap he would have washed with this morning, and then he and the Jowitts were leaving — and William, too, was turning back inside.

'Are you strong enough to come down to the beach to see them off?' asked Elizabeth. 'And then you might look in at the hospital.'

Mary Ann shook her head, but her companion was hauling her to her feet as if she were a recalcitrant child.

'Please do not, Mrs Smith.'

'It will do you good. There is no benefit to be had in sitting about feeling sorry for oneself. Forget what Mrs Jowitt said. She cannot understand how it is for you.'

How it is for me, thought Mary Ann. Elizabeth knew too much.

'I am not feeling sorry for myself!'

'You have had such a long face ever since you joined us.'

'I was on my way to the dispensary to make up some rosemary and treacle tea for the influenza patients.' It was not a lie — she had thought to do that earlier, before the letter banished the impulse.

'With ipecacuanha?' asked Elizabeth, since they had argued about this before.

'A *soupçon* — you are far too heavy-handed with it.' Elizabeth still had not let go of her arm.

On the beach, Mr Jowitt's people were bowing their heads to pray for a safe voyage.

'Will that be a Christian prayer, do you think?' asked Mary Ann, 'or one to their sea god?' She should fetch the letter now and give it to Elizabeth. She should seize the opportunity while they were alone.

'Come along, Mary Ann.'

Her companion would not let her sink back into her chair. The distance from the house to the shore was too great to contemplate. She lifted her skirt a little so that Elizabeth could see that she wore her embroidered velvet slippers.

'Shall I fetch your boots?' asked Elizabeth.

'If you like. But you know I trust you with the work. There is no need for me to know every patient.'

Elizabeth was hurrying away and Mary Ann could not help noticing that her friend's feet were once again shoeless. The soles lifting and flattening against the porch boards were thick-skinned and discoloured and made her think for a moment of the pads of a cat.

The boots were not with the others in the cupboard at the end of the hall. There were the Judge's boots, thrown in any old how and filthy from the town streets. There were his leather gaiters on a hook, and paired beneath them her own boots, carefully preserved for the next time there was need. She remembered then she had cleaned and polished Mary Ann's at the same time as her own two days ago, and taken them down to her employer's bedroom. Mrs Martin must have worn her slippers all day yesterday.

Quickly and silently she passed by the library door, which was ajar, holding her skirts away from her legs so that the Judge would hear neither footfall nor rustle and so call out for a message to be taken to his wife or to the kitchen for hot tea. Beyond it, Mary Ann's door stood wide open — it had a habit of swinging out even if it was latched — and the boots stood side by side near the slipper chair.

Oh, but there was work to do in here too — dust lay on the dressing table, the primping glass was fuzzed with it. The hairbrush was grubby, there was a pile of forgotten linen for the laundry woman who'd come yesterday and would not again for another week, there was another of close mending, and the bed had been roughly made by Mary Ann herself after her late rising. Elizabeth sank down on it for a moment, the boots in her hand.

If she didn't hurry, she would miss waving Henry off on his adventure, which would gladden her heart more than sitting in here contemplating future labours.

Mary Ann had been reading Byron again — the book had been slid in among the others on the deal shelf but not evenly aligned. She pushed it in properly and left the room wondering why Mary Ann persisted with him when she knew the damage he had done to John Elisha. Profligacy and fornication were so much the poet's persuasive ideals that everyone else could only be made dissatisfied with their dull lots. At sixteen Ish could quote deliriously from 'Don Juan':

> *A long, long kiss, a kiss of youth, and love,*
> *And beauty, all concentrating like rays*
> *Into one focus, kindled from above;*
> *Such kisses as belong to early days . . .*

The midnight of the mind which assailed Ish in letter after letter could be blamed in part on that early reading. A Wellington solicitor could not hope to live so sensual a life.

Mary Ann was gone from the porch, and Henry and Mr Jowitt were already taking their places in the centre of the waka, which was being pushed out from the shore. Slipping and sliding, waving her shawl and calling, 'Bon voyage, Henry! Haere rā!' Elizabeth tore down to the beach through the fern, taking the steeper, shorter path with the sharp decline just above the hospital. Gaining the beach with speed, she only just missed the rising midden of cockle and pipi shells, fish bones and broken glass, but caught her foot on a length of driftwood, a timber from a shipwreck that had lain there for months. Skirts flung up, she landed face down in the sand.

It was Mokihi who helped her up, the newcomer with the infected eye. His friend was there too, a man half his size with a crippled leg, who peered at her with concern as she, hot with embarrassment, was righted.

'Kei te pai?' Mokihi asked, his face sombre. She met his one good eye and nodded, seeing the kindness there, the warmth and dignity, and thought how easy it would be to respect this man. He was nobler than either of the lords of Iniquity Bay — she could not imagine him ever censorious or dismissive. He seemed to see how much she liked him, for his smile spread and his eyes lit up, and it was as if he was about to embrace her, which he must not! Gently, tenderly, he was turning her to see that the waka was heading out to sea. Her son was disappearing, the paddlers around him beginning their song, the chant ringing out in the autumn afternoon.

It was unseasonably warm but even so a little chill ran through her, a species of foreboding that had often assailed her in this place where there were daily departures and arrivals and sudden, disarming affections. It was not that her sons would never be returned to her — she would not allow herself to approach that — but that they would be hurt, irreparably damaged by some unforeseen danger, and suffer years of agonies. They were still so young and perfect. Lucky Henry — she envied him his adventure.

Mokihi was taking her hand and leading her down to stand in the shallows with the other people, then further out to their knees, where she would go no further. He kept hold, and she did too of his big, willing hand. She waved her blue shawl, scattering fine sand over both their heads.

'Goodbye Henry! Keep safe!'

But he was too far away to hear her.

It was the letter that had given Mary Ann the idea, though it should not have, because she had read of love from far more skilful pens — but it had gone very well, considering. She had kissed William on the back of his neck, just above his collar, and now, as she regained her seat on the porch, she felt quite breathless. On the beach below, a group of Natives was gathered in the shallows while Mr Jowitt's waka plied its way across the bay — Henry's fair head gleamed among the rest. The boatsong had begun already, rhythmic and carrying faintly, blown away by the westerly.

Dear William. It was not as though she had not tried before.

How had it happened this time? She was always at a loss to regain that place where the longing came from. If she knew how to approach the instinct rationally, she could perhaps learn to control herself. She retraced her steps. After Elizabeth had gone to fetch the boots, she had gone to the dispensary. No sooner had she spooned the herb into the teapot than she had heard her companion hurrying heavily down the passage and across the porch, breaking into a run and calling after Henry — and she realised that unless one of the girls came out from the kitchen, she and William were alone in the house, which was rare. It was suddenly of the greatest urgency to go to him.

William did not turn around, though he would have heard her come in. She waited for a moment, looking everywhere but directly at him. Light flooded from the high arched window over his desk, angled so that he would not cast a shadow over his papers. She lifted her gaze above his bent head. Tussock and scrub rolled away towards the small volcano called Mount Eden or Maungawhau, behind which rain clouds were gathering — another sou-westerly. They were one of the most tiresome things about living here. Mr Jowitt and Henry would get a soaking.

The silver threads in William's dark hair glittered, the pen in his hand dipped and wrote steadily on. There had been talk of installing a lady's desk on the other side of the window as companion to the Judge's grander one, but that had not eventuated — and Lord knew she needed one. First there was all the work associated with the Native Hospital and the Infant School. Then there was the stream of women from the town who required her advice and assistance. There was correspondence with treasured benefactors in England, with traders in the town, and willing ears in the Colonial Office and the Church . . . but it was as well she did not have one, for if she had, she might have been compelled to go to sit at it, rather than go to stand behind her husband.

At the touch of her lips he had turned suddenly, knocking a file of papers to the floor, and taking her hands in his to lift them to his mouth. Yes, she was sure, there was not the usual immediate recoil

— this time it seemed more willed than instinctive; he had had to struggle for it, lowering his eyes almost as soon as she met them — like a damsel, modest and true, thought Mary Ann, wondering at the incongruity while her cheeks burned. This was how it always ended.

'I must get on, dearest.' He turned away, gathering up the papers, gesturing to a pile fully a foot high. 'You see . . .'

She did see. She saw more than he thought, and it was what occupied her now, on the porch. If he had married a woman in good health, not one perpetually ill, would he have been any different? He was only thirty-seven, which was not so very old, and she was twenty-six. They had been married for only three years, there was still time.

'All these years I have longed for you,' she whispered now, with no one to hear her but the wheeling gulls. That was what he had written, the man in Port Jackson: 'All these years I have longed for you, my sweet Bess' — a diminutive her companion never used.

Look at her now, barefoot on the sand, her dress wet, clasping the hand of the new patient and talking intently with him, lifting away the bandage to look at his eye.

'I knew you as soon as I saw you,' he'd written, or dictated — but people change so much through hardship and illness. Mary Ann could hope it was a mistake, that it was another Bess the convict had lost.

'I met your son on the beach. He gave me news of his brother, which interested me greatly. I would like to write to him, but I do not know which name he goes by. If you are kind enough to respond you could tell me it and I would write to him as an old friend of his mother's.' So the letter ran, or in words to that effect.

How terrible was this new knowledge — she had wanted to believe Elizabeth blameless. What else had she left behind? Who, for example, was this Mr Griggs she talked about, the London schoolmaster? What was the exact nature of their relationship? It was as well Sarah Selwyn had gone back to Hulme Court, the Bishop's residence, after her long stay — Mary Ann might otherwise have found herself spilling over and then there would be no containing it. Sarah already had a low opinion of Mrs Smith, who was arriving now from the beach, puffing, her sea-stained blue shawl tied around her waist in Native fashion.

'I've come for the medicines. Are they mixed?'

'Not all.' Mary Ann stood. 'We will have to go to the dispensary to finish them.'

'Your boots.' Elizabeth pointed. 'For goodness sake, Mary Ann.'

But her employer went into the house as if she had not heard her. There would be no going down to the hospital together this afternoon. As she followed along behind, Elizabeth thought she sensed a change in her, something profound. There was a new resistance in her back, resilience in the set of her head, a prickling. Whether it was directed at her or the man whose library door was now firmly closed, she was not sure. Something must have happened while she was down at the beach. Whatever it was, she doubted it had occurred in the little dispensary on the eastern side of the house, with its outer door open onto the garden in case a patient should come calling, because no work had been done here that morning. Or wait — the pewter teapot was rinsed and loaded with herbs. Mary Ann had been in here.

They set to, Elizabeth scooping water from the butt outside the door and setting the pot over the spirit lamp to heat and infuse, while Mary Ann sat down at the round table to cut strips of muslin for new mustard plasters. The women worked in silence, their usual habit of industrious companionship slowly settling around them.

Through the open door there was a view of Mary Ann's chapel taking shape on the opposite hill. Little construction was going on, since most of the builders had departed with Mr Jowitt. A solitary man, a European from the town, was hefting a hogskin of seawater up the steep slope to make cement, and Elizabeth pitied him his labour.

Another Englishman, short and slight with a mop of brown hair blown about by the wind, was nailing up boxing for the cement to be poured and left to harden. It was Mr Cotton, who had managed to escape another epic visitation with the Bishop and was putting himself to use at Taurarua in between making long entries in his journals. The journey he had made with the Bishop to Whanganui had just about finished him — his bearer Renata had been very entertaining in his account of all Mr Cotton's failings.

But it was a pity he had not accompanied Henry to Orere and

Waiheke, thought Elizabeth, and then they could look out for one another like brothers. Henry was to be the only Pakeha amongst them and would be challenged at games and races, and general larking about and recklessness. Mr Cotton could be trusted to be a voice of caution at least. She distracted herself from visions of broken limbs and near-drowning by mixing the ointment for Mokihi — camphor gum, mercury, oil of cloves, and morphine — and then found herself putting it aside. The amalgam was harsh enough to draw liquor from the eye, but the crow's formula was faulty in so many ways, even in its consistency. The camphor made it clump and fester. She would leave it off and only bathe the eye with warm boiled water from now on, until it was returned to the splendour of the other.

'I will rest Mokihi's eye today,' she told Mary Ann, who did not respond, although usually she insisted Elizabeth follow the crow's instructions. Turning from the bench, Elizabeth found her employer intent on Mr Cotton on the hill.

'Mr Cotton could help you take the medicines down, since I cannot,' Mary Ann decided.

A girl from the kitchen was sent speedily to call him, and he came straight away. The two women watched fondly as he came towards the house. The dear lad, always so eager to help, even though he was less able to bear the face of suffering than Mary Ann, who was putting down her aching arm now before the egg white was quite stiff enough. Elizabeth took the bowl and fork from her and beat it up, mixing it with freshly ground mustard seed and spreading the mixture on the new plasters.

By the time Bee came in, washed and ready to share Mary Ann's sacred burden — her selfless effort on the behalf of others — the lady was resting her head on her hands.

There was always a slightly guilty cast to her face when she exaggerated her case as she did now — Elizabeth wondered if she was alone in perceiving it. The lowered profile drooped further. Really, she did not need to convince either friend.

'Is it the usual trouble?' Bee asked softly.

Elizabeth wondered what that was, because Mary Ann was often so inventive in her diagnosis. There was pain there, certainly: Mary Ann's legs were bandied from childhood rickets, or appeared so — she was vague as to whether she had had them since birth or infancy — but they were weak and made her pigeon-toed. In the process of lacing her up, when they were still in London, Elizabeth had found also a bend in her spine, where a vertebra veered away from the others. Her very skeleton ailed her — no wonder the seat of the pain travelled so emphatically all over her poor body.

Mary Ann was nodding sadly, her gaze alive and locked intimately with William Cotton's. When the Judge was away in Port Nicholson all through the summer, Elizabeth had come upon them alone in the parlour several times. On the last occasion, only last week, they'd been side by side on their knees in worship, Mary Ann's inclining head almost touching his. Elizabeth's heart went out to them. It made sense she would love him. He was so like the other William, being fresh-faced and clever and gentle, given to long searching conversations and prayer. It was a combination of qualities to excite sentiment in certain types of women, of which Mary Ann was one. She did not enjoy Bee so much when he was blithe, perhaps because the Judge maintained always a steady level of anxiety.

'If you were to leave off your sofa habits,' Elizabeth found herself saying, though she should not, because by doing so she condoned their intimacy, 'you would build your muscles and sinews, which would in turn strengthen your frame and maybe even straighten it.'

Mary Ann blushed, and the colour brought her an unnatural beauty, a flare of what she could have always if she allowed herself exercise and fresh air and nourishing food. The blood ebbed as quickly as it had come, even from her lips, so that the only colour was the fine gold chain she wore at her throat. It drew Mr Cotton's eye, and he lifted his hand dangerously close as if he would caress it — but her eyes were rolling back in her head, she was about to fall, she was fainting and Elizabeth rushed to catch her.

Between them, they helped her down the hall to her room and rumpled bed, laying her down and drawing up the coverlet.

'More pillows, Bee.' Elizabeth lifted her shoulders. 'Her breath is coming shallow.'

He took some cushions from the chair and tucked them behind her head while Elizabeth took from the cretonne-frilled chest a bottle and spoon. Out in the hall, the library door opened and the Judge's footfall sounded. Every movement rang quite as clear here as it had on the *Tomatin*, thought Elizabeth, ship and house both wooden bells. She slipped the tiny spoon between her employer's dry lips.

'What is going on?' Judge Martin came to stand at the foot of the bed. 'Speak to me, Mary Ann.' He employed his new no-nonsense tone.

It was better for him that he had inured himself more to her suffering — early in their marriage, he had shared her every pang. Elizabeth took a clean handkerchief from her sleeve and dipped an edge in the jug on the washstand.

'If you wouldn't mind, Mr Martin.' She put the damp cloth in his hand. 'I have to be getting down to the hospital.'

'Delay a moment,' he said, unable to remove his gaze from his wife.

They stood around the bed watching Mary Ann fight exhaustion, her eyelids fluttering until they opened completely and she looked sightlessly from face to face. Forgetting himself entirely, Bee laid a finger gently against her cheek. For a moment the Judge tolerated it, then bristled and would have dashed it away, but his wife was murmuring and they bent their heads to hear her.

'Mata? Are you still here?'

'Yes, dearest.' She had to get down to her patients as soon as possible, the afternoon was drawing on.

'Will you stay with me?'

'For a moment. William is here. And Bee.'

'I am here with the three who love me most.'

There was a soft anguished moan from Bee, and his eyes were filling with tears. There had never been a man to cry as easily.

Mary Ann whispered again. 'William, Bee and dearest Bess. Sweet Bess. I saw it written.'

She was delirious. Her husband mopped ineffectually at her brow and Elizabeth went to the parlour to fetch a glass of Madeira, which he might succeed in having her drink. He sometimes had more luck at it than she did. When she returned to the bedside, Bee was dabbing at his eyes, a gesture that irritated the Judge beyond measure.

'You can go now, Mrs Smith.' He took the wine from her. 'I'm sure you have enough to be getting on with.'

He held the glass to his wife, who took a sip of the wine and refused another.

'Dearest,' she said, 'the letter you brought me—' Mary Ann found Elizabeth among her loving attendants. 'It was a bill — a dressmaker I ordered from when we were in Sydney — it was paid long ago.'

Such a sad, sweet smile accompanied this announcement that Elizabeth refrained from reminding her that there had been no pieces ordered in Sydney — though Sarah Selwyn had availed herself of the tailor, as had other women of their party. The poor darling was wandering.

Taking Bee gently by the arm, Elizabeth led him to the dispensary to fetch the medicines before they made their sombre way down the hill. It was familiar to both of them, the sense of being torn between duty to the fragile spirit in the house above and the other work they must do below. If Bee wondered at the sudden elevation of her mood as she tended a particular patient, he did not remark on it.

FIFTEEN

Lady Audley's Secret

1866

For some time he had been watching the women over the edge of his lowered book. It seemed Mrs Smith was the invalid and Mary Ann the nurse, in that way women had of reversing roles. In the open world a man was either physician or patient, and if lucky neither, which was how Bee counted himself. He could see Elizabeth's legs lying along the bed and Mary Ann's narrow form bent over her, and there had been a lot of murmuring, first from Mary Ann and then from Elizabeth, who sounded for a brief time as though she were reading aloud, which she had always excelled at. In this instance she kept to an undertone, as if she was anxious for him not to hear. And then he thought, but he wasn't sure, that he could hear weeping and consoling. Eventually Mary Ann emerged from the room, closing the door after her.

'Mrs Smith will not be accompanying us to the theatre.'

'But why ever not?' asked Bee. 'She would enjoy it better than any of us.'

'She has had a shock,' said Mary Ann weakly enough to bring Bee to his feet and guide her to sit with him, 'and I'm afraid it is all my fault.'

'No, no.' He could not conceive of Mary Ann ever being to blame for anything. When he and Elizabeth were alone, he forgot Elizabeth's lowly level. Present company reminded him and he thought again, as he had so many times, that if they had not all been so affected by the giddy excitement of the voyage out, they may never have brought her so close. Of what had she accused Mary Ann?

It was a marvellous discovery that age permits more liberties than youth, though he had always expected it to be the opposite — he lifted her little wrist and kissed it, allowing his lips to linger long enough to detect her pulse, her very heartbeat, and she did not pull away. As they sat close together on the settee, there was a sense of everything clicking back into place. He could feel his thoughts going on in an orderly manner — and so many of them were focused on the wellbeing of the dearest creature who allowed him still to hold her hand. She would be now, he calculated, in her late forties, almost fifty. She looked so deathly pale.

'Shall I fetch you a drop? Mrs Smith has left her purse beside the chair.'

It was divine intervention. How pleased he was when a certain light entered her eye and she nodded — but how despairing he was to discover the spirit lamp gone out and the tea grown cold. Mary Ann was not concerned, and motioned for him to continue, sipping her tepid drops with relief.

The medicine had not yet had its full effect when they met Augustus and her husband, Bee bearing her downstairs on his newly reliable arm and triumphantly delivering her up. With that first wave of the drug Mary Ann could cross the carpet towards them almost unaided. William would know — he would look into her eyes and know that immediately had she resumed Mrs Smith, then so she had the opiates, though she had done very well without them for so long. There had been a number of remedies Mata had put at her disposal that William had not approved of, various implements and potions, and thinking of her favourites now brought a smile to her lips.

A conveyance was brought in quickly from the portico to the vestibule, which her husband and the bathchairman closed her into with the efficiency that came from practice. Oh, but she had been too heavy-handed. With her body at rest came the second rush of the drug — it swept her out to float in a warm, blissful sea. There was total absence of pain.

She lay back against the cushions and took in her surroundings. William and Augustus stood above her, and guests were passing through, on foot and wheel, none of whom she recognised. Easy chairs were set in plots and clusters in the wide room, and in one, under the window, sat Sarah. Mary Ann had the sense that she had been embroidering there again for some time, perhaps even since she had left them. Didn't she crave company at least as much as Mata did? Both had led such crowded lives at missions and schools that one would expect them to welcome peace and solitude as just reward, but they railed against it. Mary Ann pictured her friend, as she would have been as she left the sitting room, discomforted by Elizabeth's sudden appearance and her husband's unplanned exit, to say nothing of her perceived exclusion from a confidence and the alarming company of Miss Tripp. She would have decided that to sit among strangers with whom she had no connection would be the most peaceful thing. The hotel abounded with voluble invalids, so she was bound to hear of more woeful conditions than her own, which — unfortunately — always had for Sarah a cheering effect. Above the busy, concentrating fingers her face was in repose and the stricture around her mouth relaxed. Mary Ann saw for a moment the younger woman — though she would never have allowed herself that depth of peace then from any source, not from the Scots pills she continually took for her indigestion, or even from the Heavenly Father. Neither was peace permitted in any of those closest to her. One had to be in a continual state of spiritual examination.

'Mary Ann!' William was bending over her again, his face swimming up to her. 'Augustus has asked you twice now: where is Mrs Smith?'

'She's upstairs lying down,' Bee was saying, and Mary Ann saw that he was babbling again, wringing his hands, returned to his mania by the company of the men. 'She's had a shock—' But neither man was listening. Poor Bee. How he must long for Augustus to love him as he once did.

William was looking at her intently and a shadow of knowledge of her state of mind seemed to cross his face but was quickly dismissed. 'As you grow older you remind me more and more of Mrs Chapman,' he had told her worshipfully one night in their cabin on the voyage Home. 'Your silence and humility.'

She had had to take the compliment in the spirit it was intended. There were other similarities with the missionary's wife. 'We are both childless,' she could have said, or she could have pointed out their great difference, 'I was never frightened of our Maori friends,' but she whispered instead, 'Kīhai tāua i ai.' You and I were never lovers.

It was the nearest she had ever come to the hollow heart of their marriage. She had thought that now they were old — and weren't they? — in another two years she would be fifty. They could name it now, and perhaps comfort one another.

'Despite that, we have loved one another so.' She had brought her lips close to his ear.

Her husband had gone away from her abruptly, and spent the night elsewhere on the ship. When they met again the next morning, it was as if nothing had been said.

'Miss Tripp will be along directly,' she said now, enunciating carefully, 'and then we will go to the theatre.'

More time passed then; an effect of Mrs Smith's beloved little bottle, so long unaccustomed, was that she was not quite sure how much the drug interfered with one's internal clock. There was a muffled discussion taking place above her head and guests came and went, and nothing was of so much interest as the anticipation of Miss Tripp's arrival, so that when she appeared it was as if there was no interval between desiring and receiving her.

The actress was damp from her bath. Evidently she had hurried; her hair was slick and falling and her face moist — she could catch her death. She seemed delighted to observe them there, grouped as if to do her bidding, but when she detected — immediately! — Mata's absence, Mary Ann saw her enthusiasm dim. Bee explained again, and this time he was attended to.

'Oh, but she must come! She must!' Miss Tripp flew off up the stairs immediately.

Mary Ann felt herself drift in her wake and a little of her resolve ebbed away. William was bending again: 'This is quite out of the question. We will go to the Baths.'

His top hat had slipped a little over his brow, his hair being not as thick now to hold it in place, and Mary Ann giggled.

'Either that, or we will return to our room. You are not yourself, Mary Ann.'

'I am more myself than ever, dearest, and I should like to go with Miss Tripp.'

But he was behind her and taking hold of the handlebar, which was strictly against bathchairmen's rules, and began to push the chair towards the doors. Sarah stood, and so did the young woman beside her, whom Mary Ann only then recognised as being her maid. So Sarah had returned to her room, if only swiftly, to give the girl instructions. The maid carried a leather bag of dimension large enough to carry her mistress's clean change.

The Baths it was then. It was pointless to argue. They were back to their old positions so quickly — Sarah doing whatever the men wanted, always glad of their company because it brought activity and motion. Solitude and indolence made her ill, or inclined to believe she was. Mata believed Sarah's constitution so strong that she would outlive them all, and Mary Ann thought she was probably right.

The bathchairman regained control and they went along the portico and onto the colonnaded ambulatory that adjoined it, towards the Hot Baths. William laid his hand on her shoulder for a moment and she looked into his gentle eyes, glad, suddenly, that she was not going to be washed about in whatever tumultuous sea currently surrounded Mrs Smith. In her company it was too easy to find oneself ranged against others — Mrs Smith so enjoyed polarity. There had not been a chance to ask her about Miss Tripp — and after her old companion had read the letter she was not fit to be gently enquired of. Perhaps Bee could explain Kitty, who she really was — Mary Ann looked about for him — but it seemed he had not accompanied them out of the hotel.

'Where is Mr Cotton?' she asked, but her husband had fallen back to look into the apothecary's window. Ahead of her the Bishop gave Sarah his arm, and behind her the bathchairman whistled a quiet meandering tune, which came louder and softer in puffs with his steady tread. The sun had come out a little, the frost quite melted away, and there seemed now more passers-by in rude good health than those decrepit, which was cheering. There was a lovely holiday feel suddenly, further sweetened by the comfort of easeful friendship renewed. There was no need to worry — it was not as if she would not see Mata again. There would be other times before Mrs Smith returned to London, which would surely be soon. The St Anne Hotel must be a stretch for her. If only she could be invited to dine, to go some way to making it up to her for concealing the letter, but Augustus would never allow it.

Mrs Smith lay flat on the bed, all colour drained from her face and her hands folded on her breast. Kitty was reminded of the first time they met at the schoolmaster's house, and how at her own insistence she and Mr Griggs had taken Elizabeth home to her lodgings and put her to bed. It was not wise perhaps to form an affection for a lady of such advanced years, and possibly even less wise to subject her to the afternoon's entertainment. Entertainment for whom, exactly? Her conscience pained her sharply, and she sat down on the bed, taking one of Mrs Smith's inert hands in hers. Life was not a play, or a variety show — entrances and exits could be mistimed, and scenes could go on and on without a curtain to conveniently end them. The lady's breathing came too deep and too slow to be wholesome, but less noisily than it had on that first day.

'Mrs Smith?' She gave the hand a little shake. 'Elizabeth?' But her old friend was seemingly too far away to perceive either sound or touch. Kitty remembered Mr Griggs's confidence that Mrs Smith would return to the living, and aspired to that complacence in herself. Perspiration slicked the lined brow — she was hot and feverish, overdressed. By a cursory count there were at least three skirts and who knew how many petticoats.

'You rest then, Mrs Smith,' she said, in as soothing a voice as she could muster, 'at least for a few minutes more.'

A letter lay on the coverlet, the paper sea-stained and old, the writing so faint that she doubted Elizabeth could have read it. It crackled in her fingers — some of the words had washed away. 'By hand' stood clearly in the right-hand corner, and two dates, one in 1842 and the other in 1844.

'My dearest Bess,

'I will take this letter to Tusculum and have them give it to you directly. I will not shame you alone or among friends, but you must know I have seen you and the boy, who is not mine. I saw you in the garden with a priest. I met the boy on the beach.'

The next few sentences were obliterated and even though she took the letter to the window, opening the curtains to hold it into the light, Kitty could make out no other words than what might have been 'money' and, further on, 'promise'.

'. . . if your father had not accused me and we had not fought, then the fire would not have taken. You done better from it than I — it is my pride more than your shame I mind. Dearest Bess, I have longed for you all these years. You will remember my kindness when you were a girl. I was much older and seen a harder side of life. I was a gentle husband to you. I could not have been gentler, you were scarce a child when you formed an affection for me. Now I have lived so many years in this place and you in England, we are strangers. Who is it you mourn? It is not this man who has not died to you.'

Meaning was lost again, the writing clumsy with crossings-out, smudging and bleeding into the lines above and below.

A cough sounded from the corridor. Had she left the door open? It must be a guest returning to his room. Kitty hurried on — there were sentences she could decipher if she had time, but she did not — there were footsteps turning into the room beyond.

'You can send for me by the hand that passed you this, a servant woman I know from the town. She does not suspect. I told her I was bringing a message from the mantymaker for a dress you have ordered for your mistress. It you want it, I will come to join you.

'I hope to be forever and again your forgiving and loving husband who has never once forgotten you, Nicky.'

The cough sounded again, closer, and Kitty turned to see Mr Cotton crossing the sitting room and coming in at the bedroom door, flustered and scowling.

'Now we have lost them! They have gone to the Hot Baths instead.'

Kitty pushed the letter into a loop of her skirts — but Mr Cotton had not seen. His attention was fixed on his old friend.

'Wake up! Wake up!' He took the same hand Kitty had so recently held and shook it more roughly than was necessary. Mrs Smith startled, her eyes flying open to stare sightlessly at them, then closed again.

'Mr Cotton, I do not think you should!' Kitty would restrain him.

If she didn't hurry she would be late to the theatre, and she had promised. A sign had been hurriedly painted this morning and set out on the street to announce her return — there was general hope for a bigger house than in recent times.

Mr Cotton withdrew his hand and sighed heavily.

'Do you have the hour?' she asked him.

He examined his fob. 'A half after one.'

'I must go!' But she found herself coming to stand on the other side of the bed to take up Elizabeth's other hand. Such concern dragged on Mr Cotton's face, she felt bound to comfort him. 'Have you never seen her like this before?'

He shook his head.

'I have. Mr Griggs says it is a result of the voyage, the unnatural distances she has travelled. He says not all people are suited to it.' And what distances! She had run from the crime she was as guilty of as Kitty's father.

'How does he come to this conclusion?' asked Mr Cotton emphatically. 'It could only be the diagnosis of a man who has never left home.'

'Oh, but he has. He was in India.'

'There may come a time in the age of steam when we are able to make long journeys more quickly than is wise for heart and soul, but that time is not with us yet.'

'Do you have the gift of prophecy, Mr Cotton?'

'I do not — neither do I believe such a thing exists.'

'I have a sister with the gift,' she told him. 'My youngest sister,

Pamela, who was named for my mother, who died bringing her into the world. She is only thirteen.'

'I do not believe such a thing exists!' he repeated, glaring at her.

Kitty went into the other room to fetch her coat. Mrs Smith's purse sat on the settee and her medicine bottle stood open on the tea tray, risking evaporation. She corked it and put it back, the letter with it, and returned to the bedroom to give Mr Cotton an address near Spring Gardens.

'Please come,' she said, 'and bring Mrs Smith. There is a sign outside bearing my name — the bathchairman will know it.'

'When does the performance begin?'

'If you are there within the hour, you will not miss me.' She would make sure she was the final act.

Mrs Smith opened one eye and looked directly at her, and Kitty wondered for the first time if she was faking, or at least making more of her condition than was necessary.

'I have read the letter,' she would have liked to say, and a good deal more besides — and would have done if they'd been alone.

'Will I see you there?' she asked.

The expression in the eye softened, and she took it for the affirmative.

The Shakespeare Hotel was a hundred and fifty years old and not one of Buxton's finest. It was scruffy and small, and named for a long-gone theatre of the same name which was inspiration to her father.

Kitty found him in the tiny cramped office which doubled as his dressing room. A mottled mirror leaned against the ledgers while he applied the greasepaint and hairblack that returned him to the young handsome soldier he had been, brimming with military ballads and verse.

'Your sisters are waiting for you,' he said, as soon as he saw her reflection loom beside his. 'Pamela had thought to impersonate you, you are so late.'

Her sisters were in the theatre, which was once the back parlour, and so dark and dusty her youngest sister had often had to be carried out for her wracking cough. They were arguing about the number of extra chairs that would be needed. Jane, two years older than Kitty and several shades darker — and so jealous, thought Kitty, that her face seemed permanently pursed and bitter — maintained that there was no need for any.

'In other families they play charades! In ours we indulge our father with this embarrassing spectacle.'

'We will have an audience today,' said Kitty, 'I have made sure of it.'

'Mr Dickens himself has a theatre,' said their father out of the dark, arriving beside them. 'His whole family performs!'

'You are not Mr Dickens,' said Jane.

Kitty laughed and planted a kiss on her sister's cheek.

'Will you play for me?' she asked. 'I left the score on the piano this morning for you to practise. Where is the box of scarves and veils?' She went towards the small room that stood behind the makeshift stage.

'Are you going to do something new?' Pamela asked her. 'Is it your London turn?'

'Wait and see!' Kitty laid the tip of her finger on her sister's nose. She was the most English of all them, pale and thin, and the sister everyone said was the most like her. She wished suddenly she could confide in her, tell what entertaining and astonishing scenes were likely to play out before their very eyes, but perhaps Pamela knew that already.

'When are you going back?' Pamela sat on the edge of the trunk labelled 'Hats and bonnets' while Kitty rummaged in the gloom for light shawls of equal size.

'Tomorrow — I am expected.'

'Jane says you are one of many cheap acts at the Pavilion and that you have exaggerated your success.'

Kitty ignored her. She had the veils — all cast-offs of her mother's, bright Indian silks, some many years old. She would take some back to London with her.

'I have an act now,' Pamela was telling her. 'Papa says it's very good. I bring messages for whoever of the audience is in need of them. And rather a lot of people are, in Buxton.'

The child was staring through the open door to the chairs, which Jane was banging into order. The older sister had still not looked at the score. When Kitty had passed the piano it was folded just as she had left it before hurrying to the Crescent.

'Someone is here already. Two little girls have come all on their own. Third row back, three from the left. One is English, I think. The other is . . . I don't know. I have never seen anyone like her.'

'Stop it, Pamela,' said Kitty sternly. It was unnerving, but not as unnerving as the girl's related advices from their mother. It was Pamela who had foretold her sister's change in fortune a full year before it came to pass — an attachment to a gentleman who would compose songs especially for her, and that she would be set on the road to fame. 'You will be happy, my darling,' she had told Kitty in Mamma's voice. 'You will enjoy your life.'

'She is at least as dark as our other sisters,' Pamela said now, 'who by the way we have had a letter from. They would like us all to join them in India, where there are many more like us and we would perhaps be happier.' She giggled. 'The little girl is smiling at me, and such a smile!'

Kitty bundled up the scarves and went to lay them in order at the back of the stage, Pamela following behind.

'Such a warm, encompassing smile!'

'You could help,' said Kitty. 'Here. Tie these two together.'

But Pamela was making a show of listening to the ghost, and Kitty thought how good she was at it. There was no outstretched straining hand as if she would snatch the words from the air. She stood neutrally, openly, her whole body a receptive ear. She was a better actress than any of them, turning now to regard her sister with a frown.

'She says to tell you she's coming. I asked her who, and she said you know her . . . Martha. No . . . Marta.'

Involuntarily, Kitty found herself looking towards the spectre's chairs.

'Marta,' said Pamela. 'Who is she, Kitty?'

Her father had sat down at the old piano, since Jane would not —

she had vanished entirely — and was sounding a doleful note again and again, the score open before him. He was not as good a player as her sister, and Kitty wished she would come back.

'Do you see, Kitty — you come in before me — you must begin here —' he called, playing the note again, his back younger and stronger in costume, ramrod straight and golden epaulettes level.

'I know, Pa. I have sung it many times.'

'And you always come in true?' he asked. 'With no starting note?'

'Most usually. And I do believe that piano is more out of tune than ever.'

Her father laughed. 'My clever singing bird!'

There was a tug at her skirts.

'No more, Pamela!' But even as Kitty said it, she knew the tug had come too low. Two little girls, Pamela had said, and she wanted to ask her about them, but her sister was hurrying away to stand beside Pa, though not too close to be smirched by his paint.

Watching them, Pa playing and Pamela sight-reading, singing the part in her high, thin voice, Kitty felt herself relax as if someone older and wiser was telling her everything would be all right, that the old folk might not recognise one another, that she could escape having to make the introductions, but she could write to the half-brothers in New Zealand and tell them how it was for their father and half-sisters. She could describe Papa, performing his nightly shows with Pamela, while the spinster sister ran herself out at the elbows keeping the shabby hotel and their father in check. She could explain how on his good days Pa was as he was now, singing, encouraging little Pamela in her sight-reading, plying the guests — who were most often regimental men suffering impoverished convalescence from one hot colony or another — with port and ale. She could describe how on his bad days he sat slumped at his desk in mourning for his long-lost true wife and bemoaning the bills. She could introduce her half-brothers to all five sisters, two in India and three in England, whom they would likely never meet. She could write that she had seen their pictures and knew details of their lives from their mother's accounts. She could tell them that the New Zealanders and Mr Griggs had all remarked on a resemblance between herself and Henry, which was always passed over quickly so as not to abuse their mother's trust.

'Dear brothers,' she could write, 'I have been mischievous and you may chastise me, but why should not they meet again? I do not agree with Mr Griggs. Why should not two people, who were once as close as it is humanly possible to be, once again breathe the same air? You must have imagined that this could happen, that their reunion could be the result of your investigations. Mr Griggs read me part of a letter of yours, dear Henry, where you wonder why you should not know if your father lives, even if the gaining of that knowledge should meet with fierce resistance in a particular quarter. I have reason to believe it would not be as affecting to your mother as you would believe.'

Her father got up stiffly from the piano and came across the stage, dragging the faded red curtain closed behind him. Kitty scarcely noticed him, going on with the letter in her head.

'Our friend Mr Griggs is most insistent that your mother not be shamed — he will not allow her reputation to be damaged in any way. He particularly requested that I end my friendship with her and so I did, though it pained us both, until it was necessary for me to head her off at Lichfield. You see, if your mother had learned her friends were going to Buxton, and not Torquay, she could have gone there and come upon my father in far less favourable circumstances than those I now intend.'

Voices sounded in the saloon and people were coming in at the door. A young woman on two sticks was making slow progress, accompanied by a lady in a bathchair who looked so much her like as to be her twin. Behind them came Pa's dearest friend and long-time guest, an elderly officer from his own regiment who had stayed for seven years. He attended every occasion and would sometimes rise from his seat to contribute his rumbling bass to the saddest of the soldier's ballads.

'You must understand Mr Griggs is devotedly protective of your mother, even though he has described her more than once as a "tough old trooper". How do you like that?'

And we shall see very soon exactly how tough she is, thought

Kitty. I will know the instant they come face to face whether she ever loved him at all.

This is how she would finish her letter: 'It was my mother my father loved most. I do believe there is a convict in Port Jackson who holds the same place in his heart for yours.'

Kitty went to find her older sister to make sure she had added fundamentally to the price of a ticket. Pa had promised a percentage of the takings.

SIXTEEN

The Shakespeare

I AM AT TAURARUA with Mokihi, I am at Te Ngae with the Chapmans, I am with the Browns at Te Papa, with Henry at Manupirua, and I see at all these stations the love and work that filled that life. I hear laughter and sense adventure, and know the heartbreak was less than it may have been because I was inured by what had come before it in England.

Then I am delivering a child of Mary Ann, as real as a memory, tho' it never happened. She labours on a low bed in the Native Hospital, before the structure was properly enclosed. Through the open walls come the warm summer night and the sound of waves breaking gently on the shore. The baby crowns — and as I reach to catch her, a pair of strong brown hands are there before me. Gently, Mokihi takes up the child and cradles her, still slick and wet, against his breast. Mary Ann pleads for the child to be given to her — and Mokihi looks directly at me, smiling conspiratorially, tho' I have no idea what he plans. Suddenly he goes out into the dark, taking the tiny living infant. And then, somehow, in the logic of the dream, I know that the child belongs to him and wake with a start.

Standing at the window is a young woman, who in profile looks very like Henry. Her head is bent over a book or page and I recognise neither her nor the room — the chintz curtains, the battered travelling wardrobe — and I would cry out against it all, but I am swallowed again by the drug and this time I am swimming in the sea, which I never did voluntarily, tho' twice I was tipped out of a longboat into boisterous surf on the sandbar at Maketu, and each time I was terrified.

I seem to be able to breathe underwater — a child's dream — and the fish come around me as thick as a London crowd and as tame as they were at Taurarua if I paddled in the shallows and scattered crumbs. The deep water draws me out, surrounded by the gentle nudging creatures and I doubt I will ever return to the land or want to. As I swim, I recall there was a man on the beach mourning my departure but it slips my mind which man it is. At one moment I remember him as Horelock and the next Mokihi and the last Henry, but it is Bee who is shaking me now and I am returned to Mary Ann's bed in the hotel.

Bee is as out of sorts as I am vertiginous, and resents being sent for my drop, tho' he brings my purse eventually. The bottle has been tampered with — he allows he gave some to Mary Ann, who was sorely troubled. The fog that surrounds me clears enough for this to be perturbing. 'But you must not, Bee!'

'She administered it herself. I really do not enjoy a lady's bedroom, Mrs Smith.' He gestures to Mary Ann's chemise hooked over a dressing chair.

There was a letter and it is gone from my hand! Bolt upright, I grope around the coverlet for it, struggling to stand up — the letter from Horelock, or did I imagine it? Bee has stepped away in consternation.

'Whatever is wrong, Mrs Smith?'

'A letter — there was —'

It is not on the floor or surrounding furniture, and by his expression Bee knows nothing about it. Did Mary Ann put it away in my purse? A blue edge — and I pull it free to hold it again, and know as soon as I hold it in my hand that Horelock must have died soon after he sent it. He would not have let it rest, even tho' he had discovered me. He had seen my silk mourning dress; he had seen me set above him and must have known that I could not risk association. How could he have known our reunion was my fantasy at the time?

The letter is a secret I keep with Mary Ann, and it shall stay so. It makes no difference to me now, I tell myself. That is the only dignified response. Even if he had lived and come to me, and out of shame or love I had joined him, I may have had this same dreary future looming, of lonely lodgings with only the company of conjured children and, intermittently, of Mr Griggs or Mr Cotton. If he had found me out and claimed me, that future may have been the same, but I would have had a seafaring past to reflect on — Horlock, the lads and I may have worked a coastal trade out of Auckland, we would have lived aboard until our family grew too large, and then we may have come ashore and prospered. I saw it happen to others who built fine homes around that shining harbour.

But then my sons would more likely have grown to be merchantmen and sloggers, not the responsible men I helped them become! And who is to say Mr Horlock would really have been able to forgive me for my second marriage, or what scandal could have followed him from Sydney? And if he had come to find me I would not have loved Mary Ann, or Mokihi, or stood as an equal alongside many who would have scorned me at Home, and the truth would have had to be told about Henry. It is better this way. There is nothing to regret.

'Please do hurry, Mrs Smith!'

Bee is at the door again, tho' with his back to it. I attend to my appearance, briefly — washing my face and straightening my cap and gown — and tell myself over and over it is better this way, while the glass shows my ruined old face. It is better this way, I think, as Bee and I make our way down the stairs, where obediently I am closed into an odorous conveyance.

There is nothing to regret. Nothing at all.

The gypsy family are once again at St Anne's Well and I see now one of the children is very sick. Too old to be carried by her father, her thin adolescent arms and legs dangle bright and ragged against him, her face against his shoulder yellow with jaundice. There are no gypsies in New Zealand — they have yet to find their way there. I had to explain them to John Elisha's daughters when we came upon one in a fairy tale. If I was independently mobile I could gently enquire of the problem and suggest a treatment for the child — but they have their own medicines and could ignore me. The same dilemma was presented more than once during my work in New Zealand. I kept for many years a record of the remedies suggested to me — I wonder what became of it? I made a present of it for Mary Ann before I left.

The bathchairman pushes me out of the Crescent, Bee puffing along beside me.

Buxton is a gracious town, built as proud as the best parts of London and not at all like the quaint Derbyshire villages that the train passed beside. It is no little wonder — the rich have played and convalesced here, Bee says, since the Romans. The buildings are of stone, and some approach greater antiquity than others. There are terraces and shops; the ladies are fashionably dressed. Still the streets grow older and poorer until there is the sign outside an old hotel — 'The Shakespeare' — and another, crudely painted against the wall: 'The London Pavilion's Miss Kitty Tripp for One Day Only'.

The jolting cobblestones have left me bruised and nauseous and glad of the opportunity, while we are delayed behind the crowd queuing to go in, for another drop. At this rate I will have run out long before my return to London.

When I look up again, it is to see the genuine Mrs Hogg, as youthful and beautiful as she ever was. She stands just inside the narrow door and is smiling in welcome. Hikipene is beside her, holding her hand, a green Indian silk tied around her tattered blue smock like a cape. The wisest course is to take yet another drop, hurriedly, because I begin to suspect that the unbidden arrival of these spectres is the result of only a moderate state of intoxication. That and remorse. That and regret. Another sip will dissolve the sticky web and bring sleep — my potion is far stronger than Browne's, which takes a full fifty drops. Only twenty of mine will do it, a small cascade to my willing tongue.

In my last moments of consciousness I look again and the fetches are gone. In their stead is a girl of twelve or thirteen, who looks very like Kitty, the same shining black hair and delicate features, the same sloping shoulders and rich complexion. She catches my eye and gives the most delighted grin before she vanishes ahead of us into the gloom of the shabby auditorium. Darkness without and darkness within — the padded chair back cushions my heavy head.

SEVENTEEN

The Lover's Heart

WHILE HE WAITED for the performance to start, Bee pondered the thought that he had attended precisely no theatrical entertainments in the years since his return from New Zealand. In Auckland there had been a playhouse he frequented with Henry, to the voluble disappointment of William Martin and Bishop Selwyn. He supposed *The Idiot Witness or the Tale of Blood* was a novelty as crude as this promised to be. He remembered fondly the oft-repeated *Grace Darling or the Wreck of the Forfarshire Steamer* and how it had wrung his easy tears. Tears or laughter — there had to be either or both for an entertainment to be worthwhile.

This programme promised less sensation, beginning first with ballads and verse given by a strangely youthful gentleman who wore the red coat of the 65th and seemed to sport, though it was difficult to make out, the regimental badge of the Royal Tigers, which was proof of service in India. Mrs Smith was snoring so loudly he could not discern the words. Then there was a small girl who sat on a chair before the curtain and gave messages to invalids in the audience. It was scarcely Christian, but he suffered through it out of curiosity for the act to follow. The little theatre was stuffy and there was an unpleasant miasma, which rose either from the walls or perhaps from those invalids dangerously excited by the child's pronouncements. The audience was mostly of women, he noted — the bathchairmen who had brought them had gone outside to smoke and pass the time. Mrs Smith snored more quietly, which was convenient because the child's voice rose barely above a whisper. There were remedies and comforts, blessings and endorsements, all of which he strained to hear.

Just before the girl finished, she stood and gave a distinctive gesture that he recognised — she wiped her hands on her apron. Her apron was frilled, clean and ornamental, while the pinny the gesture conjured from his memory was stained calico and entirely functional. Palms flat and fingers outstretched, she passed her hands down her flanks and looked directly at him.

'Could you please wake the lady on your left?' she asked.

He felt a chill in his bowels but did as she asked, after a delay long enough to prompt her to ask again — and this time the voice that reached him was uncannily like Mrs Smith's. He shook her elbow now, since calling her name and patting her hand had not roused her.

'Taihoa,' she mumbled, that most comprehensive word that means either in half a minute or this time in two years and one of the earliest adopted by those learning the language. In her fist she clasped her beloved little bottle and she seemed in the dim light to be unusually pallid. Mr Cotton began to be alarmed. The girl on the stage had still not moved. The heads of the women who had turned to stare were now turning to one another in consternated whispering.

'Bring her nose around! Take her off the wind,' Mrs Smith said clearly, without opening her eyes.

He wondered if he should call for help and whether the girl could see that his old friend was narcoticised past rousing. He bent his head to listen at her chest — she breathed regularly. The girl did not seem to care that she was losing the crowd's attention; indeed some of the more able were getting up to leave.

'Please try again sir,' she asked. 'I have a message for her.'

'Give it to the old man to pass on,' called a wit from the front row, 'and give us Kitty Tripp!'

The soldier appeared again from the wings and whispered in the girl's ear, and the girl allowed herself one disappointed glance in Bee's direction before being led away. Bee settled again, hoping the next act would be more entertaining — Kitty was a pretty girl, he would never forget the time she sang for him alone at Doctor

Tuke's asylum. A heavy-set, unhappy-looking woman sat down at the piano and struck the first run of notes, which were close enough to remind Bee of a piping snake-charmer he had seen as a boy. Abruptly she stopped, as if she'd made a mistake, and peered closely at the music, her head nodding with the count. The curtains opened again to show Kitty kneeling. The morning's bright attire seemed to have had the addition of red and yellow Indian shawls, one of which floated around her head and put him in mind of Mary Magdalene. Her arms were outstretched in the manner of a figure on a Grecian vase, her neck arched and head thrown back in an attitude of rapture. She began to sing in high, penetrating tones.

> *I am a little maiden of the Ganges delta*
> *I serve a Hindoo princess who married in the spring*
> *She has married her love, she has married true —*

Here the piano began again with the shivery notes and Kitty sang on.

> *But he is an English captain and must sail across the blue —*

The key changed suddenly to become more magisterial and Kitty came to stand at the foot of the stage where, if she were in a proper theatre, her skirts would be in danger of the limelights. A heavy gas lamp that hung smoking from the ceiling illuminated her face and bare arms while she plucked veils from her garment and set them waving magically around her and sang on but in an even higher register. She had assumed, seamlessly and entirely, another character altogether.

> *I am that Hindoo princess and my heart is brave and strong*
> *And though I am not Christian I know always right from wrong*
> *And it's right to love an English captain who is far away from here*
> *My babe and I will search for him though he holds another dear*

She is an English governess, less noble far than I —

There was a sudden movement at his elbow. Mrs Smith had woken and was clutching at him.

'What is it?' he asked, but her eyes were rolling and closing again, her hand flopping loose and the little bottle falling under the chair in front. Mr Cotton retrieved it, and when he returned his attention to the stage the song seemed to have come to an abrupt end. The pianist had moved away from her instrument and the redcoat was once again drawing the curtain closed. It was as if he was intent on covering a misdemeanour — though Bee could not think what it could be. A grey-whiskered gentleman of military bearing stood and began on Hodd's voyager poem, which at least showed a kind of continuity with the previous act.

> *The stars are with the voyager*
> *Wherever he may sail;*
> *The moon is constant to her time;*
> *The sun will never fail;*
> *But follow, follow round the world,*
> *The green earth and the sea;*
> *Love is with the lover's heart,*
> *Wherever he may be.*

From behind the curtain and beneath the poem came the hissing of a suppressed argument, and even before the old soldier began on the second verse the younger, dark-haired soldier emerged from the far end of the stage, between curtain and wall, dragging Miss Tripp by the wrist towards the door where both paused for a moment. Bee stood to go to her aid at that instant, and could have sworn that Kitty was pointing in their direction — there was her flailing white arm in the gloom — and the solider was likewise staring, his mouth open in astonishment. Kitty took a step away as if she would draw the soldier towards them, but he renewed his hold and pulled her into the hall, closing the door after them.

Bee sat down again. After all, Kitty was of a particular breed of women more mysterious to him than the clergy wives with whom he was the most familiar, or indeed than any of his parishioners that he could recall. His conscience pained him for a moment — she had been dutiful, though erratic, in her friendship with Mrs Smith.

> ... *The sun may set, but constant love*
> *will shine when he's away* ...

continued the man with the grey whiskers, drawing the poem hurriedly to an end before following Miss Tripp and her employer from the room.

The entertainments were finished then, unless the child was to reappear to play clairvoyant, which Mr Cotton felt was to be avoided at all costs. He stood to take the controls of Mrs Smith's bathchair.

Mary Ann and Sarah took their baths in adjoining rooms. At the last half-hour Sarah asked for the connecting door to be opened so that they might call to one another. It would be at no cost to their modesty — all either woman could see of the other was her head above the bath's rim, which was at floor level.

'You may wait outside,' Sarah told the uniformed attendants imperiously, and Mary Ann anticipated the making of confidences — but for the first little while Sarah was quiet. Mary Ann was grateful; she would rather the door had remained closed, the better to meditate on recent events and drift on chloroform clouds.

Sarah's face was mottled, scarlet against the white of her bathing bonnet. One silver tendril escaped to snake along her jaw.

'If I am not mistaken,' she began, 'you have recently passed your forty-ninth birthday.'

Mary Ann nodded. How pretty the steam was as it rose, how uniform its misty strands, like ghostly reeds. There was no wind crossing a lake to blow it about in puffs and eddies, no frothing ferns or songbirds to gladden the heart. Here it was all white tiles and marble, and the ingenious pulley-chair they had lowered her on. She floated out of it, took hold of its back and stretched her legs luxuriously.

'Mary Ann?'

'Yes, I have.'

'And do you think your life's work is over?'

'No, not at all. I have told you. I intend to write my memoirs.'

'And I intend to write mine.' She had the tone of a child snatching a toy or of a man claiming an invention. 'I draw closer to it than you do.'

Sarah's age was not permitted to be enquired of, though William had it that she was born in the same year as Augustus, which made her sixty-three. Even if that was not true, she had once allowed that one of her earliest memories was of hearing horns in the street trumpeting Wellington's victory over Napoleon in a battle of the Peninsular War. Considering the war began in 1809, and unless she was a peculiarly cognisant child, Sarah must already have been two or three by then. Or older.

'Mary Ann? Do you hear me?'

'We may both write them,' said Mary Ann gently.

'The world is awash with accounts of colonial lives. Perhaps we should write our volume together. We did very well at our household compendium in Maori, did we not?'

Over the rim of the bath and across the wet slicked floor, Sarah's face was impossibly redder. There was a steady plinking of water, which could have been a very faint repetitive birdsong if they were bathing in that other place — which she did only once, at Rotorua. Mrs Smith was the devil for it, submerging far more than her waewae, which was what the doctor had ordered.

The hose gave a sudden silvery stream, and then was dry — testament to Sarah's treatment. Before they had gone in, she had instructed her attendant to perform a Scottish douche with particular attention to her abdomen, a pummelling of hot and cold hoses simultaneously. For herself, Mary Ann had wanted only to float in the chalybeate waters which so eased the pains in her back and legs. Perhaps Sarah would be so tired after her treatment she would be happy to retire to her room. That would be a blessing.

'Mary Ann?'

'I have already begun,' she said eventually, and hoped she would be forgiven for the untruth.

'Really? But you have only just returned. Would it not be wise to allow your recollections to settle?'

'I began on the voyage home.' Another untruth! It was the drug making her inventive. 'The employment of a pen is a fine way to while away long hours.'

That much at least was true to her experience. She had spent hours at her desk at Taurarua, with correspondence and lessons and working on the language — hours that had sped by. The most believable untruths were not complete. A long-ago conversation with Mata surfaced. Mr Cotton had sung her friend's praises when they returned to Taurarua from a sail on the harbour which had evidently been enlivened by a sudden, violent squall.

'But how do you know how to sail, dear?' Mary Ann had asked her. 'It is not a common accomplishment among women.'

In reply, her friend allowed that she had come from a seafaring family, which Mary Ann already knew, but would not elaborate — out of fear, it seemed now, of telling lies, of which, if one were honest, Mrs Smith was in the habit. If she had come into Mary Ann's employ earlier in London, she may have gleaned more details of that early life. It was a common disorder among the lower classes in the Colonies — the ease with which aspects of the English past could be erased. The man in Port Jackson had mentioned a shipburning.

'I find it a pleasant enough pastime myself,' said Sarah, 'but I was so occupied with attending to Augustus and helping him, I could not be so selfish.'

Mary Ann did not respond — it was the most effective way of deflecting Sarah's barbs.

'And what is it called?' Sarah asked, baldly.

'Our Maoris,' said Mary Ann. She had decided on it while the last of New Zealand had slipped below the horizon and she and her husband stood side by side at the rail. William had wept and so had she.

'Come to us at Lichfield,' said Sarah. 'We may spend our days at our memoirs — separately, if that's how you would like it — and worship and dine in company. Why should we live apart when we have been so much together?'

Mary Ann lifted her hand from the water and examined it. Her fingertips were wrinkled.

'Mary Ann?'

'Yes, Sarah, thank you. May I first discuss it with William?'

'But you are well disposed to the idea?'

Mary Ann wished she could have time to think. In New Zealand, she and Sarah had made up two of a triumvirate of ladies known socially as The Three Graces, but they had worked mostly in separate establishments — she at Taurarua at the hospital and Infant School, Sarah at Bishop's College. It was true she had enjoyed Sarah's company, particularly in the early days when she would come with little Willie to stay for weeks on end while the Bishop made his visitations. There was a pattern after that of Sarah coming for the birth of each successive child and her lying in, where Mrs Smith could help care for her. And the journeys they had made together with their husbands, hundreds of miles by ship, litter and horse, to the missions at Te Papa and Te Ngae, where very often Mrs Smith would be the first to greet them.

Mrs Smith! It was just as well she had not made the offer she had thought of earlier at the hotel. She would now have to withdraw it.

'Mary Ann?'

'I'm sorry, Sarah. I was thinking.'

'Why should you have to think?' asked Sarah, aggrieved. 'This bathwater is growing cold.'

'If you had not sent the attendant away, she would refresh it for you,' said Mary Ann.

'If I am chilled, it is more the work of your cool words,' Sarah snapped. 'Aside from your desire to play memoirist in seclusion, what other reason would you have to decline my invitation? Augustus and I would not expect any contribution to household expenses.'

'Have you discussed this with him?'

'Briefly — as an idea. Now I must not mention it again until he does, as his own initiative. Then I will agree and congratulate him on his thoughtfulness and generosity.'

Mary Ann smiled. Wisely, this was a strategy Sarah had not overused. It was how any woman in the world would survive marriage to dear Augustus, she thought: we all of us are drawn into doing his will. She shifted again in her bath and the water ran silkily over her legs under the bathing gown. The warmth and close conversation brought it back to her, how she had envied Sarah her husband when they were younger. She would imagine the private life the Selwyns must have to bring the babies into being, the babies that kept coming. And there was that repeating dream, so long ago now, where Augustus kissed her and she would wake full of longing for him. The crushing guilt that followed would have her calling before dawn for Mata to arrange her bath.

'Will you come to us, Mary Ann?'

'I had thought . . .' Mary Ann began, gathering herself. 'I had thought to ask Mrs Smith to join us in Torquay. The house William is arranging there is easily large enough for the three of us—'

'I am surprised you would even entertain the notion.' Sarah's voice was raised, and her neck straining above the bath put Mary Ann in mind of a turtle. 'She is neither friend nor servant. You could hardly believe her to be a faithful retainer when she was for ever rushing off to Maketu or Wellington after her sons. Do you know—' she dropped suddenly to a whisper — 'she had the nerve to ask my husband yet again for assistance.'

'You know what I think about this, Sarah. It would not have hurt for the Church to have given her a little cottage in Auckland. Then she would have stayed in New Zealand, likely as not.'

'Augustus thought she had been too erratic in her duty.'

'That is nonsense — she was years at the hospital and between the missions.'

'I think I should like to get out of the bath,' said Sarah.

Briefly Mary Ann considered submerging herself entirely beneath the water, cap and all. She let herself float, letting go of the back of the chair — a ducking chair it was, for the old witch she could have been in another age — and let her chin dip to the water, out of view of her friend. Sarah did not seem to comprehend that if Mata had stayed behind, then there would be no duty to her here. There were obligations that had not been fulfilled.

'I could not believe it when I saw her from the window at the gate!' Sarah was saying, her voice ringing on the tiled walls. 'In the absence of a son to drag along, she had with her poor Will Cotton, whom you will have observed is more bewildered now than he ever was at ho— in New Zealand.'

There was a soft tap at the door and Mary Ann's bathmaid came in with a pile of soft towels.

'It is my fervent wish,' Sarah said quickly to beat the closing door, 'that our husbands have already made the decision. You will come to us at Lichfield.'

EIGHTEEN

Strangers and Pilgrims

London, 1868

THOSE WHO DIE in company may have the means to be granted a dying wish. I am not dying, not yet, tho' the way my limbs ache of a frosty morning and the sudden strictures of heart and breath could be harbingers. My list of symptoms grows daily more colourful and resistant to the dose so that I imagine I will end as one of those females that enter the pages of the newspapers — found dead surrounded by empty, small, sweet-smelling brown bottles.

My wish, whether I am dying yet or not, is to be once more upon the waves. I do not mean the Thames with its sooty stay-at-home starlings and crowded, slum-ringed docks. I would like a boat to take me out as far as the mouth of the river at the very least, even if only for a sniff of the open sea.

At this lodging house there is no little maid to attend to my comfort as there was at Tollington Park. Since our journey to Buxton — which left me in such grievous debt it has taken a full two years of penny-pinching and a begging letter to Ish to absolve my necessary maintenance loan from Judge Martin — I have had various rooms in various houses, public and private. Members of the clergy both Anglican and Dissenting have given me shelter; I have gone from inn to padken to priest and back again to finish here on the Camden Road, where friendships new and resumed have fallen away.

Miss Tripp, I hear, has sailed to New York, a city less suspicious of her origins. I know she believes we British care more for class than we do for race, but it becomes an old-fashioned notion that is adhered to more in the New World. A great many people of all races and from all over the Empire have come to England since the wars of the 'fifties, and the stay-at-homes do not like it.

Bee Cotton's father died while we were at Buxton and left him nothing — the estate will go to a younger brother. How much kinder it would have been if he had died years earlier, when Bee was yet a young man in New Zealand. Bee is still at Frodsham, growing older and more demented. Rumours of his alarming and undignified conduct circulate among congregations far and wide — he has a wine cellar with a Maori proverb etched above the door, he is intemperate, he refuses to administer to his flock, he threw a book at his doctor, he is mostly in a torpor, Holy Communion is rarely given, his very church is in abject disrepair. We correspond irregularly — the medicines I made him for our pilgrimage to Buxton made him better, I am sure. I have offered him the formula, but he declines it.

Mary Ann and the Judge remain at Lichfield with the Selwyns — my letters are returned unopened. Had I a piece of the Bishop's pink blotting paper, I would draw Sarah as her husband did over and over, beaky-nosed, but with her long fingers thrusting my communications into a pillar-box.

On the Camden Road I have unpacked more than ever before in the hope that this will be the last of my lodgings — it is certainly the poorest. I have a room of my own, but must share the crowded kitchen downstairs with many others, some so penniless they make their nightly beds there, close to the fire. I venture down as little as I can, cooking over my own grate and keeping mostly to my sanctuary, which has a lockable door. I have set my travelling table on its four spindly legs; I have a bedstead and quilt, my field chest and embroidered screen. Above the fire stand my Bibles in English and Maori and my simple mementoes of that other home. There is the tiki that Mokihi gave me as a parting gift, the nosegay of flowers from the sands of Maketu. My carpet is at last unrolled, which would please Miss Tripp should she ever return. Beside my bed are the portraits of my sons so that I might look at them each night before I sleep and send my love all those long miles. I keep also Horelock's letter, worn with caressing and regret. Had I ever been able to sit with Ish again, and we were talking of this and that, I might have been able to ask him casually, 'Do you remember meeting a man on the beach at Port Jackson?'

It was so inconsequential at the time that he did not tell me.

Mr Griggs visits me still and will occasionally accompany me on an outing, such as the one I make myself ready for now. The late April day, what I can glimpse of it through my one window above the busy street, is what Henry calls a 'windy, cloudy, hang-yourself sort of day' and I call a good day for sailing. I have not seen Mr Griggs for many weeks — or anyone else for that matter — and curiously I have never once felt alone. Memories of my long and fateful life break upon me and may occupy me for hours.

A single image — Henry in the garden at Maketu, his legs encased in canvas bags for the mosquitoes, gazing along the tumultuous, magnificent coast for a friendly sail. I have this picture in my mind as clearly as if I saw it, but I did not — it is how he described it himself. It is always late afternoon at the end of summer, that particular short-lived golden light that replaces the English dusk. He is in conversation with Tohi, the chief who asked the Governor for a pacifying Pakeha after a Tauranga tribe stole and ate a Maketu child. I remember, on one of my long visits to Henry, sitting by the fire and reading aloud to my son and Tohi from *Captain Grey's Travels in Australia* and how Tohi vowed he would see it for himself. I wonder if he ever did.

I remember how the house would fill with visitors, how Henry could walk to the pah in five minutes and spend many hours among the people, how abundant were our orchard and gardens. He lives there still, with Sophia and his children, and the house prospers. Only twenty-six miles away, the mission house at Te Ngae has its roof fallen in and grown over as surely as our cottage does at Manupirua. Cherries and walnuts grow wild, the asparagus gone. It is that image I mull over longest — all that we endeavoured there gone to green obliteration. It could all be so — Taurarua, Maketu, Te Papa — and then my sons and their families would be compelled to board ships with every other Pakeha and return to London as I have, tho' few would desire it. It would mean the utter failure of all our aspirations — the expulsion of the white man. It is a fantasy, and on so many counts wrong of me to indulge it — tho' I could compile an inventory of prospective passengers the Colony would be better without, officials and sub-officials on the make, land thieves and grog-floggers. Names surface: the Native Secretary Donald McLean, who has accrued land worth hundreds of pounds; the Tarawera arms-dealer Warbrick; even Governor Grey who returned to us after his term in South Africa as a different man. He had been coarsened, his previous respect for the Maori people eroded.

I have ordered a cab and put money aside for the fare. Mr Griggs will be here directly.

If I had embarked on my account, this would be a time to set about it, a way to fill the minutes spent waiting, but I have lost heart. When I bade goodbye to the Selwyns and the Martins at Buxton, Sarah was at pains to tell me that she and Mary Ann would work side by side on their memoirs. Often I think of them in that pink and grey room at Lichfield, surrounded by the multitude of china shepherdesses. At Sarah's announcement, Mary Ann had hidden her eyes from me so that I would not see the reluctance there.

'Come to us at Torquay,' she whispered to me as I bent to kiss her. 'I will write to you as soon as I know our day of departure.' Even as she said it I did not believe it would come to pass, not because she did not want it, but because Sarah and the Judge would not.

A good hour after the appointed time there is a knock at the door and in comes Mr Griggs, flustered, without removing his hat.

'I am so sorry, Mrs Smith — I had gone to your lodgings at Reverend Harris's. I had forgotten you had moved again.'

'Yes, yet again, Mr Griggs!' It is so lovely to see him. 'Will you sit down?'

'No time! A cab waits downstairs for you and the driver is impatient to be off!' He brings me my purse and shawl, bless him.

⁂

I have the cab drop us at London Bridge and from there Mr Griggs goes in search of a boat — my dying wish! He made no rejoinder to that, save for a quizzical smile as if to say, 'And how many of those do you intend?' He is a little out of temper, I think, with ladies who are dying. The invalid Miss Jennings has been dying for years, which pastime has proved a considerable drain on his time and finances. She is almost as good at it as certain missionary wives of my acquaintance who in the face of drudge and deprivation took to their deathbeds, several times over, before it was real to them. Sophia's mother Mrs Baker was legendary in the Colony for her singing of the hymn 'Jesus Lover of My Soul' when she believed the end was near. Reverend Baker let it be known abroad that she had 'entered into its true meaning with peculiar emphasis'. She had gathered her family and the oldest native girl around her to listen to her quote in its entirety Pope's 'Cease, fond Nature, cease thy strife, And let me languish into life'; she told the poor children, Sophia among them, that she was leaving. All present wept and mourned until a doctor was called who diagnosed her condition as imaginary. It is little wonder that Sophia will run herself out to the full length of her rope before she will take some rest, that she will not succumb to her mother's 'illness' — which had as its cause the birth of five children in six years and was not at all imaginary! Sophia could lie down for a month and still be sickly — she goes about dazed and incompetent, making a mess of things. Oh, how I wish now I had curbed my tongue with that daughter-in-law — she is the one I should have drawn the closest.

So absorbed am I in meditating on my distant loved ones that I scarcely notice my surrounds — the low wall I wait on, the thickening stream of Londoners of all variety out to enjoy the first sun we have had for weeks.

At length Mr Griggs is back with the intelligence that we may take either a steamer as far as Gravesend for one shilling and sixpence or hire a small sailing boat for rather more.

'There is a darkie to take us out. I asked for his master, but he says it is his boat.'

If the choice is to wallow in a black steamboat with lurid green cabin, bilious with the movement and the stench of fish and old shoes, or to sail alone with Mr Griggs, then there is no contest.

'My treat, of course!' I remind him as he helps me up from my waiting wall and through the Saturday crowds to the steps that lead down to the river. The prospect of a sail so lifts my spirits I manage entirely without his aid down to the path, where I wait for Mr Griggs to engage the sailor. *Hine* reads the vessel's name on her yellow prow. It strikes me as an excellent name for a small ship that will buck and skip like a deer and gallop over breakers as hines will do across open tussock.

Mr Griggs hands me in, and so does the sailor, who has a wide hat and muffler wound across his face for the cold wind. He lets go the painter and we pull on the guide ropes away from the jetty until we are free of it and our sails catch the wind. *Hine* ducks between steamers and colliers, passes Billingsgate Dock with its smell of fish and the Tower with its long-lost moat, keeping closer to the north bank than the south.

'I have not sailed since the voyage home from India,' says Mr Griggs, who has removed his topper for safekeeping and sits beside me in the stern with the sudden delight of a schoolboy, squinting in the sooty breeze. I hook my arm through his and we laugh together when the wind catches and lifts my bonnet and cap so emphatically that I remove it. The wind streams through my long hair, scattering pins until it is entirely loose! All is delicious — I am as close to abandon as an old grey mare may be. The tide is running out and the breeze behind us swift — Wapping, the Pool, Rotherhithe — the steamers we pass choked and noisy with pistons and braying patrons set on their early spring trip to Margate or to Gravesend.

Mr Griggs's warm arm is banded still with black crepe for his general maid Mrs Stott, who departed this world on Easter Sunday — she made quick work of it, falling where she stood in the scullery. He remembers her all the more fondly for her rapid demise. I will make quick work of my own after this. I desire nothing more — I throw my head back and sing a few lines of a boatsong I learned many years ago, 'He tuki waka tēnei, kia kaha ai ki ngā tāngata kē', as loudly as the men I once heard sing it over and over, paddling hard in short, swift bursts, then drifting a while to catch their breaths before singing and paddling again.

'What does it mean?' asks Mr Griggs.

'It is a song to give them strength.'

It certainly gives strength to me, and I draw breath for the next couplet, but Mr Griggs is saying, 'There is certainly not much of a tune to it.'

'That is a feature of sea songs — English sailors sing as dolefully tho' less rhythmically — Tōia te hoe i te waka, kia tere ai te waka!'

I now have the full attention of our sailor, who regards me with astonishment. He clambers along the boat from the bow where he had been hauling on the foresail, leaving the sheet flying, and hauling off his hat and muffler. His eyes do not leave my face, and as I meet them for the first time I see who he is. He takes my hands in his and presses his nose against mine in that way his people have of showing their regard.

George Rupai, Selwyn's walking dictionary on *Tomatin*.

'Why have you returned to England?' I ask eventually. 'You were so glad to be home, you showed us all a clean pair of heels!'

He shakes his head as if the answer to that question is so large he could not begin on it, but then, slowly, in his own language, he tells me that he has been in London for almost ten years. His late benefactor in England (tho' he calls him kaipaua — abductor) had left him money that took a time to find him.

'The sails!' Mr Griggs stands and the little boat rocks. 'The ropes, my man!'

But George will not leave me, and despite Mr Griggs's best attempts with the tiller, the yacht begins to broach and circle alarmingly — a blackened collier looms to starboard and we almost collide. Mr Rupai leaps to turn us away, his story broken off. I would have the rest of it — my desire for the blue horizon dissipates in its wake.

We are almost at Limehouse Pier. The slums and warehouses of Limehouse Reach are the opposite of what I had hoped for.

'Me hoki ki uta?' I ask him, pointing towards the bank.

He brings *Hine* about — not hine at all, that old word for deer, but *hi-ne*, a Maori word for girl — and we slip between canal boats and lighters for the muddy shore. The explanation I give to Mr Griggs is necessarily short — this was the lad who voyaged with us on *Tomatin*, grown to middle age and returned to work the Thames, as different from a New Zealand river as could be imagined.

As soon as we are tied up, and who knows how long we will be allowed to remain so — an excise man stands with his ledger examining a cargo-laden canal boat — Mr Griggs clambers up to the crowded pier. There are hawkers and lightermen, beggars and maids, sailors and snot-nosed chavvies. There is a perambulator, battered and worn, rattling a broken wheel along the timbers with a proud young mother at its helm — what a fine new invention is the perambulator! A young soldier and the hopeful girl on his arm gaze across the river and lift their faces to the early uncertain spring warmth.

'I will go to the nearest inn,' Mr Griggs announces, 'and bring us a pot of beer.'

George points out his direction, then comes to sit beside me in the stern and hold my hand. I cannot take my eyes off him — his smooth open brow, his black thick hair coursed with silver, his deep world-weary eyes. What has he had to learn to survive in this place? False friends and true would easily have divested him of his fortune.

'I bought *Hine* with the last of it.'

'Are you entirely alone here?'

'I am acquainted with plenty, men and women and —' he looks about as if he does not wish to be overheard by the sailors and paupers above — 'and kehua.'

My benign and comforting ghosts do not agitate me as his appear to do. He is wide-eyed, the same fear blazing there that I saw when he slaughtered taniwha on the deck of the ship, those creatures he blamed for his childhood exile — but he does not allow it to possess him.

I have ghosts too, I could tell him, born of remorse and regret, but instead I ask, 'What do they say to you?'

'They tell me I must go home, but I cannot. I stole the money for myself, and my people are angry with me.'

It was your money, I could respond, but it would not be true. There have been countless attempts to civilise his people of 'beastly communism', as it is styled by the officials. They have succeeded with Rupai, tho' not in the way they intended.

'Are you married, Mr Rupai?'

He shakes his head, but happily enough — he suffers no shortage of female attention then. Were I still that girl who left my father's house to go to the sailors' dances with Horelock, I would dance with him. I would like him to spin me the length of the floor and back again.

'Did you go to your benefactor's widow when you came back? Did he have children you grew up beside?'

'He was alone in the world.' George narrows his eyes to gaze across the water to where some ragged children poke sticks into the stinking mud — mudlarks digging for coins. 'He was harmless enough. He left me mostly to the servants — I was, as Mrs Selwyn said, their "pet". She said it before me on the ship, and I have often thought on it.'

I will not enquire to his conclusions, having seen enough of downstairs life to imagine it. Doubtless he was fed and fondled and endured unwelcome caresses and castigation from any number.

'Were I ten years younger, I would insist on your return and accompany you home to strengthen your resolve.'

'I would not go.' He folds his arms across his chest, his haunted cast returning.

Three children have come to stand at the edge of the pier and look down at us. There is a boy with a fishing line and a girl carrying a marmalade kitten with a mucky eye. She wears a blue smock, clumsily made, and it is a moment or two before I recognise her as Hikipene and see that she holds Katie by the hand — Katie with a smudge on her nose and tangled hair. But those beloved faces fade away as quickly as they came, and the urchin's real face is as urgent as the narrow hand she holds out for coins. George takes from his pocket a farthing and gives it to her, the boat rocking as he stands in his heavy boots. In one swift movement she hands him the kitten and melts away into the crowd, pulling her younger sister after her.

George is so surprised that it seems at first he will toss the kitten overboard, but he thinks the better of it and instead gives it to me. It is only a few weeks old, scarcely big enough to be away from its mother.

'For you, Mrs Smith. Do you have a ngeru?' The word can mean sleek, smooth. This kitty is bony, her fur rough and the mucky eye superficial. I am tempted to use my handkerchief, but resist. Animal husbandry has rarely been my forte.

'Do you remember the puppies on *Tomatin*?' I ask him. 'The bitch whelped in the cabin you shared with Ish and we looked after them through the night after she died.'

The memory dawns on him warmly. 'I do! I do remember that!'

'The Bishop came in to see them in the early hours of the morning, bringing his little son and Mr Cotton, who was broken out of the torpor that had settled over him after the loss of his bees.'

'And Ish fainted when the pups came — he banged his head!' George laughs.

I had forgotten that. Poor Ish. I would like to tell George he was a false friend to my son, that Ish's black moods only increased after the loss of him, but he strokes the little cat so gently, with so tender an expression I do not have the heart for it.

'Ka tau te wairua i tō hokinga mai?' I ask. 'In New Zealand, I mean.'

'I was happy enough at first, when I was still a boy. I was welcomed by my family, what was left of it — there had been so much sickness. But as I grew up I remembered all the fine things of England and I wanted to see them again. I made enemies among my people for the praises I sang of this country, for my arrogance for having been here. I told them they were savages, that I would one day return, that the rich man would have forgiven me.'

'For what?'

'For not being happy with him, for wanting always to go home to New Zealand, for not returning his love.'

Mr Griggs is returned with a pot of beer and hot potatoes wrapped in brown paper, and George will say no more. Silently, he helps him down and we pass the pot, sip and eat, our host bringing a twist of salt from his pocket for our savoury. I have been in London for nearly six years, I tell him, tho' he has not asked for my story. I tell him also that I wish often that I had not returned. It comes into my mind to mention our war, which he must know of if he keeps his ears open when ships are in from those distant ports — but if the news has escaped him, then it would be cruel to advise him of it.

'Which part of New Zealand are you from?' Mr Griggs asks conversationally, but George will not give that up, merely grunting as he finishes his hot potato and reaches for another. Above our heads an oysterman walks with his pail and George calls him over to give him a penny and an old cup to fill. I would warn him against them, but his stomach must be stronger than mine — after all, he thrives on this fetid tide. Likewise, Mr Griggs does not partake — our refusal could offend a Maori host, but Rupai shrugs and concentrates on completing his own meal.

'Would you like to know what became of Ish? You remember you were cabinmates and went about together in Sydney?'

He allows himself a moment to recollect John, or not, but the memory does not entice him.

'Where do you live, Mrs Smith? What is this man to you?'

I give him my address and explain my connection with dear Mr Griggs, from which arises another chance to tell him about Ish, but still he does not enquire. He tosses the paper and scraps to be fallen upon by the mudlarks, and unties the little boat.

'Would you visit me, Mr Rupai?'

'Mata Te Mete,' he says kindly, 'I think we would be each of us made more lonely by it.'

'But would you not like to sit and remember those people so far away?'

'I have come here to forget. It is better that you keep your secrets and I keep mine.'

So bruising and perplexing is this that I make no reply.

We bob out to catch the current — the wind is blowing more strongly and we will have a job against it. It begins to rain, a skirl of it on the headwind as we tack back and forth — but our sailor is skilful and I determine, unsuccessfully, to enjoy the trip back as much as I enjoyed the course downriver. Chance meetings may change a life — or they may be as inconsequential as this drop of rain to the Thames. If I had not met with Mr Rupai, I would not be seized by this desire to make him my friend, to have him be for me everything I left behind. His thick hair streams behind him, his eyes narrow against the weather, and I could once again be in New Zealand and on my way to a settlement or Maori village to work. And if I were there, would I only be longing to be here as I was those last years? When I was a girl, my mother would chastise me for my changefulness. As Horelock's young wife, he had only to indulge my love of adventure to make me happy.

At the landing steps, Mr Griggs is impatient to be off. There is an icy drizzle, we are damp from our voyage and he is disappointed that we did not complete our assignment to reach Gravesend. He goes ahead to find a cab.

When our sailor helps me out of the boat, I keep hold of his hand for a moment.

'There are people who love you in New Zealand, Mr Rupai, I am sure of it.'

George Rupai shakes his head. 'I am making my life here and why should I not? I can determine my own fate as much as can any white man.'

'I did not mean that you . . .' But he has pulled his hand away and bends to the kitten, who picks her way towards him across a coil of rope. He puts her in my arms.

'Will you come to see me?' I try again, with a kind of shamelessness. Why should he come to visit me? I am so firmly a part of his distant past, and he is a man for the future. He must hear the desperation in my voice — I am blushing for it — because he nods. And sighs. He cannot help his kindness.

'Āe. I will come to call soon. Haere ra, Mrs Smith.'

Perhaps he is only telling me what I want to hear. As I make my way up to Mr Griggs and the waiting cab, I remember that I only gave him the address the once, and he did not write it down.

NINETEEN

London

27 March 1869

IN THE LODGING HOUSE on Camden Road, news spread that the lady on the first floor was dying. Rumour had it that she had spent her life in the Colonies, though no one was sure exactly which one. Some said Australia, some said Africa, others were sure it was India. Some said she was a Native-lover, which was evidenced one day by the arrival of a darkie about to set sail for his home in the South Seas and wanting to bid her farewell. Mrs O'Leary the landlady tried to send him away, but he pushed past her and knocked on all the doors until the one that belonged to Mrs Smith was opened to him. He was alone with her for some hours and laughter was heard from both the lady and the visitor. When he emerged, she had given him her greenstone ornament. He had tied it around his neck and he was weeping.

There was only one other friend who visited, and that was infrequently, less often than the bailiff, who was regular in his attentions — not to Mrs Smith herself, but to the families who lived crowded eight to a bed in the rooms. By his erect carriage the visitor was perhaps an old soldier or schoolmaster. On one occasion he brought with him his sickly wife, who refused to mount the greasy stairs but waited shawled and bonneted in the downstairs hall as motionless as a statue, it was said, like 'patience on a monument smiling at grief'.

On another occasion he brought with him a young girl whom he intended to act as Mrs Smith's maid, the door being so often locked against those lodgers who would bring her bread or a scrap of meat for her cat. The maid came the next day as arranged, but flew away again as if the devil himself was after her. That evening Mrs O'Leary held the kitchen inhabitants enthralled with her account of events, which was that the girl had heard the voices of children from within, that she had knocked and called until one of them had come to the other side of the door and said repeatedly what sounded like 'poota atoo', which all agreed was not the Queen's tongue. The little maid knocked again, and another child seemed to join the first, and said as clearly as if it stood beside her in the corridor, 'Mata says to let her in', and the door opened to show the room empty but for the old lady in the bed who was past care. Mrs O'Leary had gone upstairs herself then, and found it was as the girl had said — it was too late for the doctor and too soon for the priest, should anyone know which colour of priest to call.

From her capacious skirts Mrs O'Leary produced a purse of pale brown velvet with a drawstring top, from which she distributed some twenty pounds. From another pocket came a handful of small brown bottles that were shared among the assembled to assuage pain and quieten fractious infants. There were also letters — one she had removed from the corpse's very hand! She waved it aloft — from Port Jackson, no less than a convict's confession! — but she could not read it for its faded ink and ruinous creases, and neither could a keen-eyed lodger of learning, so it was consigned to the fire. The other correspondence was from the lady's sons and contained nothing of any interest. Mrs O'Leary had laboured over them in Mrs Smith's room — they were accounts of household matters and children. One of the sons appeared to be involved in a Native war in New Zealand, which country Mrs O'Leary had never heard of. She tucked the letters into the velvet purse and gave it to a ragged child who stretched her hands for the pretty thing, the same colour as the dead lady's little cat.

The caller who had visited only the day before, and so knew the end was nigh, came the following morning. Directly, he went out again to arrange the undertaker and a grave at Highgate and returned in the afternoon to sit alone with the departed. Mrs O'Leary gave him her word that he would find all as it was, but he climbed the stairs to discover that Mrs Smith's belongings had been rifled.

The carved box and greenstone tiki were gone from the mantelpiece, as was the silver-framed daguerreotype of John Elisha from her bedside. The cupboard stood open, and it was emptier than he had seen it — there was no sign even of the ancient, voluminous shawl of linsey-woolsey last worn on their river outing. There had been a pewter teapot, a china cup and her tin traveller — a cup with a folding handle of which she was inordinately proud. There remained the dried grasses and the English Bible above the fire and the Maori one by her pillow.

He hovered near the bed, taking a few moments before he was able to look into the face of his departed friend. He thought of the lines 'They who have seen Thy look in death no more may fear to die', but murmured instead, 'Dear, dear Mrs Smith — not to worry, not to worry,' which was foolish, because all her worries were over.

Under the bed was her leather portmanteau, which he remembered she had with her when she came off the ship. He began to pack her few remaining things away. The Maori Bible, when he reached for it, had a blue edge protruding from early in the New Testament — *Matiu*. It was a list that featured his own name, as well as those of the lunatic priest of Frodsham, of the Bishop of New Zealand and Mary Ann — he supposed Martin — the woman she'd cared for and of whom she had always spoken adoringly, as if she were a kind of saint. The fifth was Florence Nightingale, whom he doubted Elizabeth had ever met. It pleased him that his friend had achieved all of her objectives, except the last.

In fresher ink, more crabbed even than her correspondence from Auckland, was a single word writ large: *Why?* The lines below took some deciphering.

'*Why Henry and not John? Why the resemblance? No relation between H and Kitty, no common parent.* <u>Telegonie</u>? <u>Telegeny</u>? <u>Telegony</u>???'

The next phrase almost conquered him until he understood it read: '*but the likeness proceeding an extra stage, from N to me to Tom for Kitty.*'

It could only mean one thing — not only that there had been another husband before Captain Hogg, but that the man was Henry's father. While the revelation rocked him — to his foundations! — he saw that Mrs Smith was not as blameless as she had pretended to be, and also — this thought following rapidly after — that he had somehow always suspected it. A woman was never as tough, as resilient, as Mrs Smith if she had not a past to hide, experience to make her steely and give her a coat of armour in which to pass through the world of men — to hold her apart from them. And surely Henry didn't know the truth, for why else would he have been so determined for the investigation to proceed?

Telegony.

There had been a case of it when he was in India, he remembered, a child born to a lower-class English girl who had had a scandalous affair with an Indian several years before her marriage to an English soldier. The husband had forgiven her her past until his child was born dark-skinned, the wife passing on the characteristics of her earlier seducer. Telegony had been her defence, and she was widely believed, even though any right-thinking person would doubt the phenomenon in this modern age, especially since the publication of Mr Darwin's book.

. . . from N to me to Tom to Kitty . . .

Had Mrs Smith suspected that her husband had somehow carried from her that man's likeness — *N*, whoever he was — to pass on to his daughter by another wife? Or was it her own likeness she imagined he carried? It was a preposterous fancy and surprising in a woman who had had more than a passing interest in medicine, in the workings of the human body.

You disappoint me, Mrs Smith, not so much for your secret but for your desire to claim Kitty as more your own than she was. He looked down at his old friend's face, the closed, fine-veined eyelids, and remembered that other time, in the summer, when she had collapsed in his parlour. But there was no hope of rousing her this time to explain that if Kitty resembled Henry — and she did, he had seen it himself — then it was only coincidence. The more the Earth was peopled, the more people would look alike, the more there would be resemblances that could not be explained by inheritance. It stood to reason.

A bubbling, hissing sound — and Mr Griggs found himself looking immediately to the fire for a kettle, but there was none, the embers long dead: it had emanated from Mrs Smith herself. He had seen enough bodies in his time as a soldier to know there was nothing mysterious about it — it was the last of the breath escaping. Still, the hairs rose on the back of his neck and he moved away towards the small window, the note still in his hand.

He supposed she had not been thinking clearly at the end — but then she not been well since their voyage on the Thames with the New Zealand Native who had rejected her proposal of friendship. It was proof of her state of mind that she regarded him as representative of his entire race and believed that none of them remembered her with love. It was as if the man had been a member of a small family that had revised its opinion of her.

From his pocket he drew a page torn from a lady's notebook. He had brought it with him the previous day to read parts of it aloud to his old friend, but she had been too far gone. It might have cheered her, for Kitty had proved elusive since their return from Buxton. He read the letter now, her assurance that events in that town had conspired to spare the old people any shame. She intended to write to her half-brothers in New Zealand to tell them of her existence, and that of her sisters.

'But I must have their addresses — it is a pity they are not still Hoggs, for I understand the Colony is so small a letter may find its way without every detail of the receiver — but Smith! I do not blame her for abandoning Hogg, for is it not the ugliest name on Earth? My new husband would like to make a play on her adventures, but he will call her by something prettier.'

Mr Griggs had replied immediately by return mail that she absolutely must not write to Henry and John Elisha, that he had promised them there would be no contact unless they desired it. And they would not, most definitely! He reminded her of the Brahmin belief — she must surely already know of it — that on crossing a body of water a man loses his caste.

'It is a phenomenon that occurs naturally in the Colonies, without religion. You would stand to destroy all that your brothers have achieved there,' he wrote. 'I urge you to desist.'

Crouching at the fireplace, Mr Griggs tore Mrs Smith's list and musings to tiny pieces and scattered them in the grate. From his pocket he drew a box of safety matches, struck one and held it to the thin paper — a brief, bright flare and the fragments curled and burnt away. Mr Griggs surprised himself — there was a lump in his throat and his eyes stung, just a little.

Goodbye, Mrs Smith. Godspeed.

He made his way downstairs. In one hand he carried the portmanteau and under the other arm the scraped and banged medicine chest, which the landlady maintained was all Elizabeth had arrived with.

TWENTY

Creation's Lords

Pipitea Street, Wellington, 1869

'MY HEART IS FEELING about, as it were, for my mother.'
John Elisha Smith, Solicitor, Receiver of Revenue, Chief Registrar of Deeds, and Sheriff of Wellington, looked up from his brother's letter as his wife and sister-in-law passed in the hall, three of the children running before them, and felt the phrase resound in his head.

Henry had written the same thing, many years before, after the experiment at Manupirua, where he was suffering from a knee injury that would trouble him for the rest of his life and taking more baths in the hot mineral springs than was good for him. His letters from that place had at first been gloating — 'Do you not envy me my cosy evenings with the society of our beloved mother?' — but as time went on his tone changed, as John knew it inevitably would. It would have been better for them if their mother had married again — a widower perhaps, a healthy husband to absorb her tumultuous affections. Henry had had the worst of it. And also the best.

He carried the letter over to the window for the better light, though it scudded in the fierce wind that kicked up steely, white-capped waves in the harbour below the house. His niece Bertha, the seven-year-old who resembled his mother to an alarming degree — 'even to the bend in her neck!' was Sophia's observation — was ministering to an unwilling cat: Tip gone rangy since his diet of dotterels in the marsh had been extinguished. She examined the inside of its ear, forcing the animal to lie flat on a garden seat, stroking it tenderly. If he were a man to give expression to his emotions, he would rush now out from his study, down the hall and out into the garden, scoop the child into his arms and cover her with kisses. He would teach her it is as well to accept love as to give it; he would help her not to make the same mistakes his mother had made — showering those around her with affection but struggling to receive it herself, as if she believed herself not worthy of it and would push those who loved her away, going as far as to voyage to the other end of the Earth.

When she first began on the idea of returning Home, neither son had been brave enough to ask her 'Who is it you expect to find?', and nor could they believe that their mother was capable of returning to England in a fit of pique. She must surely have had some idea that she would reunite with their father, or that Hogg would make her his fiscal responsibility — but even when he and Henry had drawn Mr Griggs into the investigation, they were no further along. At one stage of their correspondence their old schoolmaster believed he had found a half-sister.

'I will leave my investigations here,' he had written, 'for this whole sorry business is really none of my concern. If you were to make the voyage yourselves and take up where I have left off, then you may be able to affect reunion with your parent. The young woman has vanished and your mother too ill for a final questioning. At all times her feelings were respected — all enquiries were necessarily opaque.'

Henry had enclosed the letter with this one, which John smoothed now on the sill.

'In all these years since our dearest mother left you have never fully described how it was for her on her last few days before sailing away — I look forward to hearing the account in person. I have long worried that your silence on the matter was to save me some anxiety and so did not press you on it. Was her mind really so made up all those years ago? It is difficult to tell from her letters whether she enjoys the contentment she anticipated, which I fear is a common condition for those returning. It is no secret that the ships leaving Auckland are quite often as crowded as they were arriving, but carrying a disgruntled tribe of settlers as opposed to the hopeful one. I trust she remembers at least some of her time here fondly. If only either you or I had been able to provide for her a home of her own, then she may have been able to live out her days here, visited now and again by the people she had worked for, and her grandchildren. It still galls me that she was never able to achieve pacific relations with either of her daughters-in-law, indeed set them against her from early in their acquaintance. I know my poor Sophia did her best.'

Crazed by the buffeting wind and persistent attention, the cat had scratched Bertha and run away, but the child was not crying. She had hauled herself up onto the garden seat, scuffed boots swinging, her broad brow bent to examine the long cut to the white flesh of her underarm. Neither mother or aunt was in evidence — he could hear children's voices raised from the side of the house. There were so many of them now, and mostly girls. They should be encouraged to play quietly inside.

As the uncle watched, a broad leaf fell from the tree above the seat, fluttering to the child's fair head. The child caught it up and ran its edge along the scratch, collecting the droplets of blood. She had inherited her grandmother's morbid curiosity then, and her father's stoicism. His own daughters resembled more their own mother, rather than his, which was how he preferred it. As each successive daughter arrived, he quailed at any observed resemblance.

'We are not a family in good repute,' he had noted to his brother in Spartan refrain over many years. Henry had chastised him: 'I do hope I am the only man with whom you share that opinion, and I must assure you it is not true. By your repetition of it to others you would make it so.'

Bertha had bounded off the garden seat now and was running away, the leaf discarded to blow about the lawn.

'The children are all so excited at the prospect of moving to Wellington and spending Easter with their cousins, but I think, dear brother, that I am the most excited of all. I have not gazed upon your dear face for more than ten years — aside from your picture of course. I sense you were affronted by my remarks on it, but I do not like your beard — it is in my opinion a great mistake — unsuitable to your style of face — when I see you animated I may be proved wrong. I am on circuit in Whanganui and will be with you all at Pipitea Street on the eve of Good Friday at the latest, all going well.

'We will see one another very soon, God willing. May our Saviour bless you and keep you.

I am always, dear Ish,
Your devoted brother,
Henry.'

John Elisha lifted his gaze again to the harbour. If only he could see the ship coming in now, one of the battered coastal steamers on which Henry risked his life on his voyages around the North Island for interminable meetings with the Natives. He was a born negotiator, with an instinct to search for the truth and not judge his fellow man. Always since they were boys John had aspired to be more like him — instead, as Henry wrote to him once 'Everybody comes under your lash.' He had not liked the same quality in their mother.

Ish folded the letters together, his brother's and Mr Griggs's, and put them away in his desk, his well-worn thoughts running along — surely he was never similarly opinionated, so dangerous a party to knowledge, and too partial to speaking out of turn for effect or amusement as their mother. He was not that much his mother's son. He did not resemble her physically as Henry did, and he did not have her talent for brazen appeal. How often had she taken it upon herself to call upon the Bishop or the Judge or even — unfortunately — Governor Grey to advance their case, with very mixed results? It must have been easier for Henry since she had gone back to London.

Peeking around the study door was Little Henry, ten years old, the apple of Henry's eye — his Lord of Creation.

'Young man?'

'Could you please come into the parlour, Uncle John?' The child was thin, earnest, the sort of boy who needed a brother to share some of his battles — he had only sisters. Why did the Lord not send the family sons? It was a punishment.

'Why?'

'Grandmother's portrait has shifted on the wall.'

'Has it, indeed?' He would humour young Henry, as he had so often failed to humour the older. 'And how did that happen, do you suppose?'

'Aunt says because of the earthquake yesterday.'

'Earthquake! Was it as grand as all that? I would call it a tremor.'

The child, who had spent most of his life at Maketu in the Bay of Plenty and was a veteran of seismic shifts, regarded his uncle steadily. Ish laid his hand gently on the boy's tousled head.

'Mamma made a joke and Aunt laughed, but I didn't understand it and neither did Bertha.'

'Can you remember the joke?'

'"Elizabeth must be displeased."'

He would not quiz the child, who could be precocious. Henry had enjoyed relaying the quip; dimples formed in his cheeks with the effort to suppress a smile.

'And then Aunt said, "Oh dear, what ails her this time, do you think?" And Mamma replied—'

The uncle held up a warning hand: 'Henry!' His imitation of the women was too precise.

'"— That she is not here among us the first time we are all together after so many years." And then — the front door banged shut, very, very loudly, as if Grandma had slammed it herself!' the child finished, triumphantly — just as another door slammed, shaking the house, an internal door into the echoing passage. There followed immediately a piercing infant wailing, the pitch and urgency of which never failed to set John's teeth on edge. The boy jumped, looking over his shoulder.

'Mamma says Grandma is here in spirit.'

One of the first stories John Elisha ever heard about Sophia Baker — and she was a young woman the Colony talked about, for the cruel tragedy of her childhood — was how at fifteen she had seen two bodies, Maori, laid out on Mokoia Island at Rotorua, and conceived a fanciful terror of their spirits that had unnerved the women around her, and also some of the men, and how her infection of the people spread and took a great deal of trouble to contain. Perhaps she had learned early the power of the medium, but John had presumed her to have grown into a sensible woman. His mother was convinced that she was not in the least practical, and his wife Lilias had whispered that the older children had practically no warm clothes and the younger in hand-me-downs, and autumn in Wellington! The child before him had his knee almost out of one leg of his britches and his jacket was too short in the arms.

Little Henry took his uncle's hand, confidently. 'Please? They are waiting for you.'

⁂

The portrait was indeed skewed on the picture rail, though so much was awry in the room, which thronged with infants. The older girls were playing with their dolls on the window seat and the younger on a rug spread at the feet of their mothers, who sat wide-eyed on the settee. It was unlike Lilias to be superstitious.

'What is it?' he asked shortly. 'If it is just the painting to be straightened, then surely you could have asked the maid.'

'But you know the maid has run away,' said his oldest daughter, coming into the room bearing a tea tray, which she placed on a table. One of the infants took heed of the cake and began crying for it. 'To be with her people,' Marion continued over the whining. 'There is a war on, Father.'

'Do not take that tone, my girl.' He looked at her more closely. She wore a smeary apron from the kitchen and had dark circles under her eyes.

'Be thankful you have girls first to do the work of servants,' his mother had comforted him for his abundance of daughters and paucity of sons. He should find the letter and show it to Marion. She seemed resentful, though had at least replaced the chill atmosphere in the room with one of churlishness.

'Look at your mother's portrait,' said his wife quietly, nodding at her daughter to begin pouring out.

'Yes, I can see.'

'The other pictures have remained straight,' Lilias went on. 'See

— the paintings of Mount Egmont and Loch Lomond. Why is that?'

John shook his head. His mother looked across the room, above the heads of her daughters-in-law and grandchildren, with a resigned expression that was not characteristic. The artist had exaggerated the richness of her cap — he did not remember it with quite so much lace. It was a long time since he had given the portrait perusal. Indeed, he had never looked at it so closely since defining it as 'proficient' almost a decade ago. It was painted during his mother's last weeks in Wellington before she sailed. He thought now that he could read trepidation in her face, an anticipation of the long, perilous voyage, though he had seen little of that at the time. She had been more in one of her brittle, take-no-prisoners moods, in a hurry to be gone.

'I think she looks better like that,' said Marion, who had found her grandmother a trial.

'Will you need a ladder?' asked Lilias.

He would, not being tall enough to reach above the crowded mantelpiece without disturbing the row of smaller paintings that hung beneath the portrait.

'Did you hear the door slam?' asked Sophia, clasping her thin, work-worn hands entreatingly.

'Not the first time, no, which is odd, given this house bangs like a drum when the wind runs through it.'

'Oh, no. It wasn't the wind,' Sophia said. 'It was unearthly. It was—'

'Young Henry has already told me. There will be no more of that nonsense.'

He turned on his heel and went out, there not being a cup set for him on the tray — or at least, not his own cup, which Marion knew he preferred.

The front door gaped again. The maid must have opened it, or one of the children, he thought, then remembered the maid had gone away. Closing it after him, he went across the verandah and down the steps into the garden, where he stood for a moment at the gate. Had he missed seeing the ship? It was unlikely — except for the time he was engaged in re-reading Henry's letter, he had scarcely taken his eyes away from the Heads all day. Still, his brother might appear, far below, making his way along the road that looped around from the port. He waited and watched a little longer, but the street was deserted.

What a curse this lack of servants was. Was there a ladder? Where would it be? He found himself rounding the house to the shed — he had never before been in there. The door hung unevenly and stood ajar, a drift of autumn leaves at its foot. If he waited for Henry, then they could do it together, straighten Mother on the wall. A familiar sense of inadequacy assailed him, different from the one that pursued him at his desk in the face of the usual deluge of correspondence. He felt his arms hang heavy and useless at his sides while the boisterous wind tugged at his coattails and beard more persistently than an infant got loose from its mother.

Young Henry joined his sisters at the window seat. On his way he snatched Te Kooti from little Edith, who howled at the loss of the doll. Te Kooti had a moko in fine blue wool, embroidered by Grandma. He remembered her labouring over it, bringing into play her lacemaker's lamp in order to see the stitches. In its soft, magical glow, Te Kooti's scowl had taken shape around his button eyes — Henry gripped its knitted waist above the knotted cord of its skirt, and held it up out of squealing reach. Once it had had a mouth, which had a little smile, but it was long fallen off. Te Kooti looked very grumpy indeed, and Mamma never took up a needle unless she had to. Grandma had given the lamp to him and he had kept it on a shelf in their house in Maketu until an earthquake much larger than the one they'd had yesterday shivered it away to dust.

'Hark at Uncle John.' He pointed into the garden.

His older sister followed his gaze.

'He's praying, Henry. See — his head is bowed.'

'What's Pa praying for?' asked Marion.

Suddenly, before he realised quite what he was going to do, Henry flung out an arm to open the casement, stitches popping the full length of his too-tight jacket sleeve, and tossed Te Kooti out into the garden. His uncle looked around sharply, his gaze resting on the row of assembled faces in the window and his shoulders lifting almost to his ears in a sigh. Behind him, Edith howled more loudly, setting Aunt's baby howling too.

'Poor Uncle John,' said Henry loudly, 'I expect he's in another midnight of the mind.'

'What was that?'

His mother was going to slap him for throwing the doll — she had left her place with such intent and speed — but was pulled up short by his aunt repeating more loudly, over the wailing babies, 'What did you say, lad?'

'Grandma used to say it — "Oh I do hope Elisha is not in another midnight of the mind."'

His older cousins' snorts of laughter were gratifying, but the mimicry brought him finally the delayed slap on the back of the head.

'Oh, he is always so! He is always so!' moaned his aunt.

He raced from the room, noticing as he flew by that his aunt had abandoned her upright position on the settee to languish tearfully on its cushions, and that his mother was returning to her with comparable speed, murmuring, 'Oh dear Lilias, no — you must not —'

Uncle John was gone and the doll had landed headfirst in a garden of dead things — one of its button eyes dangled from a thorn. Henry pocketed the eye and grabbed up the doll, scratching his legs on the sharp brown sticks while he posted it inside. His mother was still comforting his aunt, and all the girls were watching him, lined up at the window.

He ran away, across the garden towards the shed. The door stood ajar and it looked dark and cool in there. A person who was in a midnight of the mind might like it, so he went in to look for his uncle. It was empty but for an upended wheelbarrow and flowerpots, a rake and a spade and, leaning against the far wall, a ladder. He would carry it inside, he decided, he would put the painting right, which would cheer everybody up — but the ladder proved cumbersome. He could not help that it somehow hooked up a sack of pinecones hanging beside it and cleared a bench of old pots and crocks, nor that it lost some paint on its passage through the door. Outside, the audience of girls seemed to help it come to lie heroically over his shoulder. He carried it with no further mishap around the side of the house and inside through the kitchen passage.

With his mother's assistance and the older cousins shifting the clock and ornaments on the mantel, it was short work to rescue Grandma from the lurch of her ship. It was grand, the way the women watched him achieve the task. Aunt observed to Mamma that he was 'beginning to fill out' and Mamma made a little noise in her throat, a tiny, proud laugh.

What sort of man would he be, he wondered, as he returned to the garden with the ladder. He thought he would have a farm. He would not be a man for paper and inky fingers and interminable worries like his father and uncle. He felt his shoulders square and a new strength in his legs, which made him want to run very fast, so he took off out the gate and down the hill. There was a ship coming in and it was his father's. It was perhaps only an hour out, and he would be there to meet him.

Lying between the North and South Islands, the Cook Strait is one of the most tumultuous stretches of water in the world. Henry pondered this fact as he clung to the taffrail of his ship — if it weren't for his blessed knee he would stand upright and enjoy the ride. There was a stiff sou-westerly blowing and there had been a shower or two of rain, but now the day was blue and glaring, with racing clouds that would cover the sun only momentarily. It was fine enough for the family to make their way down to the beach — if they were to note the signal rising now on the flagstaff or were to see the ship coming in. He longed to see them all — this tour had been almost three months in duration. He would cradle his baby girl Edith and listen to Henry's prattle, he would kiss Sophia's loving lips. Three months since he'd seen them, and nine whole years since he'd seen his brother. He prayed suddenly, fervently, that he would find John buoyant and not wanting to sequester them alone together in his study, away from the women and children or his Wellington friends. On that last visit all those years ago, Ish would grudge him only ten minutes conversation with a European and five minutes with a Maori. He had been too much alone. Away from his mother and brother he had been starved of affection.

White Star made good progress up the harbour towards the port. There had been more building going on at Lambton Quay since Henry's last visit, more houses showing their roofs in the steep narrow gullies leading away from the shore. There were more ships rocking at anchor and less evidence of the original inhabitants in the bays. It was changed — all so changed — from the tents and shacks that had been their reception in 1841. Henry tried to recall the younger self, the improver who had boarded the *Brougham* at Gravesend — and could not begin to remember his hopes and ambitions. Surely none of his training as surveyor had prepared him for the anguished conscience that had assailed him almost daily from his early twenties on, whether he laboured for Church or State. The love of the people here, expressed openly and generously, was often overwhelming — he remembered Wiremu Hoete asking him to call him Papa, Sarah Jowitt sitting him down one day in her fine house on Waiheke and telling him how loved he was by a considerable number of people, Tamihana's concern for him at Manupirua; he remembered welcoming friends at Maketu and Rotorua, the kainga he visited as Commissioner and Judge. All over New Zealand, villages were depleted for the hosts' generosity and natural curiosity for the white man, their cupboards bare and love betrayed. More and more tireless men arrived from Europe — the Colony attracted the most determined of Church, State and Commerce — and more and more of them went among the Maoris with no language and only one objective. Why should the people not fight to retain their land? Why should they not go on throwing up leaders like Titokowaru and Te Kooti? Would there come a time when they did not? It was only a year since Te Kooti had last emerged from the Urewera mountains.

Among the small knot of people waiting on the beach was a man whose narrow stature and slightly stooped bearing identified him long before Henry left the ship for the wet and choppy passage in the longboat. A smaller figure was dancing back and forth around him, holding his arms out to the wind as if he was a bird and could take off. It was surely Henry, but the child was taller than he remembered. The boy had seen him now and was calling into the gale, his hands circling his mouth: 'Papa! Papa!'

Tears stung and ran in the buffeting wind — his brother and son waiting for him on the shore, together: who would ever have thought it possible? Such a simple pleasure, a simple arrival — but it brought a welter of emotion. His mother would have liked to see it, to have seen them all together just once more — and here they all were. She had put her own son on a ship when he was barely a man; she had seen his chance and taken it for him. He thanked her now for her courage, and a very different scene flashed before his eyes — a premonition perhaps, the places swapped — he and Ish side by side on the shore watching young Henry sail away for England. The generation before, the likes of the Selwyns and the Greys, had sent their sons Home to school. He would not. This was all the home his son would ever need. Elizabeth would die in London, sooner rather than later, and the last link would be broken.

The boy splashed through the shallows to take his father's hand, while John Elisha waited above. When finally the two brothers were face to face on the sand, a moment or two passed before either was able to speak.

AFTERWORD

Tricks and Mirrors

WHAT LITTLE THAT REMAINS of Elizabeth Horlock Smith's correspondence has pieces cut and torn from it, possibly because the correspondent had come too close to the truth, or even begged a certain question. True history was carefully hidden by Elizabeth herself and may never be written. More determined sleuths than I have tried to unearth her origins and life in London before 1841 and discovered virtually nothing. It is probable that Smith was an alias, and possible that Horlock was her maiden name. I dispute the latter on one shred of evidence. In her correspondence, she variously spells the name 'Horlock' and 'Horelock'. It is unlikely Elizabeth would misspell her own name — she had had more than a rudimentary education, and her letters are literate and grammatically complex. She only resumed the use of Horelock/Horlock in 1862, ostensibly to distinguish herself from other Elizabeth Smiths resident in Auckland.

The Open World is a re-imagining of her life, and also of the lives of people she knew, many of which have been comprehensively recorded — for example, Bishop and Mrs Selwyn, and Chief Justice Martin and his wife Mary Ann. It was as Mary Ann Martin's companion that Elizabeth made her way to New Zealand, along with her younger son John Elisha. Her other son, Thomas Henry, was already in Port Nicholson, working as an improver, or apprentice surveyor, for the New Zealand Company.

Elizabeth lived in New Zealand for twenty-one years, during

which time her sons married and, to a greater or lesser extent, prospered. Thomas Henry Smith is fondly remembered for his careful diplomacy as Civil Commissioner and Native Land Court Judge at a tumultuous time in our history.

In Lady Martin's memoir *Our Maoris*, Mrs Smith is mentioned only as 'my friend'. In their correspondence and journals, William Cotton and Elizabeth's sons account for the enormous amount of work she undertook at the Native Hospital at Taurarua (Judge's Bay, Auckland). She is also mentioned by Anne Chapman, a missionary at Maketu and Te Ngae (Rotorua); by Charlotte Brown at Te Papa (Tauranga); and by Sarah Selwyn, among others. She returned to London in 1863.

It seems Elizabeth was indeed a great friend of the irrepressible William Cotton, Selwyn's chaplain and librarian, who was one of the party on board *Tomatin* on the voyage to New Zealand. In his prodigious, twelve-volume journal, Cotton gives accounts of lively parties Elizabeth gave aboard the ship with the aid of her tincture the 'Cup of Grace'. Together they sailed on the Waitemata and worked hard in the service of Church and State. In reality, Cotton sailed Home in 1847. Since he so loved New Zealand, I have given him a few years extra. After various misadventures in England and what we would now call bipolar episodes, he was dubbed the 'lunatic priest' of Frodsham. The year 1865 saw him briefly resident in Doctor Tuke's famously humane Chiswick asylum. In the novel Elizabeth visits him there.

In 1868 Bishop Selwyn reluctantly returned to England to take up the bishopric at Lichfield Cathedral. It wasn't until 1874 that William and Mary Ann Martin returned, four years after Elizabeth's death. For the purposes of this novel, their returns are drawn forward to the mid-sixties.

The gunsmith Wiremu Hoete (William Jowett/Jowitt) was a regular visitor to Taurarua from Waiheke. Chief Tamihana is a famous figure in New Zealand, and really did stay overnight with Elizabeth and Henry at Lake Rotoiti. A lad called George Rupai was shipmate on *Tomatin* and vanished from history on landing. His return to London as an adult is fiction.

Mr Griggs existed and really was the schoolmaster at Tollington Park. Kitty Tripp did not exist and most probably neither did Captain Hogg and his genuine wife, though rumours of a husband of that name persisted in family lore until the mid-twentieth century.

At the end of 1867, Thomas Henry Smith brought his family to live in Wellington for three years. In the novel they arrive at Easter 1869.

Although I have based much of this book on historical fact, it is a work of fiction. If I have offended any descendants of these historical figures, either by the words I put into their mouths or by their imagined actions, I unreservedly apologise. To those descendants who are offended by the mere fact that I include them in this narrative, I offer no apology at all. Maori, Pakeha and English, they belong to all of us. This is not to say that a certain discomfort has not accompanied the writing of this book. I often sensed Elizabeth's displeasure with aspects of my account, but just as often I heard her laughter. She is my great-great-great-grandmother.

My ancestor calls out to yours.

ACKNOWLEDGEMENTS

I WOULD NOT HAVE BEEN ABLE to complete this novel without the assistance of a much-appreciated literature grant from Creative New Zealand.

Very special thanks go to my daughter Maeve Woodhouse, who accompanied me on a pilgrimage to London in 2009 and to whom this book is dedicated.

I also thank my father's cousin, Jill Williams, for her assistance, and hope that she accepts this flight of fancy in the spirit it was intended. Her late sister Glenise Rolfe's family history *Te Mete* was instrumental and inspirational.

Thank you to Christine Parker and Steve Templeton in Derbyshire for the country interlude and research assistance. Without you there would be no Buxton or Lichfield in these pages. Thanks to Pip and Cally in London for their generosity. A huge thanks to Mary and Hilz and to Jane and Keni for their support and friendship. Special love and thanks to Jane for her careful reading of the manuscript.

As always, I am immensely grateful for Harriet Allan's inspired contribution.

Jane Parkin is the most brilliant and insightful editor ever.

Heartfelt thanks to Lois Wallace in New York.

Thank you also to the staff of the Mitchell Library in Sydney and the Auckland War Memorial Museum library who allowed me to read the Cotton journals and the Smith correspondence, respectively.

Selwyn's speech, page 195, is quoted in *Mission and Moko: Aspects* of the work of the Church Missionary Society in New Zealand, 1814–1882.

'A man either says too little or too much' is from Cotton's journals. Likewise, 'Taihoa — that most comprehensive word that means either in half a minute or this time two years.'

The boatsong on page 264 is from *Renata's Journey*.

From the Smith correspondence I wove many gems, including: 'I am more tired of the Sub-officials than even of the Natives' from Elizabeth's account of the serving at the Native Conference at Kohimarama; 'Be thankful you have girls first to do the work of servants' comes from a letter to John Elisha, as do her cautions against the reading of Byron and his subsequent 'midnight of the mind'.

Mary Ann's 'sofa habits' are so described in Thomas Henry Smith's correspondence with his brother John Elisha. He also recounts Judge Martin's description of Mata Te Mete as an old hen with two chickens. I put to use his description of the manner in which time passes at Huruhi, his opinion of Carlyle, and John's jealous guarding of his brother's company in Wellington.

The following publications were helpful in my research for the book:

Our Maoris by Lady Martin, 1884; *Te Mete* by Glenise Rolfe, 1991; *Renata's Journey* by Renata, transl. 1994; *Mission and Moko: Aspects of the Work of the Church Missionary Society in New Zealand 1814–1882* edited by Robert Glen, 1992; *Never the Faint Hearted: Charles Baker* by Mary Baker, 1986; *The Best Man Who Ever Served The Crown* by Ray Fargher, 2007; *The Founding Years of Rotorua* by D.M. Stafford, 1986; *Landmarks of Te Arawa, Vol 2* by D.M. Stafford, 1996; *Ko Mata: The Life in New Zealand of Anne Chapman* by Philip Andrews, 1991; *At Home in New Zealand* by Alison Drummond and L.R. Drummond, 1967; *Taken In* by Hopeful, 1887; *Early Victorian*

New Zealand by John Miller, 1958; *Victorian Costume* by Anne M. Buck, 1961; *The Life and Times of Auckland* by Gordon McLauchlan, 2008; *Auckland, the Capital of New Zealand* by W. Swainson, 1853; *The Victorian House* by Judith Flanders, 2003; *Victorian Life and Victorian Fiction* by Jo McMurty, 1979; *Reminiscences of Sarah Selwyn* edited by Harry Bioletti, 2002; *Notes on Nursing* by Florence Nightingale, 1859; *The Six Colonies of New Zealand* by William Fox, 1851; *A Sort of Conscience: The Wakefields* by Philip Temple, 2002; *The Victorian Underworld* by Kellow Chesney, 1970; *Priest, Missionary and Bee Master: William Charles Cotton* by Arthur R. Smith, 2006; *The Lively Capital* by Una Platts, 1971; *Emperors of Dreams* by Mike Jay, 2000; *Letters from New Zealand* by Archdeacon Harper, 1914; *History of New Zealand and its Inhabitants* by Dom Felice Vaggioli, 1896; *Tamihana the King Maker* by L.S. Rickard, 1963; *Buxton: A Pictorial History* by Mike Langham and Colin Wells, 1993.

Also available by Stephanie Johnson